No Chance

MEETING

No Chance
MEETING

NO CHANCE LOVE – BOOK ONE

JAYE ELLIOT

And we know that all things work together
for good to those who love God, to those who
are the called according to *His* purpose.

– Romans 8:28

Chapter One

BAYLOR'S BRIDGE. ON AVERAGE, FOUR PEOPLE DIED THERE EVERY year. Some by accident, others not. The local paper had just bragged about how no one had died this year. Yet.

Alex pulled her old Jeep into an empty parking spot on the edge of town. The bridge's dark, skeletal trusses loomed half a mile down the road. In just half a mile, the hollow ache consuming her from the inside out could be over.

Hand trembling, she put the Jeep in park and shut off the key. Though the sweltering mid-August heat struck her as she opened the door and slid out of the vehicle, a shiver coursed up her spine and across her arms. Maybe walking this last half mile wasn't a good idea after all. What was there to see anyway besides gray mountains and a few aspens already losing their bright summertime green?

A truck rumbled past with a hot gust of wind, kicking up dust. She turned her face away and blinked the grit from her eyes. Just across the street stood the main bar in town. A strangled laugh caught in her throat. She had never set foot in that bar—she didn't even drink—but what did these so-called accomplishments mean now? Maybe a drink or two would help. As long as she could still walk a half a mile, why would it matter? Or was she just stalling?

Both destinations tugged at her, but the lure of the bar finally jarred her feet loose and led her to the open door. The dim interior offered immediate relief from the heat outside. Neon lights and signs buzzed like summer flies and illuminated a large collection of haphazardly-placed photos of men and women in uniform hanging on the walls. A throbbing ache gripped her chest, and she pulled her gaze away from them.

Only one guy sat at the bar and two others at a table near the door. All strangers, thankfully—not that she knew many people in town. Scraping together a living and contending with the ever growing dark cloud surrounding her life didn't exactly foster the time or energy to make friends. Her move to little Aspen Creek, Colorado had been supposed to help.

It hadn't.

No one seemed to notice her walk in except for the bartender, who glanced up from drying a shot glass. She ducked her head, warmth prickling through her cheeks. Her parents would be so disappointed.

She kept her head down and approached the bar, sliding up onto the vinyl-topped stool farthest from the other patrons. She rubbed her clammy palms along her jeans and drew in a deep breath. Footsteps approached. She looked up. The bartender stood directly across from her now, his towel slung over one broad shoulder. He certainly fit the image of a bartender—average height but stocky and well-toned—capable of breaking up a bar fight and throwing out unruly customers. He even had long hair pulled back in a dark ponytail.

"Mind showing some ID?"

Alex pulled out her wallet and handed him her driver's license. His gaze shifted from the card to her and back. She squirmed. She looked like an immature high schooler in that photo even though she'd just had the license renewed. Her date of birth, however, would confirm her nearly thirty years.

Finally, he handed it back. "What can I get you?"

Alex's stomach wound itself in a knot at his husky voice. What did she know about alcohol? Aside from a couple of sips of wine at Christmastime and New Year's, she'd never had a taste for it.

She cleared her throat. "Something strong." Her cheeks burned again.

One of his brows quirked ever so slightly. "Whiskey?"

She forced a decisive nod. Without a word, he grabbed a bottle and set a shot glass on the bar in front of her. He filled it with amber liquid, just like on the old westerns Alex used to watch with her family. Back when life was normal.

The bartender gave her one last look before turning away. Was that pity in his expression? Or maybe just puzzlement. Alex focused on her drink. How many of these little glasses would it take before numbness engulfed her? Friends in college had wondered what sort of drunk she would make, but only the strangers here would ever find out. She took the shot glass gingerly in her fingers. Her parents flashed to mind once more. Alex had always been the good girl. She'd tried so hard to make Mom and Dad proud. So much for that.

She brought the glass to her lips and took a gulp. Big mistake. She should have sipped it more carefully. The liquid stung her mouth and scorched her throat, almost choking her. She fought the urge to cough. Hopefully, none of the men noticed the stupid girl who had no business being in a bar drinking whiskey. The barkeeper did cast a glance out of the corner of his eye. Alex's cheeks burned almost as much as the alcohol warming her chest.

She set the half-full glass back down. What an idiotic move to come in here. She should have just walked to the bridge as planned. Still, the alluring promise of numbness if she just downed the rest of the alcohol and had a couple more kept her seated.

For a long time, she just stared at her drink. Eventually, the other patrons left, silence settling in their wake. Alex chanced a peek at the bartender. He was busy cleaning up, almost as if she weren't here. He was kind of cute. Well, more than kind of, if she was honest with herself. She'd always had a thing for guys with long hair. At least the ones who could pull it off.

She shook her head. Stupid, fanciful thoughts to have today of all days. Since when had she ever had luck with guys anyway? The cute ones never noticed her, and the ones who did always ranged from not her type to downright creepy. She sighed, every weight she had carried for the last couple of years falling so heavily she could have just crumbled right here. She was so tired. So *incredibly* tired of it all. She didn't want to carry it anymore.

A car backfired outside. The bartender flinched. He then closed his eyes and let out a slow breath. The reaction was so familiar to Alex tears welled in her eyes and clogged her throat. She cleared it quietly.

"Afghanistan?"

He looked over at her, questions in his eyes.

She shrugged one shoulder. "My brother was over there."

He gave a slow nod. "Afghanistan, Iraq, Syria. Wherever I was needed."

Alex drew in a long breath, darting a glance at the photos on the wall. The last thing she had come here for was conversation, but it had been so long since she'd really talked with anyone. Maybe she was just stalling again.

"How long did you serve?"

"Thirteen years. I would've kept serving, but I got shot up in an ambush. A year and a half of physical therapy and I can almost walk without a limp." A corner of his mouth shifted upward slightly, but didn't remain in place. "So where's your brother now?"

The giant rock in her stomach that never seemed to go away settled once again with aching intensity. She reached for the chain around her neck and tugged the dog tags out from under her shirt. Pressure wrapped around her throat. "Bethany Cemetery."

He bowed his head. "I'm sorry. How long has it been?"

"Three years. He was only two weeks away from coming

home. But a suicide bomber in Kabul brought an end to that." Tiny daggers scraped her eyes. Even three years didn't erase the pain burning a hole in her chest.

The bartender drew his brows together. "What was his name?"

"Joshua."

"Joshua . . . Jennings?"

She stilled. Did he remember her last name from her driver's license, or was there something more behind the question? "Did you know my brother?"

His chest lifted with a deep intake of breath. "Yeah."

The broken pieces of Alex's heart crashed against her ribs like shards of glass.

"I didn't know him well, but our units were working together. I was there . . . just after the bomb. I tried to save him."

She put her hand to her chest and more tears gushed into her eyes. "You were with him when he died?"

He nodded again.

The tears scalded her cheeks. "Did he say anything?"

"It all happened too fast. There wasn't time."

She lowered her head, and her teardrops left small puddles on the bar. A tearing sensation burned through her ribs with each deep sob that rose within her. She just missed Josh so much. He'd always believed in her. He'd been her anchor. Without him, nothing was right. Even her faith seemed to have abandoned her when he died. She just couldn't face life without him.

But she didn't have to. The pain could end. The sobbing settled, and cold numbness crept in to take its place. She pulled off her glasses and wiped her face.

"I have to go." She slid off the stool and opened her wallet to pay for the drink.

The bartender held up his hand. "Keep it."

She whispered thanks and turned for the door.

Time to end this.

"Alexis, right?"

She paused and looked back. "Usually, I just go by Alex."

"I'm Riley. Riley Conrad."

Alex attempted a weak smile. "It was nice to meet you, Riley."

She took another step toward the door before he spoke again.

"Want to get coffee tomorrow? Maybe breakfast over at the diner?"

The invitation echoed around her. Had he just asked her out on a date? Of all the absurdly inopportune things to happen at this moment. Just say no and walk out. It would be better that way. Then she couldn't hurt him in the end.

However, that stubborn female heart of hers that had dreamed of true love and happily-ever-after since early childhood tugged at her to accept the invitation. Here this cute and, by all appearances, nice guy had just asked her out. Every part of her screamed she would be a fool to turn him down. She had never actually been on a date before. At twenty-nine years old, that was just sad. Sure, plenty of guys had asked, just never the right ones.

She sighed. Might as well cross one last thing off her bucket list. Besides, he was the last person to see Josh alive. She craved even that small link to her brother. She turned to Riley.

"All right."

He gave her a bit of a lopsided smile, and she scolded herself for melting just a little. She wasn't some heart-eyed teenager. A hopeless romantic, perhaps, or at least she used to be, but she'd only just met the guy.

"How does eight o'clock sound?"

"Sounds good."

"I'll meet you there then."

She nodded, and this time made it out of the bar. A flutter passed through her middle. Nerves? Probably. When was the last time she had been excited about anything? Did she even remember what it felt like? Now her stomach twisted. Definitely nerves. No doubt she would succeed spectacularly at displaying her complete lack of dating experience. The whole thing would be a disaster.

Well, the bridge wasn't far from the diner. She may have postponed her plans for today, but it didn't mean she couldn't finish them tomorrow.

Riley caught one last glimpse of her dark blonde hair as she stepped out of the bar. Honestly, she'd looked far too young for him before he'd seen her driver's license. Maybe it was the rounded, dark-rimmed glasses and brown freckles that made her look fresh out of high school. He glanced at her half-full shot glass. Obviously, she didn't drink much, and he would have remembered if she'd visited before. He'd witnessed all types come in over the last several months and had developed a knack for spotting those having a rough time of it. She was definitely one of them.

Maybe that's why he'd asked her out more than her pretty face. He might not be in the military anymore, but he still had a hard time turning the other way when someone needed help. And since he had failed to save her brother's life, the least he could do was buy her breakfast.

Memories of the bomb's aftermath poured into his mind, and he grimaced. There was nothing he could have done. He knew that, but it still haunted him.

He picked up Alex's shot glass to dump the whiskey and his memories along with it. Her face took over his thoughts again. He really hadn't expected her to accept his invitation. He would have to let Bradley know he was at least attempting to get back in the game. He hadn't been on a date—a real date—since he'd enlisted at nineteen. Of course, this all depended on what sort of

7

beliefs Alex had. Bradley would warn him about getting involved with anyone who didn't have a relationship with Christ. But it was just one date to get to know her. She might not even be interested beyond that anyway.

Chapter Two

ALEX SCRUBBED HER FINGERS AGAINST HER BURNING EYES AND groaned. Where were the soothing eye drops when she needed them? This was the price of crying so much. She hadn't moved from where she'd collapsed on her bed after returning to her small apartment from the bar yesterday. She hadn't even changed her clothes. Talking about Josh had opened the floodgates of emotions she struggled so hard to keep contained. She just hadn't had the will to do anything but hug her pillow and cry. This morning, however, there weren't even any tears left to moisten her dry, gritty eyes.

She rolled over to squint at the clock. Seven-thirty.

Her date with Riley.

She bolted upright. Her head pounded, her vision closing in around the edges. She covered her face and groaned again. One sip of whiskey wouldn't give her a hangover, but her head obviously didn't know that. It surely didn't help that she'd skipped supper. Her stomach growled just for emphasis.

She had a mere thirty minutes to prepare for the first date of her life. Not even enough time to shower and wash her hair. A perfect disaster. Either that or she just didn't go. She winced. Was she really such a failure as to consider standing him up? But what else was new? The whole thing was a bad idea anyway.

She let her legs dangle over the edge of the bed. This was such a mistake. Heaving a sigh, she dragged herself out of bed and shuffled into the bathroom. One look in the mirror only reinforced her misgivings. Puffy eyes, oily skin, messed up hair. At least Riley wouldn't be disappointed not to go on a second date with such a mess. He'd probably be relieved once they parted ways.

Running warm water, she cleaned up as best she could before returning to her bedroom to find clothes. What should she even wear for a first date? Well, it was just breakfast at the old diner. Something casual would be more than sufficient. She chose a pair of jeans and a black peasant top.

Back in the bathroom, she fought with her hair until she settled with a messy bun and attempted to conceal some of the puffiness around her eyes. A smudge of pink lip gloss and it would have to do. Her chipped black nail polish didn't exactly say "well put together," but there was no time to fix that now. She had to leave if she didn't want to be late.

Grabbing her purse and phone, she rushed out of her upstairs apartment. The cool breeze sent goosebumps along her arms—much different from yesterday's weather. Though still summertime, the chilliness hinted at the encroachment of fall. She'd always loved fall, maybe because it had been Josh's favorite time of year. They'd had so much fun growing up. Her missing tears showed up suddenly, but she blinked them away. At the curb of the Victorian-style duplex she'd called home for the last couple of years waited her beat-up old Jeep Cherokee. The one reliable thing in her life these days.

Five minutes later, she pulled into the parking lot of Penny's Diner, avoiding the worst potholes. She spotted Riley immediately. He wore a dark blue button-up and jeans that were a little faded at the knees. His hair wasn't pulled back this morning, settling around his shoulders, and he leaned against a navy blue and white 1970s Ford pickup. Her pulse accelerated just a bit. Old trucks. Another weakness of hers. Typical that all outward signs would point to Riley as Mr. Right with her life in such turmoil.

Even if he did happen to be Mr. Right, she was a mess no guy in his right mind would want to sort out. She never should have agreed to this.

She pulled into the empty parking space next to the truck. Too late to turn back now. She hauled in a gulp of air and shut off the Jeep. Her heart thumped loudly as if to fill the sudden silence. Once she stepped out of the vehicle, she had to face all new territory. She might be steady with a paintbrush or pencil, but real life had a way of making her a klutz and not just with her hands and feet, but her brain too. Add an attractive man to the mix and she had the perfect recipe for certain disaster.

She unbuckled her seatbelt and opened the door to slide out. Riley stood there waiting for her.

"Mornin'."

She forced a smile. The muscles it required strained like they hadn't been exercised in ages. "Good morning."

And then came the awkward silence she always dreaded. She really wasn't cut out for this sort of thing. She needed chatty friends around to keep the conversation going. Josh was good at that.

However, Riley gestured toward the diner, and they both turned for the door. Inside buzzed with conversation and the sizzle of frying food. A couple of the tables contained families with young kids or teens that all but screamed vacationers. Though not a main tourist destination, Aspen Creek offered good fishing, camping, and hiking trails to those seeking more outdoorsy pursuits or a quiet getaway. Alex and her family had always packed up and headed to one of their favorite campgrounds this time of year. One last summer vacation before school started. She swallowed to loosen the lump in her throat.

The perky young waitress at the door—probably a local high school student—greeted them with a smile bright enough to give Alex a headache. She'd been that optimistic once too. The girl led them across the worn checkerboard floor to one of the faded red vinyl booths by the windows. The place could use an update. Alex slid into her seat and Riley across from her. The waitress placed a menu in front of each of them and asked what they would like to drink. Riley requested a pot of coffee, to which Alex nodded in agreement. She could use a strong cup right about now. Once the girl had walked away, Alex picked up the tacky laminated menu but found it hard to concentrate with the male presence seated across from her.

So much for any silly romantic notions about first dates. It took sheer willpower not to fidget and squirm. What if she spilled coffee on herself, or choked on her food, or got something stuck in her teeth? Warmth crept up her neck. If only she could be more like Mindy. Her best friend always seemed right at home in any situation during their time in college. Had she experienced such awkwardness when she'd first started dating her now-husband Zach? Alex should have called her for advice last night, but they hadn't talked in such a long time.

"Hungry?"

She looked up. Riley watched her over his menu.

"Yes."

Starved was more like it, but she wasn't going to tell him that she hadn't eaten in almost twenty-four hours.

That uncomfortable silence fell again as Alex looked back down at the menu. Even with her glasses, her eyes wouldn't focus. Not that she really needed them to. She had pretty much memorized the menu within the first couple of months of living in Aspen Creek. She peeked at Riley again. She should say something. Anything.

Thankfully, the waitress returned with their pot of coffee before she had a chance to say something stupid. "Are you ready to order?"

"I am." Alex glanced across at Riley, and he nodded.

She looked back up at the waitress. "I'll have blueberry pancakes and bacon."

The girl wrote it down in her notepad and turned to Riley. "I'll take the same, and a plate of eggs. Scrambled."

With another cheerful smile, she left to fill their orders. Alex reached for the coffee pot and took ridiculous care not to spill as she filled her mug. She then stirred in creamer and a couple of teaspoons of sugar. Josh had always teased her about her sweet tooth. He'd liked his coffee black and on the verge of boiling. She took a sip and swallowed hard.

Back to trying to get her brain to work correctly. Would this whole morning be as awkward as these last ten minutes had been? The date had barely even started. Then again, if she just died of embarrassment right now, she wouldn't have to bother with the bridge.

"I haven't seen you around. Have you been in Aspen Creek long?"

Finally, something to break the silence. Alex set her mug down. "About two years. What about you?" There, a polite response. She wasn't an absolute failure. Not yet, anyway.

"Almost a year."

She took another sip of coffee. If she kept this up, they would go through that pot in no time. She set the cup down and crossed her arms to keep from reaching for it again for at least a minute. She was a grown woman. She should be able to handle polite conversation.

"Where are you from?"

"I grew up in Denver. I had rehab there after I was wounded and then moved here. I prefer small towns."

Alex managed the barest hint of a smile. "Me too. I grew up down near Colorado Springs in Bethany. It's even smaller than Aspen Creek."

"So what do you do? Where do you work?"

A bucket of ice water crashed into the pit of Alex's stomach. As if she could ever dare to hope to escape reality for even a short time. She reached for her mug again and ran her finger up and down the handle. "Well, I did work at the post office until yesterday when I got let go. Not enough work to go around. I doubt I'll have better luck anywhere else. One of the downsides to living in a small town."

Riley's brows gathered, and he shook his head. "I'm sorry." His voice had lowered from its conversational tone and spoke of something deeper than just generic sympathy. "Things get tough sometimes. I never saw myself working in a bar, but I'm just thankful to have the job."

He studied her for a moment, and her heart gave a small hiccup. She quickly took another sip of coffee to avert her gaze.

"If there's anything I can do to help you find work, I'd be happy to."

Alex gulped her coffee, narrowly avoiding the calamity of swallowing down the wrong tube. "Thanks. I'm not sure what though." She released a long, heavy breath. "Actually, I went to school for art, but no amount of determination or optimism can guarantee success as an artist."

No, it only led to post office day jobs and bouts of un-employment.

However, his expression lifted. "What kind of art do you do?"

"I paint, mostly. But I do like to sketch sometimes."

"My family is very into the arts. My dad and brother are architects. My mom used to be a music teacher, and my sister is in fashion design."

Alex stalled with her mug halfway to her mouth again. "Wait, Conrad. Conrad Architects. Is your dad Phillip Conrad?"

He dipped his chin slowly. "Yeah."

"Wow." The Conrads were considered one of Denver's elite

families. "He designed the McKinley Art Gallery, right? It's one of my favorite places. It's so beautiful."

Riley only smiled with another brief nod, though there was something off about it, as if he wasn't keen on discussing the family business. Odd that someone from such an affluent family would work in a small town bar. But who was she to pry into other people's private lives?

"What about you? Are you into art?"

He shrugged and took a swig of his coffee. "Depends. Art means different things to different people."

She waited for him to elaborate, but he didn't. Instead, he switched the topic back to her. "What about your parents? What do they do?"

"Well, my dad's a farmer and my mom was always a stay-at-home mom." Simple and straightforward. They loved their lives, and she had loved growing up in it. However, her dreams had always been a bit beyond that. Maybe she'd been foolish.

"A country girl, then."

Unbidden, a tiny laugh escaped Alex. "Yes, pretty much. A country girl with big dreams."

Their food arrived before Riley had a chance to comment, and the waitress set their plates in front of them. Alex focused on buttering her pancakes and gathered herself for the rest of this date. So far it hadn't gone quite as catastrophically as she'd feared. Perhaps she might even call it fun to a certain degree. Interesting anyway.

She spread syrup around her pancakes and glanced at him. "So did you always want to be in the military?"

Josh had set his mind on joining the Marines just like their grandpa when he was only six years old. It was in his blood.

"No."

Another brief answer and silence. He didn't seem to have much he wanted to share in the way of specifics. Of course, Alex wouldn't push him. They were practically still strangers after all. But then he met her eyes. "I did it to get away." A smile grew on his face that projected more sadness than humor. "I guess you could say I'm the black sheep in the family."

While she didn't know the circumstances, his words tugged at her. She didn't exactly consider herself the black sheep of the family—more a very colorful sheep—but hadn't she always felt different from most of those around her?

Riley's shoulder lifted in a half-hearted shrug. "It was just a given my brother would carry on the family business. My parents probably thought I would too, but I was more into sports. They constantly tried to 'discover' my artistic talent. I made the mistake of showing interest in cooking around the time I graduated, so they sent me off to culinary school intending for me to open my own high-end restaurant. I swear my dad had already designed the place in his mind. I had just started my second semester when I dropped out and enlisted."

"I imagine that didn't go over well."

He gave a humorless laugh. "No. I've hardly spoken to my parents since."

"I'm sorry. I guess we're both kind of disappointments then. I mean, it's not that my parents don't support me. They've always supported me, but they put so much into helping me get to art school, and now I have nothing to show for it." She breathed out heavily. "Maybe I should have just made a life in Bethany like they did."

"Sometimes we've got to make our own way, even if it means disappointing those around us."

Alex nodded slowly, but it didn't erase the doubts. Had she made a colossal error in her life choices somewhere along the way? Sitting here in this booth was definitely not where she had seen herself at nearly thirty.

For a minute or two, they both focused on their breakfast

that slowly grew cold in front of them. Alex's stomach thanked her immediately after the first bite. She hadn't had much of an appetite lately, but today she could probably finish every pancake on her plate. She glanced at Riley as she chewed. He raised his coffee mug to his lips, and she studied the tattoo on the underside of his wrist partially obscured by a tattered bracelet—a simple black cross with foreign writing along the side.

"What does your tattoo say?"

He met her gaze and set his mug down. "It's Hebrew for 'paid in full'."

Her heart skipped. So he could be a believer. That made things interesting.

He nodded downward. "What do yours mean?"

She looked at her arms and turned her left one first where two small arrows had been inked into her skin on the underside of her forearm. "When things were hard and I felt like I wasn't getting anywhere, I always liked the saying that an arrow can only be shot by pulling it back." She then showed him the underside of her right wrist—the shape of the Big Dipper constellation with Josh's name incorporated into it. Her throat constricted. "I got this one after Josh died. We always loved to look at the stars and find all the constellations."

"Sounds like you two were really close."

She nodded and bowed her head, blinking hard. "He was only a year older than me. He was my best friend, even during high school. I was always the tomboy tag-along with him and his friends."

A bit of moisture leaked from the corners of her eyes, and she lifted her glasses to brush it away. "He's really the only reason I have tattoos. We grew up in a pretty conservative church, so tattoos, black nail polish, piercings, and all that were right on the verge of scandalous, at least for some people. But I always thought tattoos were beautiful and a form of artistic expression."

"You're an artist, that's understandable."

"Well, when I first wanted to get one, my parents were a little hesitant, but Josh said I should go for it." She laughed a little, though more moisture burned her eyes. "He's the one who understood me best and my personality and dreams. He always encouraged me to be myself and not be afraid of what others think. I just miss him so much. I feel like I've lost the one thing that was keeping me going."

The tears formed fully now and rolled down her cheeks. She took off her glasses and wiped at them with her napkin, but they didn't want to stop. Riley gave her a minute before he spoke.

"I know it doesn't take away the pain or the loss. Trust me; I lost some good friends over there. But your brother died a hero. It might not help, but you can be proud of him."

Alex held her eyes shut to slow the tears. "I am."

She breathed slowly in and out, working the pressure from her chest. Once confident the tears would remain at bay, she finished wiping her face and put her glasses back on. Searching for a less painful topic, she settled on a very important one.

"So . . . are you a born again Christian?"

Riley's smile alone answered the question. It was the smile of someone happy to find another believer in this crazy world. "Yeah. My best friend, Bradley, led me to Christ while we were serving. It's only been a couple of years, but I thank God every day that he got through to me. I certainly didn't grow up in a Christian home."

"I got saved when I was six." She sighed quietly. "My faith has taken a bit of a hit in the past few years though."

"It's been a rough time for you."

She appreciated his understanding. From here they spoke of lighter things, such as their favorite spots in Aspen Creek. Once they finished their meal and were on their last mugs of coffee, Alex's mind drifted back to yesterday and the fact that she had planned to finish what she had started. Nothing had really changed, but . . .

She focused on Riley. "I need to tell you something." She bit her lip. She wasn't going to do this, but the words just poured out anyway. "Yesterday, when I came into the bar, I was on my way to Baylor's Bridge. I . . . I was going to jump."

His eyes widened.

"If you hadn't asked me out, I probably would have."

He just stared at her as he processed her confession. What was it like to have someone tell you they planned to commit suicide? Actually, now that she'd said it out loud, she almost couldn't believe her own ears. This was never who she'd thought she would be.

"Are you still planning to?" His gaze bored into hers.

"I . . . don't know." She had been, yes. But it suddenly seemed more complicated than it had yesterday when she was reeling from the loss of her job and all the other emotions that cascaded in along with it. They still hounded her, as relentless as ever, but something had changed.

Riley didn't appear to know quite what to say. Alex hunched in her seat. She should never have unloaded this on him. The date had gone so well before now.

"I'm sorry, I shouldn't have told you that."

He did not respond. Instead, he pulled a pen from his pocket and grabbed an unused napkin. After writing something on it, he slid it across to her. "That's my number. Call or text any time. It doesn't matter when, I'll answer. Just don't do anything or make any drastic decisions without talking, whether it's to me or someone else. Please."

She picked up the napkin and studied the neat line of numbers. It was asking a lot. She'd grown used to shutting people out for their own safety. With a weighty breath, she nodded, and it was like grabbing a lifeline. She'd been drowning for so long. It had been a horribly long time since she had talked with God, but deep in her heart rose a whispered thanks.

Riley gave her a bit of a smile. "And if you want to have dinner sometime, you can let me know that too."

Chapter Three

ALEX LAY IN BED AND FIDDLED WITH THE DOG TAGS AROUND HER neck. All in all, she actually felt . . . okay this morning. Maybe. Had she really gone on her first date only twenty-four hours ago? A surprisingly good first date. The memories brought a tiny smile to her face. At least she had accomplished something. And Riley even wanted to go out again. She must not have made too big a fool of herself.

She turned her head to her nightstand and focused on the napkin she had placed on her clock. Riley hadn't asked for her number. He had left it entirely in her hands whether or not she wanted to have contact with him again or pursue a second date. She appreciated that.

Yet, now she had to make a decision. It was a little bit like standing at the edge of a figurative bridge. One side offered a clear choice—quick, easy, safe. She could guard both her heart and his by walking away. The other side presented a complete unknown and a huge risk. It could have more pain, more heartache—and yet, it held a glimmer of something that stirred her sense of adventure like she hadn't experienced since college. She wouldn't daydream about what might happen between her and Riley— dreams shattered far too easily—but how could she not hope for something special?

She reached for her glasses and put them on before grabbing the napkin and her phone. Taking a deep breath, she held them to her chest for a long moment. Before Josh died, she had prayed over every decision she made. It had been habitual; something she'd never imagined forsaking. Yet now she found herself so estranged from her Heavenly Father her heart ached. What did she say? Did she even know how to pray anymore? She didn't feel worthy to come to Him. Ridiculous, of course. It went against everything she had learned and believed in. He would meet her exactly where she was. If only she could get past feeling like such a failure.

She struggled to form words to a prayer, but all that really came was the intense desire for things to be different. To be the person she used to be. To be mended, somehow.

Though an incredibly weak attempt, a fragile peace she hadn't experienced in some time seeped into the painful cracks in her broken heart. She believed in God's healing hand, she just wasn't as confident in herself, that she wouldn't just fall all over again.

But today was a new day, and she would seize the opportunities it held. She raised her phone to dial Riley's number in and typed a quick text.

Hey, this is Alex. Thanks for breakfast yesterday.

She probably should have texted him sooner. What if he'd spent all day yesterday and last night wondering if she would change her mind about killing herself?

A few seconds later, he replied.

No problem. I enjoyed it.

A smile tugged at Alex's lips. She gazed at the text for a long moment, standing at that figurative edge. She didn't really have much to lose at this point. Time to take the jump.

If you want to have lunch or dinner sometime soon, I'm free any time.

Her thumb hovered over the send button for another moment. When she pressed it, her heart gave a little bloop. She had gone all through high school and college without a boyfriend. Honestly, she had given up hope of ever having one. She wasn't about to call Riley a boyfriend after just one date, but it did restore her hope. Her heart thumped as she waited, but his reply came promptly.

How about lunch tomorrow?

Alex grinned like she hadn't in forever.

Sounds great. Want to meet at the diner again around noon?

I'll be there.

She set her phone down and sighed—a comfortable sort of sigh. Maybe things would be okay after all. Could she dare to hope? She pushed her covers aside and got out of bed. In the kitchen, she prepared a pot of coffee. The bag of her favorite brand was almost empty. She would have to get groceries, although coffee might not be a luxury she could afford right now. What she really needed was to get right on job hunting. If she didn't find something soon, she would have hard decisions to face. It would be so typical to have to move back in with her parents right after finally meeting someone.

She shook her head. She needed to stop being so cynical.

The excitement high from this morning had faded, leading Alex straight back to the familiar dark mire she'd floundered in for longer than she cared to remember. She'd fought to hold on to a hopeful outlook as she filled out applications at almost every shop and restaurant in town, but most of it had died to nothing more than cold ashes.

She sank down on her worn living room sofa and curled up against a pillow. Sometimes it would be so nice to just fall asleep and not wake up. If only Josh were still here. He could always make her feel better, especially about herself. She glanced at her purse out of the corner of her eye. Finally, she reached into it and pulled out her phone. Bringing up her text conversation with Riley from earlier, she typed a new text.

I went job hunting today.

It took him a couple of minutes to answer this time. He was probably working tonight.

How did that go?

Alex blew out a hard breath.

I filled out a bunch of applications, but no one is hiring, I doubt I'll get any calls.

Give it a few days. You never know.

In a few days she would start running out of money to buy food. In a few days she might have to pack up the failure of her life here and crawl back to her parents. If she made it that far.

Her phone chimed with another text.

Maybe we can think of something during lunch tomorrow.

For some reason, that did it for Alex. Tears streamed down her face before she even knew where they had come from. She'd forgotten how good it felt to have someone there to help her out.

⤙⎯⎯⎯⟶

Today, Alex put more effort into preparing for her lunch date with Riley. She pulled her hair back into an elegant French braid, picked out a cute summery top, and repainted her nails—this time a bright shade of green instead of black. However, it was only mid-morning by the time she had finished so she sat down at her computer to pass the time. One by one, she checked the websites where she had listed her art. Occasionally, a sale or two surprised her, but not today.

Her breath leaked out slowly as she finally closed the laptop and turned in her chair to look at her easel. A half-finished canvas stared back at her. The mountains and aspen trees had sat mournfully incomplete for weeks now. Something about it just wasn't right. Maybe the perspective? Or the colors. Alex couldn't seem to pin down exactly what nagged at her about it. Actually, no painting had seemed right since Josh had died. Every canvas she had finished in the last three years sat in a growing pile in the closet. A pile that didn't make it onto any art websites. Would she ever paint something worth sharing again?

A dry ache formed around a knot in her throat. She cleared it and shook her head. She could sit here and wallow or she could focus on her date. Pushing up from her chair, she stepped into the kitchen and reorganized the countertop to use up her remaining time.

When she pulled up to the diner just before noon, Riley waited by his truck. Nerves fluttered up through her stomach, yet the awkwardness of their first date did not assault her so strongly. She stepped out of the Jeep and they exchanged smiles.

"It's good to see you."

The rather quiet, earnest way in which he said it definitely made a girl feel special, like he'd been thinking about her as much as she'd been thinking about him. A little warmth crept into her cheeks.

"It's good to see you too."

He gestured toward the diner, and they walked to the door. She'd been too nervous last time to notice his subtle limp. She probably wouldn't have at all if he hadn't mentioned it at the bar. The same perky waitress greeted them, all smiles, and led them to the same booth as before. If this happened again, Alex would start to feel like this was their table. That is, if they kept seeing each other after today. Crazy how much she hoped they would.

They both browsed their menus. After a moment, Riley asked, "What's your favorite?"

She looked up and set her menu down. "A bacon cheeseburger, fries, and a vanilla malt. At least until it starts getting cold out. Then I skip the malt."

Apparently, he liked that, and set his own menu aside to focus on her. Alex could only hold his gaze a moment. She ducked her head and brushed a stray piece of hair behind her ear. She wasn't used to being the sole object of a man's attention, but she couldn't deny it felt pretty good to be noticed. No guys had ever made her feel like she was particularly attractive.

"So which businesses did you try yesterday?"

She breathed in deeply and lifted her gaze again. She would not to let her job situation bring her down during this date. "Pretty much everywhere in town, including here." She shrugged. "Most places are fully staffed with people who have lived here for years, if not their whole lives."

Riley gave a brief nod and sat quietly for a moment, as if he were giving the situation thought before he spoke.

"Would you consider working at the bar?"

The question hung in the air before Alex. A thousand and one thoughts skittered through her brain, none actually forming into a coherent response.

"I know it's not ideal," he continued, "but I talked to Luke, my boss, about it last night. He owns the place and is willing to give you a job. You'd only work when I'm working, so you wouldn't have to worry about being there alone or dealing with anyone you didn't feel comfortable with. It wouldn't be full-time—mostly evenings and weekends. I could pick you up and drop you off back home after work so you wouldn't have to be out late alone."

Alex's scrambled thoughts still refused to settle. It was not something she had even remotely considered. "I would have to give it some thought. Um . . ." She had exactly zero experience bartending and the only bars she had ever even seen before the other day were at a couple of reception halls during family weddings and bar and grill restaurants.

"You could just try it out for a few days. It wouldn't have to be permanent. Just a way to earn an income until something else comes along. Luke is pretty flexible. He wouldn't expect you to stay if you didn't want to."

She *did* need a job, desperately. Rent would be due soon, and she wasn't sure she'd have enough, let alone for food. It would be better than commuting to Boulder for a job. While only a twenty-minute drive, she had left her apartment and life in Boulder for a reason. Josh had helped her find and move into that apartment. Being in the city just brought back too many memories. If she didn't take this job, she very well could find herself having to move back home. Sitting here with Riley, that didn't seem like a viable option. Besides, he seemed to have given the whole thing a great deal of thought to make it a comfortable solution for her.

"All right."

He smiled. "Good. Why don't you come by tomorrow afternoon? Luke will be there, and I can start showing you around."

Chapter Four

RILEY THREW A JAB AT THE OLD-AS-HE-WAS PUNCHING BAG hanging in the corner of his apartment. He tried to get a good workout in every morning since he'd been able to stand again without crutches. He didn't consider himself a fitness junkie, but it was a good way to start the day along with Bible reading. It provided good stress relief.

He'd just finished his usual routine and was pulling off his gloves when his phone buzzed on the counter. His first thought was Alex, yet he found a video chat invite from Bradley. Swiping back his damp hair, he accepted the call. A second later, his friend's face popped up, his brown hair cut in a fresh military style and his beard trimmed short. He wasn't in uniform, and the yellow wall decorated with family photos behind him wasn't the military setting Riley expected.

"Hey, man, I thought you were deployed."

Bradley grinned, the corners of his dark eyes crinkling. "I just got back over the weekend."

"That's great." His friend had been away from his family for the last five months. They had to be thrilled to have him home.

"Yeah, I got your text and had to give you a call. How are things going with this girl you met?"

The mention of Alex brought a smile to Riley's face. "So far so good. We had lunch yesterday. She's coming into the bar today to see about working here. It's not the first place I'd invite a woman to work under normal circumstances. But Luke's a good boss, and I'll be around to make sure there aren't any problems."

"Well, God knew what He was doing bringing you into her life. I know you'll bend over backwards to make sure she's all right."

Riley shrugged. "Thanks in large part to you. I wouldn't be the man I am today if you hadn't shaken things up with your incessant God talk."

Bradley's broad grin returned. The man had saved Riley's life in more ways than one. He'd pulled him to safety after the ambush just as surely as he'd helped pull Riley back from an eternity in hell.

"I had to keep at it to get through that thick skull of yours."

Riley laughed. Thank God for a friend as stubborn as he was.

"So, have you talked to your family lately?"

The question came out of nowhere. An uncomfortable bristling inside of Riley promptly swallowed his good humor. He didn't answer for a long moment. Too long. He cleared his throat.

"No."

Bradley just nodded, but even in his silence he had a way of making Riley reevaluate himself and his decisions. Though he appreciated the accountability, it didn't make it any less disquieting to know he could be doing better. Not ready to discuss it further, he changed the subject.

"When is your next deployment? Do you know?"

"There won't be a next for me."

Riley raised his brows.

"After a lot of prayer and consideration," Bradley continued, "I've decided to retire. It's time I devoted my attention to my family."

A wide smile sprang to Riley's face. "That's awesome, man. You deserve it. Heidi and the kids must be thrilled."

"Overjoyed. And this means I can come out and see you one of these days. I can bring the family to do some camping and fishing."

"What, there's no camping and fishing in Wisconsin?" Riley smirked.

"Oh, plenty, but there's no mountains. And, I'm sure you know all the best fishing spots. I haven't been fly fishing since high school. Maybe next summer we can plan a trip."

"We'll make it happen."

———

Alex's stomach quivered. First days at new jobs were always nerve-wracking, and this wasn't like any other first day she had experienced. What should she expect? Her conservative Christian upbringing didn't exactly prepare her for this sort of environment. But it wasn't like she *had* to accept the job. Today was just a trial. She could make her final decision once it was over.

After downing the rest of her morning coffee, she left her apartment. The early afternoon sun shone warmly through the aspen and maple trees that marched single file down both sides of the street. At the front of the house, she met her downstairs neighbor and landlady, Dia Santos. The older, though still spry, woman tended her rose bushes, something she took great pride in.

"Hello, Dia."

The woman looked up with a smile that always brought a twinkle of happiness and, perhaps, even a bit of mischief to her dark eyes. However, it was a little dim today.

"Alex, dear, I heard what happened at the post office. I'm so sorry you got let go."

In a small town, news traveled, especially between those who had lived here for so long.

Alex shrugged and put on a smile. "They did what they had to do."

"Just so you know, if you have to wait a bit on next month's rent, don't worry about it."

"Thank you. I really appreciate that, though I hope it won't be necessary. I'm on my way to a job interview now."

Maybe it wasn't an interview, per se, but she was meeting Luke. He could decide not to hire her even if Riley said he was willing.

"That's wonderful. Let me know how it goes."

"Oh, I will." Alex held her smile a little more tightly. What would the woman think of her working in a bar? Dia was a very devout woman, attending church every Sunday and Wednesday without fail. Still, she'd never kick Alex out. Of that, Alex was certain.

She got into her Jeep and rolled down the window as she drove to the bar. It wasn't far—only a few blocks. If Riley did pick her up and take her home when she worked, at least he wouldn't have to drive her to the opposite end of town.

The butterflies in her stomach burst into a furious flurry when she pulled up in front of the bar and slid out of the Jeep. She paused as she shut her door and looked toward the bridge. If she hadn't stopped here a few days ago, she wouldn't even be here anymore. She'd probably be buried in Bethany Cemetery next to Josh, her parents mourning over both of them. Her throat squeezed around her windpipe.

"Hey."

Alex jumped and turned around. Riley stood in the bar's open doorway. He glanced toward the bridge, but said nothing about it. Instead, he just smiled.

"Ready to learn everything you thought you'd never know about alcoholic beverages?"

A breathy laugh broke out that loosened Alex's throat. "Yes and no."

He tipped his head toward the door. "Don't worry; you'll get the hang of it."

She followed him inside the cool interior. Just seeing him boosted her confidence. Working with him might actually be fun. It was the perfect opportunity to get to know him better and hang out more often.

A couple of customers sat at the tables, but a tall, thin man with black hair and a mustache stood behind the bar and drew her immediate attention. She might have found him intimidating had she been alone, but his smile welcomed her. Riley led her around behind the counter to meet him.

"Alex, this is Luke. Luke, Alex."

Luke extended his hand. "Nice to meet you, Alex."

"You too, and thank you for letting me give this a try. I really appreciate it." Even if bartending was not something she'd ever had in mind, it was still a job.

Luke shrugged. "Riley spoke highly of you, and we can always use an extra hand."

She glanced at Riley. Was he blushing? The butterflies settled with the warm emotions that grew around her heart.

Luke pulled a thin stack of papers out from under the bar. "I just need you to fill out a few things and you'll be good to go."

She took the papers and sat down on the stool at the very end of the bar. It was just the usual contact and information forms so she finished within a few minutes. After all, she'd filled out more than a couple over the years.

"The timesheets are here." Luke showed her a clipboard. "Just put in when you start and when you finish. If you decide to stay, I'll have a check for you every Friday."

"Sounds good."

"Excellent. I'll let Riley show you around. If you have any questions, just ask either of us. I've got errands to run, but I'll be back later."

With that, he left them to their work. Alex turned to Riley. If she was going to do this job, she would learn to do it well, just like her dad had taught her and Josh to do growing up.

"All right, so it might be overwhelming at first," Riley gestured to all the liquor bottles and beer taps, "but, eventually, you'll get the hang of it. Luke has a cheat sheet here if you ever need it." He held up a laminated page full of recipes for different mixed drinks. "Most people who come in are just looking to sit back, relax, and hang out with friends. Things get a bit rowdy on Fridays and Saturdays, but as long as I've been here, we haven't had any real trouble. But you don't have to deal with anyone you're not comfortable with. Just let me know and I'll handle it."

She nodded, fighting not to let her nerves take over again. She'd seen how fellow college students could get on the weekends and the trouble it caused. The last thing she'd imagined then was working at a place where she might have to deal with people like that regularly.

Riley lowered his voice and motioned to the shelf under the bar. "Luke keeps a pistol in the lock box down there, just in case. You know how to use one?"

She nodded again. Growing up on a farm and in a military-oriented family, she had been around and learned to properly handle firearms at a young age. Not that she ever wanted to be in the position to have to use one for anything other than recreation.

"Good. There's never been a need for it, but Luke likes to be prepared."

From there, Riley went on to show her where all the glasses and utensils were located and taught her about their most popular drinks. Her head spun with the information, but then every job had a learning curve.

Customers came and went, never more than two or three at a time. Riley seemed well acquainted with most of them. After helping clean the tables, Alex sat down with Luke's cheat sheet to learn more about mixed drinks. Josh would laugh so hard if he could see her now. He always found humor in things. She missed his laugh and good-natured teasing.

Before the emotion and heartache could gain a foothold, she looked up. She and Riley were alone in the bar right now. She watched him put away clean shot glasses before asking, "So, do you see yourself here for a while, or is it just until something else comes along?"

He turned to her. "Depends on what comes along."

"I know you said you never planned on going into the military. Did you have any dreams, you know, before you parents sent you to culinary school?"

He remained silent for a moment before shaking his head. "Not really. Kind of hard to have dreams when your parents are bent on orchestrating your life for you."

"I suppose so. What about now? Do you have any dreams for the future?"

He shrugged, not looking at her, but gave the distinct impression he did have something in mind.

Maybe just a little coaxing. "There must be something you hope to do or accomplish."

He raised his eyes to her again. "Open a coffee shop."

Her brows shot upward. How many times would he surprise her like this? She could have guessed a long list of things he might be interested in, but a coffee shop wouldn't have been one of them. It was much better than any of her guesses.

Now that he'd said it, he seemed to gain confidence. "I've had my eye on that place over on Martin Avenue."

Alex knew exactly where he was talking about. The old industrial building had once housed the local paper before being converted into a coffee shop. However, the owners had closed it up and moved almost a year and a half ago. So far no one else had seen it as a sound investment and it sat empty. It was a shame. She had loved to go there for coffee, especially around the holidays. The atmosphere was always warm and cozy. She would love for it to open again.

"That sounds like an amazing idea."

He smiled but wasn't as enthused. "Unfortunately, I'm not in any kind of position to make such an investment. I've been saving as much as I can, but the down payment on the building is going to take a while, let alone enough for equipment and supplies."

"Well, I still think it's worth pursuing."

His smile widened, and her heart warmed again at being able to encourage him. Everyone needed validation sometimes, especially dreamers.

"Do the owners know you're interested?"

"I've talked with the realtor, but I can't get serious about a loan until I have the down payment."

"How much more do you need, if you don't mind me asking?" Not that Alex could help. She could barely afford food at the moment.

"About ten grand."

That was a lot, and a hefty commitment on top of it, but most dreams took risk. She knew that well. "I'll pray about it. I know God will provide what you need if it's part of His plan." Her faith might have taken a serious plunge, but she did believe what she said. And praying for and believing in someone else's dream came a lot easier than it did for her own.

Chapter Five

A WEEK INTO HER NEW JOB AT THE BAR, ALEX ACTUALLY FOUND herself picking it up rather quickly. Though she turned to Riley often for direction, she was getting used to taking orders and serving customers. She had even begun to recognize some of the regulars. Old Mr. Jenkins from just down the street was one of her favorites. He was a hoot and never failed to make her laugh with some outrageous story. As Riley had warned her, Friday and Saturday night were a bit hectic, but she had managed with her sanity intact.

But the best part was how well she and Riley were getting along. They had gone on two more dates and had spent hours working together. Somewhere deep down, she had feared they would get tired of each other. However, the more time she spent with him, the more she *wanted* to spend time with him. And, as far as she could tell, he was just as eager. Though she never said it aloud, she tentatively started to consider him her boyfriend. A real boyfriend. Her high school self would have melted into a giddy pile of mush. If only she could have assured herself back then that this day would indeed come.

Today, however, she would have to settle for missing him. It was her day off, and he had an appointment with his physical therapist. They probably wouldn't see each other until tomorrow. Well, she wouldn't mope over it like a love-struck teen. She would make today count. It was high time she got back to her art and took advantage of the whisperings of creativity that had been so absent.

She grabbed a granola bar for breakfast and brewed a mug of coffee from a bag Riley had bought her. She'd never tried it before since it was pricier than she was used to, but he promised it was the best around. Judging by the smell curling up with the steam, she wouldn't be disappointed. She fixed it with sugar and French vanilla creamer and took a sip. Her eyes closed at the smooth, rich flavor. Grabbing her phone from the counter, she typed a quick text.

You should never have bought me this coffee. Now I'm addicted.

A minute passed before her phone chimed a reply.

I told you it was the best.

She grinned and texted him back.

Drive safe today.

I will.

Satisfied, Alex carried her mug, granola bar, and phone into the living room. She was ready to get to work; however, the teal cover of her Bible sitting on an end table next to the sofa caught her eye. For days she had told herself she would make time to read it, yet every day slipped by with the promise unfulfilled. She sighed. Of course, she *wanted* to read. Her heart ached for it, in fact. But she still felt so . . . unworthy.

She straightened her shoulders. She would do it today. The hesitation and feelings of shame did not come from God, which meant they only came from one other source. She would not let Satan succeed in dragging her down. Setting her coffee on the end table, she curled up into the corner of her happy yellow couch and picked up her Bible. The cover and pages were well worn with use, though unfortunately not from the last couple of years.

She opened it up to one of her watercolor bookmarks where she had left off trying to read Psalms just after Josh died. Her heart constricted with the pain but with longing too. She closed her eyes and whispered into the stillness of her apartment.

"I feel like I've made such a mess of things I can't even come to You, Lord. I know that's not true, I'm just finding it hard to get past how terribly I've failed in the last couple of years. After Josh died, I should have clung to You, but I just sank deeper and deeper into my grief. I'm still afraid I'll fail again, but I want to change. I really want to change."

Riley came to mind.

"Thank You for bringing him into my life. I've never met anyone like him. Please help us both to pursue You, individually and in our relationship. I've never had this before. I don't want to do anything to ruin it."

She went on to pray silently for Riley and his dreams about the coffee shop. She also prayed about her parents, about her art, and about everything surrounding it. She hadn't truly prayed in so long she only now realized just how much she had to pray about. Almost an hour had passed before she even opened her Bible.

A while later, a chirp from her phone drew Alex out of her reading. It wasn't Riley's text tone, and she frowned. However, a smile replaced it when she picked up the phone and read Mindy's name. She opened up the text.

Hey girl! How have you been? It's been way too long! We desperately need to catch up. Give me a call when you have the chance.

Had Alex received the text two weeks ago, she would have ignored it for a few days, hoping Mindy just thought she was busy and forgot to call. She tapped on Mindy's name to bring up her contact information and stared at the call button. She would have to be honest about how she had been lately. Mindy would know just by her voice if she tried to conceal her struggles. Did she really want to delve into it? However, today had become about making things right. She hit call. The phone rang twice before Mindy's voice filled her ear.

"Alex! I'm so glad you called!"

"Hey, Mindy," she said through a smile.

"It's so good to hear your voice."

"Yours too." Really, her friend's bubbly enthusiasm was like a balm. She should never have avoided calling.

"How are you? I've been worried. I haven't heard from you in ages."

"I'm okay." Alex paused for a moment. This would probably turn into a three-hour call. But that was okay. She needed this, hard as it might be. "Well, I'm okay right now. Things were pretty bad a couple of weeks ago."

"What happened? Are you sure you're okay?"

Alex nodded, even though Mindy couldn't see her. "Yeah, I am. I lost my job at the post office."

"Oh, Alex." She could just imagine Mindy's delicate face scrunching up to commiserate. "Will you be able to afford rent? I can send money. Don't hesitate to ask. Any luck finding another job?"

Her friend's rapid-fire questions drew a quiet laugh from Alex. "Thank you for the offer, but yes, I'm working again."

She paused once more. So far, no one else knew about the recent developments in her life. She wasn't exactly scared to tell Mindy about her job, but hesitancy lingered.

"So where at?" Mindy asked when her silence stretched out.

"Well, um, I'm bartending."

One heartbeat of silence.

"Huh. Well that's interesting."

Alex detected the surprise in Mindy's voice but no judgment. "It's not quite like it sounds. I mean, the job is, but the circumstances are a little out of the ordinary."

"Do tell," Mindy replied, now all interest.

"Well, I'm seeing someone."

Mindy squealed, and Alex had to take the phone away from her ear.

"Alex, that's awesome! What's he like? How did you meet? Seriously, I want to know *everything*."

She laughed. Where did she even start? "His name is Riley. He's former-military. He's cute. He loves coffee as much as I do. And he's really sweet."

Mindy squealed again, more quietly this time, and Alex could just picture her bouncing up and down in excitement. She was the textbook definition of over-the-top. "Do you have a picture of him you can send me?"

"Not yet." Alex was self-conscious taking selfies to begin with. She hadn't yet worked up the guts to take one with Riley. She should though. She would probably wish she had in the future.

"Aww," Mindy whined.

"We've only been going out for a week and a half. It's not like we're halfway to getting engaged or anything."

"All right, so tell me more. Details, Alex, details."

She smiled, but it faded. In order to tell Mindy *how* she and Riley had met, she would have to tell her *why* they had met. Her stomach formed a tight knot. Riley was the only person in the world who knew what she had almost done.

"I met him at the bar. He works there."

"Okay." The slow way in which she said it hinted at her confusion. Alex was not someone who would just randomly walk into a bar.

"I . . ." Alex bit her lip. "I went in there for a drink. I thought it might help when I . . ." She swallowed hard, and barely whispered the next bit. "When I jumped off of Baylor's Bridge."

Mindy gasped. After a moment of suffocating silence, she practically cried Alex's name.

"I know. I just . . . things were really hard and I, uh . . ." She didn't really have a good excuse or explanation.

"Are you really okay?" Mindy asked, her voice low and a bit choked.

"Yes, I am." It felt good to say it with even an ounce of confidence. "Thanks to Riley. We started talking while I was sitting at the bar and when I was about to leave, he asked me out for breakfast. He changed my mind, Min."

A little sob came over the phone. "I'm so glad, Alex."

She breathed in deeply. "So am I."

"You should've called me when things were bad. I would've been there in a heartbeat."

Alex sighed. She had no good excuse for that either. "I know, but you're four hours away."

"I would've driven twenty if I'd known what shape you were in!"

Alex hung her head. "I know. I'm sorry."

"Well," Mindy said as if working to compose herself, "this seems like the perfect time to give you my news."

Alex was all ears. Were Mindy and Zach going to have a baby?

However, Mindy told her, "Zach got promoted."

"That's awesome," she replied. "Tell him congratulations for me."

"Actually, you can tell him yourself. He's being transferred . . . to Boulder."

Alex's heart thumped. "Wait, you're moving to Boulder?"

"We are!" Mindy's enthusiasm returned full force. "And he has training next week. I plan to come with him so we can start looking at houses, and it's definitely time you and I spent some quality time together."

Alex grinned, her eyes getting watery. "I'd like that."

She hadn't seen Mindy in almost two years. They had a lot of catching up to do. No doubt her friend would have more to say about her near-suicide. And with her friend living in Boulder, maybe she could face the city again without the memories being too painful.

"We'll be coming up Monday," Mindy said. "When are you free next week?"

"Well, I'm supposed to work evenings Wednesday through Saturday."

"How about we plan on me coming over Tuesday morning and we'll see from there?"

"I'll be waiting for you then."

After saying goodbye, Alex set her phone down and smiled. A visit with Mindy was sure to energize her. Though Mindy had gone to school for photography, not art, they both had an artistic view of the world. If anyone could get her excited to paint again, it would be Mindy.

She closed her Bible, which still sat in her lap, and took a silent moment to thank God for meeting her where she was and giving her such a wonderful surprise. She still had a long way to go, but this morning she was on a good path. Finally.

She looked at the clock. It was noon already? No wonder her stomach grumbled. She hadn't even finished her granola bar. Time to make lunch and then, maybe, she could get to work on a painting.

Alex perched on her artist stool in front of her easel, lightly adding shadows to her painting. The mountain meadow she worked on wasn't quite to her liking, but she'd determined to keep on. She wouldn't get anywhere if she kept giving up on pieces. Maybe, in the end, it would actually turn out. It still didn't quite dispel the fear she might never paint again like she used to. She had feared for a long time her talents had died with Josh. But when she'd admitted it to Riley at work the other day, he'd encouraged her that maybe she just needed a little more time, and that Josh wouldn't want her giving up. That had been the most encouraging thing anyone had told her in a long time. Josh had always wanted her to succeed. If nothing else, she had to push forward for him.

A knock tapped the door. She paused and frowned. She almost never had anyone show up at her door. Maybe it was Dia. She set her paintbrush down carefully and wiped her hands on a rag. At the door, she parted the curtain over the window. A grin sprang to her lips, and she opened the door to Riley.

"You never said you were stopping over here."

"I wanted to bring you something." He held up a bag of coffee. "I stopped at a shop in Denver after my appointment. I think you'll like this one."

She took the bag and brought it to her nose to breathe in the delicious caramel-laced scent.

"It smells heavenly, but you shouldn't spend all your hard-earned money on me. Not when you're trying to save up."

"Isn't that what a girlfriend is for?" He seemed to gauge how she would respond to being called his girlfriend.

She answered with another grin. Now it was official. "I suppose. Still, I don't want you going overboard. I don't require gifts. Time is much more precious to me."

"Then would you like to get dinner tonight?"

"I'd love to. I just have to clean my paintbrushes." She took a step back and gestured inside. "Do you want to come in?"

He nodded, and she let him through. He stepped into the small kitchen and dining area of the apartment and looked around. Besides her dad, Alex had never had a male presence here before. She never would have invited just anyone in, but she felt safe with Riley. He hadn't proven to be anything less than a perfect gentleman.

She waited a moment to see if he'd say anything. After his brief perusal, he turned to her. "It's a nice place."

"Thank you. I'm thankful to have it. Dia is very flexible as far as rent, and it's a lot cheaper than most apartment buildings." She motioned toward the wide doorway into the living room. "I just need to get my paintbrushes before they dry."

She walked to her art table and collected the brushes and her paint palette. When she carried them to the kitchen sink and began cleaning, Riley stepped to the doorway of the living room and looked in at her work.

"That's a beautiful painting."

Alex shrugged. "I'm still not happy with it. I don't know why. Maybe it's just me."

"I think it's just you."

She appreciated his words, even if she didn't entirely believe him. After setting her brushes on a paper towel to dry and wiping her hands, she turned away from the sink.

"I just need to change, and then we can go."

Alex hurried to her room where she changed into a pair of jeans and grabbed a flannel shirt just in case it got chilly later. It was feeling ever more like fall, especially in the evening. She slipped on a comfortable pair of moccasins, grabbed her purse and phone, and joined Riley back in the kitchen.

"Ready."

They stepped outside and descended the stairs down to Alex's small, private porch. Dia was just coming out the front door with a pitcher of lemonade and a basket sure to contain homemade sweets she set on her antiqued patio table. Tonight was the weekly knitting get-together she hosted. She'd invited Alex more than once, but there was nothing like the thought of joining a knitting club to make her feel like a spinster.

"Alex," she said cheerfully when she looked up. Her gaze drifted to Riley and then back to Alex, sparkling with curiosity.

Alex paused with Riley at her side. "This is Riley Conrad. We work together and . . . he's my boyfriend. He's taking me out to dinner tonight." She shared a quick smile with Riley.

Dia looked positively delighted. This would certainly dominate tonight's conversation with her friends.

"How wonderful! I'm very pleased to meet you, Riley. I'm sure you'll take very good care of that young lady."

Alex had no idea if she said it in a completely innocent manner or if it was actually more of a challenge. She almost giggled to think of Dia giving Riley a subtle threat behind that pleased smile of hers.

Very seriously, he promised, "Yes, ma'am."

Her smile turned to one of satisfaction. "Enjoy your evening."

"You too," Alex replied.

She and Riley walked to the street where he'd parked his truck. He opened the door for her, just as he did whenever he picked her up for work. She had been positively thrilled to ride with him the first time. There was just something about old trucks that couldn't be beat.

When Riley got in, he said, "I have an idea your landlady could be dangerous if provoked."

Alex laughed outright. "You caught that then? I'm thinking the same thing. I could just see her gathering up her friends and coming after you with brooms and knitting needles if you break my heart."

He glanced over at her, his smile teasing, yet serious at the same time. "I'll have to make sure not to break your heart then."

She was pretty sure her face was glowing as they pulled away from the house.

They picked up burgers and malts to-go from the diner and drove to a park overlooking the creek the town was named after. Riley backed his truck up to the stream, and they took seats on his tailgate. With no one else around this evening, everything was perfectly quiet except for the sounds of nature. Alex didn't mind living in a quiet town like Aspen Creek, but there were plenty of times she missed the country. Evenings like this helped.

They talked about Riley's appointment, and Alex told him about her phone call with Mindy. He said it would be no problem for her to take off as many days as she needed next week. He was adamant, actually, that she should spend time with Mindy.

Chewing a bite of her burger, Alex eyed the braided bracelet Riley always wore around his tanned wrist. Though it had probably faded over time, it looked like nothing more than an old piece of rough string. It surely held some significance if he never took it off.

"Where did you get your bracelet?"

He glanced at it. "A little girl in Afghanistan gave it to me. I taught her and her brothers how to play tic-tac-toe in the dirt."

"Aw." The thought of that brought a grin to Alex's lips.

He pulled out his phone and, after scrolling through it, he handed it to her. A picture of him in full military gear with three dark-haired Afghan children lit up the screen. The little girl couldn't have been more than six years old. Alex's heart melted into a warm puddle at the sight of Riley sitting and smiling with them.

"That's adorable." She handed the phone back. "You have to send it to me." She'd cherish it forever, probably giving it a place on the wall in her living room with her other special photos.

When they finished their burgers and malts, they took the bag of wrappers to the trashcan and walked down to the stream where an old log had been used as a bench for years. Carved initials, names, and hearts covered the worn surface. They sat down, shoulders and elbows brushing. A bit of a flutter passed through Alex's chest to be so close to him. Romantic comedies and romance novels didn't quite prepare one for a real life relationship. What she hadn't anticipated was how comfortable she would feel around him after so short a time. She had always been awkward and self-conscious around strangers, either not knowing what to say or rambling nervously. But with Riley, that wasn't the case at all. Even in silence, she didn't feel pressured to say anything at all. Just enjoy Riley's company, like now.

After a couple of minutes, he finally spoke.

"Do you like to fish?"

Alex nodded enthusiastically. "I do. My dad used to take us all the time, and then Josh and I went whenever he was home. We were always going to learn how to fly fish." She let a quiet sigh escape. Too many plans would now remain unfulfilled.

"I could teach you."

She looked over at him, meeting his eyes and smiling. "I'd like that."

He held her gaze. She hadn't noticed until now just how blue his eyes were as he looked deeply into hers. No one had ever looked at her like that before. Her heart beat like wings about to take flight. He bent toward her, and she found herself leaning in to meet him. His lips pressed against hers, stealing her breath away. He kissed her gently, tentatively, and then pulled away slowly. Only then did she notice the way he cradled the side of her face with his hand. Her brain had puddled into mush, and all she could do was grin. He smiled right back, sending warmth cascading all through her.

When he pulled his hand back, she found herself missing the presence of it against her cheek. But her brain did solidify again, allowing semi-coherent thoughts to form once more.

"Do you want to go for a walk?"

Alex only nodded, still a bit breathless.

Riley stood and extended his hand to her. She took it, and he helped her up. Instead of releasing her hand, he kept it captured in his, and she happily left it there. Ever since she was young, she had dreamed of the little things like handholding. She could hardly wrap her mind around the fact it was happening now.

For the next while, they followed the well-worn paths others had left along the creek, serenaded by crickets and trickling water. They talked and laughed, discussing fishing and other outdoor activities they made plans to do together. When dusk settled, Riley led her back to his truck.

Back at Alex's apartment, he walked her up to the house where they stopped on the porch. Light streamed through the downstairs windows, and conversation and laughter from Dia and the other ladies drifted from inside. Alex smiled. Would she catch anything about her and Riley?

She turned to him, her grin widening. She hadn't smiled this easily in years.

"Thanks for a perfect evening."

She could easily fall head over heels with that smile he was giving her.

He nodded. "I'll see you tomorrow."

Alex remained on the porch as he turned and walked back to his truck. She gave him a little wave just before he drove away and then climbed the stairs to her apartment door. The moment she let herself inside, she released a long, happy sigh, not even caring how ridiculously dreamy and love-struck she probably sounded. Life was too short not to savor such moments.

Chapter Six

ALEX HAD JUST FINISHED CLEANING UP THE KITCHEN AND STARTING a load of laundry Tuesday morning when someone knocked on the door. Trust Mindy to show up ASAP. She opened the door, a huge grin springing to her face at the sight of her friend.

"Alex!" Mindy practically squealed. She had Alex in a tight hug before even making it all the way through the door.

Alex squeezed her back, laughing at her friend's abundant energy. She didn't know where it all came from. Even during college finals, Mindy hadn't slowed down. Instead, she'd been a bundle of exuberance fueled by caffeine. A part of her missed those days. Everything had seemed so exciting and possible then.

She pushed away the twinge of melancholy the memories stirred as they parted. Mindy, however, grabbed her shoulders and said in a no-nonsense way, "We are going to have the best time while I'm here. Got that?"

Alex laughed again, looking up at her friend. Mindy stood a couple of inches taller than her, not counting her affinity for heels. Tall, willowy, with a dark bob of wispy hair and smooth skin that always looked sun-kissed no matter the time of year—Mindy was as near perfect as a girl could get. Add to it her own unique style that blended casual, Bohemian, and a touch of high fashion, and it was little wonder Zach had fallen for her so hard. Alex really did envy her self-assuredness. But the great thing about Mindy was how she strove to project her confidence and joy into the lives of those around her. Alex always felt better about herself just being in Mindy's presence.

"Got it," she responded with a firm nod. She had every intention of enjoying this visit to the fullest.

Mindy then looked around the kitchen and dining room. "Oo, I love what you've done in here. And something smells divine."

"Thanks. I just put in chicken a bit ago. I thought we could have chicken salad sandwiches for lunch."

"That sounds delicious. I haven't had them since college. I never remember to make some." Mindy set her purse and keys down on the counter and turned back to Alex. "All right, now please tell me you have a picture. I've been absolutely dying with curiosity."

Alex laughed. "Well, we did go for a walk the other night, and I finally took a selfie with him." She'd been a bit embarrassed to ask, but he hadn't minded at all.

"Lemme see!"

Mindy crowded in at her side as Alex picked up her phone and opened the photo app. She brought up the photo of her and Riley, slightly self-conscious.

Mindy snatched the phone from her. "Oh my, he is cute. And just look at how adorable you two are!" She was like a kid let loose in a candy store. "You have no idea how insanely excited I am for you. Please tell me he's treating you right and it's serious and you'll stay together forever."

Alex had a feeling she would laugh a lot today. "Yes, he's treating me very well. He's very sweet and chivalrous. Seriously, I wasn't sure there were any guys left like him. And I think it's serious. I love being with him and working with him." She shrugged. "We get along really well and . . . it just seems right."

"Oh, you're smitten, aren't you?"

Alex glanced down, practically feeling her cheeks turning

pink. "Maybe." She looked up again, battling a bashful smile. "Still, I'm trying not to be too silly or foolish about it, especially since I've never dated before. I don't want to fall head over heels for a guy before I know if it's wise."

"Is there anything you're unsure of?"

"About him?" Alex shook her head. "No. About me making stupid decisions or messing everything up? Yes."

"Hey, give yourself a little credit. You made it through college and have been making it on your own all this time. All of that was new when you started, but here you are. And if he's half the guy he should be to deserve you, he won't scare easily. Just imagine what Zach puts up with being married to me."

Mindy could definitely be a handful.

"Besides," she continued, "if you're both praying about the relationship and for guidance, then you're way ahead of most couples out there. That makes all the difference."

Though Alex still struggled to reach the place of deep faith she'd relied on earlier in her life, she did pray about her relationship with Riley. More than she had prayed about anything in years.

She moved toward the kitchen counter. "Do you want coffee?"

"Always." With a cheeky grin, Mindy slid onto one of the barstools on the opposite side of the counter.

Alex filled the coffeemaker with the coffee Riley had brought her after his appointment. While waiting for it to brew, she peeked over at Mindy, who was checking her phone.

"He kissed me the other night."

Mindy's eyes shot up, and her phone rattled on the counter. Her mouth fell open with a squeal. It was a good thing Alex had given her the news now instead of after handing over the coffee or her friend might have choked in her giddiness.

"Your first kiss! Oh, you must tell me! Did you like it?"

Alex's cheeks competed with the heat coming from the coffee pot. What kind of question was that? "Yeah," she mumbled through an attempt to wipe the dreamy grin from her face.

Mindy laughed. "It's so funny seeing you blush. I don't think I ever have before." She leaned over the counter a little. "So it was a good kiss then?"

That set her face on fire. "I mean, yeah, I think so. It's not like I had anything to compare it with."

"Oh, you'd know if it was a bad kiss."

Alex hid her face behind a cabinet door as she reached for the coffee mugs, letting herself grin fully. It was a good kiss.

Composing herself, she set the mugs on the counter and closed the cabinet. Mindy still watched her intently, her eyes sparkling with an abundance of delight and mischief. While her friend was sure to have a gazillion more questions, Alex shifted the subject to let her flushed cheeks return to normal.

"So you and Zach. Any babies on the way?"

Mindy raised a brow and gave her a look that told Alex the Riley subject was far from over.

"No. No babies on the way."

"And is that by choice or . . ."

"By choice."

Alex had no reason to doubt her.

"Don't get me wrong. I adore kids as much as the next person, but let's face it, kids change everything. Zach and I are perfectly happy at this point in our lives to be husband and wife. We're not quite ready to cross the parent bridge just yet."

"Well, remember, after your parents, I'm the first one who needs to know about it when you do."

"Of course." Mindy cast her a mischievous grin. "After all, now that we're moving to Boulder, you can be our free babysitter when the time comes."

"You can pay me with coffee."

All morning and late into the afternoon, Alex sat with Mindy in the living room catching up. They had so much to talk about. Of course, Riley came up in their conversation many times. Alex told Mindy all about work and what she knew of Riley's family. That led to lighthearted teasing about Alex marrying into wealth.

Though the talk remained light and carefree, one particular topic hovered unspoken between them. Finally, as the late afternoon sun streamed in through the windows, a lull settled between them. Mindy just looked at Alex for a long moment, her expression slowly sinking, the usual twinkle in her eyes growing dim.

"Were you really going to do it?"

Alex let out her breath slowly, her mind slipping back to that day. She could still feel it so strongly. "I don't know. I wanted to. Whether I actually would have when I got there . . ." She shrugged. It was hard to say exactly what would have happened in that moment. Would the pain have won? Or would something inside of her have fought harder to live? "I just don't know."

Mindy's eyes filled with tears. "I'm so sorry you felt that was all you had left. I had no idea things were so bad."

"It's not your fault. No one knew. Everyone thought I was just busy . . . and that's what I let you all think. My parents don't even know. You're the first one I've told besides Riley."

Mindy leaned closer to her on the couch and took her hand, squeezing it. "Listen, I don't want you to *ever* feel like you only have one option again, do you hear me? You don't have to do this alone. It doesn't matter when or where, you pick up that phone and call me, all right?"

Alex took a deep breath. "All right."

Chapter Seven

MINDY RETURNED BRIGHT AND EARLY THE NEXT MORNING WITH a box of pastries from Boulder. Alex already had a full pot of coffee brewed in preparation, so the two of them prepared their mugs and sat down at the table across from each other with the pastries between them. Alex picked out a donut with a generous coating of white icing. She bit into it, savoring the melt-in-yourmouth sweetness.

"Mmm, these are divine!" Mindy said around a bite.

Alex gave a hearty nod. "They were always my favorite when I lived there. Mind if I save one for Riley?"

"Not at all. Take two, actually. I went a little overboard, but everything just looked so good." Mindy took another bite and chewed contentedly for a moment. "Speaking of Riley, any chance I can meet him before Zach and I have to go back to Trinidad?"

"Well, he's working through Saturday, but we could bring lunch over to the bar. It's always pretty quiet until later in the afternoon."

Mindy's expression crinkled mischievously. "I've never hung out in a bar before."

Alex just laughed and wiped her sticky fingers on a napkin. "Let me text him and make sure it's okay."

She composed a text with her plans to which he promptly replied. "Looks like we've got a lunch date at the bar."

Mindy gave her a silly grin. "Wait until Zach hears about this."

"When are you two leaving?"

"Well, Zach finishes training on Friday. We thought we'd stay the weekend to look at houses. Providing we can get a hotel, of course. The company only reserved us one through Thursday night."

"No need for a hotel. You can stay here."

"If it won't be a bother . . ."

"A bother? Come on, I'd love to have you and Zach stay. I'll have to work on Friday and Saturday since those are the busiest days, but I can give you a key. Just make yourselves at home. And if you're not in any hurry to leave on Sunday, we could even have dinner and I could invite Riley. Luke gives us Sundays and Mondays off while he and his girlfriend work."

"Oh, oh, oh!" Mindy bounced in her seat. "Denver's first game is on Sunday. We could make a party of it!"

Alex hadn't paid attention to football since Josh died. The two of them and their dad had been huge Broncos fans back in the day. She desperately missed those lazy Sunday afternoons and evenings when the three of them would sit around the TV cheering on their team while Mom worked on knitting or one of her other craft projects.

"That sounds great." Maybe she could recapture some of the team spirit.

"Perfect. And if there's any chance you can get off work Saturday, I want you to come house hunting with us."

Alex shook her head. "I wouldn't want to be a third wheel. I'm sure you two would enjoy the time together."

But Mindy insisted. "You have such an artistic eye. I'd love your input."

"Well, I can ask."

Mindy settled back in her chair, looking perfectly pleased, as if it were a done deal.

Alex took another big bite of her donut and then wiped her mouth with her napkin. "How does your dad feel about your move?" Since Mindy's mom had died when she was only three, it had always been just her and her dad. They were super close.

Mindy shrugged. "It's hard, of course, but he understands and wants the best for us. Half of me hates the thought of moving away from him, but the other half can't wait to start somewhere new. Other than college, I've never lived outside of Trinidad."

Alex nodded. It was hard to venture away from the familiarity and safety of home, but a good thing too. "Well, I'm really excited for you to be in Boulder. I've had a hard time going back there, but I think it will be different once you're there."

"I should hope so, after all the fun weekends we spent there between studying."

Alex laughed. Boulder had been one of their favorite destinations when they'd had to get away from Denver for a while. It was why she had chosen to get an apartment there after college in the first place. She would focus on those memories instead of the ones that brought pain.

"So, do you guys have any particular houses in mind?"

"Yes." Mindy reached for her bag at the end of the table and pulled out her tablet. "Zach and I have been looking at realty sites and set up showings for our favorites." She brought up a realty app, and Alex moved around to the other side of the table to see.

For the next couple of hours, they looked through house photos and discussed possibilities for each one. Alex really did enjoy dreaming up ways to decorate the different rooms. Perhaps interior decorating was her second calling. She wasn't sure she could give up art, though, no matter how miserably she was failing at the moment.

Around noon, the two of them grabbed their purses and headed out to Mindy's SUV. They stopped at a local place for sub sandwiches and then drove over to the bar. A twinge passed through Alex's belly as they got out in front of the bar and approached the door. What if Mindy found a reason not to like Riley? How would Alex deal with the devastation? The questions must have been written all over her face.

Mindy grabbed her arm and leaned in close, almost smashing the bag of subs between them. "Don't worry. From everything you've told me, I'm sure I'll love him."

Alex blew out a huge breath. "I just hope you don't spot something about him that I haven't." She could just see herself falling for a guy and missing all the red flags.

"Give yourself more credit. You might be new at this, but you've always been good at reading guys."

Alex didn't hold nearly that level of confidence, but she kept it to herself as they entered. Riley stood behind the bar, breaking into a smile when he saw her. A flutter passed through her chest. She wasn't sure if it helped or just elevated her nerves. Her heart probably wouldn't slow it's uncomfortably up-tempo rhythm until she and Mindy left.

He stepped out to meet them, and Alex made introductions. Though perfectly comfortable with both Riley and Mindy, right now she felt one step away from stumbling over her words. Why did her nerves always have to take over at such inopportune times?

Mindy shook Riley's hand, the metal bangles and turquoise beads around her wrist clinking. "It's so nice to meet you, Riley. My visit wouldn't have been complete without getting to meet the guy Alex has been telling me about."

He offered a charming smile, and Alex's cheeks heated up again. Who knew Mindy would be such an instant expert at making her blush?

"It's nice to meet you too. I'm glad you and Alex are getting to spend time together. Sounds like you had a lot of fun in college."

"We had a blast," Mindy replied as the three of them moved toward the bar. "Actually, if not for Alex, I wouldn't be married to my best friend."

"Really?" Riley seemed genuinely intrigued.

Mindy nodded, and Alex let her tell the story while she set the bag of subs on the bar and distributed them.

"Our first year in college, she invited me to spend Thanksgiving with her family. That's when I met Zach. I know a lot of people dismiss the notion of love at first sight, but I'm not sure what else to call it."

"It was definitely love at first sight," Alex said, calmed by the pleasant memories. "I saw the way your eyes lit up when you first saw him. And his did too."

The two of them took seats at the bar, while Riley stood across from them. He poured them each a glass of soda, and they dug into their subs. Mindy and Riley did most of the talking. Though Alex kept waiting for something catastrophic to happen, they each seemed to enjoy the other's company. And Riley kept sending glances and smiles Alex's way, even when she wasn't an active part of the conversation.

Once they had finished the meal and Riley had the latest customers taken care of, Mindy put on a smile Alex was sure could persuade just about anyone.

"So, Riley, do you think you could possibly get Alex out of work on Saturday? Zach and I are looking at houses, and I would love her artistic expertise."

Alex quickly jumped in. "If not, that's perfectly fine. I don't want to take advantage of Luke's generosity or skip out on work when I've only just started here."

Riley shook his head. "Go ahead. If things get too busy, I'm sure Kat would come in."

Alex hadn't met Luke's girlfriend yet, but Riley said she was nice and always pitched in if it got busy. "Are you sure? It doesn't even have to be for my whole shift. Mindy and Zach can drop me off here as soon as we get back to town."

"Whatever you want to do is fine."

Alex found it hard not to just smile at him. "Thanks. I really appreciate it."

"No problem."

"Awesome." Mindy grinned and then gave Alex a prompting look.

"Mindy and Zach are staying at my place this weekend and we're planning a little party for the Broncos game. Would you like to join us? Then you could meet Zach."

"I'd love to," Riley replied. "I probably would've ended up just hanging out down here with the rest of the customers. Do you want me to bring anything?"

"I guess if you have something particular you'd like to snack on. Mindy and I are already planning to get pizzas."

"What time?"

"Any time before noon is fine." She certainly wouldn't complain about spending extra time with him.

With the party plans settled and a couple of new customers walking in, Mindy and Alex said goodbye to Riley and headed outside. When they got into the vehicle and Mindy turned in the direction of the antique shop she wanted to check out, Alex looked over at her.

"So?" She held her breath.

"That boy is in love with you."

Alex forced the air out of her lungs in a gust. "Come on, Min, we've only known each other for a couple of weeks."

"Pooh-pooh me all you want, but just remember I told you so. Maybe he doesn't even realize it yet, but the eyes don't lie. He's as smitten as you are."

Alex just shook her head. However, deep down, she couldn't help feeling distinctly pleased. "And, if that were true, do you think it's a good thing?"

Mindy sent her a bright grin. "I do."

Chapter Eight

ALEX AWOKE TO SUNLIGHT STREAMING THROUGH THE LIVING room windows on Saturday morning. Though the rays warmed her face, the air in her apartment had a definite crispness to it. Not long now and she would be wearing sweaters and boots. She stretched out on the couch and yawned. It had gotten late last night. Mindy and Zach had arrived shortly before suppertime, and they'd spent hours talking around the kitchen table and then sitting comfortably in the living room with mugs of coffee.

She reached for her phone to check the time. Just after six-thirty. With another yawn, she pushed aside the throw blankets wrapped around her and got up. She would have to hurry with breakfast to have it ready in time for them to eat and get to their first house showing. Grabbing the clothes she'd laid out last night, she padded quietly to the bathroom.

After dressing and pinning her hair up in a bun, she entered the kitchen and gathered ingredients for a batch of French toast and bacon. She also put on a full pot of coffee. Between the three of them, they would probably have it finished by the time they left.

She stood at the stove frying breakfast when Zach walked in a little while later, his dark hair still damp from a shower. Alex sent him a smile. "Good morning."

It had been so good to see him yesterday. The two of them shared so many memories of Josh, and Zach was as close as family. He and Josh had been inseparable growing up. And wherever they had gone, Alex usually had too, whether it involved riding their bikes into town for ice cream, playing video games, or constructing stick forts in the woods connecting their families' properties.

He echoed her with a grin, his brown eyes as kind and approachable as always. He had the perfect calm and grounded personality to blend well with and sometimes temper Mindy's spunk. And despite how many would have mistaken him as a total nerd between his IT job and the blue Captain America t-shirt he wore, Alex knew better. He was a country boy underneath who just happened to also be a computer geek. He was a unique blend, just like her and Mindy. It was no wonder the three of them got along so well.

"Breakfast smells good," he said.

Alex thanked him and gestured to the coffeemaker with her spatula. "Coffee should be ready. I made it strong like you like it."

Zach helped himself, pouring a large mug of the fresh, steaming brew and drinking it black like Josh used to. "Mm, that's good. What brand is it?"

"The bag is by the toaster. Riley bought it for me at a shop in Denver."

Zach leaned against the counter and studied the coffee bag. "Mindy's been telling me about him."

Alex glanced over at him, waiting.

He smiled. "All good things."

A smile touched her face as well. "I'm glad you'll get to meet him tomorrow. Neither of us really have close friends here in Aspen Creek, so it would be great if the four of us could hang out once you and Mindy move to Boulder."

She paused to flip a piece of French toast and then looked at Zach again. "Did she tell you about Riley and Josh?"

He nodded slowly. "Yeah."

Emotion clouded his eyes, and Alex's throat squeezed. They'd both lost a brother.

She cleared her throat. "I'm just about done with this. Will Mindy be ready soon?"

Zach blinked, the emotion fading. "She should be." His smile returned. "Although, she's not very speedy in the morning. At least not until she gets her coffee."

Mindy happened to walk in right then. She smacked him lightly on the shoulder over the counter. "I heard that."

He feigned innocence. "What did I say?"

She shot him a little smirk and walked straight to the coffee pot. Fixing her mug, she looked over at Alex. "You didn't have to go to all this trouble to make breakfast for us. We could've grabbed something on the way."

"I like cooking for people. I never get the chance to cook for anyone but myself."

"Well, it does smell delicious, so thank you."

In a couple of minutes, Alex brought everything to the table. Zach said a quick prayer for the meal, and they dished up. Around bites of syrupy French toast, they discussed the houses they planned to look at and exactly what Mindy and Zach hoped to find.

With full bellies and travel mugs, they set out for Boulder. Alex sat in the back seat as they drove along the winding roads and peered out the window. Here and there she spotted leaves beginning to change to autumn golds and reds. Mindy and Zach talked and teased each other, and Alex listened with a smile on her face. They were as close to a fairytale couple as she figured could exist in real life. She had prayed so fervently for such a relationship during her late teens and early twenties.

The twenty-minute drive brought them to the outskirts of Boulder. Zach pulled into one of the driveways after Mindy pointed out the right address number, and they parked in front of a nice-sized colonial-style home with white siding, charcoal gray shutters, and a huge front porch.

They got out of the SUV and met the realtor—a tall, blonde woman in a professional navy blue pantsuit. She greeted them enthusiastically and handed Mindy and Zach each papers of information about the house before leading them inside. The first thing Alex noticed upon entering was how much the previous owners liked color. So many houses had drab beiges and creams, but every room they entered sported a different shade, ranging from cool aqua, to spring green, to soft orange. Tasteful colors. Nothing too over the top.

The bright aqua tile flooring in the kitchen drew a half gasp, half delighted squeal from Mindy. Alex laughed quietly at the way she grabbed Zach's arm as if projecting her excited energy onto him. She then studied the white cabinets and stone backsplash. It was a modern kitchen, yet still held a country feel. With brightly colored appliances and dishes, it would make the perfect kitchen for someone as creatively colorful as Mindy.

They toured the second floor next, though Alex had begun to tune out the realtor, letting her own thoughts wander. While she loved her little apartment, she dreamed of what it would be like to have a house of her own—to have a separate painting studio and office instead of trying to fit it all into the living room.

And what would it be like to share a life with someone the way Mindy and Zach did? Riley jumped to mind, but she brushed the thoughts away. She wouldn't get ahead of herself and start dreaming about a future that was in no way guaranteed. Mindy might have said Riley was in love with her, but they had never said anything of the sort to each other. Alex wasn't even sure exactly what she felt for Riley yet. Yes, she did feel something that grew a little bit deeper every time they were together. She did care deeply for him, but she wouldn't go all in and call it love.

At least not love like Mindy and Zach shared. It was far too early for anything like that.

"What do you think?"

Alex snapped from her musings when Mindy appeared in front of her, her face glowing.

"I think it's beautiful."

It might seem a bit big for only two people, but it wouldn't be just the two of them forever. And they had their two dogs back home, an adorable English bulldog and a lovely golden retriever. Plus, Mindy loved entertaining and having guests. A larger house would make that much easier.

"It really suits you."

Mindy grinned as if on the verge of squealing again.

"Well, my wife might be sold already," Zach said to the realtor as the two joined them, "but we should probably take a peek at the other houses, don't you think?" He put his arm around Mindy, smiling down at her.

"Very well," Mindy said with an exaggerated sigh. "Let's see the others."

They spent all day in Boulder, stopping for lunch at a local diner and then grabbing burgers to eat in the car on their way back to Aspen Creek for the night. Alex had just finished hers when they pulled up in front of the bar. She climbed out, pausing at Mindy's open window.

"Remember, my apartment is yours. Make yourselves comfortable."

"We will. Thanks."

Zach leaned toward the window. "Just don't be surprised if the coffee is all gone when you get home."

Alex giggled. "I'd be scared to see Mindy on that much caffeine."

Zach laughed now. Mindy just shook her head at them, but said, "Don't worry. We'll save you a cup or two."

"All right, I'll see you later, but don't wait up for me if you're tired."

"Tired?" Zach scrunched his face. "Nah. There's coffee for that."

"Just drive," Mindy told him in mock exasperation.

Still laughing, Alex waved to them as they pulled away from the bar and then walked inside. Quite a few customers occupied the tables and barstools, as she had come to expect for Saturday nights. Luke stood behind the counter, while Riley cleaned a table across the room. He sent her a smile when he saw her. Alex returned it as she headed into the back room to hang up her purse and tie on her little work apron. When she walked out again, she met Riley behind the bar.

"Hey, how did it go today?" he asked.

"It was fun. I was a little nervous about how I'd feel about visiting Boulder, but I was fine. It's different knowing that Mindy and Zach will soon be there. We looked at some really nice houses, although I think Mindy has her heart set on the first one we saw. It really suits her and has a nice big yard for their dogs, so I wouldn't be surprised if that's the one they settle on." She looked around the bar. "So, what can I do?"

"Why don't you see if they need anything?" Riley gestured to a group across the room.

Alex headed over to the table occupied by four older gentlemen, including their regular, Mr. Jenkins. He greeted her happily and introduced her to his friends. Of course, he promptly launched into one of his tales. Alex laughed with them and listened for a couple of minutes before she moved on.

She still had things to learn about all the different drinks, but waiting on the tables came easily enough. Though subjected to a good amount of flirting, it was never too forward or inappropriate, thankfully. Most of their patrons seem to be decent people.

Whenever she did need to get someone a drink, Riley was there to show her how. For the most part, she spent her time clearing tables and washing glasses. While she was behind the bar with Riley, they chatted, and she told him what she and Mindy were planning as far as food for the game tomorrow.

When the bar closed at eleven, Alex helped with the final cleanup and then followed Riley and Luke out. Saying goodnight to Luke, Alex climbed into Riley's truck. The short drive home passed in silence, except for the low hum of the Christian radio station. Occasionally Riley switched it to country, but he always changed it back.

He pulled up to her apartment and put the truck in park, though he left it running. Light still filtered through the curtained windows of Alex's living room. No surprise there. Mindy always had been a night owl. Alex unbuckled her seatbelt and looked over at Riley. "I guess I'll see you tomorrow then."

"I'm looking forward to it."

She held his gaze for a moment and watched it settle on her lips. Her heart thumped the way it had when they'd sat on the log by the stream. She'd thought of that kiss so many times since then. Had secretly hoped for another. He leaned toward her, and she slid over just enough to reach him for a brief but no less magical kiss.

Her heart as light as her head, she smiled at him and murmured, "Goodnight."

Sliding back to her door, she got out of the truck and just about floated up the walkway to the house. On the porch, she glanced back and could just make out his smile in the light of one of the street lamps as he waited to make sure she made it inside. A sigh left her of its own accord. Maybe Mindy wasn't quite so far off after all.

She climbed the stairs and entered her apartment. Mindy, clad in a comfy pair of pajama pants and t-shirt was putting a mug away in the cabinet, and Alex caught a glimpse of Zach watching TV in the living room.

"Hey," Mindy said, looking over her shoulder.

Alex echoed the greeting but the plastic grocery bags on the table distracted her. "What's this?"

Mindy walked to the table and pulled out football-shaped paper plates, napkins, and an assortment of other football-related items. "Can't have a party without party supplies. Zach and I picked them up after we dropped you off."

Trust Mindy to go all out, even for just a four-person party.

She walked around the table to Alex's side, leaning in to whisper by her ear, "He kissed you again, didn't he?"

Alex's jaw dropped. How did she know? She snapped it closed, but her cheeks burst into flames. She shook her head, doing her best to sound serious. "You have to stop doing that. Honestly, Min, I've never blushed so much in my life."

Mindy just grinned wickedly. "Then you'll to have to stop walking in with that obviously dreamy look on your face."

Alex opened her mouth again but had no decent comeback. Was it really that obvious?

"Are you two talking about kissing in there?" Zach's voice joined them from the living room.

Alex threw her hands up. "You stay out of this."

In answer to his hearty laugh, all Alex could do was laugh too.

It was good to have friends around again.

Chapter Nine

ALEX'S APARTMENT BUZZED WITH ACTIVITY LATE THE NEXT morning as she and Mindy mixed up a batch of buffalo chicken dip for the game. The kitchen was too small for them all, so they sent Zach happily to the living room to watch pre-game coverage.

"Just wait until we can have parties at my house," Mindy said, dicing up chicken. "I can't wait to decorate for the holidays."

Of course, Mindy would be super optimistic about the house she had loved. Zach had talked to the realtor this morning and officially made an offer. Alex prayed the owners would accept. The sooner Mindy and Zach moved to Boulder, the better.

"That house would look beautiful decorated for Christmas," she agreed.

Mindy practically shivered with excitement. "I can hardly wait to have a place of my own and not have any limitations on what I can do with it."

"That *would* be nice." While Alex liked her apartment, she could appreciate the prospect of total creative freedom.

A knock at the door interrupted the conversation. Alex's heart fluttered. It must be Riley. She wiped her hands and opened the door to him, taking in the sight of his Broncos t-shirt and navy-blue flannel with the sleeves rolled up. She did love a man in flannel. They shared a quick grin, and she stepped back to let him inside. Zach appeared from the living room. She introduced the two of them and, as they greeted each other, Mindy sent her a knowing little smile. Alex narrowed her eyes and shook her head. Thankfully, she stood behind Riley so he didn't catch the exchange.

A few nerves pinched Alex's stomach like the afternoon she'd brought Mindy to the bar, but within minutes, Riley and Zach talked like old friends. The anxiety subsided, and she smiled at the festive atmosphere. Once Mindy and Zach moved, she would be happy to make such gatherings a regular occurrence.

Riley sat in Alex's living room with Zach to watch the pre-game while the girls worked in the kitchen, chatting away. The sound provided a cheerful backdrop he hadn't experienced growing up at home. While he and Mark had never missed a game, they never celebrated sports as a family. Game days usually consisted of him and Mark, and maybe a friend or two, sitting in front of the TV with a bag of chips. Depending on how the game went, they'd get louder and louder until Mom or Dad would come in and yell at them to keep it down. Not that it did much to quiet a group of rowdy teenage boys.

Between discussing the game and the players, Riley and Zach talked about work. Riley liked Zach. He had the kind of smarts and education that would have impressed Riley's parents but the easy-going, laid-back sort of personality Riley gravitated towards.

Twenty minutes before the game, Mindy stepped into the room. "Alex and I are going to go pick up the pizzas."

"Want me to get them?" Zach asked.

"No, we've got it."

The two of them headed out, leaving Riley and Zach to listen to the sports commentators give their projections for the game and which players to keep an eye on. Denver had picked up a couple of rookies in the draft Riley looked forward to watching. He'd once thought he could play pro. His senior high coach had even encouraged him to try for a football scholarship. Of course, his parents hadn't stood for that.

"I hear you tried to save Josh."

Snapped out of his memories, Riley looked over at Zach. He wasn't looking at him, but Riley nodded slowly. "I did."

Zach sat in silence for a moment before he asked, "Was there any chance?"

Riley breathed in and let the air out slowly. He could still see the carnage left behind after the smoke cleared—gaping wounds, missing limbs, blood and gore everywhere. The air had reeked with charred flesh. "No, there wasn't."

He glanced at the framed photograph he'd noticed on the wall when he'd sat down—a picture of Alex and Josh on some mountain trail, both grinning. It was the first time he had seen Josh's face since the bomb. Riley might not have known him well, but he'd seemed like a good guy. Someone he could've been friends with. "There's nothing anyone could've done."

Zach nodded, his emotions hidden behind a solemn mask. But Riley understood what it was like to lose friends. You didn't fight and risk your life every day alongside someone and not feel like family. He'd lost more than one brother before his own wounds sent him home. He still had this nagging guilt sometimes that he was here and they weren't. He'd gotten off easy, with just a few scars and barely a limp to show for it. Too many others had lost so much more.

"Josh, Alex, and I were always more like siblings than friends," Zach said after another moment of silence. "He was the best man at my wedding. He was only home for a couple of days, and it was the last time I saw him."

He cleared his throat, his posture going straighter. Now he did look at Riley, right in the eyes. "Since he's not here, I try to look out for Alex like he would have. His death really broke her. Even more than we realized before she told Mindy what she almost did. She seems to be doing better than she has in years since she met you. I just want to make sure you'll take care of her."

Riley hadn't expected the big brother speech, but at least someone around Alex cared enough to give it. "The last thing I want is to hurt her. I'm not in this just for the fun of it. I've been down that road before, and I know it doesn't lead anywhere worthwhile. I care about Alex. A lot. I just want her to be happy."

Zach nodded, seeming satisfied. "Good."

While he might not need Zach's blessing to keep dating Alex, he did value it.

Shortly before kickoff, the women returned carrying three boxes of pizza.

"Here's extra cheese for Alex, pepperoni for Zach, and one with everything," Mindy named each one off as they set them down.

Zach rubbed his hands together like he was about to do a high dive right into the box.

Alex laughed at him. "You and your pepperoni." She then turned. "I'll be back in a minute. Min, you can bring the dip in."

She disappeared for a couple of minutes and returned wearing a Broncos jersey. Riley smiled to himself. He appreciated a girl who enjoyed sports, and that slim-cut jersey looked real good on her.

Mindy sent her a pouty look. "Aw, if I'd known we were going to have this party, I would've packed my jersey."

She was the only one in the room who didn't sport some sort of team apparel.

Zach looked up at her. "Don't worry, hon, we won't hold it against you."

Mindy raised her brow at him.

"I'm sure I still have a Broncos t-shirt hanging in the closet," Alex said. "You can wear it if you can find it."

Mindy's face lit up, and she disappeared down the hall, while

Alex carried bags of chips, soda, and cups from the kitchen. Mindy returned with only a couple of minutes to spare, now wearing a slightly-faded Broncos t-shirt.

With the game about to begin, Riley started getting up to let Alex and Mindy take his spot on the couch, but Zach stopped him.

"Nope, you just stay right there. Min gets her own seat during games. Trust me, she needs it."

She cast him a stern look, but humor lurked behind it. "I may get a *little* too into games sometimes."

"Which includes whacking innocent bystanders in the nose with her elbow."

"Hey, it's not my fault you leaned forward."

Zach shook his head dramatically. "I thought I was gonna end up in the ER with a broken nose. Then I'd have to explain that, no, my wife doesn't beat me, she just thought swinging her arms around and yelling at the TV would whip the players into shape."

"Oh, stop. It didn't even bleed."

"No, I just sported a black eye for a week." Zach glanced over at Riley. "Try explaining that to the guys at work."

Mindy rolled her eyes and shook her head but wore a little smirk on her face.

"Anyway, the moral of the story is: never let Mindy sit within arm's length of anyone during games."

Alex laughed heartily at their exchange, more so than Riley had heard since they'd met. He liked the sound, and it just reinforced his desire for her to be happy.

***

"Yes! That's my boys!" Mindy said, pumping her fist.

Alex grinned, quietly sharing in the excitement of the team win. It had been a fantastic game—competitive, yet clearly dominated by the Broncos, just like she loved it. Those were always her dad's favorite types of games. She imagined him sitting at home with Mom, quietly pleased. At that moment, a longing compressed her ribs, nearly taking her breath away. It was getting close to a year now since she'd seen them. The saddest part was that they were only two hours away—close enough she really had no excuse for not visiting.

Before melancholy could drag her down, she focused back on the football talk around her. Still discussing the game, they all rose and carried the dishes and leftovers into the kitchen. Mindy and Zach would have to leave now, and part of Alex had dreaded it all day. Despite how close they would soon be, even temporary goodbyes were hard since Josh had died. She just never knew when they would be the last.

Riley said goodbye and headed home as soon as they cleaned up. Alex closed the door behind him and worked in the kitchen while Mindy and Zach packed up their things. Once they were ready to leave, they gathered at the door.

"I'll send you the photos I took today," Mindy said, holding up the camera that was like her baby.

She'd snapped pictures all afternoon. Alex was sure there were a billion of her and Riley on the SD card.

"I can't wait to see them, just . . . don't post them on Facebook yet. You and Zach are the only ones who know about Riley and me. I don't want Mom to see them and feel bad I haven't told her yet."

"I won't." Mindy offered an encouraging smile. "You should definitely call her. I know she'd be very excited to hear about the two of you."

"I will."

"And be honest. Tell them everything. They need to know."

Alex drew a deep breath. That would be difficult. But Mindy was right.

Mindy then took her hands, giving them a squeeze. "I'm very happy you and Riley found each other. I can see it has been really good for you. Just remember to be vigilant. When you're with someone, emotions and feelings can get overwhelming and lead to some not-so-good choices. Just be on guard. It's worth it. Trust me."

Alex nodded, her cheeks growing a bit warm, but she did take Mindy's words seriously. "I will."

Her friend's grin broke out full force. "Really, I'm very excited for you. I know you've been waiting a long time. I'm so happy Zach and I will be able to hang out with you and Riley like this whenever we want. Hopefully we'll be back very soon."

"Can't wait."

"And remember," Mindy said, squeezing her hands again, "you call me any time, for whatever reason."

With a quick hug goodbye from each of them, Mindy and Zach left the apartment. After waving at them from the balcony and watching them drive away, Alex stepped back inside and closed the door. Except for the TV, it was quiet. And empty. Before she could stop it, heaviness descended on her heart.

Chapter Ten

ALEX SCOWLED. HER HALF-FINISHED CANVAS STARED BLANKLY back at her, paint slowly drying on her brush and palette. It wasn't right. None of it was right. Why couldn't she do this? In all her years of painting, she had never had so much trouble before. Inspiration used to come faster than she could finish a painting. Why couldn't she summon the excitement to create anything that made her happy now?

After a long time, she hung her head and forced out a breath. She had said goodbye to Mindy and Zach a week ago. For the first couple of days, she'd shoved aside the emptiness of her apartment. The emptiness inside *her*. Despite her determination to fight it, old, dark emotions crept in—hopelessness and despair lurking in the still-painful wounds of her heart. Even at work with Riley, she couldn't seem to shake the suffocating shadow.

And she hated herself for it. Things were finally going right! How could she still feel this way? But it was as if the grip of depression had never truly released her, only loosened its hold temporarily to let her believe she had escaped before swooping back in to swallow her once more.

She slid off her stool with a long sigh and walked into the kitchen to clean her brushes and palette. Was this the last time she would do this? If it brought nothing but frustration and pain, why persist? She had not produced a single decent painting since her dad had called her to deliver the awful news about Josh. The things that had always defined her were gone, and that hurt nearly as much as losing her brother. Without them, who was she? She glanced at her phone. She should call Mindy. She knew she should. But admitting how weak she was—that she was already sinking again—ate at her. How could she be so weak? She set the brushes aside and grabbed her purse. She had to get out. She needed air. Forcing herself to pretend everything was fine, she left the apartment. Fake it 'til you make it, right? When she climbed into her Jeep, she put her keys in the ignition and turned it. Nothing. She tried several more times, but the engine wouldn't even turn over.

"Come on." A flood of moisture seared her eyes. "Don't do this to me." Her Jeep was always so dependable. How could it give out on her now? She rested her forehead against the steering wheel and fought to compose herself. Finally, she reached for her phone and dialed Riley's number. He answered after the second ring.

"Hey, what's up? Everything okay?"

"Um, yeah, mostly." Alex drew a steadying breath. Her voice threatened to wobble. So much for pretending everything was okay. She'd make a lousy actress. "You know a lot about vehicles, right?" She remembered him talking about how he used to work on trucks with his grandpa.

"Yeah."

"Do you think you could come and take a look at my Jeep? It won't start."

"Sure, I'll be right over."

"Thank you." She prayed it wouldn't be a serious problem. Even though she was working again, she didn't have the money to spare for expensive vehicle repairs.

She sat in the Jeep with the door open to let in the crisp air until Riley pulled up and parked just in front of it. He got out and lowered the tailgate of his truck, reaching for an old toolbox.

"Pop the hood and try to start it again."

Alex did, and the Jeep still refused to show much sign of life. Sure, it was an inanimate object, but it still felt like a slap in the face. She slid out of her seat and stood beside the engine as Riley looked it over. He grabbed a wrench from his toolbox and went to work. Alex watched him for a couple of minutes and then walked over and sat on the tailgate of his truck. They were both quiet. The silence left Alex uncomfortable, but she wasn't in the mood to talk either. She supposed she should be paying attention to what he was doing in case she had trouble again. The thought of mechanics, however, just gave her a headache.

Some time later, Riley tried to loosen a bolt when the wrench slipped and slammed his fingers against the engine. He yanked his hand out and swore under his breath. He then glanced at Alex and winced. "Sorry. I'm working on that. Not an easy habit to break."

She slid off the tailgate. Josh had struggled with that too. "Are you okay?"

"Just scraped some skin off." Blood welled from the gouge in one of his knuckles.

"I'll get something to clean it and a Band-Aid."

She followed the cracked cement walkway back to the house and up to her apartment where she gathered what she needed from her medicine cabinet. Riley still worked on the Jeep, blood oozing down his finger, when she carried the supplies outside. She set them down on the tailgate.

"Here, let me see."

He turned to her and held out his hand. She soaked a cotton ball in peroxide and wiped away the blood and grime from the wound. The gouge continued to bleed, but she wrapped a Band-Aid around it.

"Thanks," he said and returned to working on her vehicle.

A little over an hour later, he grabbed a rag from his toolbox to wipe his hands and then opened the door of the Jeep to reach in and turn the key. Immediately, the engine roared to life. Smiling, he turned it off, shut the hood, and tossed the keys to Alex.

"Good as new."

She attempted a weak smile but ended up looking down at her feet. If only her life could be fixed as easily. "Thanks."

"No problem." Silence hung between them for a moment. "What's going on, Alex?"

She looked up, meeting his eyes.

"You haven't been yourself all week."

She let a sigh escape. She didn't want to talk about it. Why couldn't she just be strong enough to get a grip on things without dragging everyone else into her mess? But she couldn't just ignore him. He'd press her if she didn't open up.

"I've been trying to paint, but . . . I just don't think I have it in me anymore. I haven't been happy with anything I've done since Josh died."

He remained silent for a long moment, looking down at his hands as he wiped them on his rag. Alex didn't know how to interpret the intense look on his face. Was he disappointed in her? Disappointed to be dating such a weak individual who couldn't even get her life together? She gulped.

Finally, he met her gaze again, and she braced herself, though not for the words that actually left his mouth.

"You've got to let him go."

Her weak defenses evaporated. "What?"

"Your brother. He was your security blanket. He's gone, Alex."

All the air left her lungs as if she'd been viciously punched in the stomach. The tears she'd battled all morning rushed into her eyes as phantom cords wrapped around her chest, strangling her voice. "I know he's gone. What do you think is the first thing I remember when I wake up every morning?"

He just looked at her steadily. "Maybe you know it, but I don't think you've accepted it. You relied on him to make sense of things for you, but you can't keep doing that. He's not coming back. You can't keep waiting for him to help you figure things out. You've got to let him go and move on."

Her heart thundered in her ears. How could he say that to her? He didn't understand. How could he? Hot tears poured down her cheeks, and she couldn't look him in the eyes. She squeezed her fist around her keys, the sharp edges digging into her fingers.

"Thanks for fixing my Jeep," she gasped out.

She turned and strode toward the house. He called her name, but she did not stop or look back. He'd ripped open every wound inside her, ignited fresh agony from the past. How could he do that?

The tears flowed faster, almost blinding her as she climbed the stairs and entered her apartment. Inside, she sank down on the couch and hugged her knees to her chest as one sob after another tore through her.

Riley pulled into his parking space behind the bar and shut his truck off. Instead of getting out, he heaved a sigh and just stared at the worn brick wall of the building. That certainly hadn't gone as he'd hoped, not that he'd planned to have such a heavy conversation with Alex today. Sure, the thoughts had been on his mind, but he probably could've found a better time to say it. He didn't blame her for walking away. That was understandable.

But would she be all right after hearing such a stark truth? What if his blunt honesty drove her back to the bridge? He rubbed his forehead, his blood running cold. Maybe he should go back. He glanced at his watch. It was nearly time to open the bar and Luke was out of town until this evening. Riley could call Kat, but what then? He couldn't just camp out on Alex's porch to make sure she didn't do anything drastic. Her landlady would probably call the police on him if he did that. At this point, he could only see one good option.

"Lord, I just wanted to help her. Maybe I did a poor job of it, but whatever she thinks of me, don't let her do anything drastic." His chest ached as if run over by a tank just saying it aloud. If not for his responsibility to Luke, he would have turned his truck right around and slept in the street if he had to. "Hard as it is, I've got to leave her in Your hands. Help me trust You. But most of all, heal her."

———

Alex didn't want to open her eyes. To do so would mean facing the misery that had kept her up crying most of the night. Even when the tears had dried up, her body still went through the motions. Everything ached—her eyes, her throat, her entire body. But her heart worst of all.

Amidst the heartache, guilt wrapped around her. She had been so angry when she'd walked away from Riley—so angry he would hurt her like this when she trusted him. Yet, once the anger had burnt itself out, she realized how she may have hurt him when she had walked away. He'd only been trying to help her. She could see that now. In response, she had treated him badly.

Moisture built beneath her eyelids and leaked from the corners. She'd finally met someone, and not just any guy, but one who cared enough to be honest with her, and she'd walked away from him. Would it be over now? Had she just destroyed the best thing that had happened in her life in years?

It was after nine-thirty by the time Alex dragged herself out of bed. She shivered at the chill in the apartment. Not bothering to get dressed, she stayed in her flannel pajama pants and walked to her closet where she pulled out an over-sized Marines hoodie that had belonged to Josh. She clutched it in her hands and closed her eyes to ward off the tears before she slipped it on. In the bathroom, she braced herself against the sink and peered into the mirror. Her pale, blotchy skin and dark, red-rimmed eyes said everything. Misery.

Washing her face did little to revive her or erase her ghoulish appearance, and she barely summoned the energy to pull her messy hair back in a ponytail before wandering aimlessly into the living room. She didn't have the stomach for breakfast right now. Sitting down on the couch, she turned on the TV, not bothering to notice what was on. She just didn't want to sit in silence.

Staring without really seeing, she didn't move until her phone chirped from the table next to the couch. Riley's text tone. Her heart jumped while her stomach simultaneously did a nosedive. Would he call things off? Would he tell her that they were over?

Bracing herself for the worst, she picked up the phone and blinked the text into focus.

I'm outside if you feel like talking.

A little cry escaped her lips. She put the phone in the pocket of her hoodie and got up. Slipping her moccasins on at the door, she unlocked it and walked out. At the bottom of the stairs, she found Riley waiting on the porch, leaning back against the railing. He met her eyes, his expression both sad and searching. If there was any bit of anger left in her, it evaporated in an instant. She descended the last step and walked right into his arms without a word. He closed them around her as she buried her face against the soft fabric of his flannel shirt. Tears leaked from her eyes, but she found comfort in being held.

His voice vibrated in his chest, deep and husky.

"I'm sorry. I didn't mean to sound harsh yesterday, I just—"

"No," she cut in. She pulled away to look up at him. "You were right. Part of me has never wanted to believe Josh is really gone. I haven't wanted to move on. I think that's why, all this time, I've harbored the idea that it was just better—easier—to give up. Both on my paintings and . . . life."

"He wouldn't want you to give up on anything. He would want you to soldier on, just like he did, no matter how tough things got."

Alex nodded, the tears still rolling down her cheeks. Riley pulled her closer again, and they just stood there like that for several minutes while she let her emotions drain. When she finally had the tears under control, she pulled away slowly and wiped her face with her sleeves.

Riley offered her an encouraging little smile. "I brought coffee." He nodded past her.

Two Styrofoam cups sat on the little table against the house. They each took a chair on either side of the table, and Alex brought her coffee to her lips. She let out a huge sigh after she swallowed the first sip, the warmth soothing her throat.

"Thank you," she said, glancing at him.

He nodded, and they sipped their coffee in silence for a few minutes. When he looked over at her, he seemed a little uncertain at first but then asked, "Want to go for a drive?"

"Sure."

Alex stood up and followed him to his truck. Anything had to be better than sitting alone in her apartment. He pulled away from the house and drove through town, following the route they always took to work. However, when they reached the bar, he turned right instead, toward Baylor's Bridge. A knot coiled in Alex's stomach, and she glanced at him. He kept his eyes on the road ahead, his profile set and determined. She shifted against her seatbelt, her heart rate elevating. She would have walked this way if she had kept going that day four weeks ago instead of stopping at the bar. Her tongue turned to dry wood in her mouth.

At the bridge, Riley pulled over and shut off the truck. They sat for a moment with Alex's thumping heart filling the silence in her head. Finally, he turned to her. "You look this way every time I bring you to work."

She lifted her brows. She hadn't even fully realized she did that.

Before she could say anything, he opened his door and stepped out. Questions rang in her mind as he rounded the front of the truck. Why had he brought her here? Why had he gotten out? What was he planning to do? A shiver passed through her, goosebumps rising along her arms.

When he reached her door, he pulled it open and peered in at her. "I won't make you get out. You can stay right there, and I'll drive you back home. But sometimes we have to face our demons to move forward."

She swallowed hard, her throat aching in response. She let her gaze slide back to the bridge. Her limbs froze in place. She didn't want to get out. She would much rather hide from this particular demon for as long as she could. But then she looked back at Riley and slid from her seat.

Her feet settled on the pavement, pebbles crunching under her moccasins. Riley took her hand and guided her toward the bridge. Her feet dragged, but she followed him, all the way to the middle where the distance between the bridge and the rocky ravine below was the greatest. The place where one would jump if they intended to end it all. They stopped at the guardrail, and she chanced a glance over the edge. Though the bottom wasn't much more than a fuzzy distance without her glasses, her heart stuck in her throat, and she gripped the rough, cold edge. She had really intended to do it. To jump off right here.

"I think you're holding onto it as a last resort—your escape route if your life comes crashing down again."

She gulped, tears clogging her throat. She didn't want to admit he was right.

"Don't do it, Alex. Don't have an escape plan. I don't have all the answers, but I know life shouldn't be lived that way. No matter what happens in the future, with us, with your family, with your paintings, I don't want to think you might take your life. God put you here for a reason. I know what's happened doesn't make any sense and there's nothing anyone can say that makes it all right, but somewhere in it all, God's got a plan. He had a plan for Josh that meant taking him home early, but He's still got a plan for you. You wouldn't be here otherwise. And I know that plan doesn't involve you jumping off this bridge."

Her tears returned once more, fast and heavy, as if they would never stop after this. A sob broke free and then another and the strength drained from her body. She sank to the pavement, shaking with the heart-wrenching sobs that attacked her. Everything rushed in, all the pain and loss and emotions of the past three years.

Riley sat down beside her and wrapped his arm around her shoulders. She leaned into him, crying harder than she had since that day her dad had called her, barely able to give her the news over the phone. She'd been to Josh's funeral. She'd been with her family as they'd come to terms with his death. But right here where she had wanted to end her own life, she finally said goodbye. Goodbye to her brother, goodbye to the future she had envisioned, goodbye to who she had been before.

Life had changed, and she could not reclaim her old life, no matter how hard she fought to hold onto it. After all this time, the hard truth crystalized that underneath the pain and the loss, she'd been angry with God for taking her brother away—for leaving her without his support. Her heart pained with the realization. She had never wanted that. She had begged for His comfort, yet at the same time had turned away from Him.

Tears of grief mixed with tears of sorrow over how far she had fallen. She didn't know how long she cried. It could have been an hour, it could have been three. However long it was, she cried until the tears were utterly spent and she had no strength left at all. And yet, somehow, she felt lighter in the midst of it.

At last, she lifted her head from her hands and blinked to clear her vision before looking over at Riley.

He hadn't moved, hadn't stopped holding her. He'd sat right there with her for however long had passed. He looked into her eyes now as if seeking something from her.

"I won't do it." Her voice barely reached a hoarse whisper. "I won't have an escape."

He let out a long breath, telling her just how much her promise meant. "Good."

They sat for another moment more before he stood up. He reached down and helped her to her feet, putting his arm around her as they walked back to his truck.

They drove in silence back to her apartment where he parked and looked over at her. "Go in and rest. Don't come to work tonight. Luke and I can handle it."

She only nodded, in no shape to deal with work today. She unbuckled her seatbelt and reached for the door but paused to look at him again.

"Thank you, Riley. For everything."

He smiled gently. "No problem. Just call if you need anything."

Chapter Eleven

WHILE THE INTENSE EMOTIONS AT THE BRIDGE WOULD TAKE TIME to recover from, a day to rest and a night of deep sleep revived Alex. She rose in the morning holding firmly to a determination not to let any of the lingering heaviness drag her down. Her first mission after brewing a cup of coffee was to put away her painting supplies. During a lull at work last night, Riley had called her. He'd suggested she take a break from painting to gain fresh perspective. How long the break would last, she could not say, but for right now, she would focus on her life outside of art—on her relationships, especially her relationship with God.

The remainder of the morning, she spent reading and praying, sometimes remembering. It was time to get excited to pursue God's path for her again, whatever that path meant or where it led. She shed a few tears, but they were more cleansing than simply grief. Though still tired by the time noon rolled around, she found enough strength to face work again.

After a quick lunch, she got dressed and freshened up in the bathroom before Riley arrived to pick her up. She slid into his truck, and he looked over at her before they pulled away.

"How are you doing?"

She took a deep breath. "All right, I think. I put away my painting supplies and spent most of the morning reading my Bible. I'm sure it helped."

He smiled. "Good."

As they drove away from the apartment, Alex mulled over something Mindy had mentioned during their visit that had come to mind this morning. "Have you ever been to church around here?"

Riley glanced at her and shook his head. "No. I should. Bradley keeps encouraging me to find a good place, but . . . I've never been to church aside from weddings. I guess I wasn't keen on just walking in when I didn't know anyone."

Alex understood the reluctance. She wasn't keen on that either.

"Perhaps we could go together? At least we would know each other. Mrs. Santos has invited me multiple times."

"Sounds like a plan."

"I'll find out what time the service is and let you know."

"I can pick you up on Sunday then."

Now she smiled. She hadn't been to church in years, but the thought of attending with him replaced some of the apprehension with comfortable warmth in her chest. Now she just had to ignore the nagging fear of what people would think of them since they were both bartenders. It shouldn't matter. It was just a job, but Alex had experienced enough to know it *did* matter to some people. At least Riley would be there with her.

When they arrived at the bar, Luke was working on inventory in the back, so they prepared to open. Alex set all the chairs around the tables while Riley plugged in lights and turned on the computer for the register. They then flipped on the neon 'open' sign in the window.

In the waiting silence before their first customers, Riley spoke tentatively. "I don't know what you'll think of this, but have you ever thought about seeing someone about how you've been feeling?"

Alex paused in the midst of putting glasses away to look at him. "You mean, like a psychiatrist?"

"Yeah."

She considered it quietly for a moment. The thought had crossed her mind, but spilling her life secrets to a stranger wasn't the most appealing prospect. "Not really."

"I'm not saying you should, but it might help. There's no shame in seeking help when you need it."

She let a quiet sigh seep past her lips. "I wouldn't even know where to go."

"That's why I brought it up. I know someone—Dr. Gracin. I used to see her while I was recuperating in Denver. She's easy to talk to, and I think you'd like her. She usually works with veterans, but I think I could get you an appointment with her if that was something you wanted."

She didn't respond right away. It was hard to admit she needed psychiatric help. Yet, to deny it would be ridiculous. She swallowed against the constricting pressure in her throat. Hadn't she spent all morning determined to do what she had to in order to get her life back together?

"Okay."

His smile bolstered her. "I'll give her a call tomorrow morning."

Nerves prickled Alex's insides, but if she was honest with herself, she really did need all the help she could get to make sure she wouldn't sink again.

The next morning, Alex maintained her goal to start her day with Bible reading, and she already enjoyed the routine. It spawned confidence in herself that she had struggled with for so long. And even though the looming prospect of church this weekend stirred anxiety in the pit of her stomach, it also ignited a spark of hopefulness she prayed wouldn't find itself crushed.

About an hour and a half later, she closed her Bible and cleaned up her apartment. She had just finished putting laundry away when her phone chimed with a text from Mindy.

We got the house! Oh yeah, and I got those photos from our party edited and sent to you. Been busy packing!

Alex smiled and texted back how excited she was. She could just imagine the whirlwind at their apartment. Mindy must be bouncing off the walls. Alex then grabbed her laptop and checked her email. The photos Mindy had sent brought a smile to her face as she clicked through them. She loved the photos of her and Riley. Now she would have to get one framed to hang next to the photo of her and Josh. If only he and Riley could have known each other long enough to become friends.

Before the emotions could gain a foothold, she closed the laptop. However, the photos brought her parents to mind. She still hadn't called them or told them about Riley. They deserved to know about such an important step in her life. If only she had talked to them more recently. Why did the long silence in between have to make calling now so difficult? What would she even tell them? Still, she missed them deeply, and it was time to reconnect.

She picked up her phone again and tapped her parents' contact. It rang a couple of times before her dad's deep but soothing voice answered.

"Hey, Dad." Alex smiled into the quiet emptiness of her apartment, her eyes smarting already.

"Hi, sweetheart," he responded, his voice lifting. "How have you been?"

"Well . . . good and bad, but I'm doing pretty good now." She paused. Though she had planned to tell them about the bridge, she couldn't do it over the phone. She had to see their faces—had to let them see hers. "I have exciting news."

"Let me get your mom and put it on speaker."

Alex waited a minute for her mom to join them.

"Hi, Alex."

"Hi, Mom."

"It's so good to hear from you." Mom's warm voice was earnest, perhaps even emotional too.

"I know, and I'm sorry I haven't called in so long. I've been having a rough time."

"Oh, sweetheart, you should've let us know."

"I know." Alex winced, guilt needling her ribs. "But things are getting better. Actually, I called to tell you I've been seeing someone for about a month now."

"Oh, that's wonderful!" Of all people, her mom knew how deeply she had always desired to meet someone and get married.

"Yeah. I can't even begin to tell you how much he has helped me these last few weeks."

"So he's a nice boy then?"

Alex laughed a little. "Yes, he's very nice. I think you'll really like him."

"I'd love to meet him. Do you think you could bring him out for a visit sometime?"

"Well, we haven't talked about anything like that yet, but I think he'd like to." Her dad's voice was noticeably absent in response to her news. "What do you think, Dad?"

"I agree with your mom. I'd like to meet him. Make sure he's good enough for my baby girl."

Alex laughed again. Of course Dad would be happy for her, but he wouldn't be sold on the idea until he got to know Riley face to face. "I don't think you have anything to worry about. So far he's been everything I've ever dreamed of and more."

"Tell us what he's like," Mom said.

So Alex did, managing to avoid the precise details of how they had met. She hesitated to tell them about her new job, but they took it well, especially when she assured them Riley kept her safe during the late nights at the bar. They all grew a little emotional when she told them about how Riley had known Josh. This particular detail seemed to warm Dad up to the idea of her dating. She emailed them her favorite photo Mindy had sent while they were talking, and she giggled when Mom exclaimed over how cute Riley was. It wasn't a long phone call, but long enough to reconnect after the silence. Just before she hung up, Alex promised she would call again soon.

When she did set her phone down, another bit of weight lifted from her shoulders. While she would still have to tell them how deeply she had fallen over the summer, for right now, it was good just to have the connection with them again.

Shortly before one o'clock, Riley pulled in to pick her up as usual. While she buckled herself in his truck, she told him about her phone call and how her parents had responded to the news about the two of them. He seemed genuinely glad she had talked to them and that they were happy with what was going on.

As they neared the bar, she looked over at him. "Would you feel comfortable visiting them with me sometime? I know that's kind of a big step."

"Sure. I'd love to meet them."

She let out a breath and smiled to herself. Everyone always made such a big deal of taking someone home to meet their parents. Deep down, she'd worried Riley would think things were moving too fast. And maybe they were moving fast, but so far the progression between them seemed natural and comfortable.

"I'm not sure when. I know it's a bad time to try to get off work with football season, but my mom will probably call and try to arrange something soon."

Riley shrugged. "I haven't taken off except for appointments since I started working for Luke. He's not going to mind if we take a weekend."

Thank God for that blessing. She'd never worked for anyone as wonderfully flexible and understanding as Luke. He treated the two of them more like family than employees.

"Speaking of appointments," Riley broke into her thoughts. "I talked to Dr. Gracin this morning. Like I said, she usually works with veterans, but I made a deal with her. If you want to, she can see you on Monday."

Alex's breath froze in her chest. First church on Sunday and then visiting a psychiatrist on Monday—two things that sent little spasms darting through her stomach. "What kind of deal did you make?"

"She agreed to see you if I came in for an appointment too." He cast her a sheepish look. "I've neglected to keep seeing her since I left Denver."

Alex had to smile despite the nerves she wrestled with. "I guess if you're going, I'll go."

Chapter Twelve

ALEX STOOD IN FRONT OF THE BATHROOM MIRROR SUNDAY morning and carefully applied her makeup. The butterflies in her stomach didn't exactly make her hands as steady as when she was painting. Once she was satisfied, she slipped on all of her favorite rings and a layered necklace that contrasted nicely with her long, navy blue cardigan and jeans. She might not have Mindy's sense of style, but at least the effort produced a satisfactory result.

She walked out to the kitchen and glanced at the clock. Riley would arrive soon. She grabbed the mug of coffee she had brewed right after getting out of bed and sipped it while she waited. She'd nibbled a bit of a granola bar for breakfast but had trouble finding her appetite. The clock ticked away the seconds inside the quiet apartment, and she jumped a little when a much louder knock echoed at the door. She shook her head to herself and scolded her nerves. It wasn't like she was going to court or anything like that.

Grabbing her purse and Bible, she opened the door and stepped out to join Riley. She shared a hopeful smile with him. He looked particularly handsome this morning in a pair of dark wash jeans and a dusty red button-up.

"Ready?" he asked.

She drew a calming breath. "As ready as I'll ever be."

Neither said much on the short drive toward the middle of town. When they pulled up to a white church, it looked like a photo from a calendar with the leaves changing on the two giant maples towering near the back of the building. It even had a steeple. Alex had heard it was one of the original buildings from when the town was founded sometime in the 1890s.

The parking lot was nearly full, but Riley found an empty spot in the far corner. Together, they got out and walked toward the church. A cramp pinched Alex's middle. Churches shouldn't be scary. They should be the most welcoming places in the world. However, she couldn't tamp down her anxiety at facing the unknown. Riley took her hand as they neared the stairs. Just that small gesture infused her with courage.

They walked inside and found the foyer full of people greeting each other and conversing before the service. Alex recognized a few individuals from working at the post office, but most of the congregation consisted of strangers.

Now what? She should do something since Riley had no experience in church outside of weddings, but she'd always been shy growing up. Even now she wasn't one to just walk up and introduce herself. She'd surely bumble it if she tried.

Before she could get too caught up in her head, an elderly woman bustled toward them. A gentleman around the same age followed more slowly. Now Alex recognized the woman from Mrs. Santos's knitting group, though she couldn't recall her name.

The woman smiled brightly upon reaching them, her white hair, which was much longer than most women her age, braided over her shoulder. "Alex, dear, Dia said you might come this morning. I'm so glad to see that you made it."

"Thank you . . ." Alex hesitated. "I'm sorry; I'm not the best with names."

"Amelia," the woman supplied readily. "Amelia McKary. And this is my husband, Ed." She gestured to the gentleman, who had just reached her side. His kind expression put Alex at ease. He looked like an old cowboy with a full gray mustache, leather vest, and a worn pair of black boots.

"And you must be Riley." Mrs. McKary turned her attention to him.

"Yes, it's nice to meet you." He gave Mrs. McKary a charming smile and shook hands with Mr. McKary.

Alex didn't have to worry about trying to fill any awkward silence. Mrs. McKary immediately started telling them all about the church. The gregarious woman then took them around and introduced them to different people. Most of the women around Alex's age either had babies on their hip or small children racing around their legs. She seemed a little behind, but then again, Mindy didn't have children yet either. And Alex wasn't sure she was ready for the craziness of kids anyway. She struggled just to keep herself stable these days.

In just a few minutes, everyone filed into the sanctuary for the service. Alex and Riley found empty seats about halfway to the front. The rustling and murmuring around them grew quiet when the pastor stepped up to the pulpit—Pastor Ellis according to the bulletin. His mostly white hair gave him the appearance of having been at this for a while. He seemed to have a calm, friendly disposition that encouraged Alex. Someone with a dour, intimidating personality wouldn't have given her much comfort at the moment.

After a couple announcements, everyone rose for worship. Alex greatly enjoyed the opportunity to sing the old hymns that were so familiar growing up. She had forgotten how much she liked to sing with a congregation. All the voices together made up for her lack of talent in the music department. Josh always used to tease her about how out of tune she was when they sang karaoke during family get-togethers. None of that mattered when her voice blended with the others. She did, however, pick out Riley's voice now and then, and it sounded far more in tune than hers. Not a surprise considering his mom had been a music teacher.

Pastor Ellis's message appeared to be part of an ongoing study in First Timothy. Though Alex's nerves from meeting new people left her mind a bit scattered, she managed to focus and enjoy the message. She liked Pastor Ellis's way of teaching and the stories and examples he shared in between passages. He didn't sugarcoat things, yet came across as sort of a loving and encouraging grandfather.

After the closing prayer, conversation built around them. Alex looked at Riley, once again not quite sure what to do, whether they should just leave or stick around. Before she could ask him, she spotted Mrs. Santos weaving her way through the crowd, smiling and greeting people along the way.

"I'm so glad you made it." Her enthusiasm engulfed them when she neared. "We're all so happy whenever we have new faces on Sunday morning. I hope you enjoyed the service."

"I did," Alex replied.

Riley agreed.

"Oh good, I hope you'll consider coming back."

"I would like to." Alex glanced at Riley who nodded. Maybe he would tell her differently later, but he did seem to have enjoyed it as much as she had.

"Come, let me introduce you to Pastor Ellis." Mrs. Santos waved them along with her as she wound her way back toward the pulpit.

At the front of the sanctuary, Mrs. Santos greeted Pastor Ellis with the warmth of an old friend and motioned to Riley and Alex. "These are the two I was telling you about. Alex is my renter, and this is Riley Conrad. He works for Luke Cahill."

Pastor Ellis shook both their hands. "I'm very pleased to meet you. Thank you for coming out this morning."

Alex smiled easily at him. "I very much enjoyed your message."

"Oh, thank you. I'm happy to hear that," he said, both genuine and humble.

Alex liked how approachable and open he seemed. Some pastors were intimidating or more given to judging than loving. He looked with interest at Riley. "You wouldn't happen to be related to Phillip Conrad, would you?"

"He's my father."

Alex detected a slight hesitation at the connection.

"Really? God had a different calling for me, but I always had an interest in architecture."

"It's an interesting job," Riley said, but didn't get into any of the details of the family business.

Pastor Ellis then turned his attention back to Alex. "And I hear you're an artist."

She nodded. "Yes." Or at least she hoped she still was. That was yet to be determined after her time away from it.

They talked with Pastor Ellis for another few minutes before saying goodbye so he could see to the rest of the congregation. Though Mrs. Santos probably would have introduced them to everyone, Alex and Riley took their leave. It had been a good first experience at a new church, and Alex wanted to leave it at that until next time. Once they were back out in Riley's truck, he looked over at her as he turned the key.

"Well, that wasn't so bad."

She smiled and agreed. "Do you think you'll want to go next week?"

"I think so." As they pulled out of the parking lot, he asked, "Feel like getting lunch?"

"Yes, please." She was suddenly starving, and an after-church lunch date sounded perfect.

Chapter Thirteen

WELL, SHE HAD SURVIVED CHURCH. NOW ALEX JUST HAD TO survive her first visit to a psychiatrist. Riley picked her up around nine o'clock on Monday morning. It was a rather dreary day— gray clouds and spitting rain. Even so, the cab of his truck was warm when she got in. Falling leaves and rain pelted the windshield as they pulled away. Too bad she had been too distracted to think of filling a travel mug with coffee to drink on the way. Then again, caffeine might not have been the best thing for her jittery nerves anyway.

The forty-five-minute drive to Denver consisted of brief small talk. While Alex tried to focus on Riley's attempts at conversation, her anxiety had her mind going in circles. Thankfully, he seemed to understand.

When they pulled up to a large behavioral health clinic, she took a couple of deep breaths to try to slow her racing heart. Deep inside, she fought the urge to bail. What if she went in there only to discover she really hadn't made much progress? What if she was still just as much of a mess as she had always been and all her efforts were failures?

Riley strode around to her door and opened it. Alex sat frozen, more than a little like that day at the bridge.

"Don't worry. Dr. Gracin is good at what she does, and I know you'll like her. Trust me, this is a good thing."

With another gulping breath, she nodded and slid out. She would trust him.

Together they walked into the building and entered a comfortable waiting area. Riley checked them in at the receptionist's counter and they sat down with clipboards to fill in documents with their current information. When they finished, they sat quietly for a minute or two. Just across from Alex hung an art print by James Moretti, her favorite contemporary artist. She focused on the impressive, sweeping landscape to lose herself in studying the brushstrokes.

It didn't work.

She rubbed her palms on her jeans. Then Riley reached over and took her hand, holding it on the arm of the chair between them. She looked over him, and his smile melted into her like the warmth of a cozy fire. Already her eyes stung. She would be a blubbery mess before this ended. She just knew it.

"Thank you for bringing me today. I couldn't have done it on my own." She bit her lip before confessing, "I'm afraid. I'm scared that once I start talking, I'll crumble." She had been fighting to hold things together for so long.

"Maybe that's not such a bad thing. Sometimes things have to crumble to be rebuilt stronger."

She swallowed the large knot in her throat. If she wasn't careful she would crumble right here, but the way he held her hand was like a lifeline and brought her courage.

After another moment, he spoke again. "Do you want to go first, or do you want me to so we can leave as soon as you're done? I don't think I'll be in there long."

She nodded a bit too enthusiastically. "You can go in first."

Only a minute or two after that, a woman walked out from one of the doors down a short hall. She was tall and thin, and about the same age as Alex's mom. However, her short, straight brown hair gave her a youthful appearance. Her gaze settled on Riley as she approached them, and she smiled kindly. Riley stood, and Alex imitated him.

"Riley, it's good to see you again. It's been a while."

"It has."

Alex detected just a bit of chagrin in his voice, but then he motioned to her. "This is Alex Jennings."

The woman's warm brown eyes turned to her now. She reached out her hand, and Alex took it.

"I'm very pleased to meet you, Alex."

She swallowed again so she wouldn't choke on her dry throat. "You too."

Dr. Gracin looked between the two of them. "Who's coming with me first?"

"I will," Riley said.

He offered Alex one more quick smile before following Dr. Gracin to the room she had just left. Alex slowly sank into her seat. A clock ticked above her, and she clutched her purse. Closing her eyes, she prayed for calmness. This could only help, right? Riley clearly thought so, and he had asked her to trust him. It was kind of like having a bad injury, just like when she had torn open her knee on a barbed wire fence when she was little. No one liked to remove the bandage for the first time and expose what was underneath. Her heart had been wounded for a long time, and she had tried to keep it bandaged as best she could. Now Dr. Gracin would remove that bandage. She just hoped, like her knee, the exposure would eventually help it heal.

Twenty minutes after they had left, Dr. Gracin's door opened again. Alex's heart gave a bruising thump against her ribs. Riley walked out first. Whatever they might have talked about in there, he seemed only focused on her. Alex stood, still gripping her purse as if it were a shield.

"Are you ready, Alex?"

Her attention shifted from Riley to the doctor. Her kind smile held understanding, which did boost Alex's courage. She stepped forward. Before passing Riley, he looked her in the eyes.

"You'll be fine."

She flashed him a weak smile, more grateful than she could ever say for his confidence in her. She then followed Dr. Gracin into her office.

It was a cozy room, with comfortable chairs and more Moretti art on the wall amongst others. Dr. Gracin motioned her to a plush armchair, and Alex sat down stiffly, forcing herself to release her white-knuckled grip on her bag. The woman then took a seat across from her, a clipboard in hand. Alex had seen therapy sessions on TV, but still had no idea what to expect. Despite how comfortable the chair was, she couldn't relax and perched on the edge of it. She fought to keep her knee from bouncing.

Dr. Gracin's gaze settled on her with a gently prompting expression. "Tell me about yourself, Alex."

"Um . . ." She licked her lips and awkwardly rattled off the normal list of everyday information.

Dr. Gracin followed up by asking her standard questions about her life and family. After that, she offered Alex a look of understanding and compassion. "Riley tells me you've had thoughts of suicide."

Alex swallowed hard, the tears now coming on with a vengeance to burn her nose. "More than thoughts. I was on my way to do it when I met him."

From there it all broke open. Alex's tears flowed freely as they discussed her plans and what had happened to Josh. She talked about her failing art career and how much she wanted to make her parents proud but felt like she was failing them as much as herself. Talking about it hurt every bit as deeply as Alex expected. Yet, it did help to let it all out and receive understanding and constructive feedback. She even managed to get her tears under control after a while. By the time they finished over an hour later, she was exhausted, yet not nearly as wrung out as the other day at the bridge.

"I'm going to write you a prescription," Dr. Gracin said as she finished up the paperwork. "I expect it to help you significantly."

She explained the anti-depressant she prescribed and handed the script over. Alex glanced at it before smiling and sticking it in her purse. "Thank you."

They both stood, and Dr. Gracin opened the door. Alex walked out into the waiting room where Riley rose to meet her. His eyes searched hers, and Alex smiled to let him know it had gone well. Better than she'd expected, actually. He'd been right.

They both made appointments to see Dr. Gracin again in a couple of months and left the building. Outside, Alex released a huge sigh of pent up stress before filling her lungs with the damp, yet fresh air. She felt so much lighter now that she didn't have the appointment hanging over her.

Inside the truck, Riley started the engine and asked, "So, do you want me to take you home, or would you like to grab a coffee? There's a good place not far from here. They've got sandwiches, too."

As tired as she was, she couldn't say no to an invitation like that. "I could use a good coffee."

They pulled out of the parking lot, and she folded down the visor in front of her to look in the mirror. Her eyes were a bit red and puffy, but at least she had not worn any eyeliner or mascara this morning that would have smeared everywhere. She looked a little rough, but not a total mess. A bit of a miracle, really.

Deeper into the city, Riley pulled into the parking lot of a café with an old world look to the front. The warm lights welcomed them inside, and Alex breathed in deeply of the rich coffee scent permeating the place. It gave the impression of an old pub and may have once been a bar. Quite a few people sat at the high round tables or in the booths along the windows. It was an excellent place to spend a cool, wet day like this, and she wished all the

JAYE ELLIOT

more that Riley could open a coffee shop in Aspen Creek. The town desperately needed one, in her opinion.

They ordered their coffees and sandwiches and claimed an empty table in the corner. For a while, they quietly talked about their appointments between bites and then sipped their coffee as raindrops chased each other down the large window near the table. Alex looked out at the parking lot and the glow of the street lights before turning her attention back to Riley.

"How far does your family live from here?"

He swallowed a sip of coffee and set his mug down. "My parents and brother live on the other side of the city. My sister has an apartment not too far from here." He looked out the window then, a faraway look taking over. A moment later, his expression lifted a little. "My granddad lives in an assisted living place just down the street. Best money can buy, though I know he hates it. He'd rather be out in a cabin somewhere, tinkering with his trucks, fishing, and sketching the wildlife."

"Wait, your grandpa is an artist?"

Riley shrugged. "I wouldn't exactly say that. It's more a hobby, but he does enjoy it. Maybe he once wanted to make something of it. I'm not sure. I just know he gave up a lot and worked hard to put my mom through college."

This piqued her curiosity. His grandfather seemed like an interesting person. And from how Riley talked, his grandpa was the only person in his family he was close to.

"Do you want to go visit him?"

He frowned slightly. "Today?"

She nodded.

"We don't have to do that."

"I don't mind. Really. I'm intrigued by him."

She hadn't expected to meet part of Riley's family today of all days, but she could sense his pleasure and eagerness to introduce them.

As soon as they finished their coffee, they left the café and drove a couple of blocks down the street to a sprawling assisted living community. He was right when he said it was the best money could buy. The place looked like it had everything, including its own chapel.

"We'll check the common area first," he said as they entered the main building. "He usually spends more time there than in his apartment, talking about the good old days with his buddies."

He guided Alex down a long hall. They passed several elderly inhabitants along the way. Riley smiled at each of them, even greeting some by name. He looked over at Alex and said, "Once I was able to leave the hospital, I spent a lot of time here visiting with my granddad and his friends."

She grinned at the thought of him sitting around with a bunch of old ladies.

At the end of the hall, a large room opened up, filled with chairs, couches, tables, and a TV at each end. A whole wall of windows overlooked a spacious garden that surely provided an abundance of colorful blooms in the spring and summer. Groups of elderly men and women sat around talking or taking part in various activities.

Alex followed Riley around the perimeter of the room to a table where three men played a game of cards. As they drew near, one of them looked up, and the brightest grin split his face.

"Riley!"

The man rose, seeming quite spry for his age. Riley walked straight to him and gave him a hug. "Hey, Granddad."

His grandfather slapped him on the back just before they parted, his grin just as wide. "It's mighty good to see you. It's been a while."

"It has. I'm sorry. I guess I got caught up in work and settling in at Aspen Creek. I should have called."

His grandfather just waved his hand. "You're young and

busy. No harm done." Behind his thin, wire-rimmed glasses, his eyes twinkled the same shade of blue as Riley's. "Well now, who's this fine-looking young lady?"

Riley turned to Alex with a smile and held out his arm, drawing her closer. "Granddad, this is my girlfriend, Alex Jennings. Alex, my grandfather, Joseph Preston."

His smile grew even brighter, if that was possible, and he held out his hand for Alex to shake. Though his skin was wrinkled, his grip was strong.

"I'm very pleased to meet you, Alex. It's about time Riley found himself a good woman."

It was impossible not to grin at his enthusiasm. "I'm very pleased to meet you as well, Mr. Preston."

He laughed then. "Mr. Preston. No, that's far too polite for friends. Call me Joe."

He then introduced them both to his friends, but they didn't remain long. When their seats were empty, Alex and Riley joined Joe at the table.

"Looks like you've been doing well for yourself in Aspen Creek," Joe said to Riley. "Where are you working?"

"I'm bartending. It's not a prestigious job, but it pays the bills and I meet a lot of interesting people." Riley sent a warm glance at Alex that nearly set her to blushing.

This brought his grandfather's attention back to her. "And what about you?"

"I actually work at the bar with Riley as a day job, but I'm trying to make a career as an artist."

Joe perked up. "An artist? It's getting harder nowadays, but I like to sketch once in a while. Birds and other wildlife, mostly."

"That's what Riley told me. I'd love to see some of your sketches."

He chuckled. "Oh, they're not that good. Just something to pass the time when the inkling hits."

"I'm sure they're lovely, and I don't believe art is ever a waste of time."

Joe's infectious grin returned. He looked at Riley. "I like this one. You better hang on to her. Much better than those whiny girls you used to bring home during high school."

Riley rubbed his neck. "Yeah, well, I wasn't very smart in high school."

His grandfather chuckled again and asked Alex more about herself. After a time, he took them up to his little apartment to show her his drawings. She sat on a loveseat with Riley and flipped through an album of pencil sketches of birds, deer, and other local wildlife.

"These are beautiful." She glanced up at Joe, who sat in a recliner across from them. "Did you ever take any art classes?"

"Me? Oh, no. Didn't even make it all the way through high school."

"Well, your natural talent is impressive. You could probably sell some of these."

He shrugged. "I was never in it for any money. It's just my way of enjoying the world around me."

Alex had to agree. Though she did hope to make a living from her art, at its core, it was something she did for herself. Something that brought her joy, or was supposed to.

They spent all afternoon with Riley's grandfather, even having supper with him. Alex loved hearing his stories. Life was so different back when he was young. Sometimes she wished she had lived back then, during simpler times.

After they helped him clean up and put away the dishes, they prepared to head home before it got late.

At the door, just before they left the apartment, Riley turned to his grandfather. "Would you mind keeping this visit between us? I haven't talked to anyone else since Alex and I started dating."

His grandfather gave a little smile, his eyes twinkling. "Don't worry, your secret's safe with me."

They traded goodbyes, and Alex gave the old man a hug and a promise to come back to visit him.

Once they were well on their way back to Aspen Creek, Alex looked over at Riley. He hadn't said a word since they left Denver.

"I love your grandfather." It was clear where so many of Riley's good qualities came from, including his adorable smile.

He glanced at her, but this time that smile didn't quite reach his eyes. "He's always supported me."

Alex watched him for another long moment of heavy silence. Despite how well today had gone, something definitely bothered him. "Are you okay?"

He didn't answer right away. She sensed he wanted to speak, but the words wouldn't seem to come. In all they had experienced in these last few weeks of dating, Alex didn't think she had seen him look as emotional as he did when he glanced over at her again.

"I've been saved for almost three years now. I was here in Denver for almost a year after I was wounded. But in all that time, I haven't once tried to share my faith with my family."

Those guilt-ridden words hung in the cab around them. Alex didn't how to respond at first. For the most part, everyone in her family was a Christian. She had no idea what it was like to be the only one.

"It's not too late." But what comfort was that, really? They both knew how abruptly life could end. Trying for something more encouraging, she said, "I'll pray you'll have the opportunity to tell them."

It wouldn't be easy, though, considering their almost non-existent relationship. However, he thanked her. Maybe she had managed to encourage him a little.

"So why does your grandfather live in an assisted living community? He seems pretty well able to take care of himself."

"He had a heart attack a couple of years ago and is pretty forgetful about his medication. And his eyesight's not that good." Still, he seemed better off than most.

Riley paused for just a moment before he said, "It's because my parents don't feel like having him underfoot. They have plenty of room but, to my knowledge, never offered to let him stay with them. Instead, they just pay for his living."

"Oh." She shouldn't have asked, especially since he was so down already. She scrambled for something to cheer him up. "I meant it when I told him I would come back and visit. I really do want to."

Finally Riley smiled, for real this time. "He'd love that."

Chapter Fourteen

THE CHILLY, RAINY WEATHER CARRIED ALL THE WAY OVER INTO Tuesday, but Alex didn't really mind. Riley had his truck all warmed up when he came to get her for work, and while the bar was no coffee shop, it was cozy in its own way. She almost laughed to herself at the silly thought, but she had woken up with a pretty good outlook on life. She hardly dared to hope she had passed through the worst, but a little spark of it rested in her heart.

Work started out slowly with only one brief customer. To amuse themselves, Alex started a guessing game of random facts about each other. This drew more than a bit of laughter between them.

When it came around to her turn again, she said, "Your favorite superhero growing up was Batman."

Riley shook his head. "Superman."

"Really? Huh, I had you pegged for a Batman guy."

He chuckled. "Batman didn't have heat vision. Homecoming queen?"

"Oh my goodness, no. Never in a million years."

"Come on, I think you would've made a great homecoming queen."

She laughed at the sheer absurdity of it. "I was definitely not homecoming queen, but you're not too far off. Josh was homecoming king during his senior year." He was the popular one, and she'd been perfectly happy with it that way.

Since they'd brought up high school, she had another guess. "High school quarterback?"

He just grinned. "Running back."

"Seriously? I so thought I had that one."

"I liked running into guys more than I liked throwing the football." He paused to think for a moment before he gave her a knowing smile. "You were the middle-school girl with braids, glasses, and braces."

She laughed dryly this time. "The awkward middle-school dork, you mean? Yeah, that was me."

"I'm sure you were cute in braces."

"Try telling that to the cool girls. It was okay though. I had too much fun with Josh and his friends to really care." Now it was her turn, and she had just the guess. "You first grew your hair out in high school."

"I did, though not quite this long before I had to cut it when I enlisted."

"And let me guess, your parents hated it?"

"Yes, they did. I guess that's why I did it."

"Is it still why?"

He considered the question for a long moment as if he'd never consciously thought about it before. "Maybe. I don't know. I guess it's just my way of being my own man. Not conforming to what others expect of me. Why? Do you not like it?"

"No, I do. Actually, I kind of have a thing for guys with long hair. I think it started with a major crush I had on Sully from *Dr. Quinn, Medicine Woman* when I was little. We all used to watch it every week, and Josh teased me relentlessly."

Riley grinned. "Good reason to keep it then."

"Yes. Don't you dare cut it."

He just looked at her for a quiet moment in that way that quickened her pulse, like he was thinking about kissing her. No doubt he was because she was sure thinking about kissing him.

However, he must have thought better of it. They were at work, after all. Instead, he slowly moved past her, down the bar.

"Do you want coffee?"

She raised her brows at him. "I always want coffee."

He glanced at her with a bit of a crooked smile. "Good, 'cause I want to show you something."

What was he up to? She stepped closer as he turned to an espresso machine tucked in amongst the liquor bottles behind the bar. She'd always wondered about it but had never asked. Riley gathered ingredients and coffee supplies from the shelves below the bar, and Alex watched quietly as he worked the machine. The strong, earthy scent of hot coffee masked the ever-present hint of alcohol. He brewed a little of the espresso into a cup and then picked up a pitcher of steamed milk. With impressive skill, he drizzled it into the coffee to create a perfect flower-shaped pattern. Alex widened her eyes, a grin taking hold. He'd said he had a passion for coffee, but she had no idea he could do this.

He handed her the mug. "On slow days I like to practice." He laughed, a little self-deprecating. "I even have a couple of costumers who come in just to ask for a latte." He paused, and something changed about his expression, a vulnerability, as if he were sharing a closely guarded secret about himself. "My parents would laugh, but I always considered this a form of art."

Now she read that look in his eyes—a deep longing for approval. He probably had no idea how clearly it shown in his gaze as he looked at her, waiting for her to respond.

"It's beautiful," she said earnestly. "And it *is* art. It doesn't matter what anyone else thinks."

He smiled then, not a full grin, but it displayed just how much her words meant. A desire to encourage him and see him pursue this passion of his filled Alex near to bursting. If she could make it happen right here and now she would.

"How did you learn to do this?"

He shrugged. "Online videos and practice."

She took a sip of her latte. She hated to ruin the design, but the smell was too tempting. Not only did Riley make a very pretty coffee, it was delicious too. "Are you going to have one? I'd love to watch you make another."

Happily, he turned back to the machine.

Despite the slow start to the day, the bar filled up once evening rolled around and people left work. Alex kept busy cleaning tables and bringing orders to the counter for Riley to fill. It still surprised her how well she had settled into this job. A big part of that was because of Riley. They worked well together, and his presence provided her the confidence to do her job.

With this confidence in tow, she approached a table occupied by four young men she hadn't seen in here before. They were all in their early to mid-twenties, or so she assumed since Riley would have checked their IDs before serving them. They laughed rowdily as she neared the table, their beer glasses almost empty.

"Can I get you gentlemen anything?"

They all quieted and looked up. The one nearest her, a guy in a dark hoodie and flat-billed cap, eyed her slowly up and down. "Well, hello, gorgeous. When did you start working here?"

She cleared her throat. Sure, she was getting used to the flirting, but her skin prickled at his tone. "Recently."

"I've been missing out then."

He eyed her again, and the goosebumps intensified. Even here, the guys were usually not so forward. Now she realized her error in not approaching them with more caution. She composed herself and spoke in a professional tone. "Do any of you want a refill?"

The guy leaned toward her, a leering grin curling his lips. "None for me, but your company would be nice."

Before she could move, he reached out to slide his hand down her back and lower. She quickly slapped it away and took a step back. She breathed hard, her chest tightening around the hard thumping behind her ribs, and her face flushed. The creep just laughed like it was the most amusing thing in the world.

Alex spoke through her teeth. "If you don't want a refill, then I'll leave you to the rest of your drinks."

"Ah, don't be that way." The cap-wearing jerk looked like he was about to reach for her arm when Riley's strong, masculine presence arrived at her side, blocking his reach.

"Hey, if you want to walk out that door instead of being thrown out of it, you'd best watch yourself." He practically growled at the guy. "A lady tells you no, you keep your hands off, got it?"

Rather than backing down, the guy just smirked and looked up at him as if Riley weren't all muscle and couldn't shove his head through the wall if he had a mind to. Such boldness sent shivers down Alex's back. Finally, the guy peered around Riley toward the counter.

"That you on the wall over there?"

Alex glanced over her shoulder at the photo of Riley and his friend Bradley in Afghanistan, amongst the photos of other soldiers Luke honored at the bar.

Riley just stared the man down. "You mean that photo of the men fighting so punks like you would have the freedom to keep being punks? Yeah, that's me. Now you better keep your hands and eyes to yourself. Unless you want to find out what thirteen years of military service can teach someone about how many different ways a body can be messed up."

The guy laughed to himself, a bitter, condescending sound. "What's the matter, Captain America? Am I butting in on your territory?" He tipped his head toward Alex.

Riley gave him a look that could have incinerated him on

the spot. His voice lowered to a quietly dangerous edge. "Are we going to have a problem?"

The man sat back lazily. "No, no problem."

"Good."

Riley took Alex by the arm in a firm but reassuring grip and guided her toward the bar. They hadn't gone far before the guy called after them, "Better watch your back."

Riley paused mid-step, and Alex could almost feel the tension pulsing from his hand into her arm. Several bad scenarios rushed into her mind. She thought about where Luke kept the gun behind the bar. What was she supposed to do if Riley and the guy went at it? But then he urged her on, and she released a slow breath. Behind the counter, he sent the men another scathing look before turning to her.

"You all right?"

She nodded, though her heart pounded furiously. Even her hands trembled a bit. Thank God she had Riley around. She didn't like the memory of the guy's hand on her, but no harm had actually been done.

"Just stay away from them. I'll handle anything else they need."

"Thank you."

His taut expression melted into a slow smile. "No problem."

Her smile broke out as well. She was beginning to love this catchphrase of his. He probably had no idea how often he said it. But being around him really did make her feel as though there were no problems that couldn't be fixed.

Chapter Fifteen

A WEEK AND A HALF AFTER THE BAR INCIDENT, ALEX MET RILEY outside just before eight in the morning. The crisp early October day was just the kind Josh had loved, and Alex breathed in deeply as she climbed into Riley's truck. Today would be perfect for helping Mindy and Zach move into their new house. Much better than working in the heat of summer. She could hardly wait to see them again. She couldn't believe a month had passed already since their football party.

Before pulling away from the apartment, Riley handed her a Styrofoam coffee cup.

"Tell me what you think of this."

Ever since he had revealed his talent for latte art, he'd begun having her try different coffee blends he hoped to someday serve in his own shop. Alex was more than happy to lend her thoughts and suggestions to the endeavor.

She took a sip. Frothy whipped cream came first, followed by coffee sweetened how she liked it and laced with a definite taste of chocolate.

"Mmm," she breathed, even before she swallowed.

He grinned. "You like that one?"

Alex nodded enthusiastically. "I think it might be my favorite so far. It definitely belongs on your specialty menu." She took another appreciative drink. "This is so good. It's like a coffee, hot chocolate combo. You know, if you added a bit of peppermint, this would make a fantastic holiday blend."

After a sip of his own coffee, he agreed. "Maybe I should hire you to come up with more ideas and be my official taster."

She sent him a playful look. "No need to hire me. That's what coffee-loving girlfriends are for." Though, now that she thought about it, she would jump at the chance to work with him if he did open his own place. "Any progress with being able to buy the shop?"

"No," he responded with a hint of true disappointment. "If I was smart, I'd sell this truck and buy something more fuel efficient, but I don't think I can bring myself to do it."

"You could also stop taking your girlfriend out so often and buying her so many gifts." She projected humor into her words, though she was being serious. Neither of them was in a position to spend that kind of money.

However, he just gave her a lazy smile. "Where's the fun in that?"

Alex couldn't bring herself to argue with him when he made her feel so special. So she happily sipped her coffee and enjoyed the ride to Boulder.

A large moving truck sat in front of Mindy and Zach's new house when they arrived. Parking at the curb, they climbed out and met Zach as he hauled a large plastic tote out of the back of the truck. He set it down to greet them, and Alex gave him a hug before he turned and shook hands with Riley.

"Mindy's been baking most of the morning, preparing for you to get here."

Alex shook her head. "She didn't have to go through that much trouble. We could have just snacked."

Zach shot her a skeptical look. "Try telling her that. I think she was just anxious to try out her new kitchen."

Alex laughed. Of course Mindy would go overboard. It was practically her middle name. "So, is there anything we can help bring inside?"

Zach swept his arm toward the truck. "Whatever you can carry. It all has to come in at some point. We'll try to get most of the smaller stuff out first, and then Riley can help me with the furniture."

The two of them climbed the ramp, each grabbing a box before following Zach to the house. Just inside, they set the boxes by the already large pile taking up half of the entryway. Alex wouldn't have relished the prospect of having to unpack them all. Then again, Mindy was a bit of an organization freak. She probably enjoyed the process.

"They're here," Zach called out.

In answer a dog barked, followed by the scramble of toenails. A big, broad-headed golden retriever barreled into the room first, a stocky brown and white English bulldog at its heels.

"Hi, puppies!" Alex exclaimed.

Zach's retriever, Shadow, bounded up to her, his tail wagging frantically. It was a not-so-closely-guarded secret that Alex had seen Zach cry while watching the movie, *Homeward Bound*, when they were kids. She and Josh had been sure to tease him about his name choice when he'd first gotten his dog a few years ago. She knelt down, scrubbing her fingers into the retriever's luxurious coat. Mindy's little Bella nosed in between them and pawed Alex's leg seeking attention too. She laughed and rubbed the bulldog's wrinkly back. Last time she had seen either of them, Bella was just a roly-poly puppy. Though she still had her wrinkles and adorable smooshed face, she had quadrupled in size.

Shadow turned his excited energy to Riley now. Alex smiled as he rubbed the dog's ears comfortably, earning an appreciative groan from Shadow. There was nothing more attractive than a guy who liked animals.

Mindy walked in then, the scent of warm cinnamon sugar wafting in with her. Alex straightened to give her best friend a hug.

"I'm so glad you could come today." Mindy nearly squeezed the breath from her lungs. "It's so much more fun to unpack with friends."

"Happy to help."

Mindy stepped back. "I just took a pan of cinnamon rolls out of the oven. As soon as they are cool, I'll ice them. I made chili for later."

"It sounds delicious."

Mindy beamed. She just plain loved doing things for people, and Alex loved her for it.

Mindy then slapped her hands together. "All right, now that I'm done in the kitchen for a while, we can get this unloading party started."

Over the next several hours, the four of them took many trips back and forth from the moving truck to the house, with plenty of breaks in between for conversation and enjoying the warm, gooey cinnamon rolls. Once they had all the boxes unloaded, Riley and Zach went to work on moving the furniture and hooking up the electronics. While they were busy, Alex joined Mindy in her gorgeous new kitchen to help unpack.

"Are you enjoying church?" Mindy asked as Alex handed her an assortment of brightly-colored plates to put in the cupboard.

"We are. Yesterday was only our third time, so we still feel like the new people, but we are gradually getting to know more of the congregation. I really like Pastor Ellis. He's very kind and has always made a point to talk to us after the service."

"I'm so glad you have a place to go. Zach and I were just talking about it yesterday. There are churches we could try here in Boulder, but we want to join you on Sunday."

"Really?"

"Yeah. We don't mind the drive. It's only twenty minutes."

Alex grinned. "I'm so happy you're so close now."

Mindy's expression matched. "Me too." Her eyes then narrowed searchingly. "So how are you doing? You seem a lot better since last time. Did your appointment help?"

"I think it did. I still have days I feel down. Not as much when I'm busy at work or with Riley. Nights are probably when I struggle the most, but my medication should be kicking in."

"I'm glad you agreed to get help. Zach and I have been really worried."

"I'm sorry." Alex did hate to have caused such concern for them.

"I'm just happy things are improving." Mindy's impish smile returned. "And things are still good with you and Riley?"

Alex couldn't hold back a grin of her own. "Very. He's so sweet all the time and very protective of me."

"I'm so glad. You needed a guy like that. Honestly, I was a little worried when you first told me about him, that he would be kind of hard, you know, with everything he's been through and working at the bar. He looks it, but it's funny how often those kinds of guys have the softest hearts."

Alex agreed, the incident at the bar coming to mind. Riley had looked like he could have taken that guy's head off right there at the table. He definitely had a fierce side, yet he'd turned right around with that heart-melting smile and made her feel perfectly safe.

Later in the evening, once the house actually looked like a home, Zach built a small campfire in the backyard where they gathered around with mugs of hot chocolate and told stories. Riley and Zach shared about their days of playing high school football, and Riley even offered up a few stories about his siblings. Though he'd told Alex a little about them, they always seemed to avoid the topic of his family. It was good to hear of the fun things he had done. She liked hearing what he was like as a child.

Eventually, the conversation worked its way to more recent history and Riley's time in the military.

"So you were medically discharged?" Mindy asked

He nodded.

"How many times were you shot?" Zach said. "If you don't mind my asking."

"Technically, five. My vest stopped two of the bullets, but not these two."

Riley pushed his fleece-lined flannel jacket away from his neck and pulled down the collar of his shirt to expose two distinctive scars below his left shoulder. Alex had never seen the evidence of his wounds. Her stomach bunched up toward her ribs. Had those bullets hit a bit lower, he probably would have died where he'd fallen. Despite the heat from the flames, a wave of cold washed through her.

"I caught another bullet just above my right knee that shattered my femur."

They all grimaced, and Mindy put her hand over her knee as if she could feel it.

"That's so awful," she said. "I'm so thankful you recovered from it."

Riley sent her a warm smile. "So am I. Could've been a lot worse. I happened to be the first one in the line of fire and the only one seriously injured in the ambush."

Alex's throat ached, constricting her airway in response to all this talk of war. What must Josh have faced over there and in his last moments here on earth? She hoped he hadn't been in terrible pain. She'd thought about asking Riley for details, but she could never bring herself to do it. And what would have happened if Riley had died too and she had never met him? He was such a big part of her life now. A true Godsend. She couldn't imagine her life without him.

Everyone must have noticed how quiet she had become, and Mindy, in her upbeat way, changed the subject to church. From here on, the conversation remained lighthearted. By the time they left for home, Alex was able to leave her morose thoughts behind and simply rejoice in the fact that God had saved Riley's life and brought him into hers.

Chapter Sixteen

ALEX PULLED A CRISP DUTCH APPLE PIE OUT OF THE OVEN AND set it on the counter to cool. She glanced at the clock. She had about forty-five minutes to finish getting ready. After a wonderful morning at church with Mindy and Zach yesterday, Riley had invited them for supper tonight to watch the Monday night game together. Alex looked forward to having supper with Riley. He might have only done one semester of culinary school, but if his food was as good as his coffee, they were in for a real treat.

And, hopefully, the evening out would help dispel the cloud that had followed her around since waking up from a bad dream this morning. Why did something always have to happen when things were going well? At least making the pie to bring for dessert had served as a distraction. Her mom's family recipe was the perfect fall-time dessert for when the game started. Plus it was one of Mindy's favorites.

After cleaning up the kitchen, Alex headed to her room to change out of her flour-dusted clothing. She matched a pair of jeans that had a fashionable rip in the knee with her Broncos t-shirt and a flannel shirt. In the bathroom, she brushed out her hair from its messy bun and applied just enough makeup to look put together.

By the time she finished, she figured Mindy and Zach must be on their way. Slipping on her favorite camel-colored leather jacket, she grabbed the pie and her purse and headed out to her Jeep. It hadn't acted up at all since Riley had worked on it, but it would give her peace of mind this winter to know she had his expert assistance if it did.

At the bar, she pulled up into the employee parking space next to Riley's truck behind the building and let herself in through the back door. The buzz of conversation up front told her customers were already gathering, and that number would only grow as game time neared. She peeked around the corner to see how full the room was.

Kat worked with Luke tonight. Alex had finally met her a couple of weeks ago. She was the kind of woman who wouldn't take trouble from anyone, least of all the male patrons. Alex wasn't sure how she managed it with her petite stature and pretty dark pixie cut that weren't at all intimidating. Confidence and personality made up for it though. She wore a long-sleeved t-shirt tonight, but Alex had seen her full sleeve tattoo of a colorful peacock. She did, after all, work as a freelance tattoo designer in her spare time.

Kat's outgoing personality reminded Alex a bit of Mindy. She gave off a strong older sister vibe, especially when she'd heard about Alex's confrontation with the four guys. Apparently, she'd had her own clash with the instigator of the group, Tony Vargas. Unlike Alex, however, she hadn't required any assistance. But Alex didn't mind. She was glad Riley had come to her rescue.

Her phone chimed, and she glanced at it. A text from Mindy said they would be there in about ten minutes. When Alex looked up again, Kat was on her way from one of the tables with a tray of empty glasses. She caught sight of Alex and grinned. As she rounded the end of the bar, she said, "I don't know what Riley has cooking up there, but I caught a whiff of it a while ago, and it smells delicious."

"He said he was making spaghetti."

"Lucky girl. You can just head up and knock on his door." She gestured to the staircase in the back room leading to the apartment above the bar.

Before turning, Alex watched Kat slide comfortably around Luke and lean close to ask, "How come you never make me spaghetti?"

"Maybe because the last time I tried to cook something I nearly burned our place down," Luke answered.

Alex laughed at them. While she didn't agree with their living arrangement, they made a cute couple.

Still laughing quietly at the banter that continued behind her, she climbed the stairs. She had never been up to Riley's apartment before. Pausing at the door, she caught the delicious scent of garlic and tomato. She balanced the pie in one hand and knocked. Riley opened the door a moment later with a smile and invited her inside.

"Mindy says they'll be here in a few minutes," Alex said as she glanced around the studio-like apartment.

"Good, supper is almost ready." He nodded at the pie. "That looks good."

"Thank you." She set it on the kitchen counter and then slipped off her coat. Riley took it from her to hang on a hook behind the door.

As she took in the surroundings, movement caught her attention. A sleek, black tuxedo cat with a white chin and white paws waltzed toward her from the living room area of the apartment. He paused and peered at her with vivid yellow eyes.

"Well, hello there, handsome." She bent down and reached out her hand, wiggling her fingers. The cat padded toward her, sniffed her hand, and then rubbed against it affectionately. Alex rubbed his neck and ears, eliciting a loud purr. "Aren't you a gorgeous boy? And very well cared for, by the looks of it."

She glanced up at Riley. How had he never shared this delightful little secret with her? "You never told me you had a cat."

He ducked his head, his cheeks going a shade darker. Alex wasn't sure she had ever seen him look so embarrassed.

"That's . . ." he cleared his throat, "Tux. I found him scrounging in the dumpster last fall covered in grease and scared half to death. He was still pretty small then. I brought him in to clean him up and was going to take him to the shelter the next morning, but . . ." He shrugged as if he had no explanation for how the animal had wormed its way into his life.

Alex fought to subdue her grin so as not to make him any more uncomfortable than he was already. "I love cats."

Riley cleared his throat again. "I better check the sauce."

He stepped into the kitchen and busied himself at the stove. "Need any help?"

He shook his head. "No, I've got it."

Alex scooped Tux up into her arms and took a seat on one of the barstools at the counter. The cat snuggled into her lap. She watched Riley prepare two delicious-looking slabs of cheesy garlic bread to put into the oven. Finally, she peered around the apartment again. Though bigger, it wasn't quite as nice as hers. Still, Riley kept it well-maintained. All it really needed to spruce it up was some artwork on the walls, throw pillows, and perhaps a rug or two—just to add color to the place.

She halted her thought process. He was probably happy with it just the way it was, and she definitely did not live there.

She fixed her attention back on Tux, who had taken an interest in the threads hanging from the rip in her jeans. The playful twitch of his tail made her giggle.

A couple of minutes later, someone knocked on the door. Alex slid from the stool and set Tux on the floor as Riley stepped away from the stove to let Mindy and Zach inside.

"Sorry if we've kept you waiting," Zach said as they crossed the threshold. "My wife just doesn't know when to hurry."

Mindy shoved him lightly. "Watch it, or you'll be sleeping on the couch tonight."

"Not at all," Riley assured them with a laugh. "I was just finishing up."

After taking off their coats, Mindy and Zach both scanned the apartment.

"This is nice," Mindy said. She had always wanted to share a studio apartment with Alex during their time in college. They had almost rented one together but couldn't quite fit it in their budget.

Riley thanked them, and Alex took over introducing Tux who wove between her legs and rubbed against her ankles. It would be less embarrassing for Riley that way, especially in front of Zach. However, she knew for a fact Zach liked cats even if he might deny it with his dying breath. He'd spent just as much time playing with kittens in the barn hayloft back home as she had growing up.

The four of them talked happily, and Alex and Mindy set the table with black, stoneware dishes from the cabinet. Riley took the garlic bread out of the oven a few minutes later, toasted to a bubbly golden brown, and they carried the food to the table. Just before they took their seats, Riley pulled a bottle of red wine from a cabinet.

"My parents sent this last Christmas. I've never had any reason to open it, but I figure tonight's as good a time as any."

Alex eyed the bottle. "That looks expensive."

"It is. My parents wouldn't bother with anything less."

Mindy's mischievous smile showed up. "I've never had any expensive wine before. I'm starting to feel like I'm dining at a restaurant in Italy."

Riley laughed as he pulled the cork from the bottle. "My cooking's not that good."

"I don't know; that garlic bread is making my mouth water just looking at it."

Alex agreed, and they all sat down. Before they passed the food around, Zach said a prayer. He was always good at that. They then filled their plates. Alex's first bite of spaghetti was just as delicious as she expected. All the spices in the tomato sauce blended together perfectly, without being too overpowering. When she tried the garlic bread next, she was convinced she could eat a whole loaf by herself. Had Riley actually gone into the restaurant business, she was sure he would have done well.

Mindy and Zach appeared to enjoy it just as much as she did. Halfway through the meal, Mindy raised her wine glass to Riley. "To the chef."

Alex and Zach raised theirs in toast as well, and Riley just smiled in thanks.

They stayed at the table talking until just before the game started. After helping Riley put away the uneaten food, they gathered around the TV. Riley had an armchair pulled up near the couch just for Mindy, which Alex found hilarious. She sat down on the couch next to Riley, leaning against his shoulder. About a quarter of the way through the game, he lifted his arm and draped it over the back of the couch behind her. He gave her a little smile, and Alex snuggled in closer. Right now, she couldn't think of any place she would rather be.

A couple of hours later, the game clock ran out with Denver up by fourteen, forming the perfect end to a perfect evening. Still stuffed to near bursting with their dinner and slices of halftime pie, they all pushed themselves up and headed toward the door. Mindy and Zach slipped their coats on and thanked Riley for the excellent meal. As they were about to leave, Mindy turned to Alex.

"Are you coming?"

"I'll leave shortly. I just thought I'd help Riley finish cleaning up." There were still dishes to rinse and things to put away.

"Okay," Mindy said, but Alex caught the look of caution her friend sent her way.

They said their goodbyes and headed out. Once they were gone, Alex helped Riley with the remaining dishes. They laughed and discussed the game a bit while she washed and he dried. It was fun to talk football again. When the kitchen was spotless, Alex leaned back against the counter, quite content. If only every evening could be so nice.

"Thanks for having us over tonight. I really enjoyed it, and you really are an excellent cook."

"Thank you." Riley stepped closer to hang his dish towel from a hook on one of the cabinets. He then looked at her again. "I think this is the first time this place has really felt like home to me."

She gave a slow nod. Aspen Creek had never truly felt like home for her either until just recently. Not until she'd met Riley. "That's important."

She stared at him as silence fell between them. She had never been so drawn to anyone before—to his kindness toward her and the way he looked at her as if she was the only woman in the world who mattered to him. He embodied every hope and dream she had ever had from the moment her little-girl heart had first understood the concept of love and romance. It was terrifying yet thrilling at the same time to feel so deeply for someone.

He moved closer and bent to kiss her. She leaned into the kiss. It started out soft and gentle. He wrapped his arm slowly around her back, drawing her closer. The kiss deepened, over-whelming her senses with only the acute awareness of him.

A warning triggered in her mind like an electric jolt. She broke off the kiss and scooted away to put some distance between them. Her heart raced and she was a little bit dizzy, but one thing was very clear—she was perilously close to making a terrible mistake.

"I-I'm sorry. I think I should be going." Her cheeks flushed like she'd shoved her face in a hot oven, and trying to catch her breath and stammering like a fool did not help. She couldn't bring herself to look at Riley. Panic sent her mouth into motion before her brain could fully catch up and slow her down. "I just . . . a long time ago, I made a commitment between me and God that I wouldn't cross a certain line until I was married and I feel like this is getting too close to that line and I just . . . I can't break that commitment."

The height of embarrassment burned through her cheeks again. She probably sounded like an idiot. No one seemed to care about such things these days. The select few like her and Mindy probably were like alien lifeforms to most people. Oh, Riley was going to hate her. What if this was it? What if it was over after this?

She closed her eyes, preparing for the worst. "I'm sorry if that upsets you."

She swallowed hard. A heartbeat of silence and then he answered.

"I'm not upset."

She finally brought herself to look at him, and true to his word, she could find no evidence of indignation in his calm demeanor. "You're not?"

"No. I respect your decision and your conviction. It's pretty rare these days." Now he looked away, lines deepening in his forehead. He drew a deep breath and let it out slowly. "Honestly, I wish I had made the same commitment, but before I came to Christ, I can't say I always made the best decisions."

He looked at her again, waiting for a response. There was something almost fearful in his eyes.

She nodded slowly, but she couldn't judge him for his past, especially not for the life he had lived before getting saved. After all, only a few weeks ago, she'd been about to get drunk and throw herself off a bridge. He wasn't the only one guilty of poor decisions. "I understand."

His expression smoothed, the apprehension fading. His eyes held hers earnestly. "I promise I won't do anything to jeopardize your commitment."

Alex's own relief washed through her. Those words meant so much. She didn't want this to be a battle she fought alone. "Thank you. I just really, really don't want to ruin anything between us by not honoring God."

"I agree."

She smiled bashfully. "And thank you for putting up with my weirdness. I've just never been in this position before or even had a reason to have this conversation with anyone. Sometimes I overthink things and panic and then I just talk too much." She shrugged.

He chuckled and gave a lopsided smile that threatened to melt her inside. "I like your weirdness." He then pushed away from the counter. "I'll get your coat and walk you down to your Jeep."

She breathed a long, steadying breath and thanked God first for the warning and then that Riley was such an honorable and understanding man. If not, her perfect night could have ended disastrously.

They left the apartment and walked out the back door. Just as they reached the Jeep, Alex's phone chimed. She pulled it out. "Just Mindy checking to see if I'm home yet."

Riley glanced at the lit-up screen. "You've got a good friend."

She smiled down at her phone as she typed a response that she was leaving now. "Yes, I do."

She unlocked the Jeep and slid into her seat. Riley stood at her door for a moment, looking in at her.

"Be careful walking up to your apartment. Text me when you're inside."

His concern for her was more than enough to melt her heart. "I will."

He then closed her door, and Alex started up the Jeep. She gave him a little wave as she backed away from the building and pulled into the street. Alone in the vehicle, she drew in another calming breath, her heart rate still above normal. That kiss was going to stick in her mind for a very long time. She couldn't help but savor it just a little, though she gave herself a very stern mental warning not to foolishly put herself in that position again. She'd probably overreacted, but that kind of thinking could lead to trouble. Better to be safe than very sorry later.

Chapter Seventeen

Midweek, Riley picked Alex up for work as usual. Wednesdays were always the slowest as far as the afternoons went. Fewer tourists passed through now that the weather had turned colder. After rearranging some glasses to gain a bit more shelf space, Alex focused on Riley, who tinkered with his espresso machine. She hesitated at first. She wasn't going to bring this up, but . . .

"How many girls were there before me?" The question left a slightly bitter aftertaste, but she would not judge him for his past. That wasn't an issue; however, the uncomfortable thought of him with other women, especially intimately, soured her stomach.

He turned to her slowly. Maybe he would just try to brush it off or avoid the subject. But his expression sobered, regret robbing the light from his eyes.

She shook her head. "You don't have to talk about it if you don't want to."

"No," he murmured. "You should know." He paused. This was probably even more uncomfortable for him than it was for her. "I dated a couple of girls during high school. Nothing serious. But just before junior year, I started dating a girl named Amber. We were together until college. I think everyone expected us to get married. When I enlisted, she told me she wouldn't wait for me. I haven't spoken to her since." He cleared his throat. "There were a few random girls I saw over the years on leave, but I'm certainly not proud of that."

Alex processed the information in silence for a minute. It's not like any of it surprised her. It could be worse, she supposed. She drew in a long breath before speaking. "Well, Amber obviously didn't deserve you."

That brought a hint of a smile to his face, but he said, "I can't blame her. That's a lot to ask of a person."

Maybe, but if he were to go back into the military right now, Alex would wait. It would be torture, but she would do it.

Now he stood silently for a moment before he said, "I'm sorry."

His truly remorseful tone touched her heart. It had always been her deep-down desire to meet someone who had made the same commitment to purity she had, but she wouldn't dwell on something God had already forgiven in Riley's life.

"I'm in no position to condemn you for anything, Riley. We're new creations in Christ, remember? That was the old you. I am just incredibly blessed to know the new you."

His smile returned, emanating relief and happiness. Seeing it eliminated any nagging doubts she might have had. He had made mistakes. So had she. What mattered was the man he was now, and she loved that man.

Church on Sunday morning was as enjoyable as always. Alex was so glad Mindy and Zach had decided to join them instead of finding a church in Boulder. Even though it was only their second time attending, the two were very popular already. Mindy had a way of drawing people with her bubbly and energetic personality. Alex was more than happy to follow in her wake.

After visiting with the congregation for a while, they all headed over to Alex's apartment to watch the game that started at noon. When it ended a couple of hours later, Mindy, who was buzzed on caffeinated soda and nearly bouncing out of her seat, suggested they go bowling before she and Zach headed home. Alex had never visited the local bowling alley since she'd never had anyone to go with, but it did sound like fun. When Riley and Zach agreed, they all piled into Mindy and Zach's SUV and drove across town.

Though the old building was a little rough on the outside, the well-maintained interior offered a dozen bowling lanes to choose from and the only other bar in town. A few people were already playing as they walked up to the counter. The slightly heavyset man dressed in a black polo shirt greeted them. Alex recognized him from the bar, and he apparently knew Riley pretty well.

The four of them rented their shoes and paid for a couple of games before heading to the farthest open lane. They played teams at first—Mindy and Zach against Alex and Riley. Alex really didn't know what she was doing. She and Josh used to go, but she'd never learned the proper technique. It was all just for fun. Riley was probably the best of the four with Zach coming in close second. They better understood the concept of how to bowl, while Alex and Mindy just hoped for the best. It led to many laughs, especially when Riley and Zach got more competitive and humorously trash-talked each other. Soon, Alex laughed so hard her stomach hurt. She would thank Mindy later for taking lots of photos and videos on her phone. These were definitely memories she wanted to hold close.

They'd been playing for about an hour when Alex turned from their lane and caught sight of another group entering. Her stomach did a nosedive. Tony Vargas and his three friends sauntered up to the counter, not yet noticing them. She caught Riley's eye. He'd seen them too.

She pulled her shoulders back, determined not to let it bother her. After all, the guys had probably been emboldened by alcohol that night at the bar. Maybe here they would maintain some civility. Maybe. She fought to ignore the sense of unease bubbling insider her. Her fortitude wobbled when the guys chose the lane only two away. No doubt a purposeful decision on their part. Mindy and Zach must have sensed the tension between her and Riley because they had all fallen very quiet.

Alex did her level best to ignore the men before Tony called out, "Hey, gorgeous."

She glanced their way. Some girls might find his slick, bad boy vibe attractive, but his flattery, dripping with predatory undertones, wouldn't get him anywhere with her.

By this time, the jerk was engaged in a stare-down with Riley. What made the guy so brash? Surely he could see Riley was not someone he'd want to mess with. Tony may have been a tad taller, but he certainly didn't have Riley's broad shoulders and toned muscles to back up his attitude. Such antagonistic behavior, especially toward a superior opponent, had danger written all over it.

"Captain America." He gave Riley a mocking salute. "You boys feel like sharing the women?" He nodded to both Alex and Mindy.

Mindy gave a sassy toss of her head and held up her left hand. "Married woman."

If only Alex could easily summon that kind of attitude. But then, Tony might just find that even more amusing. And she didn't have a wedding ring to hide behind.

"Too bad," Tony said with a little smirk. His leering gaze landed squarely on Alex. "What about you? Want to share a drink now?"

She narrowed her eyes. While she didn't have Mindy or Kat's attitude, she left no question about her disinterest. "No thank you."

She fixed her attention on collecting her bowling ball since it was her turn, and they still had half a game left to play. For the next few minutes, they tried to ignore Tony and his minions. It wasn't easy, though, with their obnoxious laughter, boisterous shouting, and occasional catcalls. When Alex was up again, she fought to tune them out but still completely missed the few remaining pins.

"Hey, sweetheart, you want me to come over there and show you how it's done?"

Alex wanted so badly to walk over and knee him right where it would hurt the most. The way Riley glared at him said he would probably do a lot more than that given the chance. With a sigh, Alex walked back to them.

"I don't want to play anymore."

Mindy agreed. "We should get going anyway."

They changed back into their shoes and slipped on their coats.

"Leaving so soon?" Tony asked in mock disappointment.

They ignored him, but he stepped into their path, cutting their escape short. His three friends lingered a few feet behind. Alex sucked in her breath, her heart thumping in her throat. Blustery talk was one thing, but blocking their way was far more serious and scary. Thankfully, Riley stood between her and Tony.

"Move," he said in a low voice.

"Come on, you don't have to leave." Tony peered at Alex as if she would really make such a stupid decision as to stay behind.

"I'll only say this once more. Get out of our way." Riley's voice promised consequences if Tony didn't comply.

Tony glared at him but then smirked. His next words about Alex flushed her face and even her ears with heat. She'd never heard someone say such lewd, vile things before, at least not towards her.

Riley's fist smashed right into Tony's face, sending him stumbling back into one of the tables. Zach jumped in to keep Riley from going after him, and Mindy pulled Alex back toward the counter. Tony's friends hurried to help him up, but he shoved them off, cursing as he spit blood at his feet. He spun around and made a move toward Riley, but the guy behind the counter stepped between them.

"Hey! That's enough. You four, out, now." He pointed to Tony and his friends and then to the door. "And don't come back."

Tony sneered at Riley over the man's shoulder and wouldn't budge until his friends convinced him to go. They slunk out of the building, Tony sending a menacing glare back at them before disappearing out the door. Satisfied that there would be no more trouble, the manager turned to Alex and the others.

"Everyone all right?" He looked specifically at Alex.

She nodded, her mouth dry. "Yeah." Her cheeks still burned with the echo of Tony's insult in her head.

The manager turned to Riley. "If the cops show up, I'll let them know you were provoked."

"Thanks," Riley said, sending angry looks toward the door. "Sorry about starting that in here."

Alex only now realized how everyone was staring at them. One woman even had her hands clamped over a little girl's ears. It had probably been quite a scene for this usually fun and family-friendly place.

The manager shook his head. "From what I heard, he deserved it."

They returned the shoes to him and left the building. Thankfully, Tony and his gang were nowhere in sight as they climbed into Mindy and Zach's SUV. Once inside, Mindy launched into a tirade about how loathsome Tony was and what she'd like to do to him. After a while, Alex tuned it out and glanced over at Riley, who shared the back seat with her. He caught her eye and leaned closer to murmur, "Sorry I lost my temper. I should've just walked you away."

Alex couldn't help smiling just a bit. "I'm probably wrong for saying this, but I thought it was awesome, and I'm glad you hit him. Guys don't seem to defend a lady's honor any more these days."

Now Riley smiled too. "I'll defend your honor any day."

With a grin, Alex reached over and wove her hand into his, quite happy with this modern-day knight of hers.

Chapter Eighteen

AFTER RILEY'S CONFRONTATION AT THE BOWLING ALLEY, ALEX WAS afraid Tony might show up at the bar again looking for trouble. He seemed to harbor a particular hatred for Riley. She couldn't figure out whether it was just because of her or something deeper. Maybe he was the type who just liked to watch the world burn. His attitude certainly pointed to that. However, three weeks passed without a sign of him or his friends, thankfully.

Now that November had rolled around, the weather was consistently cooler, and they'd even had their first bit of snow flurries earlier in the week. The holidays would be upon them in no time. Alex looked forward to the festivities. Holidays had always been lonely while single. This year she could look forward to experiencing them for the first time in a relationship.

After cleaning up a table at work, she brought her tray around the counter to join Riley. None of their customers seemed to need anything right now, so she took the opportunity to bring up a phone call.

"I talked to my parents this morning. Veteran's Day is next week. I was thinking of heading down there for the day if it's all right with Luke. My family always gets together and makes care packages."

"I'm sure that would be fine."

She paused for a moment before speaking again. "I also thought—if you wanted to and Luke could make it work—maybe you could come with me." It wouldn't be the easiest visit considering the occasion. She would surely have painful emotions to face, and a part of her just really wanted him there for support.

He stopped working to look at her, seeming to see everything she wasn't saying. "I'll ask him."

She smiled, warmth beating in her heart. "Thanks. I'd really love to have you there, and I know my parents really want to meet you."

———

Though a last-minute request, Luke gave both of them off the next Friday. Alex rose early to prepare for the two-hour drive to her hometown. Not that she'd been able to sleep particularly well. Her family always made a point to visit the graves of their family members who had served on every military holiday. That meant visiting Josh's grave. Not only that, but she hadn't seen her parents in almost a year. Now she was bringing Riley home to meet them. She just prayed they would love him and everything would go smoothly. Every time she introduced him to someone close to her, she felt as though disaster loomed just on the horizon even if the feelings were unfounded.

After a quick shower and drying her hair, she changed into a cozy cable-knit sweater, skinny jeans, and a pair of knee-high boots. She'd just finished a quick breakfast when Riley showed up. He had a tall cup of coffee waiting for her in his warm truck—his special chocolate mocha she loved so much. She wrapped her fingers around it and took a sip as they pulled away. The hot liquid seemed to warm her straight to her soul.

She breathed an appreciative sigh and then looked over at him. "Are you nervous about meeting my parents?"

He shrugged. "Not really."

That's good, because she was. They were quiet for a little while as they drove out of town, but then Riley asked her about Bethany. Thankful for the distraction and escape from sinking too far into her own head, she told him stories of growing up in the small town. She even found herself able to laugh while recounting some of her misadventures with Josh, Zach, and their other friends. Once they were deep into conversation, the trip passed quickly. Before long, they drove into Bethany, and Alex gave directions to the farm.

She gazed out the window at all the familiar buildings they passed on the way through town. Other than a couple that sported fresh paint, everything looked almost the same. Quiet and quaint—just how she had always liked it. American flags hung from almost every street light, and many hung in the windows of the shops. The sight of the little local bakery tucked in next to the post office made her mouth water with memories of her favorite sugar cookies.

Her nerves took over again when they passed through the outskirts of town and drove along an old country road that went on for miles before disappearing toward the mountains in the distance. They were nearly home. How many times had she and Josh ridden their bikes up and down this road? She even recognized the exact place where she had crashed her bike into the ditch after attempting to imitate Josh and ride without holding the handlebars. She smiled slightly to herself, and then drew in a long breath.

Only a couple of miles outside of town, a weathered red barn came into view at the end of a long gravel driveway. A few horses grazed in the wide open pasture, with a herd of dark cattle farther out. In the other direction stood the line of trees marking the woods where so many adventures had taken place.

"Turn in here," she said quietly when they reached the driveway.

Riley drove slowly up the path leading toward the barn and into a large yard dotted with mature maple and aspen trees. Tucked between them stood the old, white-trimmed yellow farmhouse with a wide wraparound porch Alex had called home for nineteen years. And even though she had lived away from it for the last several, she still considered it home. It was where all of her happiest memories resided . . . well, most of them. Aspen Creek had developed its own special memories.

They pulled up to the house and parked alongside her dad's farm pickup. Once Riley shut off the engine, Alex unbuckled her seatbelt and took another deep breath.

"You all right?"

She looked over at him. "Yeah, I guess I'm just a bit jittery."

His mouth quirked with an encouraging little smile. "I'm sure we'll get along just fine."

She let out a humorless laugh and shook her head at herself. "Sorry. You're the one who is meeting them for the first time. I should be the one assuring you."

His smile only widened. "Don't worry about it."

He got out of the truck and walked around to her door. Alex could just as well have opened it herself, but it gave her an extra moment to calm her nerves. The screen door of the house slapped shut as she crawled out and looked up to see her parents on their way down the porch steps. The sight of them drove home just how much time had passed since her last visit. Her eyes stung as she walked forward to meet them. Her dad reached her first.

"Hi, Dad," she said as he wrapped her up in a warm, secure hug.

"Hey, sweetheart," his deep voice rumbled in her ear. "It's good to see you. We missed you."

"I missed you too." Her throat clogged.

They parted and he smiled lovingly down at her, the corners of his eyes crinkling. He had always been rather stoic and quiet, yet he possessed a sparkle in his eyes that displayed how much he loved his family. Though a simple man, his convictions and thoughts ran deep, and Alex knew he would do whatever he could to make her happy. She had always considered herself a bit of a daddy's girl, and she'd had no idea just how good it would feel to see him again until this moment.

She then turned to her mom, greeting her with a tight hug as well. Though a simple country girl herself, Mom was all grace and gentleness. Alex barely recalled the few times she had witnessed her mom raise her voice. She had always thrived on creating a warm, welcoming home for her family and friends, and Alex respected her for that.

Before either of them could say much, Alex heard Dad say, "You must be Riley."

She turned as he offered his hand to Riley. "I'm Daniel."

"Pleased to meet you, sir," Riley said, shaking Dad's hand.

Dad then gestured to Mom. "This is my wife, Laura."

"Ma'am," Riley greeted, shaking her hand as well.

"I'm so glad you could join Alex today," Mom said.

A brief moment of awkward silence followed. After all, Alex had never brought a boyfriend home before. None of them knew exactly how to proceed. A welcome distraction came in the form of a dog barking. Two cattle dogs bounded up to them, and Alex bent to scrub the first dog's mottled gray coat.

"Hey, Archer. I've missed you, buddy." The dog leaned against her leg and gazed up at her, his tongue lolling out as she rubbed his ears. She reached for the smaller dog that sniffed her curiously. "I haven't met you yet."

"That's Trigger," Dad said. "Archer's been teaching him the ropes this past summer, so we'll be in good hands once it's time for him to retire."

Alex patted the younger dog's head and straightened.

Before any silence could linger, Mom motioned them toward the house. "Please, come inside."

Alex and Riley followed her parents up to the porch. The old, worn rocking chair from when Alex was a child still sat near the door. She recalled long-past summer nights of sitting on her mom's lap as they rocked and listened to the nighttime crickets chirping. Inside the house, warmth enveloped them immediately, saturated with the delicious scent of beef and baked goods. Alex's mouth watered. "Mmm, that smells so good." Mom smiled. "I put a roast in for lunch and made the cinnamon bread you love."

Alex couldn't wait. Nothing tasted as good as beef raised right here on the farm and her mom's cinnamon bread.

They hung their coats on the coat tree in the corner and kicked off their shoes before Mom guided them all into the living room. A fire burned in the large fireplace. Alex sure had missed the coziness of wood heat and curling up next to the fire to read. They claimed spots on the leather couch and loveseat, and Alex prayed once more this would go well. No doubt her parents would want to find out as much about Riley as possible while he was here. He had this one chance to make a good first impression, not that she doubted him. It was just her own nerves and fears that fought to betray and overwhelm her.

"So you're one of the famous Conrads?" Dad said conversationally.

Riley shook his head. "My dad and brother are the famous ones. I doubt most people even know I exist, which is fine by me. I have no interest in the spotlight."

Was that why he hadn't wanted to become a chef?

"I'm perfectly happy keeping to myself and living in a small town like Aspen Creek," he continued.

Dad's small smile encouraged Alex. "Nothing beats a small town."

"Especially if you grew up in a city like Denver. I sure don't miss the rush."

"So you were a city boy then?" A teasing glint flashed in Dad's eyes.

Riley laughed. "City boy with a country heart, thanks to my granddad. He taught me to appreciate the country life by taking me camping and fishing. My parents would tell you he corrupted me, but I'm glad he did."

This seemed to break through any lingering awkwardness, and they all talked easily for over an hour.

Shortly before eleven, Mom leaned forward to get up. "We're supposed to meet your grandparents at the cemetery in about twenty minutes, so we should probably get going. We'll come back here for lunch afterward."

A knot formed in Alex's stomach, shattering the comfort she had been lulled into. They hadn't come here just to sit and visit all day, as much as she wished they had. She nodded, and they all stood. Mom checked the roast once more, and they gathered in the entryway to put on their coats. Outside, the four of them climbed into the silver, extended-cab truck Alex's dad had bought a few years ago. Josh had borrowed it to take his girlfriend out on dates. It was better than the rust bucket he'd driven throughout high school. She smiled a little at the memory. She'd actually liked that junkie old truck before it had bit the dust shortly after Josh enlisted.

On the way back into Bethany, Dad and Riley discussed the local businesses, but Alex remained silent, mentally preparing and fortifying herself. At the other side of town, they pulled into the cemetery. Alex hadn't been here since Veteran's Day a year ago. She prayed it might be easier this time since Riley was helping her let go. In the past, her brother's grave had clashed violently with the heartbroken denial she'd carried around too long.

They parked next to a dark sedan and got out. The occupants of the car exited as well, and Alex smiled to see her grandparents—Mom's parents, Walter and Allison, and Dad's mom, Rose. They greeted her with all the enthusiasm one would expect of grandparents. She gave them each a tight hug, relishing their abundant love for her.

She then introduced them to Riley, to which they were nothing short of enthusiastic. Riley and Grandpa Walter seemed to hit it off immediately. He was an easygoing sort of man, much like Riley's grandpa.

They stood around the vehicles and talked for a few minutes before reality settled in once more. The conversation slowly died, and they turned toward the gate leading into the cemetery. First they stopped at a gravestone near an ancient maple tree. The name engraved on the stone read *Benjamin Jennings*, Alex's grandfather. He'd died of a heart attack when she was fourteen. That had been a hard time, especially for Josh. He'd always wanted his grandpa to see him make it into the Marines.

Grandma Rose stepped forward and knelt near the gravestone. Carefully, she arranged the small flags and flowers Mom had brought along.

"I still miss you every day, darling," Grandma murmured. She kissed her fingers and touched the gravestone. Alex leaned closer to Riley. She wanted a lifelong love like that.

Her dad helped Grandma back to her feet, and they stood there in silence for a moment before he said, "Thanks for your service, Dad."

Everyone quietly nodded in agreement with his words.

Finally, they moved on, a little deeper into the cemetery. Alex looked ahead, and her chest constricted, the weight pressing painfully against her heart. Tears burned her eyes when they stopped in front of Josh's grave. Mom handed her half of the remaining flowers, and Alex helped her arrange them around the gravestone. When she stood up again, the tears had leaked over, leaving hot trails down her cold cheeks. She just missed him so much.

Riley's hand pressed against her back and rubbed it slowly.

She looked at him. His eyes were misty, and she realized this was the first time he'd seen the grave of the man he'd tried to save. If only he had been successful. What would life be like now? What if the three of them could have been best friends? Then again, she might never have met Riley had things been different.

Before she could plunge too deeply into wondering about a life that would never happen, Grandma Rose spoke again.

"Imagine, he and his grandpa together, trading their war stories and worshipping the Lord." Tears wet her cheeks, but a wistful smile graced her face. "Just think of the people they've met."

Alex nodded, forcing herself to imagine it instead of dwelling on the loss. The pain inside her heart still ached keenly though. That would never completely go away. She leaned into Riley's side as the tears flowed again, and he wrapped his arm securely around her as if it would hold her broken pieces together. And, in a way, it did. Without him here, she might have fallen apart completely. He'd been her strength these last few months, and she thanked God once again for bringing him into her life.

They stood at the grave for some time, occasionally sharing memories or words of encouragement. Riley told her grandparents the story of how he had known Josh. Mom and both grandmas cried, and even Dad had to wipe away a couple of tears.

By the time they turned to go, the cold air had chilled Alex to the bone. The weather was much chillier than she'd expected, and even with her boots and a pair of heavy socks, the frosty ground left her toes icy. She shivered, and Riley kept his arm around her as they made their way back through the cemetery. Alex held her head down, but when they reached the gate and paused, she looked up. A young couple walked toward them. The dark-haired woman carried a blanket-wrapped bundle in her arms. A fresh stab of pain pierced Alex's heart at the sight she had not been prepared to face today.

Swallowing the aching lump in her throat, she attempted a smile as the woman's face lit up.

"Alex! I didn't know you were coming down."

"It was a last minute decision." Her voice sounded hollow in her ears. Fighting her emotions, she introduced Riley. "This is Lisa, an old friend of mine, and her husband, Evan."

They greeted each other, and then Lisa folded back an edge of the blanket to reveal the pudgy sleeping face of a two-month-old baby. "And this is little Trevor."

Alex forced a smile, though the ache in her chest only intensified. The baby was adorable, and she longed to hold him, but she kept her arms at her sides. Holding him would only hurt worse. They spoke briefly before parting, Lisa telling Alex they should catch up sometime. Alex nodded, though her words remained trapped in her throat this time, and she wasn't sure how much longer she could maintain her smile.

When they finally reached the truck, she climbed in and remained silent all the way home. Tears burned mercilessly. Somehow, she managed to hold them in check until they reached the house. Everyone got out and started for the porch, but she hung back.

"You go on," she told her parents and Riley. "I just . . . I need a minute."

She turned away from them and walked toward the barn. At the wooden fence surrounding the horse pasture, she leaned against it and the tears gushed over. Hitching sobs followed, one at a time, tearing through her chest. She had thought she would manage after leaving Josh's grave, but seeing Lisa had punctured the frail wall surrounding her emotions. It had shown her with painful clarity what life could have been but wasn't.

Someone touched her shoulder, and she looked up into Riley's overwhelmingly compassionate gaze. She stepped into his arms, wrapping her own around him. He held her while she cried out her tears, just like the morning on the porch. He didn't try to shush her or attempt to make things better. He just let her pour out all her grief.

After a few minutes, the sobs and tears subsided. Resting her head on his chest, she explained, "Lisa was Josh's girlfriend. Trevor could've been my nephew."

Riley didn't say anything, but he rubbed her back, and Alex let out a long sigh. Finally, she pulled away and took off her glasses to wipe her face with her nearly numb fingers. She drew in a long, cold breath to compose herself. She didn't want to be a weeping mess during lunch. Everyone else was holding it together. She could too.

"So which one of these beauties is yours?"

Alex had no idea what Riley was talking about until he tipped his head toward the pasture. She slipped her glasses back on and looked over at the horses, a few of which had moved closer, curious what the fuss was about. A smile tugged at her lips.

"The gray paint right over there. Flynn."

"Maybe we can come down here again and go riding sometime."

Now her smile did form, and she nodded. "I'd love that. I haven't been riding in forever." And she had certainly missed it. Especially when her dad used to get her up early and they'd go riding together, just the two of them. They had always shared a special love for horses.

She shivered again, her teeth chattering.

Riley rubbed her arms. "Ready to go in and warm up?"

She nodded, and they turned toward the house. Inside the entryway, he helped her slip off her coat and hung it up for her. She glanced in a small mirror above the refurnished dresser along the wall. Though she'd obviously been crying, her glasses and cold-reddened cheeks disguised it a little.

The two of them walked into the kitchen where her mom and grandmas prepared the food for lunch. Alex offered to take it to the table, and she and Riley each grabbed something to carry into the dining room. Dad and Grandpa had already set the table, and Alex situated the food in the middle.

A couple of minutes later, they all took their seats. At one end of the table, Grandpa said a prayer before they began the meal. Though the emotions of today still lingered, Alex enjoyed this time spent with family. They talked and laughed, and once again, she found herself immensely thankful for how well Riley fit in. They all seemed to adore him, and it did her heart a lot of good.

The two of them stayed for most of the afternoon, visiting with the family and helping them put together military care packages. Once evening encroached, they prepared to leave. They said goodbye to Alex's grandparents in the living room and followed her parents to the entryway. Slipping her coat on, Alex turned to them and gave them each a long hug. Riley shook hands with Dad, and then Mom surprised Alex by giving him a hug. She'd never show such affection for someone she didn't think was good enough for Alex. The gesture left her heart happy.

"Don't be strangers now," Dad told them. "I know it's a bit of a drive, but we hope you'll come back soon. In fact, if you don't have any Thanksgiving plans, we'd love to have both of you. You're welcome to stay through the weekend depending on your work schedules."

Alex glanced at Riley and said, "We'll talk about it." Luke did close the bar for Thanksgiving and the following weekend. She would love to spend those days here at home, but she wouldn't make any plans before talking to Riley.

With final goodbyes, she followed him out into the chilly evening. She buckled up in his truck and rubbed her hands together, waiting for the heat to warm up. As they pulled away from the house, she waved to her parents on the porch and then fixed her gaze ahead. Though the emotions had taxed her, it was so good to see them. She hadn't realized how much she'd needed it.

She and Riley were quiet most of the way through Bethany, but once they hit the highway heading north, he looked over at her.

"I like your family."

"I'm so glad. They really seemed to like you too." She doubted her dad would have invited him to spend a holiday with them if they didn't. "So, do you have any Thanksgiving plans?"

"Nothing more than I had last year—sitting in my apartment watching football by myself."

"Well, that's no way to spend Thanksgiving. How do you feel about my parents' invitation?"

"I'd be happy to spend it with them. Honestly, it'd probably be the most normal family Thanksgiving I've ever had."

"Good, I'll call them tomorrow and let them know we're planning on it then."

Silence fell again for a couple of minutes as she thought about her family and then about his. As far as she knew, he hadn't received any calls today. Looking over at him again, she asked, "Does your family ever get in touch on days like this?"

He shook his head. "No. I wouldn't exactly call them patriotic. They probably don't even realize what today is. I mean, they acknowledge there are men and women protecting and fighting for this country; it just doesn't fit into their perfectly constructed world."

"I'm sorry. I'm sure that must hurt."

He shrugged. "Sometimes. I try not to think about it."

Considering all this, it had probably been as good for him to spend time with Alex's family as it had been for her.

Chapter Nineteen

THANKSGIVING MORNING, ALEX ROSE WELL BEFORE THE SUN despite having worked so late the night before. Both she and Riley wanted to get to Bethany early enough to help her mom with the huge family meal.

Grabbing a granola bar for breakfast, she ate while checking to make sure she had packed everything she would need for the next few days. She was quite aware that this was the first time she and Riley were going away together for more than just a day trip. Of course, since her parents would be there the whole time, there wouldn't be anything inappropriate about it, but it still felt like a momentous step in their relationship. What would it be like to be together all the time? Was it too early to start seriously considering moving toward marriage? She shook her head. She wasn't going to get into that with herself today. It was the holidays, and she was determined to enjoy everything about it. Questions about the future, while perhaps exciting, might just lead to anxiety.

When he arrived to pick her up, she was more than ready to start their vacation. It would be wonderful to spend more than one day back at home. This might give them the opportunity to go riding like they had talked about last week. It would be nice for her parents to bond more with Riley too.

They drove out of Aspen Creek just as the sun peeked above the horizon. As they crossed Baylor's Bridge, she shifted in her seat to look over at him.

"Thank you."

He glanced at her, his brow furrowed at the rim of the dark beanie he wore. "For what?"

"For bringing me here that day and helping me let go. It hasn't been easy, but it really helped."

He kept his eyes on the road but the corner of his mouth lifted. "No problem."

They drove into Boulder twenty minutes later and pulled in at Zach and Mindy's house. They had decided to carpool since Zach and Mindy were heading down to Trinidad for a couple of days with Mindy's dad before driving back up to Bethany for a weekend with Zach's family. The lights were on in the house, and both Zach and Mindy met them at the door. How much bribing and coffee had Zach needed to get Mindy out of bed so early? Despite not being a morning person, Mindy was as bright and cheerful as ever.

Alex and Riley helped them load the last of their things, including Shadow and Bella, into the SUV, and they all got in. Christmas music already played on the radio, and Alex enjoyed the festive atmosphere.

Laughter punctuated the ride down to Bethany, particularly in response to Mindy and Zach's banter. Alex especially enjoyed their recounting of their first meeting, which had taken place exactly ten years ago today. Where would Alex and Riley be in ten years? She glanced over at him. Together still, she hoped, and more than just girlfriend and boyfriend.

They made good time and arrived in Bethany around eight-thirty, plenty of time to help Mom with meal preparation. When they pulled up in front of the house, all four of them climbed out. Though Mindy and Zach still had another two hours to travel, they didn't want to drive away without saying hi to Alex's parents. Mindy had to use the bathroom anyway. Apparently, she had guzzled down almost two cups of coffee before Alex and Riley had shown up and then another two during the drive. Alex had always teased her during college about having a small bladder, so she was probably close to bursting about now.

Letting the dogs out to explore and dash around with Archer and Trigger, they all trooped up to the porch. Alex opened the front door to let them in.

"Mom, Dad, we're here," she called, unzipping her coat. The house smelled as delicious as it had when they'd arrived last week, though today she smelled turkey and apple pie spices. Nothing said Thanksgiving like that scent combination.

Dad walked into the entryway first, followed shortly by Mom, who wore a ruffled, red plaid apron Alex had given her for Christmas a few years ago. It saw a lot of use but had held up well so far.

Alex met both of them with warm hugs. They then greeted Riley, Mindy, and Zach. By now, Mindy was bouncing on her toes. Though not at all unusual for her, Alex did take particular notice of it.

"Mind if I use your bathroom?" she asked Mom.

"Not at all. You know where it is."

Mindy flashed a thankful smile and quickly excused herself. As soon as she was gone, Alex burst into laughter.

Mom raised a brow. "Coffee?"

"Four cups," Zach said with a long-suffering sigh.

They all laughed now and walked into the kitchen. Alex set a canvas grocery bag on the counter and unpacked the food she and Riley had brought while Dad asked Zach about their new house and work. The three men then discussed the Packers and Lions game on later. Besides her Broncos, Alex had always liked the Packers, so she was rooting for them to win today.

Mindy rejoined them a couple of minutes later, and Mom set a large plate of pumpkin cookies on the counter.

Zach's eyes lit up. "My favorite."

"I made them especially for you."

"Thank you." He gave her a quick kiss on the cheek before grabbing a cookie and taking a big bite.

Pumpkin cookies had been Josh's favorite too—a special treat their mom always made for Thanksgiving morning. In his absence, Zach was like a surrogate son.

With their bathroom breaks taken care of, Mindy and Zach prepared to leave. On their way out the door, Mom handed Zach a red plastic container.

"For the road," she told him.

He peeked inside, and Alex caught sight of more cookies.

He grinned. "You spoil me. I'm going to be so fat after this weekend."

Mindy reached for the container. "Don't worry, I'll pace you."

But he lifted the box of cookies high above his head, out of reach. "Uh-uh, no way. I'm not giving up my special holiday treat."

Mindy just shook her head and shared an amused smile with Alex.

With quick hugs and goodbyes, they saw them out. Mom then turned.

"Riley, if you'd like, I can show you the guest bedroom. I prepared it this morning."

"Thank you, Mrs. Jennings." Riley picked up the duffel he had brought along.

Before leading him away, Mom said to Alex, "And I put fresh sheets on your bed. We haven't changed anything since you were here last."

While her mom showed Riley to the guest bedroom down the hall, Alex grabbed her own duffel and headed up the oak staircase leading upstairs. She passed her parents' large bedroom just to the right of the stairs and walked down to her doorway on the left side of the hall. The old white door stood open, and she walked into the room of her childhood and teen years.

Like her mom had said, they hadn't changed anything. Art prints hung on the walls, as well as some of her early paintings. The black iron bed occupied the same spot and the white wardrobe probably still contained some of her high school clothes. It was a cozy room that overlooked the barn. She had spent so many hours daydreaming of being an artist and what life would be like at this age. She let out a quiet laugh. Good thing she hadn't known then of the heartbreak she would have to face.

She set her duffel by the wardrobe and sat down on the edge of the bed, running her hand along the purple and white quilt. Ten years ago, she and Mindy had sat here after their first couple of months in college, ready to take on the world. And then, of course, there were Mindy's not-so-subtle questions regarding Zach. Alex had teased her a little, but she'd loved the idea of Mindy and Zach together right from the start.

Smiling at these memories, she stood up and headed back downstairs. She met Riley on the way into the kitchen where her mom was at work again.

"So, what can we do?" Alex asked.

"Well," Mom said, taking stock of everything, "I haven't rolled out the pie crusts yet, and I'm still working on the stuffing."

Rolling up the sleeves of her sweater, Alex stepped to the corner cabinet to grab another apron for herself. Her mom loved aprons, so there were multiple to choose from. She grabbed a green one with white ruffles and then pulled out a black one. Biting her lip in an attempt to smother a grin, she turned to Riley.

"You have two options: an apron with ruffles and lace, or this one. It's the only manly one we have."

She held up the black apron. The front displayed an image of the insanely ripped torso of a gladiator.

He took one look at it and laughed. Alex shrugged, smiling a bit bashfully.

"Josh and I thought it made a funny gift for Dad on Father's Day."

He chuckled again and took the apron. Mom laughed when he put it on, and so did Alex, but her cheeks threatened to grow warm. It was hilarious to see her dad wear the apron, but a little different when her very attractive boyfriend wore it. Maybe she should have just left it stashed away in the cupboard.

She quickly busied herself with the pie crusts, while Riley worked on a chocolate soufflé. Mom took great interest in this, and Alex smiled when she ended up talking to him more than actually working on food. He seemed to enjoy explaining the process and giving her tips he had learned in college. The interaction between them warmed Alex's heart and brightened her whole day.

She wasn't sure where Dad had gone until the front door slammed, and he walked in with a pail of potatoes. He spotted Riley in the apron and shook his head slowly.

"So this is what happens when I leave my two girls alone in the kitchen with another man."

Alex cast him a look. "Dad."

He sent her a wink, threatening to make her blush again. He then smiled at Riley. "Looks better on you than it ever did on me."

Alex shook her head now and turned back to the counter to lift the pie crust into a pan without breaking it. Her dad sat down nearby to start peeling the potatoes, and the four of them talked contentedly. Having Riley there . . . it almost made the family feel complete—something Alex hadn't experienced since Josh died. His death had made her an only child, and things weren't the same when it was only her and her parents. The house felt too empty. Riley changed that.

They worked in the kitchen for hours, though Alex enjoyed every minute of it. Mom tuned the small countertop TV in to the parade and then switched it to the game at noon while they finished the meal. Shortly before one o'clock, Alex's grandparents arrived. They welcomed them at the door and helped them carry things inside. Grandma Allison had brought one of her home-made pumpkin pies, while Grandma Rose supplied a green bean casserole. Alex didn't know how they would eat all the food, but she couldn't wait to dig in.

Ten minutes later, Alex's aunt and uncle, David and Jill, showed up. They were the only members of Alex's extended family besides her parents and grandparents who had stayed in Bethany and always celebrated Thanksgiving out here at the farm. Alex was pleased to see them and a little disappointed her cousins couldn't make it. She recalled grand Thanksgiving days of rambunctious play and the house full of kids. But they all had families and lives of their own now. Everything changed with adulthood.

With everyone present, Alex helped the other women set the table and arrange the food amongst pumpkin and autumn leaf centerpieces. Everyone found seats, and Dad offered a thankful prayer. Right after he said 'amen,' they passed the food around, and the feast began amidst cheerful talk and laughter.

Riley was a big hit with David and Jill. He seemed so much a part of the family already. Alex prayed that would never change. She couldn't imagine a more perfect Thanksgiving except for if Josh could be there too.

"So is anyone braving the city tomorrow morning?" Uncle David asked around bites of turkey.

Dad shook his head, serving himself a second helping of potatoes. "I'm not setting foot near any store tomorrow."

"Oh, come on. Where's your sense of adventure?" David joked.

"It has nothing to do with my sense of adventure, rather my lack of patience for stupidity."

Alex had to press her fingers to her lips to keep from laughing out loud with her mouth full. Though more used to big cities than her dad, she had to agree. Black Friday sales turned some people more than a little bit crazy, and she had no intention of risking life and limb just for a bargain.

She gulped down her food. "I'd rather go out for a nice, quiet ride tomorrow."

Dad nodded to her. "That's my girl. After breakfast, we'll take the horses out. Feel like joining us, Riley?"

"Absolutely," he said with a smile, and Alex beamed at him.

Chapter Twenty

ALEX BURIED HER HEAD DEEPER INTO HER PILLOW AND PULLED the covers up to her ear as she released a long sigh. She always slept better in this little bedroom than she did anywhere else. And the fresh flannel sheets her mom had put on were heavenly. Why had she never bought herself any flannel sheets for her bed back home? She would definitely remedy that as soon as she had the chance.

Dimness still cloaked the room as it did in the mornings this time of year. She was in no great hurry to get up, especially when she considered how many people had been lined up outside of stores at the crack of dawn. She shivered just thinking about standing in the cold. Nope. A warm bed, lazy morning, and then a trail ride suited her just fine.

She dozed for another half an hour or so before lifting her head to peer at the clock on the dresser. A little after eight. But it felt good to sleep in. Last night had gotten late. After their meal and kitchen clean-up, everyone had crashed in the living room to watch football. Once the later game ended, Mom had brought out the game of Balderdash, an old family favorite. Alex had laughed until her stomach hurt from more than just food. They'd played for a while before her grandparents and David and Jill left. Alex, her parents, and Riley had then spent a quiet evening talking until heading to bed.

Still, she didn't want to waste away too much of the day, so she pushed back the covers and got up. She managed to find a pair of flannel-lined jeans in the wardrobe that still fit and pulled on a fleece-lined hoodie to keep her warm during their ride.

On her way downstairs, she caught the strong scent of coffee and bacon. Her mouth watered. She always loved breakfast at her parents' house. When she walked into the kitchen, she found Mom sitting on one of the barstools at the kitchen island, sipping a mug of coffee while Riley stood at the stove wearing that ridiculous apron again.

"Good morning," Mom said as she walked in. "Riley offered to make breakfast."

He glanced at Alex with a smile that never ceased to make her just a bit giddy inside.

"Well, if he can cook breakfast as well as he can cook spaghetti and garlic bread, it will be delicious." Alex grabbed herself a mug and poured some coffee.

"After the soufflé yesterday, I believe it."

"It's nothing fancy," Riley told them as Alex paused at his side to watch him flip a perfect golden-brown pancake. "It's actually my grandma's pancake recipe. I just tweaked it a bit."

Alex nodded to the sauce pan simmering on the back burner behind the bacon. "What's that?"

He gave her a mischievous look. "Secret recipe."

Whatever it was smelled fruity and delicious. Alex was pretty sure it involved blueberries, which were one of her favorite fruits.

She joined her mom at the island and added a generous amount of sugar and pumpkin spice creamer to her coffee. Right away, she could tell Riley had made it. Even here, without all his supplies, he made the best coffee. She sighed after she swallowed the first sip.

Mom gave her an exaggerated nod. "I know. I'm tempted to keep him here just so he can make the coffee every morning."

Alex grinned. "Wait until you try his special blend. Riley, you have to bring stuff to make it next time we visit."

He glanced over his shoulder and nodded. "I'll do that."

Mom smiled at them both, and Alex detected more than simply a reaction to what they'd said—something deeper. That's when it occurred to her how easily she and Riley spoke of visiting again. No doubt it was very noticeable to her mom, especially since Alex had not been good about keeping in touch in recent years. She returned her mom's smile with a silent promise things would change.

A few minutes later, Dad came in from feeding the animals, his hair tousled from a stocking cap. Riley was just finishing a large skillet of scrambled eggs, and they all grabbed plates to dish up. Riley revealed his "secret recipe" to be a maple blueberry syrup he'd put together for the pancakes. Alex was dying to try it. They brought their plates to the table, and after a quick prayer, picked up their forks.

Alex's first bite of the blueberry-drenched pancakes was heavenly. They were so light and fluffy. So were the eggs. Better than anything she had eaten at the diner. If she ate Riley's food often, she would be absolutely spoiled.

"These eggs are amazing," Mom said after a couple of bites. "You have to tell me how you did it."

Riley smiled. "It's mostly the spices and making sure not to overcook them, but the actual secret ingredient is pancake batter. Just a little in with the eggs. A lot of restaurants do that. But your fresh eggs make a big difference too."

For most of the meal, they talked about Riley's cooking, and he opened up a bit about his parents and why he'd joined the military. He even told Alex's parents about his dreams for the coffee shop. They were very intrigued by the idea, especially Mom. She had always thought it would be fun to have her own little shop.

On the flip side, Alex could sense from Riley's body language how much her parents' interest motivated him. She understood how painfully he must have always desired the same enthusiasm from his own parents.

When they finished breakfast, they carried their dishes to the kitchen sink where Mom said, "I'll clean up. You three go on your ride."

"Are you sure, Mom? We can stay and help. It won't take long."

"Of course. It's a beautiful morning. Go enjoy it."

Eager to do just that, Alex, her dad, and Riley filed to the entryway and pulled their coats on. Dad lent Riley a pair of insulated riding boots and gloves, and they stepped outside into the crisp air. Sunlight sparkled on a fresh dusting of snow that had fallen overnight, and the air was still. Alex puffed out a clouded breath as they headed to the barn, the dogs leading the way. She could hardly wait to get back in the saddle.

"Have you done any riding, Riley?" Dad asked.

"I took some lessons as a kid, but I haven't ridden since high school."

"You can ride Rudy, then."

Alex fell into step beside Riley. "He's Josh's horse. He's very calm and won't take off with you or anything."

Riley chuckled softly, his breath cloud mingling with hers. "Sounds good."

At the paddock gate, Dad gave a shrill whistle, and the horses trotted up to meet them. Dad led his tall black gelding he used with the cattle out first, and Alex grabbed Flynn's halter. She gestured to the stocky bay standing patiently nearby. "That's Rudy."

Riley walked up to the horse and rubbed the gelding's nose before taking hold of the halter. They led the three horses from the pasture and into the cross ties in the barn. There they brushed their thick winter coats before gathering saddles and bridles from the tack room. Alex quickly saddled Flynn, all the usual motions coming back to her easily. She then walked over to help Riley, laughing together as he fumbled with the cinch strap.

Back outside, they mounted up and headed off slowly toward one of the trails to the woods, the dogs dashing ahead of them. Though he hadn't ridden in many years, Riley sat a horse well, another thing Alex found attractive. She was a country girl, after all, and did love a cute cowboy. She would have to get him a good hat sometime. The thought of him in a dark Stetson and his long hair left her quite smitten. She'd fight anyone who pressured him to cut it.

They took all the familiar trails Alex, Josh, Zach, and their friends had ridden all the time. She pointed out different areas that were burned into her memory for one reason or another, including where she'd gotten herself tangled up in barbed wire and ripped her knee open. The ride was a wonderful yet painful trip down memory lane, because Josh was such a part of those memories. They were an inseparable duo. Even now, wherever she went, she carried pieces of him with her. It was why she always wore his dog tags. She didn't expect that to ever change. Didn't really want it to.

However, she fought hard to keep the painfulness of it from overwhelming the enjoyment of the ride. She focused on Riley and her dad discussing the cattle and the rest of the farm. The two of them made a good pair, and her dad was only ever talkative with people he liked.

After a long ride around the many acres of land her parents owned, they arrived back at the barn. Alex dismounted, a little stiff-legged. She would be sore come tomorrow. Her poor muscles weren't conditioned to horseback riding like they had been when she was young.

They unsaddled the horses, brushed them down, and let them back out into the pasture. On the way toward the house,

Dad said to Riley, "I noticed last week you've got a pretty nice truck."

"Thanks. It was my granddad's."

"You know a lot about those old trucks?"

Riley shrugged. "Quite a bit."

"Well, I've got a '69 Chevy in the garage I've been working on that was my dad's. It hasn't run in years. I'm not quite sure what's wrong with it. Maybe a fresh set of eyes will see something I missed."

"I'd love to take a look at it."

Alex picked out the eager lift to Riley's voice. He really did love his trucks.

"I'll go see if Mom needs help with anything and you two can look at the truck," she said. After all, it would be good for Riley and her dad to do a little male bonding.

Dad nodded. "Let us know if you need anything."

He and Riley headed off toward the big, heated garage, discussing the truck along the way. Alex smiled after them and hurried up to the house, a little chilled now. Inside, she pulled off her coat and boots and headed into the living room. Mom sat on the couch with a Christmas novel in her hands.

She glanced up with a smile. "How was the ride?"

"Wonderful. I always forget until I'm out there on Flynn how much I miss it."

"You are welcome any time." There was a subtle nudge behind it.

"I know, and I plan to a lot more."

This added distinct happiness to her mom's soft expression.

"So where are your dad and Riley?"

"They're taking a look at Grandpa's old truck."

Taking a seat in her dad's cozy recliner, Alex held her hands out to the fireplace and mulled over the thoughts in her mind. She hesitated to speak at first—she didn't want to sound silly or naive—but she truly hoped for answers. She looked at Mom, who seemed to sense her hesitancy and patiently waited for her to speak.

"I know you and Dad were high school sweethearts, but was there a moment you knew he was the one or did you just sort of always know?"

Mom smiled softly. "In a way, I think I always knew, even before we started dating, but there was definitely a point I knew without a doubt he was the one I wanted to spend the rest of my life with."

Alex nodded slowly and took a deep breath. "Do you think there's a time in a relationship when it's too early to feel that way?"

Mom's eyes crinkled. "I think it's good to be wise and to take the time to be sure, but I also know every person and relationship is different. Sometimes, especially if it's something you've been praying about, you just know even if it hasn't been that long."

Alex released a quiet sigh, her mind settling. And then, because she'd already made it ridiculously obvious, she said, "I really like Riley . . . I really think I love him."

Mom's smile never faded. "I think you do too."

"He's been so good to me. He has helped me more than I thought anyone could. But even more than that, when he talks about owning a coffee shop, I want to do everything in my power to help him. I want him to succeed and to follow his dreams. I want him to have everything he's ever wanted."

"That's exactly what true love is—wanting the best for the other person, even above your own desires."

Riley fiddled on his truck now and then, but he hadn't worked on a truck with anyone like this since college. He didn't regret joining the military, but he did miss the time he could have spent working on trucks with his granddad. Working on this Chevy with Alex's dad wasn't quite the same, and he was still getting to know the man, but it was a bit like recapturing the past.

While they worked, Daniel told him about Alex's grandfather, and Riley talked about his own. Granddad would have loved it here on this farm instead of that fancy assisted living place. And he'd be obsessed with this truck. Maybe that's why Riley felt determined to see it running.

As they worked side by side under the hood, Daniel said, "You're the first man Alex has ever dated, let alone brought home to meet us."

"That's what she told me."

"Must be something particularly special about you then."

Riley glanced at him and shook his head. "I doubt that. She's the special one, and I'm just blessed to have met her."

He reached down to tighten a bolt but something had definitely changed in the mood. He straightened and found Daniel giving him a keen look. The man was more the quiet type and always quick to smile, but Riley sensed a lot more too him than first impressions would lead a person to believe. Others would likely pass him off as some small-town farmer who simply got by on a high school education. Riley saw much more than that. The man was far from ignorant. Riley had a feeling he was a pretty good judge of character and even better at weighing whether or not a person deserved his respect. Suddenly, Riley was very anxious to earn that respect.

"So what are your intentions toward my daughter?"

Riley set the wrench aside before speaking. Better make sure he knew just how he wanted to answer that question. Before he had a chance, Daniel continued, "Sorry to spring this on you. I'm not sure how many fathers take a vested interest in their daughter's relationships these days, but Alex is very important to her mother and me. She's our only daughter— our only child, now—and I'll do whatever I can to make sure she doesn't get hurt."

"I get that. So would I if I had a daughter." Riley paused for one heartbeat. "You don't know me well enough yet for my word to mean anything, but my intentions are honorable."

Daniel sized him up, weighing his every word. "What is this relationship to you? Are you in it for the long haul, or are you just seeing where it goes?"

"I'm definitely in it for the long haul and committed to making it work. I have no interest in messing around and then disappearing when things get tough. I honestly can't imagine Alex not being part of my future."

Daniel nodded slowly and seemed pleased with that answer, offering Riley a hint of relief. He'd faced a lot of enemies over the years, but nothing was quite as scary as this man who could very well decide Riley had no place in his daughter's life.

"I don't mean to sound disrespectful," Daniel said, "especially considering what you've done for our country and how you tried to save my son. But," the word hung heavily between them, "military service alone won't convince me that you're worthy of my daughter. And, in a father's eyes, every guy who takes interest in his daughter is a scumbag until proven otherwise."

Despite the way his stomach had decided to tie itself in a knot, Riley had to laugh at that, and Daniel offered him a wry smile.

"I don't blame you, especially these days." Riley paused, any mirth fading. If he looked back on his life, he certainly didn't think of himself as a shining example of the kind of man a father would desire for his daughter. Especially if he compared himself to the men he'd gotten to know at church who had grown up in good Christian homes.

He thought, too, of his family and how he'd made no effort in the last few years to reconcile with them. How, even now, he felt bitterness toward them stirring in his chest. Some men would have gone to them immediately after changing and shared their faith, yet he constantly struggled to find such desire. This lack weighed on him more and more these days.

"The thing is, sir, I don't know that I am worthy of Alex. I made some big mistakes and poor decisions before I came to Christ. Things I pray every day will stay in the past and won't mess things up now. And I'm still a whole long way from perfect."

Daniel's expression relaxed just a bit. "Aren't we all?" He drew a breath. "I like you, Riley, which is saying a lot. I just urge you to take great care with Alex. After her brother died . . . she was broken. I just worry what having her heart broken again might do to her."

Daniel had no idea just how deeply Riley understood that. "I'd die before I'd do anything to break her heart." And he truly meant it. He would rather die himself than do anything to drive Alex back to that bridge.

Daniel nodded again, and Riley got the distinct feeling he'd earned the man's approval.

"Good." Then, with a hint of a twinkle in Daniel's eyes, his lips twitched. "Because you'd wish you were dead if I got my hands on you."

After one second of silence, his smile broke out, and Riley gave a low chuckle. "I believe that."

With that settled, Daniel turned his attention back to the truck. "So, do you think she'll run?"

"Only one way to find out." Riley gestured to the cab.

Daniel got in and turned the key. After only a brief hesitation, the engine roared to life. After a couple of moments, Daniel turned it off again and stepped back out.

"I'm not sure what you did, but thanks for helping me get it going."

Riley shrugged. "It just needed a little fine tuning."

Daniel rubbed his hand along the slightly-faded red paint around the door. "I learned how to drive in this truck. I was only twelve at the time."

He laughed, and Riley joined in.

"I always planned to give it to Josh after my dad died and I ended up with it. Now I'm thinking I should give it to Alex. What do you think?"

Alex did love old trucks, especially if it had once been meant for her brother. "I think she'd really like that."

Daniel nodded slowly. "Maybe for her birthday this spring. Seems like a good thirtieth birthday present, right?"

"For a country girl like Alex, definitely."

Daniel smiled. "This stays between you and me."

"Yes, sir."

Chapter Twenty-one

LIGHT TAPPING DREW ALEX OUT OF A DEEP SLEEP. HER ROOM WAS still dark, though it hinted of morning, and the hall light streamed in through her partially open door. She lifted her head and squinted groggily at the silhouette in her doorway.

"Dad?"

"Feel like going for a ride?"

A slow smile stretched across Alex's lips. While her bed was warm and comfortable and it would be freezing out, she wouldn't let this chance pass. "I'll get dressed and be down in a few minutes."

"I'll get the horses ready."

The door closed, and Alex stretched out before pushing aside the covers. She shivered at exposing herself to the cool air, but no amount of comfort could replace these special moments with her dad. It had been a weekly ritual growing up—to get up at the crack of dawn and go for a ride. She had shared many of her deepest desires and dreams with him during these rides. They'd always ended with him telling her that he was praying for her. Those were some of her most cherished memories.

She slipped on her flannel-lined jeans and a sweater before quietly making her way downstairs. Most of the lights were off except for in the entryway. After a quick trip to the bathroom, Alex slipped on her riding boots and bundled up in her coat, hat, and gloves. When she stepped outside, the cool air immediately prickled her face, but it was fresh and still and perfect.

Snow squeaked and crunched under her boots as she walked toward the barn. Just before she reached it, Archer and Trigger bounded out to greet her. She paused to rub them both under the chin and then continued on. Inside the barn, Dad had just finished saddling Flynn. He smiled at her.

"I wasn't sure if you would want me to get you up."

"Absolutely."

They led the horses outside. Alex groaned as she mounted, her legs straining with soreness from yesterday's ride.

Dad looked over at her as she adjusted her feet in the stirrups. "Are you going soft on me?"

She puffed out a breath. "Hey, it's not my fault I can't have a horse at my apartment in Aspen Creek."

He laughed quietly, and she joined in as they set out toward the trail. Though the sun had not yet risen, its glow lit up the horizon ahead. Everything sat very still and quiet except for the crunch of the horses' hooves and their deep, even breaths. Alex and her dad did not speak at first, but then she asked him about the farm and how things were going. They talked a little about town and the people she had known growing up, and she mentioned how hard it had been to see Lisa and Trevor. She would have loved to be an aunt right now. She would never be one unless she got married and her brothers- or sisters-in-law had children. Even then, it wouldn't be the same. It was a tough fact to come to terms with. It had to be hard for her parents too. They could have been grandparents. Now it was all on her whether or not that would ever happen.

Twenty minutes into their ride, they reached a rise that offered an excellent view of the farm and the perfect vantage point to watch the eastern horizon. It had always been a special place. She had witnessed so many breathtaking sunrises from here, quite a few of which had spawned her early paintings. They stopped now, watching the sky that turned golden with the imminent rising of the sun.

After a few moments of silence, Dad asked, "How are your paintings coming?"

Alex let out a heavy sigh as she looked over at him. How did she even answer that? With the truth, obviously. "It's been difficult. After Josh died, I seemed to have lost the ability to paint. No matter how hard I tried, I just couldn't create anything that made me happy. For a while, I thought that part of me was gone. I'm doing better now. I'm taking it slow and not putting too much pressure on myself, but I think I'm getting somewhere, thanks to Riley. He has helped inspire me."

Dad smiled, though Alex grew more somber. "I'm afraid I'm not even close to making it as a successful artist. I'm sorry."

His smile sank into a frown. "Why are you sorry?"

She winced. She hadn't meant to start such a difficult conversation; however, these rides had always been about opening up and sharing such things. "Because you and Mom put so much into sending me to art school. I know it was a gamble and maybe even foolish of me to attempt something so uncertain. I just hate that it hasn't amounted to anything."

Dad shook his head. "We never thought it was foolish or a gamble."

"But surely it would've been better if I'd gone to college for something more practical."

"I'd never have wanted you to do that. I'm so proud you've pursued this dream despite the obstacles. I never would've wanted you to settle for anything less."

Alex's eyes stung, and she squeezed Flynn's reins. "But I feel like I've let you down. I took a huge chance on something so risky and so . . . outrageous considering how simple things are here. I just wish I had something to show for it. Maybe I should've just stayed here in Bethany, gotten married, and had a family like you and Mom did."

"Alex, you haven't let anyone down, least of all your mom and me. You're an artist, a *real* artist. That's what matters. Success isn't measured in monetary gain. Not in my eyes. I would never have wanted you to stay here in Bethany and wonder if you should've taken the chance to pursue your dreams. Dreams aren't easy to walk away from happily."

Alex stared at him for a long moment, furrowing her brow. He seemed to be talking from experience.

A slight smile lifted his lips. "Yes, I had dreams growing up too. From the time I was a little boy until high school, I wanted to be a pilot."

"Really?" She remembered him talking about flying when she was little, but she had never realized it was a true dream of his.

"Very much so. For a time, I even considered joining the Air Force. I didn't tell your grandpa that, of course."

He laughed, and so did she.

She took a moment to wrap her mind around her dad as anything other than the farmer she had always known. "So why didn't you become a pilot?"

His smile softened. "Because, in the end, the dream that truly mattered most to me was marrying your mom and raising a family. I didn't just settle for this life. I chose it because I wanted it. There have been times I've wondered what it would've been like to pursue flying, but I don't have any regrets. I don't want you to either. Whatever happens with your art, I'm glad you did everything you could to pursue it."

She breathed in deeply, her airway compressing. It seemed her dad understood her dreams more than she had ever thought. The fact that he was happy and proud of her for becoming an artist soothed an ache she had carried for years.

She cleared her throat, though her voice was a little raspy. "Thanks, Dad."

He gave her an encouraging nod and smile. They both turned their attention back to the horizon as the sun finally peeked above it, its rays lighting up the frosty trees and snow-white landscape. It was just as beautiful as Alex always remembered, and a fresh desire to paint sprung up within her.

They sat there for a few minutes more before turning toward the house. Along the way, Dad said, "I had a good talk with Riley while we worked on the truck yesterday."

She looked over at him. She knew how protective he was of her. "You didn't threaten him, did you?"

He gave her a bit of a rascally grin. "Maybe a little."

"How'd he take it?"

"Like a man." He gave a firm nod. "Now, you know this isn't easy for me to say. In my mind, no man will ever be good enough for my little girl . . ."

Alex laughed a little. "I know."

"However," he continued, "I think Riley is a keeper."

Her heart skipped. "Really?"

He nodded slowly. "I trust him to take care of you."

She grinned, getting teary again but for good reasons this time. "You have no idea how happy that makes me. I really love Riley, and it means the world to me to hear you say that."

Emotion lurked in Dad's expression as well. "I've been praying for a long time for God to bring someone into your life to take care of you. I think it's safe to say that prayer has been answered."

Had they not been on horseback, Alex would have thrown her arms around him. "Thank you."

After a warm meal of stovetop blueberry oatmeal and caramel cinnamon rolls, everyone dressed warmly and headed out to the truck. It was a Jennings family tradition to get a Christmas tree the Saturday morning after Thanksgiving. Though Alex wouldn't be around much to enjoy the tree, she was happy to help her parents carry on the tradition—even happier to include Riley, especially after her conversation with her dad earlier. That conversation seemed to change everything. She couldn't stop smiling at Riley. In fact, he was probably beginning to wonder what was wrong with her. Still, it felt good to smile and be so happy.

They drove into town to the tune of Christmas music on the radio and then out to Gibson's Tree Farm nearby. When they arrived, Dad parked in front of a large barn, and they got out. As they closed the truck doors, Mr. Gibson met them looking a little bit like a thin, country Santa Claus with his white beard.

"I just finished getting the team hitched," he told them.

For three generations, Gibson's Tree Farm had prided itself on taking customers out in a horse drawn sleigh or wagon to find their trees. It made for the perfect, old-fashioned Christmas tree cutting experience that drew people from miles around.

They waited outside as he led his team of powerful Belgian horses pulling a red wagon out into the yard. They climbed aboard and took seats on the wooden benches along each side. Alex snuggled in close to Riley across from her parents. He put his arm around her shoulders as they pulled away from the barn and headed off towards the lines of trimmed pine trees in the distance. Bells jingled on the horses' collars, and Alex smiled at how perfectly Christmassy it was.

Along the way, Mr. Gibson looked over his shoulder to converse with them. Alex didn't say much, just enjoying the ride and being close to Riley. Once they were in the midst of the snow-dusted trees, Mr. Gibson pulled the horses to a halt and turned in his seat.

"Go have a look around and take your time. When you've found the right one, I've got the saw here." He held up a bow saw that looked like it had been around long enough to cut hundreds of Christmas trees over the years.

They climbed down from the sleigh and tromped through the snow. Alex initially followed her parents, but then they spread out to widen the search. She wrapped her arm around Riley's, sticking close to him as they inspected the trees they passed. She'd always dreamed of moments like this—of sharing the fun holiday spirit with someone special.

"I hear my dad threatened you yesterday."

Riley chuckled. "He did."

"He also told me on our ride this morning that you're a keeper."

His brows lifted toward his hat a little, but he looked happy. "So what do you think? Am I?"

She tipped her head to give him a teasing look. "I don't know. I've never dated anyone else. Are you?"

"I don't know either, but I do know you are."

She squeezed his arm. "You're definitely a keeper."

They wandered through the trees for a while before meeting up at one particular tree. It appeared to be about the perfect height, full of lush branches and lacking any obvious bare spots.

"I think this is the one," Mom said.

Alex walked around it with her dad, inspecting it from every angle and then nodded. "Yup, I think so too." It would look lovely in the living room with all of their family ornaments.

"I'll get the saw," Dad said.

When he returned, he knelt down, and Riley helped him cut through the tree's trunk at the base. While watching them, Mom gave Alex a little nudge. She looked over at her. Mom wore a mischievous smirk on her face as she formed a snowball in her gloved hands. She nodded her head toward the men. Alex bit her lip to keep from laughing and quickly scooped up her own handful of snow.

The moment Dad straightened, Mom threw her snowball and it smacked him in the shoulder. He and Riley both turned right as Alex threw hers, which hit Riley squarely in the chest. He glanced down and then exchanged a look with her dad. Alex giggled.

Dad released a long sigh and shook his head. "How old are you two? You really should have thought this through before you started something you couldn't finish." He bent down, slowly and deliberately forming a snowball. Riley did the same.

Alex backed away as a childlike giddiness took hold, fluttering up through her stomach. Riley straightened, forming a perfect snowball in his hands, a sparkle of mischief in his eyes.

"You wouldn't," she said, taking another step back.

"Hey, I didn't start this."

He exchanged another look with her dad before they both threw their snowballs. Alex shrieked and dove for cover behind a nearby tree. Riley's snowball missed, but Mom wasn't so lucky, judging by the smack of snow and her gasp. Alex scrambled to form another snowball as an all-out war ensued. She ducked and dodged Riley's projectiles as she sent her own his way, though she was a hopelessly bad shot. She avoided most of his; however, one exploded near her neck that clearly hadn't come from him. Bits of snow snaked icily down her collar. She hunched her shoulders.

"Dad! That's not fair!"

He just laughed. "All is fair in love and war, and I say this is a bit of both."

The battle continued.

Using trees for cover, Alex worked her way closer to Riley, trying to get in a good shot. Josh would have taunted her that she threw like a girl, which was completely true. Eventually, she found herself right on the other side of a large tree from Riley. They circled it a couple of times until Riley jumped out right in front of her. She screamed again and turned to run, but he caught her around the waist and pulled her backward. They fell to the ground, and she landed lightly on top of him before rolling off. She let herself fall back into the snow, laughing and trying to catch her breath. When was the last time she had played in the snow? She felt so wonderfully alive right now. She never wanted to have another dark and gloomy thought or lose hope on life ever again.

Riley lay laughing beside her, and footsteps approached as her parents walked up to them.

"Shall we call it a draw?" Dad asked.

"A draw? You murdered us." Alex reached for her hat slipping off her head and waved it in the air like a white flag. "We surrender."

Dad grinned. "Does that mean we get to take you home as our captives?" He put his arm around Mom and pulled her closer.

Alex laughed. That didn't sound too bad.

Dad then reached down to help her up before offering a hand to Riley. They stood brushing snow off their clothes, and Riley helped her dump out the snow caught in her hood. If they didn't head home soon, they would be soaked and freezing. They hadn't exactly dressed for a snowball fight.

Returning to the tree, Riley helped Dad haul it back to the sleigh. Mr. Gibson gave them a little grin. No doubt he'd watched the entire battle. After loading the tree onto a rack, he took them back to the truck.

At home, they all changed into dry, comfortable clothes. Riley helped Dad bring the tree in and start on the lights while Alex and Mom prepared another lunch of leftovers. Once they had eaten, they all gathered in the living room, where Mom turned on some oldies Christmas music and brought out the boxes of ornaments. Alex loved decorating the Christmas tree, and today was especially wonderful. They sipped coffee, enjoyed the fire and music, and hung the ornaments.

When they were getting close to finishing, Mom and Dad disappeared into the kitchen. Alex happily stood at the tree with Riley, arranging what was left. She let herself daydream a little about what it might be like to have their own Christmas tree. Ever since her talk with her mom yesterday, she was experiencing more of those types of dreamy imaginings.

In the quiet, Riley asked, "Have you told them anything about the day we met?"

Alex paused. Her stomach pinched, and she let out a long sigh. "No." She'd been meaning to, and now they were leaving tomorrow. "I know I need to. Maybe sometime tonight." She closed her eyes for a moment and then looked at him. "Pray for me. And for them. It's going to be hard."

He nodded and said quietly. "I will."

Alex brushed her teeth in the little bathroom across from her room. The house was quiet as they all wound down for the night. After supper, they'd sat in the living room, sipping coffee and enjoying the glow of the Christmas tree. Alex had tried to enjoy it to the fullest, however, she kept thinking about what Riley had said. She had to tell them. She had to. It would just be so, so hard.

After rinsing her toothbrush, she looked at herself in the mirror and sighed. There was no easy way around this, and if she didn't do it now, it would have to wait for another time. It was better to get it over with. She switched off the bathroom light and walked down to her parents' bedroom door. She could tell the light was still on inside and heard her parents talking.

"God, please help me." She raised her hand and knocked on the door.

A moment later, Dad opened it. "What's up, sweetheart?"

She licked her lips. She hated herself for what she was about to put them through. "I know it's late, but could I talk to you and Mom?"

The subtle sobering of his expression was only a mild precursor to what she knew would come.

"Of course."

He opened the door wider, and she stepped into the bedroom. Both her parents were already in their comfortable flannel pajamas, and Mom was in bed, gazing at her questioningly. Dad closed the door and then walked toward the bed. He gestured to it.

"Want to sit down?"

She nodded and walked toward them, sitting cross-legged at the end of the bed while her dad sat on the edge. She had worried them. She could tell by their drawn expressions, as if they were trying to read what was on her mind. If only this were like the times when she and Josh were little and they used to come into the room in the morning and jump onto the bed with their parents. Oh, to be so young and innocent again. Now instead of grins and laughter, their faces were growing more serious by the second.

"It has nothing to do with Riley," she blurted out first. She could just imagine what sort of conclusions they might have jumped to. For all she knew, they might be expecting her to break the news she was pregnant or something. She didn't want them thinking badly of him for even a minute. "Everything between us is good. This is something completely different."

They actually did look a little relieved for a moment before the seriousness took over again. She drew a deep breath. Where did she even start? Was there any good way to explain this without breaking their hearts?

No. Not something like this.

"Before I met Riley, things were really bad," she began, praying she could do this without completely breaking down. "Worse than I ever admitted."

"Oh, honey." Mom looked like she wanted to reach out and hug her, but Alex pushed on. She couldn't stop now, and it would only get worse.

"I've really struggled for the past three years. I lost sight of things and let my faith grow so weak I thought it was dead. I've come to realize I was mad at God for Josh's death." She paused. Tears had formed and she knew she couldn't stop them, so she let them fall. "Over time . . . I just sank lower and lower until I couldn't see any way out except . . ."

Her voice died in her throat. How could she say it? It would hurt them so much. She squeezed her eyes shut for a moment, begging God to help them all. She opened her mouth again, her lips and voice trembling. "The day I met Riley, I was going to kill myself."

Mom gasped, and covered her mouth, her eyes welling with tears, and Dad looked like he had lost her even though she sat right there.

The words poured out now along with the tears. "I went into the bar to get drunk and make it easier. If Riley hadn't been working that day and hadn't asked me out, I don't think I'd still be here."

A heartbreaking sob escaped her mom. She crawled out from under the covers and toward Alex, pulling her into her arms. They both cried together. The bed shifted, and Alex felt her dad's strong hand grip her shoulder.

"I'm sorry," Alex cried. "I'm so, so sorry."

Chapter Twenty-two

ALEX HAD TO DRAG HERSELF OUT OF BED THE NEXT MORNING. HER body was leaden, her head throbbed, and her nose was stuffed. She might have thought she was sick if she didn't know the exact cause for it. Crying late into the night and not being able to fall asleep for hours produced such symptoms. Had her parents slept at all after she had finally gone back to her room to try to sleep? She wasn't sure they could after hearing their child confess to being suicidal at one point. It might have been good that she had told them, but it wouldn't feel good for a while.

Her stomach gurgled nauseously. First there was last night and now church this morning. She hadn't visited her home church since Josh's funeral. She wasn't sure what sort of impression she and Riley would make, especially if people asked questions and found out about the bar. Most probably wouldn't think anything, and it didn't matter if some did. Yet, the lingering emotions after last night just plain made her scared to face anyone who might not understand. She was even a little scared to face her parents this morning.

She drew back her shoulders and pulled in a deep breath. Hiding never helped or solved anything. After packing up her things so she wouldn't have to take the time later, she dressed in the outfit she had prepared for church—a pair of warm tights, a brown wool skirt with lace trim that would go well with her boots, and a cranberry sweater. She set out the necklaces and rings she wanted to wear and then went into the bathroom to fix her hair in a French braid and apply some makeup. Once she was finished, she grabbed her bag and headed downstairs. She couldn't put it off all morning.

The scent of cinnamon oatmeal met her as she approached the bottom of the stairs—something easy before church, though Alex wasn't sure she would find much of an appetite. She set her bag down off to the side and stepped into the kitchen. Riley was the only one there, standing at the stove stirring a steaming pot. He had on one of her mom's plainer aprons, yet it still had a touch of feminine ruffles. Laughter was the last thing Alex felt, yet a slight giggle bubbled out. He turned to look at her and then glanced down at the apron.

"The other one didn't seem quite appropriate for Sunday morning." He shrugged.

She just smiled tiredly. This little bit of humor was exactly what she needed. Without a word, she walked up to him and put her arms around his middle. She just desperately needed to feel safe right now. He wrapped his free arm around her, holding her close at his side.

The stubble on his chin pressed against her forehead. "Rough night?"

"Yeah." She breathed in deeply of the earthy, masculine soap or whatever cologne he had used. "How are my parents this morning?"

He was silent for a heartbeat. "They seemed quiet, but I think they're all right. I offered to take over breakfast so they could finish getting ready for church."

She released him and stepped back. She didn't want to distract him too much and burn the oatmeal. He took a moment to stir it before focusing on her again.

"It's good you told them."

"I know," she sighed, "but it doesn't feel good."

A moment later, Dad walked into the kitchen in a pair of

dark jeans and a green button up shirt with the tie not yet tightened. His eyes found her immediately and he smiled. He walked toward her.

"Good morning, sweetheart." He placed a soft kiss on her forehead. "You look very lovely this morning."

She smiled up at him. "Thanks, Dad."

Mom walked in next, also smiling. Honestly, both her parents looked halfway exhausted, but neither of them mentioned last night's conversation. They had already discussed it enough. Now they just had to let it sink in and move forward. It pained Alex to think her parents would probably look at her differently for a while. How could they not, knowing what she had intended?

They carried bowls of oatmeal and mugs of coffee to the table to eat. The conversation seemed a little slow to get going, but talk of the holidays and the tree led to more cheery stories of Alex's childhood.

"We should get together sometime and watch some of our old home videos," Dad said.

A year ago, Alex would have had to be dragged kicking, screaming, and crying to watch those old videos. It would have been too hard without Josh. However, the thought of it now didn't seem quite so terrible. "That would be fun."

Once their bowls were empty, they rinsed them in the sink and finished getting ready for church. Without the apron on, Alex took note of how handsome Riley looked in a light blue shirt and charcoal gray tie, especially when he slipped on his black leather jacket as they prepared to leave. She pulled on her own jacket and said quietly, "You look very nice this morning."

"Thanks. You always look nice."

Alex opened her mouth to respond that he had never seen her at her worst, yet that wasn't true. The day he'd taken her to the bridge, she'd cried her eyes out and hadn't even changed out of her pajamas. So she just smiled and let the compliment have its intended effect and warm her heart.

On the way to church, her parents and Riley talked, but Alex just watched the scenery pass out her window. She really hated this feeling of going into a situation where she just didn't feel she belonged. No doubt most of that was just her and not even so much the church, but the emotions were hard to shake. Why did the thought of seeing all of her old acquaintances today make her feel like a failure? Of course it wasn't true, but everyone had always seemed so perfect and in control of things compared to her.

Riley's hand closed around hers and squeezed it. She looked over at him, and he leaned toward her. "Hey, don't worry about this morning. Anyone who judges you obviously doesn't know you like I do."

It was just a simple statement, yet it drew a smile to Alex's lips. He was right, and nothing else mattered. He also knew her too well.

She squeezed his hand in return and murmured, "Thank you."

He nodded and kept her hand tucked in his until they pulled up to the same church building she'd attended with her family since she was little. It wasn't as pretty or as big as the church in Aspen Creek, but it was serviceable. She drew another deep breath, fighting the nervous energy building inside of her. Dad parked, and Alex got slowly out of the truck. Her grandparents were just exiting their car nearby and everyone headed toward the church together, Bibles in hand. Alex waited until Riley was at her side before following. He took her hand again and leaned close to say, "Everything will be fine."

She shook her head, more to herself than to him. "I feel like such a weakling. This is my home church and here you are walking in as a stranger. I shouldn't always have to rely so heavily on you to make me feel better."

He drew her closer, and his shoulder pressed against hers. "Don't worry about it. I don't care for one second what anyone here will think of me, and you shouldn't either. In a few hours, we'll be heading back to Aspen Creek and none of it will matter. I guarantee you, not a single person in this building has their lives completely figured out. Only God is perfect. So don't let the perfect picture people want you to see make you think there's not something broken behind it."

It was nothing Alex didn't already know, but hearing him say it made all the difference. The anxiety finally calmed, and his confidence boosted hers. She leaned into him, adoring how he made her feel safe, even from her own silly and unsubstantial fears.

"I love you."

The words slipped out so easily and naturally she didn't even realize the full import of what she'd just said until he looked at her. An invisible blow jabbed her right in the gut. Had she said it too prematurely? Would he think it too soon? She scrambled for an explanation, but the way he smiled at her silenced it.

"I love you too," he murmured.

And the rest of Alex's fears melted away. Tears needled her eyes. She was more than a little bit of a mess, yet for some reason he loved her anyway. She swallowed down the tears, determined not to make a scene, and just shared a smile with him. Not a single doubt entered her mind that his words weren't true. He loved her.

By this time, they had reached the steps leading up to the door. She snapped out of her blissful daze to focus on moving her feet. It wouldn't do to trip and fall in front of Riley or the other people on their way in. But if she did, Riley would catch her and then just laugh adorably. Her pride would be the only thing bruised.

With careful navigation, they entered the church without incident. People were congregating and laughing, and the scent of coffee drifted from the refreshments table. It didn't smell nearly as good as the coffee Riley made. Alex scanned the mingling groups—the women in their dresses and the men all suited up in their Sunday best. She recognized most of the faces. Older people and couples outnumbered those Alex's age about two to one. Quite a few children ran around, however, and she was sure most of the people she had grown up with were married and well into starting their families.

Lisa stood amongst a group of other young women. Alex's heart ached at the sight of little Trevor, but the moment between her and Riley outside quickly dulled it. Nothing would deflate that for a good long while.

Then she spotted Mindy winding her way through the crowd, and her spirits lifted even higher. Mindy always had that effect.

Riley released her hand and offered to take her coat. She slipped it off and thanked him as he took it to hang up with the many others on the hangers against the wall. Mindy reached her, looking fresh and perfect as always in a black blouse, red plaid skirt, and tall black heels.

"Hey!" She grabbed Alex's hands and lowered her voice conspiratorially. "So how was it spending four days with Riley? Is he getting along with your parents?"

"Yes, very well. They really seem to like him a lot. Dad even told me he's a keeper."

Mindy grinned, releasing the tiniest squeak of a squeal. "That's wonderful." She paused then, and must have noticed something in Alex's expression, because she said, "So everything is okay?"

Alex glanced over at her parents. Just the thought of last night dumped ice into her stomach. Though they smiled and talked happily with friends, she wouldn't forget how tired they looked earlier. She faced Mindy again. "Last night I told Mom and Dad about the bridge."

Her exuberant expression sank into one of compassion. "How did they take it?"

"About as well as can be expected. I'm not sure they got much sleep last night. I didn't."

Mindy cast them a sad look but offered Alex encouragement. "It's good you told them."

"Yeah, I just hope they'll be okay."

"They will be. It'll just take a little time for them to process."

Alex took a deep breath and nodded. She darted a quick look around to make sure no one was close enough to overhear. She hadn't felt at all like smiling earlier, but now she couldn't quite hold one back as she whispered, "I told Riley I loved him as we were walking in. I don't know where it came from, it just came out."

Mindy's eyes grew huge. "Oh! How did he respond?"

"He said he loved me too."

Oh, the immense restraint it must have taken for Mindy to hold back the giddiness emanating from her, but her grin said it all.

"I am *so* happy for you," she said in an exaggerated whisper.

"You don't think it was premature, do you?"

"Not if it's how you feel. I get being cautious, but you've got to be honest with each other too. It's better than dragging it on and on to see who's going to say it first and dilly-dallying because you're afraid of scaring someone off." She rolled her eyes. "I hate that in the movies."

Alex giggled. She did too. She didn't want to play games, and she certainly wanted honesty in her relationship.

Any further conversation would have to wait as everyone started to file into the sanctuary. Alex joined Riley and her parents, and they took seats in one of the middle rows. Pastor Stevens took the pulpit. He looked just like Alex remembered, though definitely older and more weathered. She happily joined in as they sang their hymns and then opened her Bible as Pastor Stevens indicated.

Though she fought to concentrate, she often found her mind drifting to Riley. She couldn't believe they had exchanged those three words everyone craved to hear. It hadn't even been some magical moment. Nothing even worthy of a romance novel. She'd just blurted out the words as if talking to her mom or dad. And yet, everything about it was perfect. She was so comfortable with Riley, cared about him so deeply, that to tell him she loved him was no scarier or harder than it was with family.

She glanced at him once and caught his eye. Was he having as hard a time concentrating as she was? His quick smile told her probably.

When the service concluded, everyone rose. A pinch darted through Alex's stomach again. Why did this after-church mingling have to potentially lead to awkward situations? Of course, she could hardly blame her old friends and acquaintances for being curious about her life now. They were certainly quite aware of Riley.

He stayed by her side as they all made their way slowly toward the foyer. Just as expected, a lot of people were eager to chat and ask how she was doing. She tried to avoid talking about work, but bartending eventually did come up. Reactions ranged from relatively well-hidden surprise to commiseration on how hard it was to find a job.

Thank God, she somehow maintained her confidence. Still, she got the distinct impression that Mrs. Sullivan—who used to teach Sunday school—wasn't very impressed with Alex's life choices and or with Riley. She kept eyeing his long hair as if she wanted to take a scissors to it. The interaction between them became quite comical, especially when Riley spoke to her with such abundant politeness and a bright smile. That caught her completely off-guard and sent her away in a bit of a huff.

Finally, they reached their coats and managed to say goodbye. Alex breathed in a huge gulp of fresh air as they stepped outside. It had gone better than she'd expected, but she was more than ready to curl up in front of the fire back home.

On the way to the truck, Riley said, "Well, at least we gave them all something to talk about."

Alex laughed lightly, her nervous energy trickling out with it. "I like your outlook."

He shrugged. "If you're happy with who you are and where God has you, just smile and own it. God never intended for us all to be exactly the same."

She nodded firmly. "Smile and own it." She liked that. It reminded her of all the times Josh had told her that she should just go for it. "I think you might have seriously peeved Mrs. Sullivan with that outlook though."

Dad glanced over his shoulder from where he walked just ahead of them with Mom. "That's good. She needs something to stew over for the next month."

He winked, and Alex just laughed again. So what if they all talked about her and Riley? Words only had the power she gave them, and she wouldn't give up any.

———

Back at home, Alex, her parents, and Riley enjoyed a warm lunch and gathered in the living room to watch the game while waiting for Mindy and Zach. Alex curled up in the corner of the couch nearest the fire, and Riley sat next to her. Thankfully, her parents seemed better than they had earlier. Dad and Riley talked a lot about the game, while Mom mostly listened and worked on one of her crochet projects. Alex was quiet too. In fact, she almost dozed off a couple of times.

Shortly after the game ended, Mindy and Zach showed up. They all talked for a little bit in the kitchen before it was time to leave. The sun was nearly setting when Alex and Riley carried their bags out to the vehicle. After stowing hers in the back, Alex turned to her parents. It was harder to say goodbye today than it had been last week. No doubt they couldn't help but fear they might not see her again. She hated having caused such a worry for them.

She reached her mom first and gave her a long hug. In her ear, Mom said quietly, "We're here for you, Alex. We know how hard it is. We're always here if things get bad. Please don't leave us like that."

"I won't, Mom." Alex took a step back and looked her in the eyes. "I already promised Riley that I wouldn't have an escape. I'm determined not to let myself sink that far again, at least not without letting someone know I'm struggling. So please, don't worry."

Mom smiled and nodded, though tears wet her eyes.

Alex turned to her dad next. He hugged her tightly, offering his own words of encouragement. "We love you, Alex, and are so proud of you. You call us any time you need us, all right?"

"I love you too, Dad. And I will, I promise."

They said goodbye to Riley then, and Mom gave him a noticeably long hug. They would probably never see him quite the same way again. He might have failed to save Josh, but he had saved her life.

It was hard to get into the SUV, but Alex already planned to come back as soon as she could. She waved to her parents as they pulled away, and prayed God would calm any of the fears they had for her. She also prayed she would never again sink low enough those fears would have any merit.

As they left Bethany behind, Alex propped her elbow against the door and leaned her head against her hand. It had been both a lovely and emotional holiday weekend. She forced herself to dwell on the good moments instead of the hard ones, and smiled at the memory of the snowball fight and the exchange between her and Riley this morning.

"Are you all right?"

She looked over at him. "Yeah, I'm just really tired."

He tipped his head and patted the middle seat between them. "Why don't you slide over and you can rest against me?"

With a smile, Alex unbuckled her seatbelt and slid over. She caught Zach give her a wink in the rearview mirror. Once she was buckled in again, she leaned against Riley and rested her head on his shoulder. She let out a long sigh and closed her eyes, so thankful to have him.

Chapter Twenty-three

RILEY SAT ON THE COUCH IN HIS LIVING ROOM ON MONDAY morning with his laptop open on the coffee table. He had about an hour before he had to head down and help Luke open the bar. Enjoying the leftovers Alex's mom had sent with him, he watched a few videos on latte art and scrolled through articles on opening a coffee shop. He and Alex's dad had talked about it a bit while working on the truck. Daniel had encouraged him like his own father never had and had given him a fresh dose of enthusiasm to think about it seriously again. If only he could get the money he needed for a loan.

Tux jumped up onto the couch beside him and dropped the ring from a milk jug in his lap. He picked it up and tossed it across the room. The cat dashed after it and brought it back to him for probably the dozenth time already. Well, if he was going to have a cat, at least he had one that acted like a dog and played fetch.

His phone buzzed next to his laptop and then rang. The screen displayed Mark's name in bold letters. Out of everyone in his family besides Granddad, he was probably the closest to his brother. There'd never been any true animosity between them. Mark may have been the golden child, which was irritating growing up, but Riley had always looked up to him.

He picked up the phone and accepted the call.

"Riley, hey, how's it going?" His brother's voice came through the speaker.

Riley closed his laptop and rested back against the couch. "Not bad. You?"

"Busy, as usual."

They went through the standard niceties with Mark telling him all about their latest design projects and clients. Tux came back to Riley, having grown bored with the milk ring. He jumped up to the back of the couch and settled on Riley's shoulder. Ever since Riley had let him sleep there as a kitten, it was his favorite spot. Riley reached up with his free hand to scratch the cat's head. Tux started to purr loudly, and Riley had to turn his head away so the sound wouldn't reach the phone.

"So I see you're dating." Mark's comment came after a brief pause in the business discussion.

Alex had asked if she could start posting about them on Facebook. He'd said yes, of course, but that meant it was only a matter of time before his family took notice.

"I am."

"She looks like a nice girl. How long have you two been going out?"

"About three months."

"Jen says you spent Thanksgiving with her family."

Riley should have guessed it was their younger sister who would be up on all this. The couple of brief times he'd seen her while in the hospital she'd been on her phone every five seconds. He had no doubt she used more social media accounts than he even knew existed. Part of the fast-paced fashion world she lived in.

"Yeah. It was a nice time."

"So it's serious then?"

He winced as Tux dug his claws into his shoulder and reached up to pry them out as he answered, "Yes."

A slight pause sent a twinge to Riley's gut that this conversation was about to head in an uncomfortable direction.

"Mom's surprised you never let us know about Alex."

And that twinge was right. "Define 'surprised.'"

"She's disappointed."

Riley blew out a hard sigh. "It's not like my life has been of interest to them before."

"You know that's not true," Mark said. He'd always been the one trying to smooth things over between Riley and their parents. Riley was grateful for the concern, but sometimes he'd rather his brother just leave well enough alone. Besides, it wasn't like their parents had made much effort either.

"Their interest in my life choices has only ever been disapproval. Things are good between me and Alex. They can't blame me for not wanting to subject our relationship to their scrutiny."

Mark paused again before saying, "You're not going to like this, but Kayla and I are having dinner with them Sunday night. They want you and Alex to join us."

Riley closed his eyes and rubbed his forehead. "So they sent you as messenger boy?"

"Mom wasn't sure you'd answer if she called."

She could have tried, at least. Riley sighed again. Putting them off would just upset them even more. Every instinct he possessed fought to keep his relationship with his parents and his relationship with Alex as separate as possible. However, that wasn't realistic, especially if things were as serious as he believed they were. It wasn't good any way he looked at it.

"I'd have to talk to Alex first."

"Well, just text me and let me know if you're going to make it. Dinner is at six."

They traded brief goodbyes, and Riley set his phone aside. After the enjoyable weekend in Bethany, the last thing he wanted to think about was introducing Alex to his parents. He could just imagine how nervous it would make her, and his mind already conjured up horrible ways in which his parents might treat her if she failed their expectations. Knowing them, they probably held a poor opinion of her already simply because he had picked her. Everything he did was wrong in their eyes. With that kind of track record, they surely expected nothing less with Alex.

He closed his eyes and rubbed them.

Lord, I need You to work in this. I don't know what to do.

Alex didn't see Riley until Wednesday when he came to pick her up for work. After spending four days together, she'd missed him. Not that she'd ever admit to anyone just how wistfully she had pined for him at moments. Yet, when they'd talked on the phone something was off. Now, riding in his truck on the way to the bar, she detected it again. He seemed subdued, perhaps even a little distant. A pang passed through her stomach. Was he rethinking what he'd said in the parking lot? Now that he'd had time to think about it, had her declaration of love scared him off?

She gave herself a stern mental shake. She trusted Riley, and she would not let her thoughts run away in wild speculation. Instead, she would do the mature thing and talk about it instead of simply wondering and forming conclusions.

"Are you all right?"

He glanced at her, a hint of turmoil in his eyes. "My brother, Mark, called on Monday."

There, see? It had nothing to do with her. "Is everything okay?"

"Unfortunately, when it comes to my family, nothing is ever okay. I guess my mom is upset I never told them about you."

"Oh." Alex wilted in her seat. "Sorry. I shouldn't have put anything on Facebook."

He shook his head. "No, I wanted you to. It's my fault I never told them."

They pulled up behind the bar, and he shut off the truck. However, instead of getting out, he just sat there for a moment before looking over at her.

"I guess I never told them because I didn't want that part of my life to touch my life here. I didn't want it to touch us." His brows scrunched. "Problem is, I don't think my parents will settle for that. Mark called at my mom's request. They want you and me to join them for dinner Sunday night."

Alex shifted in her seat, that pang in her stomach intensifying. The Conrads were such an affluent and formidable force, and their strained relationship with Riley made it difficult for her to summon the desire to get to know them. The mere thought of sitting down to dinner with them was enough to send her straight into a panic attack.

"I'm not asking you to go." He probably read the fear on her face. "I won't put you in that position."

She stared at the dash and drew a deep breath. This was Riley's family they were talking about. True, they might be estranged, but they were still family. Deep down, he cared about them despite the hurt that no doubt resided on both sides. Whether there was hope for future reconciliation or not, the last thing she wanted was to make the chasm between them even wider. Not if she had the power to avoid it. Though the idea of meeting them literally terrified her, she would not give in to fear.

"We can go . . . if you want."

She felt like she had stepped off the edge of a cliff, yet she trusted both God and Riley to break the fall. It's not like she had to do this without both of them at her side.

His eyes widened. "You'd go to dinner at my parents'?"

"If you think it'll help smooth things over, then yes. I'll go with you."

He just looked at her for a moment as if thinking it over. It was probably as hard for him to go as it was for her. She couldn't quite tell what he was thinking, but perhaps in amongst the convoluted emotions she caught a hint of relief.

The week passed with a subtle but ever-present mood of impending doom. At least, that was how it seemed to Alex, and it certainly affected Riley. His patience ran uncharacteristically thin, especially when the bar grew busy toward the end of the week. He was always quick to apologize whenever he was a little short with her, and she was careful not to take it personally. She didn't envy the intense pressure that must have weighed on him as the day drew nearer. Her own anxiety levels threatened to rise, but she surprised herself with how well she managed it. She found herself much more concerned with Riley's state of mind than her own.

At church on Sunday, they enjoyed a Christmas-themed message by Pastor Ellis. It was the most normal Riley had seemed all week, despite the dinner being set for tonight. While he was busy talking to Zach and some of the other men after the service, Alex slipped away for a private moment with Pastor Ellis. She waited until he finished speaking to one of the older gentleman of the congregation before she approached him. He smiled at her, as open and welcoming as always.

"Alex, Donna told me that you and Riley had a wonderful Thanksgiving."

She nodded with a smile. Pastor Ellis's wife had commented on and liked nearly all her Facebook photos. "Yes, we did. I'm really glad my parents had a chance to get to know him." She glanced over at Riley. "I don't want to take up much of your time, but I have a quick prayer request."

"How can I help?"

"I'm meeting Riley's parents tonight. They invited us for dinner; however, Riley has always had a strained relationship with them. He hasn't even talked to them in over a year. There's a lot of hurt between them, and I know tonight will be very difficult for him. I just really want him to be okay."

"Of course," Pastor Ellis said. "I will pray tonight goes well and that no more harm will be done. I'll also pray for healing between them in the future."

"Thank you so much. And do please pray for their salvation. I know Riley thinks about it and is bothered that he hasn't yet shared his faith."

Pastor Ellis nodded. "You can count on it."

She thanked him again and rejoined Riley. Though they talked with Mindy and Zach for a little while, they did not linger at church. Mindy gave them both words of encouragement as they said goodbye, and Riley took Alex home. As they sat in his truck in front of the apartment, he said, "I'll be back to pick you up around five."

She nodded, fighting all instincts of panic. "What should I wear? I've never been to a formal dinner like this before."

"Wear whatever you're comfortable in. You don't have to try to impress them. Their opinion of you doesn't affect mine." He offered her a small smile, one of the few she had seen this past week.

"What are you wearing?"

"Probably just jeans, a shirt, and tie. I don't plan on anything more than that."

"All right. I'll see you later then."

She got out of the truck and followed the path up to her porch. Inside her apartment, she spent the rest of the afternoon nearly emptying her closet to find the perfect outfit, changing her mind more times than she could count. In the midst of it, she whispered prayers. It was the only way she would keep her sanity. That and the happy Christmas music from the radio she turned on.

Once she finally settled on an outfit, she sat down at her laptop to distract herself. Occasionally, she texted Riley to see how he was doing and offer him words of support. It was definitely a role reversal, but she was happy to be his strength the way he was always hers.

An hour before he would show up, she changed into her dinner outfit and spent a long time in the bathroom working on her hair. She tried a lot of different styles before managing to create a simple, yet elegant low bun with a few wisps of hair framing her face that she took a curling iron to. She worked on her makeup next, carefully applying eyeliner and a rosy lip gloss. She had already repainted her nails earlier in a dark red that seemed appropriate for the time of year as well as classic and elegant.

When Riley knocked at her door, she let him inside. Closing it against the chill air, she stood in front of him. "Well, what do you think?"

She'd chosen a pair of thick black leggings, knee high boots, and a long wine-red sweater trimmed in elegant lace. Josh's dog tags hung tucked out of sight inside her shirt, and she wore a long, layered silver necklace with feather charms Mindy had given her for her birthday in college. She'd tried to be both formal and true to her personality.

He looked her up and down, taking his time, and smiled. "You look beautiful."

Warmth bloomed in Alex's cheeks, enjoying his perusal perhaps a bit more than she should. It felt good to know he found her attractive.

She took a moment to look him over as well. He had on well-fitting dark jeans that looked great with his leather jacket. Though it was zipped up, she spied a deep blue collared shirt and black tie underneath. He had his hair pulled back neatly tonight, no doubt because of how much his parents probably hated it.

"And you look perfectly handsome," she told him.

He seemed to smile a lot easier than he had earlier. Maybe he had finally resigned himself to this and was prepared to let whatever happened happen.

She retrieved her coat and he helped her slip it on before they headed down to his truck. It was dark out already, but it gave them a chance to enjoy the Christmas lights along the way.

For the forty-five minute drive to Denver, they talked about almost anything but tonight's dinner. It seemed they both wanted to avoid the topic for as long as possible. However, when they spotted the city lights ahead, they grew quieter and said very little as they drove into a ritzy Denver neighborhood. When Riley pulled into a paved driveway, Alex's breath caught in her chest. This was it.

Chapter Twenty-four

ALEX GAWKED AT THE HUGE WHITE HOUSE IN FRONT OF THEM, decked out in pine boughs, Christmas lights, and red bows. She let her mouth hang open a moment. It looked like something that belonged on the front of a magazine highlighting the city of Denver. Of course, how could she expect anything less from the founder of Conrad Architects? No doubt Riley's dad had designed the house. A smaller, yet no less impressive, guesthouse sat off to the side and a little behind. A red brick wall rimmed the property—beautiful, yet intimidating.

Riley parked in front of the house next to a black luxury car, and then quietly reached up to adjust his tie. Alex had a feeling he was stalling. Finally, he looked over at her.

"Ready for this?"

She gave a firm nod. She may not feel ready, but tonight wasn't about relying on him to make her feel better. Tonight she was here to support *him*. With a nod of his own, Riley reached for the door handle, but Alex put her hand on his arm to stop him.

"Hey."

He paused and looked back at her.

"Just smile and own it."

This managed to bring a smile to his face, and he even laughed a little before leaning over to give her a quick kiss. Alex grinned as he pulled away and got out. While she waited for him to round the front of the truck, she whispered a quick prayer for tonight. At her door, he opened it and took her hand. They walked toward the front door together, and she leaned into him. "Remember, we'll be heading back to Aspen Creek later and it won't matter what happens here."

The words were as much for herself as for him. She did hope to make a good impression with Riley's parents tonight and make him proud.

At the door, he reached out and rang the bell. It was noticeable that he didn't just let himself in. She had no problem doing that back home. Then again, this hadn't been home to him since he was a teenager. Had it even felt much like home to him then? Home was supposed to be warm and safe—a haven from the rest of the world. Instead, he had sought to escape it by joining the military.

The door opened, snapping her from her thoughts. A tall, willowy woman stood silhouetted in the doorway, dark hair curling around her chin and just above her shoulders. She wore a black lace dress with white from the under layer peeking through, and a stylish black cardigan that projected sophistication. Self-consciousness pricked Alex, but she reminded herself that she was perfectly happy with her own style.

"Riley," the woman said, not with the depth of warm love Alex's mom would have used in greeting, yet it wasn't cold either. This was probably awkward for her too.

"Hey, Mom," Riley responded, reserved.

She gestured them inside. They stepped into the immaculate foyer furnished with mirrors and elegant Christmas decor. The arched doorways leading into the other rooms of the house were beautiful. Alex had never seen such a place and had to stop herself from gawking again. She watched Riley's mom give him a light hug that was as awkward as their greeting.

"I'm glad you made it," she told him.

He nodded and turned as if to introduce Alex when an imposing figure entered the foyer. She immediately recognized

Phillip Conrad from advertisements for the family business. He seemed even bigger, bulkier, in person with piercing eyes and sparse silvery hair. Alex had heard he was quite a few years older than his wife, yet they did make a commanding couple. She saw a bit of Riley in both of them, yet none of the sweet acceptance she so loved about him.

He straightened beside her, his expression guarded. "Dad."

"Riley," his dad greeted him coolly.

They shook hands, though it was like watching two business acquaintances interact rather than family. If only Alex could somehow make the moment less awkward. Finally, Riley turned and drew her closer with a hand to her back.

"Mom, Dad, this is Alex Jennings."

Mrs. Conrad smiled and shook her hand lightly. "I'm pleased to meet you, Alex."

Alex responded in kind and then shook Mr. Conrad's hand as well. Though intimidated by his size, she made sure her grip was firm enough to make her dad proud. Riley's dad didn't really say anything. Probably waiting to pass judgment until he had a chance to analyze her. Every nerve in her body tensed, and she just prayed she wouldn't make a fool of herself at least.

"Let me take your coats," Mrs. Conrad said. "Mark and Kayla are waiting in the living room."

Riley helped Alex out of her coat. She smoothed her sweater and clasped her hands, fiddling with her rings. Riley's mom then led them out of the foyer and into a huge sunken living room with a cathedral ceiling. A Christmas tree towered in one corner, decorated to perfection in gold and crystal ornaments, and a gas fireplace burned warmly against one wall. Floor to ceiling windows overlooked a large yard and what appeared to be an in-ground pool.

Movement drew Alex's gaze from the beautiful view to the long, black sectional couch near the fireplace where a man rose to his feet. He had short hair and a neatly trimmed goatee. Though he was dressed in a well-tailored suit like Mr. Conrad, Alex found him far less intimidating. The stunning red-headed beauty who joined him, however, gave her pause. She was all sleek red dress and legs. Alex could only dream of such a slim, curvy figure. She had always been on the short side like her mom and more stick-thin than curvy. This woman gave off the impression that she belonged here and had full confidence in that.

Alex's gaze faltered, but she looked up again when the man spoke.

"Riley." He wore a genuine smile and stepped forward, giving Riley a quick hug.

This was the most love anyone had exchanged in the house tonight, and Riley even smiled. He turned and held his arm out for her to join him. "Alex, this is my brother Mark and his wife, Kayla."

Mark offered his hand to her. "I'm pleased to meet you, Alex. It's been a long time since Riley has had a woman in his life."

She shook his hand and smiled, greeting him as well. She glanced over at Kayla, who merely inclined her head in greeting. Alex couldn't tell if she was aloof or just more the observant, quiet type.

"Shall we sit?" Mrs. Conrad gestured to the couch. "Dinner will be ready shortly."

They took their seats on the long sofa, Alex tucking herself in close to Riley. She wasn't sure if she did it more for her own comfort or his. Despite the warm fireplace, the air felt particularly frosty in here, and Riley's rigid posture didn't relax at all. She imagined this taut, focused expression he wore was the same as the times he'd gone into battle. *Lord, please let this get easier and more comfortable.* Now she understood Riley's mood all week. So far this was anything but pleasant.

Mr. Conrad peered at them, looking as if he were sitting in an office rather than a living room. "And how is work, Riley? Are you still at that bar?"

"I am."

"Do you see yourself there from now on, or do you have bigger plans?"

Riley cleared his throat. Would he bring up his dream of the coffee shop?

"I don't intend to stay there indefinitely. It depends on what comes along in the future."

His dad didn't look impressed. "Success is not built on chance, but hard work. You can't just sit around and hope for a better future. You have to get out there and make it happen."

"I'm fully aware of that, Dad," Riley replied, his voice as taut as his expression. "I'm working on it."

Mr. Conrad appeared to have a thing or two to say about that, but his wife cut in, her eyes on Alex. "What about you? What business are you in?"

Caught in the spotlight, Alex felt like a sheep singled out for slaughter and not a quick death either. A slow and painful one more likely. Yet, if they focused on her, they couldn't scrutinize Riley, and this hostile conversation was quickly forming an emboldened desire to protect him that she never realized she possessed.

"I work with Riley at the bar a few days a week." She sensed his dad gearing up for what would probably be a cutting remark to that, but she pressed on. "However, I'm an artist. I have a Bachelor of Fine Arts degree."

Mr. Conrad's furrowed brows shifted upward at this, and Mrs. Conrad's face brightened. "An artist, really? What artists do you aspire to?"

Alex named off some of her favorites who had inspired her over the years, particularly James Moretti. She had picked out numerous pieces of his art on the walls, none of which appeared to be prints. Every name seemed to draw more and more interest from Riley's mom. Even his dad looked at her without the hard, analytical expression he'd been wearing just moments ago.

"I went to school for music," Mrs. Conrad said, "but art would have been my next choice. Tell me, have you had any success in selling your work or displaying in any galleries?"

"I have sold a few pieces online, but I haven't had success with any galleries. The last couple of years have been difficult for me personally, so I haven't pursued different avenues as much as I should have or made any connections that could help me."

"I would love to see your work. Do you have any photos?"

"I do, yes." Alex reached for her phone in a pocket of her leggings. The longer she kept their attention on her, the less Riley had to deal with them. She brought up a photo folder on her phone with her art and handed it to Mrs. Conrad to look through.

The woman swiped through each one, her husband leaning over to see as well. Alex licked her lips and glanced at Riley. He looked almost as nervous to hear what they would say as she was.

"These are beautiful," Mrs. Conrad said at last, handing the phone back. "You're very talented."

Alex let out a slow breath. While she wouldn't have put too much stock into their opinion had it been negative, she couldn't help but be pleased by their approval. "Thank you."

"I'd be happy to help you make connections. In fact," Mrs. Conrad looked at her husband before focusing once more on Alex, "next weekend is our annual Christmas party. You're more than welcome to join us and bring your portfolio. I could introduce you to James Moretti."

Alex's eyes grew huge. "You know James Moretti?"

"Yes," Mrs. Conrad said with a smile that was one of the most genuine gestures Alex had witnessed all evening.

That certainly explained all the Moretti art around the house.

"He's been a friend of ours for several years," Mr. Conrad said. "Riley could've told you that if he'd been around during that time."

Like a dousing of ice cold water, any bit of comfort Alex had been lulled into fizzled. She glanced at Riley. He wouldn't look at his dad. Instead he had his gaze firmly locked on the fireplace, his jaw muscles strained. Something hot burned to life inside of Alex. Mr. Conrad might hold the key to her art dreams, but she wouldn't just sit and let him dig at Riley the whole night.

"Well," she spoke carefully, "if he had been here, he wouldn't have been at my brother's side when he died."

Mr. Conrad's brows creased. She'd probably caught him off guard with that comment. Good.

She forged on. "My older brother was a Marine. Three years ago, he was killed by a suicide bomber. Riley was there when it happened and tried to save him."

Emotion thickened her throat, but she held it at bay. She wasn't exactly trying to guilt trip or manipulate their emotions, but they did need to know Riley hadn't simply been off gallivanting. He'd served their country heroically and made it back alive, by the grace of God, when so many others had not. He cast her an appreciative look. She had the feeling they would dismiss anything he said about his service, but it might have more weight coming from someone else.

They didn't seem quite sure how to respond. Finally, Mrs. Conrad spoke with true compassion. "I'm very sorry for your loss."

"Thank you," Alex murmured. They said nothing about Riley, but she wouldn't push the issue.

A moment later, a middle-aged woman in a white apron stepped into the room and let them know dinner was ready. Mr. and Mrs. Conrad rose and led them all to the dining room. Along the way, Alex reached for Riley's hand and squeezed it tightly. They were in this together. He gave her a quick smile.

223

At the long dining table set with white linens and expensive silverware, Riley pulled out one of the ornate oak chairs for her. It was no wonder he had such fine manners. She had a feeling his mom would have been quite strict about that while they were growing up.

Once they were all seated, the cook brought them plates of lamb chops and vegetables. Alex had never experienced such a formal setting before. What if she spilled or knocked something over? Humiliation burned her face just imagining it, but she calmed herself and carefully placed her linen napkin in her lap.

In between bites, they continued their conversation. Both of Riley's parents asked more about Alex's art career and then about her family. She got the impression they didn't have too high an opinion of her parents, but she didn't let that bother her. They would never know her mom and dad the way she did. They both praised her on pursuing her dreams and not letting her simple upbringing hold her back. Alex just thanked them and let it be. Riley didn't say much of anything, which was probably for the best.

Once the main meal concluded, the cook cleared away their plates and brought slices of chocolate cheesecake to the table. Though quite full, Alex couldn't say no to the fancy dessert. Before any of them could try it, however, Mark called for their attention.

"Before we start dessert, Kayla and I have news to share, and we thought tonight would be the perfect time since most of us are together." He focused on his parents. "Mom, Dad, you're going to be grandparents."

Mrs. Conrad's entire face lit up. "You're going to have a baby?"

Mark and Kayla both nodded with wide smiles.

"When are you due?" Mrs. Conrad asked.

"The end of July," Kayla told her.

"This is wonderful news," Mr. Conrad joined in. He hadn't been so animated all night. "Perhaps it'll be a strapping boy to carry on the family legacy."

Kayla answered with a glowing smile. "We are hoping for a boy. I promise we'll let you know the moment we find out."

Mr. Conrad beamed at them. "You two will make fine parents."

Beside Alex, Riley offered congratulations to his brother and his sister-in-law, and she did the same. Though Riley smiled through it all, it didn't quite reach his eyes. It had to be hard to witness how proud his dad was of Mark. Alex could sort of imagine it. She'd never been jealous of Josh, but she knew what it was like to feel like your sibling was better than you. All younger siblings probably experienced it at some point. If only Riley's parents could see in him what she did. He was different from them, yet a far better man than they gave him credit for.

Mr. and Mrs. Conrad remained caught up in baby talk during dessert. Alex and Riley just listened quietly. About the time the cook cleared away the rest of their dishes, Riley spoke up.

"We should be heading back to Aspen Creek before it gets too late."

They all rose from their seats. Riley and Alex traded polite goodbyes with Mark and Kayla, and then Mr. and Mrs. Conrad led them to the foyer where they put on their coats.

"I hope to see you next weekend for the Christmas party," Mr. Conrad told Alex.

She smiled, but said, "I'll have to see if I can get off since I work on Saturday."

His gaze zeroed in on Riley. "You'll see that she can make it, won't you? You don't want her to miss this opportunity."

Riley put on an obviously fake smile. "I'll talk to our boss."

Alex shifted uncomfortably, hating to be in the middle of this. It wasn't like Riley was in charge of her work schedule. She forced her own smile when Mr. Conrad's attention returned to her.

"If James likes your work, I'm sure the two of us could get some of your pieces into the McKinley Art Gallery."

"That would be amazing." Though not likely to happen, Alex couldn't stifle the giddiness that fluttered through her at the prospect. It wouldn't just be amazing; it would be a dream come true. However, it would depend largely on the Christmas party, and her attendance was uncertain at best.

She thanked him anyway for the invitation, and they traded their goodbyes before Riley opened the door and ushered her out. She could sense his desire to escape the place, and she couldn't blame him. In his truck, she buckled her seatbelt and shivered. She couldn't wait for the cab to warm up. Riley turned the key and then reached up to loosen his tie.

They were both quiet as they pulled away from the house and left the neighborhood behind. Finally, as Alex was holding her chilled fingers up to the heat vents, Riley spoke.

"My parents sure thought highly of you."

She looked over at him, trying to read his face, but it was hard with just the light from the street lamps and dash. "Is that okay? You're not upset about it, are you?" She would hate for their acceptance of her to cause more pain for him.

"No," he said as if he were surprised she'd wondered. "Actually, I feel like I did something right in their eyes for once."

"For what it's worth, I think you've done a lot of things right."

He sent her a quick smile. It was tired, but real.

She reached over and rested her hand on his arm. "Don't worry about talking to Luke about next weekend. It's too short notice, and I don't have to go to that party."

"Of course you do." He said it as if there were no question about it. "My dad's right; it's an opportunity you can't miss. I'm sure I can work something out with Luke and Kat. I'll just offer to work Sunday instead."

Alex couldn't imagine he had even the slightest desire to attend this party, so he was doing this entirely for her. "I can go alone. You don't have to take me." She was a grown woman. She'd been doing things on her own for years.

He looked over at her with an expression that was both serious and tender. "Yeah, I do."

Chapter Twenty-five

RILEY CALLED AS ALEX WAS MAKING COFFEE THE NEXT MORNING to let her know Luke had given them both Saturday night off so they could attend the party. Emotions swirled up inside her like a flurry of snowflakes—exciting but leaving her a bit cold at the prospect. She couldn't even imagine meeting James Moretti, let alone have him analyze her paintings. It scared the living daylights out of her. She would have to be extra careful to act professional and not make a stammering fool out of herself. Her palms grew sweaty just thinking about it.

Not only that, but she had never attended this sort of party before. Christmas parties back in Bethany involved getting together with family and sitting in the living room with mugs of hot chocolate. Either that or gathering at the church for potluck. She was pretty sure the Conrad's party wouldn't be anything like either of those scenarios. What would she even wear? She didn't know the first thing about how to prepare for this type of social event.

But she did know someone who could help.

Immediately after hanging up with Riley she dialed Mindy.

"So how was dinner?" her friend asked by way of greeting the moment she answered.

"It was . . . uncomfortable. Mostly for Riley, I mean. His parents seemed to like me just fine, surprisingly, but there is a lot of tension between them. It was pretty painful."

"Well, at least they like you. That's got to earn him some brownie points with them, right?"

"I hope so." She sighed but then went on to inform Mindy about the Christmas party and James Moretti.

Mindy was ecstatic for her, of course, and couldn't wait to find out how the meeting would go. Her enthusiasm and assurance that he would love Alex's work did help assuage a little of her fears. After letting Mindy's giddiness run its course, Alex came to the real reason she had called.

"Problem is, I have no idea what to wear to the party. This isn't your typical family get-together. This is a ritzy holiday party like you see in the movies. I mean, Mr. Conrad and Riley's brother wore full suits just to dinner last night. I took a peek at Mrs. Conrad's Facebook photos of their party last year, and it looked like a red-carpet event. Everyone was dressed like you wouldn't believe, especially Riley's sister-in-law. I feel like an awkward teenager next to her, and I don't even know where to begin to get ready."

"Three words," Mindy responded. "Little black dress."

Alex scoffed. "Like I have a little black dress." She'd never had an occasion to even want one until now.

"Then we're just going to have to get you one."

"It's not like I have a lot of time. The party is on Saturday."

"You're off tomorrow, aren't you?"

"Yeah."

"Then come over in the morning, and we'll go shopping. I guarantee you by tomorrow night, you'll be all set to shine at that party."

Alex laughed. She didn't expect to do much shining, especially when placed next to women like Kayla, but she appreciated Mindy's confidence in her. "All right. I'll be there around nine."

"I'll see you then."

Alex ended the call and stared at the screen until it shut off. She didn't quite trust Mindy not to go overboard with this shopping trip. Then again, she really did need all the help she could get.

The future of her whole art career could rest on making a good impression on Saturday.

———

Mindy was waiting for Alex with a tall travel mug of coffee when she arrived in Boulder. Alex left her Jeep in the driveway, and they both ducked into Mindy's bright yellow, somewhat-beat-up Volkswagen Beetle she'd driven since college. Zach would have preferred she drive something safer, but he'd relented in letting her keep it. It was a fun little car, and Alex had always known Mindy to be a careful driver.

Driving into the heart of Boulder, Mindy took a sip of her coffee and asked, "Anything specific you would like to look for today?"

Alex shook her head. "You know a lot more about fashion than I do. I think I'll just leave it in your hands."

Mindy grinned as if she'd just been given a new doll to dress up for Christmas. "Okay, so there's this adorable boutique I noticed the other day. We'll try there first." She squealed a little. "You're going to look so cute in a black dress."

"If you say so."

Mindy cast her a sideways look. "Give yourself credit. You're a perfect mix of pretty and country girl. You landed a great guy with your quirky small-town charm, and with the perfect dress, a bit of makeup, and the right hairstyle, you'll fit in great at this party."

Alex shrugged. "If only I could put on confidence as easily as a new dress or makeup. I'm afraid I'll make a complete fool of myself in front of Moretti and turn into a babbling fangirl."

"Take deep breaths." Mindy drew one for emphasis. "And just think of it as business. You are a professional businesswoman, and remember, this Moretti had to start somewhere too. He wasn't born with a paintbrush in hand."

Alex laughed. "I suppose you're right."

"Of course I am." She then started randomly singing along with one of the Christmas carols on the radio, and Alex laughed harder.

A few minutes later, they pulled up in front of one of the lovely shops that graced Boulder's streets. The two of them had spent some time here during their college breaks, though they'd both been too poor at the time to do much shopping.

They got out of the car and hurried into the boutique, out of the cold. Alex pulled off her gloves and stuffed them in her coat pocket as she looked around at all the racks of clothing, displays of shoes and jewelry, and a wide assortment of purses and other accessories. She had no idea where to even begin. Most of her clothing came from secondhand stores. She found lots of great items that way and didn't go broke doing it. This occasion, however, did call for more than a lucky thrift store find. She looked to Mindy for direction.

Without missing a beat, Mindy strode toward a rack along the nearest wall. She inspected a couple of the dresses hanging there before a woman in a cute pink blouse and heeled boots approached them.

"Is there anything I can help you with?" she asked cheerfully.

Mindy turned to her with a smile. "My friend has a very important Christmas party this weekend." She stepped up behind Alex and put her hands on her shoulders. "We're looking for something classy and elegant. I'm thinking black."

The woman grinned. Yes, Alex was definitely a doll for dress up, but she didn't mind. She would enjoy the experience.

"I will pull some pieces for you and see what you think."

The woman whisked around the store picking out dresses from various racks while Mindy ushered Alex toward the fitting rooms.

"Isn't this fun?"

"Yes." It wasn't every day a girl got to dress up fancy. "I just hope I'll be able to afford groceries once we're finished."

Mindy linked her arm with Alex's. "Don't worry. If whatever you choose is way overpriced, I'll help you pay for it."

"You don't have to do that."

"This is a very important occasion. I want to help out any way I can."

"Just having you here to help me get ready means a lot. I'm not sure what I would've done on my own."

Mindy smiled happily at her, and they sat down on one of the padded benches in front of the curtained dressing rooms. While they waited for the woman to bring them dresses, Mindy cast Alex a mischievous look.

"So if this is a formal event, does that mean Riley will be all dressed up and dapper in a suit?"

"I guess I hadn't thought about it," Alex admitted. "Probably."

Mindy nudged her. "Handsome Prince Charming is going to show up at your door to pick up his princess and take her to a ball."

Alex shook her head and laughed at the same time. "I don't think either one of us qualifies as your stereotypical prince or princess. And a '79 Ford pickup isn't exactly a carriage."

Mindy just tossed her hair. "Works for me."

A minute later, the other woman brought them several dresses to choose from. "Why don't you start with these and I'll see what else we have."

Mindy picked through them, discarding the ones that were too short or revealing. Finally, she handed Alex a knee-length, ruched satin dress with thin straps. "Try this one."

Alex eyed it. It wasn't anything she was used to, but she carried it into the dressing room. She changed into the dress and zipped it up as best she could before glancing in the mirror and stepping out from behind the curtain so that Mindy could see.

Her friend studied her for a moment, but the fact that she didn't light up said enough.

"I feel like a little girl dressing up in her mom's clothes," Alex told her.

Mindy nodded. "Yeah, it's not quite your style. It's too . . ." she wrinkled her nose, "cocktail hour. We need something that is elegant, but still matches your personality."

She handed over a black lace dress. For the next few minutes, Alex tried on each of the outfits. Some she liked and some she didn't. This obviously wasn't wedding dress shopping, but none of them spoke to her as 'the one.' Maybe she just wasn't used to dressing up like this. She would probably have to let Mindy pick for her. They seemed to have narrowed it down to two when the woman came back with one more dress.

"I just found this one. I thought we were sold out, but this is the last one we have in stock."

Mindy took it and held it up. The soft, silky black fabric did look promising. So did Mindy's giddy grin.

"If that's not a sign, I don't know what is."

Alex took it into the dressing room, slipped it on, and peered into the mirror. It was a chiffon A-line dress, fitted snugly at the waist, with a hi-lo skirt, subtle sweetheart neckline, and see-through lace sleeves that reached her wrists. It wasn't anything like the snug little cocktail dresses that were so plentiful and definitely not her style.

"What are you thinking in there?" Mindy asked from the other side of the curtain.

Alex must have spent more time looking at this dress than she had all the others. She pushed the curtain aside and stepped out.

"Ooo." This time Mindy's brows lifted and her eyes widened a bit. "That looks fabulous on you." She walked around Alex, inspecting it from every angle. "It fits you well too. What do you think?"

Alex's smile creeped out. She imagined this was as close to being a princess as she was going to get. "I like it."

Mindy's grin broke out full force. "And you know what? I have the perfect pair of black velvet heels that would go amazing with this dress."

They hadn't always been able to wear the same clothes; however, they'd always shared shoes. And Alex was glad because she didn't have anything that would go with the dress. She only owned two pairs of simple heels that were probably a little worn out by now.

She turned to look in the mirror again. The dress made her seem taller and not quite so lacking in feminine curves. Now she would just have to wait to see what it looked like with Mindy's shoes and her hair and makeup done.

"Do you think Riley will like it?"

Mindy grinned over her shoulder at their reflection. "Girl, he's not going to be able to keep his eyes off you." She gave Alex a sly wink. "Just so long as he keeps his hands off."

"Mindy!" Alex's cheeks flushed.

"I'm just sayin'."

Alex shook her head. "So how much is it?" She was afraid to look for the price tag. "Am I going to have to starve myself for the next three months?"

"Let's see." Mindy searched the dress until she found the tag in the back of the collar. Alex felt a little tug and Mindy stepped away, the tag in her hand. "You won't starve because I'm buying it for you."

"What? Mindy, no. How much is it?" She stepped toward her and reached for the tag. "Give me that."

Mindy held it up over her head the same way Zach had done with the pumpkin cookies.

"You know you won't be able to reach it, especially since I'm in heels."

Alex let her arm drop. "Come on, Min. I can't let you buy me a frivolous party dress."

"Of course you can." She backed up, grinning. "I'll take care of this and you can change back into your clothes. We still have to find appropriate accessories to go with it."

Alex sighed. A dress like this couldn't be cheap, but Mindy was stubborn when she set her mind to something.

"Will you at least tell me how much it is?"

"Nope," Mindy said over her shoulder as she headed toward the registers.

With another shake of her head, Alex stepped into the dressing room once more where she took another look at the dress. She did love it. Somehow it instilled confidence, like she was actually a grown woman and had a handle on things. She didn't feel like she had no business wearing it. Though she still couldn't hold a candle to movie star-ish Kayla, she didn't actually look too bad herself. She allowed herself a little grin when she thought of Riley seeing her.

Back in her normal clothing, she carried the dress to the registers where Mindy chatted with the clerk. The woman gave her a big smile as she took the dress from Alex to wrap up and bag for her.

Meanwhile, Mindy led Alex over to the jewelry selection to find something to go with the dress. In the end, Alex bought a couple of dainty gold and black rings that would match perfectly and a dangly pair of black earrings. She had more than enough necklaces at home. She was sure she could find something that would work.

With their shopping complete, they headed to a local diner for lunch. Sitting in their booth with warm ham sandwiches, they talked more about last night's dinner, and Mindy encouraged Alex about the party. Alex could hardly eat with so many mixed emotions. She was scared out of her wits to mingle with everyone, but she couldn't wait to meet Moretti. Would he like her and her paintings? Or would all her dreams be crushed in one fell swoop? She honestly didn't know how she would take rejection from him.

"So," Mindy said after a bite, "I'll come over Saturday afternoon before you leave and help you get ready."

"You don't have to do that."

"What's the point of living only twenty minutes away from your best friend if not for times like this?"

Alex would be grateful for Mindy's help and expertise, especially if her hair chose not to cooperate, which usually happened right when she needed most for it to work out.

"Thanks, Min."

Chapter Twenty-six

ALEX CHECKED THE WEATHER RADAR ON HER PHONE AGAIN, careful with her freshly painted black nails. Though dry, she figured she couldn't be too cautious. She could just see herself chipping them right before it was time to leave. Her head tugged back as Mindy worked on pulling her hair up into an elegant holiday up-do. Staring at the huge blue blotch on her phone screen, she winced.

"Not looking good?" Mindy asked, spritzing Alex's head with hairspray.

"It looks like there's a lot of snow coming. It just depends on whether or not it will hit us." She drew a deep breath in a fight to calm the butterflies that had been relentless all day. Of course there would be a potential blizzard tonight of all nights. "Maybe I should call Riley."

She tapped on his name and held the phone to her ear as she stared at her closet door. Mindy wouldn't let her see what she was doing until she finished. It was a little scary, but Mindy was the expert.

Riley's phone rang twice before he answered.

"Have you been looking at the weather?" she asked.

"Yeah, it looks like the worst of it will be north of us and hopefully won't get here until later."

"Do you still think we should go?"

A noticeable pause followed the question. Though he'd put effort into not being as moody as last week, this party must be

239

the very last thing he had any desire to do. He'd probably be grateful for any excuse not to go. And, if she was honest, a little piece of her wanted an excuse too.

But when he spoke, he sounded nothing but confident. "It'll be fine. I don't think it's going to hit us. And a little snow is the reason I have a truck."

Alex couldn't help but smile. Josh would have said something similar. "Okay. I guess I'll see you in a little bit then."

They said goodbye and hung up. Alex gazed for a moment at his picture on her phone. What was he doing to get ready? Would he spurn convention and wear jeans with a shirt and tie like he had the other night, or would he dress formally too? She didn't mind either way, but she was more than a little curious what he would look like in a suit. And even though she'd laughed at Mindy, she couldn't quite get her friend's Handsome Prince Charming comment out of her head.

After a bunch of pinning and more hairspray, Mindy finally finished with her hair and moved on to the makeup. Alex closed her eyes as Mindy applied eyeshadow and liner. While she worked, a knock came from the apartment door, but Alex remained still. Zach was in the living room watching TV, so he could answer it. A second later, the door opened, and she heard him greet Riley. The two of them talked, and Alex fought to keep her knee from bouncing. She didn't know if it was just the nerves about tonight or anxiousness to see Riley. Probably both.

When at last Mindy announced she was finished, she helped Alex slip on the velvet heels she had loaned her. They were a lot taller than Alex was used to, but she had taken Mindy's advice and worn them around her apartment during the week to get used to them. She was fairly certain now she wouldn't fall and break an ankle. Hopefully. Tonight it would actually be a good thing she was a bit short—otherwise these heels would have made her taller than Riley.

240

She stepped to her mirror to take in her reflection. Her smile began slowly, growing wider at Mindy's handiwork. Everything from the stunning up-do to the smoky eye shadow to the deep red lipstick was perfect. She actually looked like she could walk a red carpet, and it was all Mindy. If she had not bought the dress or made her up like this, Alex would not be nearly so ready for this party. She turned to her.

"Thank you so much. It's perfect. I really do feel a little like Cinderella."

Mindy grinned. "I'm glad you think so, because you look stunning."

Alex hugged her then, thanking God for such a wonderfully kind and caring friend.

Mindy tipped her head toward the door when they parted. "Shall we show your prince?"

Alex laughed lightly, the butterflies all aflutter once more. They stepped out of the bedroom and down the short hall to the kitchen. The moment Riley caught sight of her, he stopped mid-sentence in his conversation with Zach. It was every girl's dream reaction, and Alex couldn't stop from grinning. He didn't even have to say anything—his eyes said it all—and it felt pretty good.

Though he wore his leather jacket, he did have on suit pants and a pair of polished black shoes. He looked awfully fine and princely standing there, and her heart joined the butterflies in fluttering a bit. Their lives were no fairytale, but she believed this moment was worthy of one.

As she drew nearer, Zach put his hand on Riley's shoulder and murmured something. This was the only thing that broke Riley's attention away from her. He glanced at Zach and nodded.

"I will," she heard him say quietly.

She stood in front of him now, and they shared a smile, his eyes holding with hers.

"You look beautiful," he said, his deep voice sending a little shiver through her.

"Thank you."

A moment later, he reached into his pocket and pulled out a long, thin black box. "I got something for you."

He opened the lid. Contrasted against the white satin lining lay a gold North Star necklace studded with tiny sparkling white gems.

Her mouth dropped open, and all that came out was a breathless, "Riley."

"I know how much you like the stars," he said.

She looked up into his eyes, shaking her head a little. "You shouldn't have." The necklace probably cost more than this dress Mindy had bought her. "You should've saved—"

He interrupted her with a gentle, "Turn around."

Alex snapped her mouth shut and complied. He put the necklace around her neck and clasped it. It hung perfectly just above the neckline of the dress. She looked down at it, her eyes suddenly watery, and then turned back to him.

"Thank you. I love it."

That's when Alex noticed how intently Mindy and Zach stood watching them, almost as if they were proud parents. Her cheeks flush a little. Mindy then sprang into action, grabbing her phone.

"Before you two are off, I need to get a photo. Alex, your mom made me promise to text her one."

Alex smiled and shifted to Riley's side. He put his arm around her as they faced Mindy, who quickly snapped several photos.

"Perfect," she said with a grin. She then grabbed the long, black wool peacoat she had loaned Alex and helped her slip it on.

"Drive safe," Mindy instructed, "especially if it does start to snow before you're on your way back. If it gets bad, remember, you're welcome at our house."

"We will," Riley told her, and Alex had complete confidence in his care.

"We'll lock up for you," Mindy said.

Alex gave her a quick hug and then turned to Riley. At the door, he offered his arm, and with a grin, Alex slipped hers around it. He led her down the stairs and to his truck, steadying her. She glanced up at the sky and could tell it was heavy with clouds, though no snow fell yet.

"Don't worry. I'll get you home safe."

She sent Riley a grateful and trusting look as he opened the truck door for her and helped her in. She buckled up as he got in the driver's side, and then she checked her purse for the hundredth time to make sure her portfolio was in there. It was easy to forget, in the whirlwind of preparation, the whole point of tonight. It wasn't the party but rather her meeting with James Moretti. She so desperately wanted it to go well. It was a once in a lifetime chance. If she messed it up, she probably wouldn't get another.

She focused on breathing deeply like Mindy had told her. She must have been doing it louder than she thought because Riley asked, "Will you be all right?"

She forced a smile. "Mmhm." But she immediately shook her head. "I'm just scared to death." And fighting every urge to panic. How had she even survived college and decided to be an artist, anyway?

"You'll do fine, and we can leave any time you want. Just tell me and we'll go."

She let her breath out slowly, willing her nerves to quiet down, and tried to think about something other than Moretti. Any preplanned words or speeches would just fly right out of her head upon meeting him anyway. She recalled dinner last Sunday. At least Riley's parents liked her. That certainly made things easier, though they still intimidated her. It probably wouldn't take much to turn their opinion of her. And then there was Kayla. It shouldn't matter, but she was just so . . . perfect. Even in this dress, Alex was still just a country girl at heart.

"Out of curiosity, what does Mark's wife do?"

"She was a model. Now I think she works as a consultant for the agency she used to model for."

That explained it then. She knew exactly how to project herself around others. Alex had never been good at that.

"Hey."

She looked over at Riley.

"She's got nothing on you."

Alex smiled at him. "You're sweet."

"I mean it. I'd choose you any day."

His words warmed her heart and boosted her confidence. He probably didn't even realize how much it meant to her considering how many drop-dead gorgeous women like Kayla there were out there. "Thank you."

With a silent prayer for peace and guidance tonight, her nerves calmed a little. She looked again at Riley. "And thank you for taking me tonight. I know how difficult it must be."

He shrugged. "I've been through a lot worse. I can handle an evening with my parents."

"Just remember, I love the man you are, and it doesn't matter to me that you work at a bar and maybe don't have life all figured out yet." She hoped her words would be as comforting as his were to her.

Though he kept his eyes on the road as they drove out of Aspen Creek, she could see his smile.

Chapter Twenty-seven

EXPENSIVE LUXURY AND SPORTS CARS LINED THE DRIVEWAY AT the Conrad's house. Riley had the only truck that Alex could see, and not one of the cars appeared to be more than five years old.

"No blending in here," she said dryly.

Riley snorted. "No chance."

When he'd parked, he opened her door and took her hand to help her out. She steadied herself on Mindy's stiletto heels and grabbed her purse. Riley offered his arm again, and they walked toward the lit up front door. About halfway to the house, Alex released a nerve-filled laugh.

"What's so funny?"

"Everything. I never could've imagined myself dressed like this and walking into this sort of Christmas party. It's so out of my comfort zone it's ridiculous."

"Just be you and don't worry about the people inside."

Alex gave a short nod and drew a long breath of the frosty air.

At the door, he rang the doorbell. While they waited, she asked, "Do you think you'll see a lot of people you know tonight?"

"Probably family I haven't seen since I enlisted."

She got the distinct impression he didn't look forward to it. It would probably be like her visiting her home church. Too many people to possibly judge his life choices, and most if not all would be doing it without a hint of Christ-like love.

Before either of them could speak again, the door opened. Mrs. Conrad stood on the other side and welcomed them with a smile. "Riley, Alex, I'm so glad you were able to make it. Please, come in."

They stepped into the foyer, greeted by the buzz of voices, Christmas jazz, and an appetizing aroma of food. They slipped off their coats, and Riley helped his mom hang them up. This gave Alex a chance to check out Riley's suit. Under his black suit jacket, he wore a light blue shirt and darker striped tie that made his eyes look bluer. Forget him not being able to keep his eyes off her; she would probably stare at him most of the night.

He turned and caught her watching, and she smiled shyly. He gave her a long look in return, as if to say that if she was going to look at him like that, then he would do the same. She hoped his mom didn't notice the exchange, but Riley didn't seem to care in the slightest.

"Everyone is in the living room," Mrs. Conrad said.

Alex snapped her attention to the other woman, and they followed her.

"Help yourselves to the drinks and hors d'oeuvres."

They stepped into the living room where thirty or so people mingled. Mr. Conrad loomed across the room with Mark, talking to a couple of other men. Kayla stood nearby with a group of women, dressed in a burgundy off-the-shoulder cocktail dress. But Alex didn't pay much attention. Instead her gaze zeroed in on a man in a white suit jacket and navy vest with a red tie and red handkerchief in his front pocket. His black hair was slightly messy, yet in a completely stylish way, and he had a perfectly trimmed goatee. He was quite handsome and certainly stood out amongst the guests.

"Oh." Her heart rate sped up. "That's him. That's James Moretti." She could hardly believe she stood in the same room.

"He seems interesting."

She gave a little breathless laugh. "Well, he is an artist."

"Riley!"

They both turned at the female voice right as a young, dark-haired woman rushed up and threw her arms around his neck.

"Hey, Jen," he responded with a chuckle, hugging her back. "I'm so glad you came." The girl, who was around Alex's age, stepped back, talking rapidly. "I was so disappointed I couldn't make it to supper last Sunday." Her gaze then shifted. "You must be Alex."

She nodded, sharing the young woman's smile.

"It's so good to meet you. I was so excited when I saw your photos on Riley's Facebook."

Riley quickly stepped in to say, "Alex, this is my baby sister Jennifer."

"Jenny, please, or just Jen. Jennifer is so old fashioned." She rolled her eyes dramatically.

Alex laughed and greeted her. She could definitely see Jen as the baby of the family. She had that slightly spoiled, happy-go-lucky, everything-is-perfect type of vibe. After all, Alex was the youngest child herself, though life had given her a different view of the world.

A young man sauntered up to them. He too wore a white suit, though he paired it with a magenta shirt and didn't pull it off nearly as well as Moretti. This guy was clean shaven and had a bit of beach boy surfer hair going on.

He came up behind Jen and put his arms around her. "Are you going to introduce me, babe? Or should I be jealous of you hugging other men?"

Jen giggled. "Of course not. You've seen pictures of Riley before. Riley, Alex, this is my boyfriend, Trey."

He greeted both of them with a flashing grin Alex had no doubt was dangerous. She could tell when Riley shook his hand he was not impressed, judging by the way his jaw muscles twitched. Especially when Trey's gaze slid unabashedly down the length of Alex's dress. Jen didn't seem to notice, but if Alex caught Riley giving another woman that kind of look she would seriously question their relationship. Noticing a pretty woman was one thing. Ogling her was a different thing entirely.

Riley cleared his throat. "How is it you know my sister?"

Trey nuzzled Jen's neck, making her giggle again. Alex only just kept from rolling her eyes. She didn't have a problem with public displays of affection, but this was just silly.

"My dad owns Lily Vahn."

Clearly he expected that to mean something, but when neither Alex nor Riley reacted, Jen said, "That's the fashion company I work for."

"So," Alex said, searching for an easy topic, "you design clothing?"

"I do. I used to draw dresses all the time growing up. I can't believe I get to do it for a living. My mom tells me you're an artist, and well, I did creep on your Facebook profile a little."

Alex just smiled. After all, she had done her own creeping. "Yes."

"Wait until you meet James. He's eager to see your work. He and Dad were talking about it when he arrived."

"Really?" Alex glanced toward the artist. He happened to catch her eye and gave her a slight nod and smile. She returned it before he was once more caught up in his conversation with the other guests.

Her heart thumped her ribs, and she had to fight her inner fangirl. Her favorite artist actually knew she existed.

Other acquaintances of Riley's started to gather around, and he introduced her to them. Most were extended family. Though everyone was nice, some were less genuine than others. One man Riley introduced as his cousin Quinton practically towered over the two of them. He was a bit gangly with a noticeably receding hairline. And he loved to hear himself talk. First he went on about everything that was wrong in their military. Then, as soon as he heard Alex was an artist, he launched into a dissertation on the arts and how lacking modern art was as if he were an expert on the subject. Alex just smiled and nodded. It was really all she could do since he never gave her an adequate chance to speak. Not that she particularly wanted to.

At last, Riley excused them both and guided her toward the refreshments table. Along the way, he murmured near her ear, "You have no idea how badly I wanted to punch him in the face while we were growing up."

Alex put her hand to her mouth to stifle a laugh. "I can just imagine." She had a sudden pang of longing for Josh to be here. He'd been an expert at verbal sparring. She would've loved to see him take on Quinton and could perfectly imagine the knowing little smile her brother would have sent her way once Quinton was good and worked up.

Moisture burned her eyes, and she blinked hard. Now was not the time or place to let her emotions take hold.

They reached one of the tables along the wall laden with platters of hors d'oeuvres. She hadn't eaten much all day, so she picked up one of the small crystal plates stacked to the side.

"No paper party plates, huh?"

He shook his head. "Definitely not."

She perused the different platters and put some shrimp, cheese, and little toasts topped with what appeared to be a cream cheese spread and salmon onto her plate. She had no idea what more than half of the hors d'oeuvres actually were, but it all looked good.

"Want a drink?" Riley asked.

"Is there anything non-alcoholic?" She didn't want to try any wine on a nearly empty stomach.

He inspected the bottles of wine and champagne before lifting one no one had opened yet. "Sparkling cherry juice?"

"Perfect."

He poured a glass for her and for himself. They stood off to the side of the gathering while Alex sampled the hors d'oeuvres and enjoyed this moment to collect herself. She didn't know how she could be so excited to meet Moretti while so terrified at the same time. At least he appeared to be a nice guy, judging by his smile. She just prayed he wouldn't turn out to be the snobby sort or a jerk. She'd admired him for so long.

"Riley?"

It was the second time tonight a female voice had called his name. Alex looked over as a rather petite woman in a short, slim black dress with a deep sweetheart neckline approached them. Her blonde hair was a few shades lighter than Alex's and resting on her bare shoulders in perfect curls.

"Amber."

The surprise in Riley's voice resonated through Alex like a lightning strike. *This* was Amber? Before she could stop it, her insides prickled. It was one thing to know Riley had been with other women, but to have one of them standing right in front of her caused more of a reaction than she expected. She drew a deep breath to keep the stormy turmoil swirling up in her middle from displaying itself on her face. She wasn't sure if it was jealousy, fear, or a tangled combination of both, but she worked to calm herself. Riley was not the same man he'd been when he knew Amber.

If only that reassured her.

With a pristine smile, Amber stepped forward to give Riley a hug before he even seemed to know what was happening. He touched his hand lightly to her back but did not hold it there.

"It's so good to see you," she said, parting after only a brief moment. "I was hoping you'd be here tonight."

The smile on her face waited for his response, but only an awkward silence stretched between them as he glanced from her to Alex and back.

Finally, he cleared his throat. "Amber, this is my girlfriend, Alex."

Amber's delicate brows rose before her gaze shifted to Alex. "It's a pleasure to meet you."

Sure. Alex didn't believe that for a moment, and she responded automatically but with little emotion. She had never considered herself a jealous person, but this was just plain uncomfortable.

"So, Riley," Amber's attention swung back to him, "what have you been up to? I heard you were living in this little town . . . what was it?"

"Aspen Creek," he answered, his voice sounding taut to Alex.

"It must be quite interesting for you to leave all of the opportunities here in Denver."

"It's quiet." He cleared his throat again. "I heard you married Dean."

"Oh." Amber waved her hand like it was inconsequential. "That ended over a year ago. We're both better off for it."

Alex shifted and forced her fingers to loosen around her glass of sparkling cherry juice. She didn't want to shatter it or something. If Amber was divorced, she had nothing stopping her from attempting to rekindle a relationship with Riley. Not that Alex believed Riley could be swayed, but the mere threat left her battling a gnawing ache in her core. She drew a deep breath and prayed the woman wouldn't come between them in any way. She also prayed for peace from the nagging discomfort inside, whether it be jealousy or fear. Of the many scenarios she had imagined for tonight, this one caught her off guard entirely.

She almost whispered thanks out loud when Mr. Conrad joined them. He wasn't exactly an ideal rescue, but at least it made this awkward trio less uncomfortable. He greeted them with a smile before his attention turned solely to Alex.

"I'm so glad you made it. James is quite anxious to meet you."

"Really?" She fought to ignore Amber's presence and focus on why she was here.

"Yes. If I'm not interrupting, I'll introduce you to him."

"Not at all," she said, perhaps a bit too eagerly. "I'm very anxious to meet him as well."

Mr. Conrad gestured across the room toward Moretti, and Alex followed him. Behind her, Riley excused himself. She glanced over her shoulder to see him leave Amber standing alone. However, she quickly gathered up her scattered thoughts and focused on meeting Moretti. Her heart rate elevated again. She had to be professional. She *had* to make a good impression.

Drawing near, she realized James Moretti was shorter than she'd first noticed. In her heels, she might even be a smidge taller than him. Maybe she should have worn different shoes. But then, nearly all the women in this room were taller than him in their heels and he didn't seem bothered in the least.

When they reached him, he turned with a grand smile, and Mr. Conrad took over introductions.

"James, this is the young woman I was telling you about, Alex Jennings."

"Miss Jennings, it is a pleasure to meet you." His voice was smooth yet genuine. He was probably quite the heartthrob within his circles.

"I'm sure it's not nearly as great as my pleasure at meeting you, Mr. Moretti. Your work has been hugely inspirational to me."

"Thank you. It's always both gratifying and encouraging knowing you've inspired someone, especially another artist. Have you, by any chance, brought samples of your own work?"

"I did, yes."

"Excellent. I would love to see them."

Alex wanted to pinch herself. Could this be real? She tamped down her glee to release later in private. "I could get my portfolio now, if you'd like."

"Please do."

She nodded and turned. Though she expected to find Riley behind her, he appeared to have been snagged by some of his old acquaintances along the way. He caught her eye and cast her a quick smile. She grinned back, and focused on walking carefully and ladylike to where she had left her purse in the foyer. She would die of mortification if she tripped and fell in front of all these people, but especially in front of Moretti.

She collected her portfolio from her purse and headed back to the living room. On her way in, she caught a glimpse of blonde as Amber, like a bewitching siren, waltzed her way straight toward Riley. Alex bristled again but fought to shake it off. *God, I really don't want this to bother me, especially not right now.* Too much rested on this moment.

She set her focus on Moretti, firmly ignoring any nagging urges to check where Riley and Amber were and if they were talking. The moment she handed over her portfolio to Moretti, all worries of Amber evaporated. Now only a deep, stomach-turning fear engulfed her. She was about to have an artist—a real, established artist—critique her work. She had to fight not to feel sick. Maybe she should have saved the hors d'oeuvres for later. *Just don't faint.*

She stared at Moretti's face as he flipped through the photos she had taken of her best pieces. He was very silent but slowly nodded his head as he studied each piece. Alex could hear her heart pounding, and it seemed to have clogged her throat. Or maybe that was her stomach. She had to keep swallowing, though it didn't help much.

At last, Moretti looked up and said, "Your work is good. You have real talent and a lot of potential."

She released a huge sigh. "Really?" She took another quick breath. "I mean, thank you so much. I can't tell you how much that means to me."

Kindness warmed his smile. "I was where you are once. I understand."

She let out a breathless laugh. All the emotions seemed to rush to her head and almost made her dizzy.

"Perhaps we can talk about getting some of her pieces into McKinley?" Mr. Conrad joined in.

Moretti nodded. "Absolutely."

Alex felt as though she'd died and gone to heaven.

If Riley had forgotten why he'd enlisted and then moved to Aspen Creek, tonight served as a stark reminder. He hated all the fake smiles and how everyone micro-analyzed his life. Worse, he hated their fake sympathies over how he hadn't done anything worthwhile in their eyes. Why couldn't he be around real, hardworking people? Not this group so deluded by their own self-importance they couldn't see beyond earthly accomplishment.

And that was the most aggravating part. He should be overwhelmed with concern for their souls, yet he only wanted to escape them. A poor excuse of a witness for God's love and salvation he made.

As if it couldn't get much worse, he spied Amber making a beeline for him. He'd hoped when he'd walked away with Alex that was the end of it. They had parted painfully in the past, and now she represented a life he had no desire to revisit.

She smiled and exchanged words with some of the other guests as she passed them, always on top of her game. She had a tendency to get what she wanted, and that's what scared him. He hadn't seen it clearly when they were together, but time had shown him how much she had manipulated him with her pouty looks and his attraction to her.

Crossing his arms, he steeled himself and sent a prayer heavenward for aid. She sashayed up to him with a flirty look that used to get him to do almost anything.

"You walked away rather abruptly."

"I was busy." He didn't care if he sounded short. He looked around for Alex. She stood with his dad and the artist, her smile beaming. It must be going well then. At least that.

His attention snapped back to Amber when she rested her hand lightly on his arm. He swallowed hard. While he wasn't attracted to her anymore, her touch brought back everything he fought so hard to forget. He'd been with her in a way he should have saved for his wife—for Alex if that was where their relationship was headed—and to have such a glaring reminder standing right in front of him nearly sent him running for his truck. He hated confronting this now, but all sin had its consequences. Unfortunately, the sins of his youth were catching up to him. He prayed silently for strength and that the consequences wouldn't end up hurting Alex too.

"Amber—"

"You never called me when you got home," she cut in.

She could play innocent all she wanted.

"Why would I have?"

"Riley, we were practically engaged when you left."

"I never proposed."

"Well, I'm sure you would've eventually."

He didn't want to admit he'd been thinking about it. It seemed so foolish now. He hadn't had half the feelings for her that he had for Alex. Just a dangerous mix of lust and skewed, shallow emotions he'd mistaken for love. If he'd stayed in Denver and married her, he'd probably be divorced now.

"You were married. There was no reason to call."

"Well, I would've thought friendship at least would've warranted letting me know how you were."

"We didn't part as friends, Amber."

"I don't consider that entirely my fault. You did leave me."

He breathed out hard and shook his head. "Listen, it was nice to see you, and I'm sorry things didn't work out with you and Dean—"

"I'm not."

She gazed up at him, waiting for a reaction he wouldn't give her.

"I have a girlfriend, remember?"

With that, he turned and walked away. He didn't care if it was rude. Joseph hadn't worried about politeness when he'd fled Potiphar's wife.

He headed in Alex's direction but took a detour when he caught sight of a ridiculous white and magenta suit at the refreshments table. Trey. Riley had caught him checking out not just Alex but other women in the room all evening. Jen was making a horrible decision in dating him, but she probably wouldn't listen if Riley tried to tell her that. Though they got along, she wouldn't see it as his place to intervene considering how long he'd been separated from the family. His next best option was to confront Trey, man to man. Jen probably wouldn't appreciate it, but someone had to say something, and he wasn't in the mood to let it slide.

Trey grinned and said Riley's name rather loudly, as if they were old pals. No doubt more than a little alcohol contributed to his good mood. Man, he hated these spoiled rich kids. They thought they could get away with murder.

He cut right to the chase. "I don't know if Jen told you, but I was in the military for thirteen years."

"She did mention that. Kind of the Rambo of the family, huh?" He gave Riley a pathetic punch to the shoulder.

Riley glanced down, imagining himself grabbing Trey's wrist and putting him on the ground. The temptation was real, but he kept it contained. "Let's just say I learned a lot about taking guys out, but that's not the point of this conversation. The point is, if you keep eyeing up my girlfriend and other women when you're supposed to be dating my sister, then we're going to have a problem, and trust me, you don't want that. I suggest you learn very quickly what it means to be a gentleman and take things seriously. If not, you and I are going to have a problem."

Trey's face went blank.

Riley forced a cynical smile. "Good talking with you."

He gave Trey his own punch to the shoulder. The other man grunted and reached up to rub his arm as if bruised. Riley smiled a little wider to himself as he walked away to rejoin Alex.

Chapter Twenty-eight

WHEN WAS THE LAST TIME ALEX HAD TALKED ART WITH SOMEONE who fully understood the topic and the lifestyle? Probably not since college. Despite her extreme nerves earlier, James Moretti managed to put her so at ease it was like talking to an old friend. His advice was invaluable, and she couldn't wait to implement it in her own life. Riley joined them eventually, sticking close to her after his conversation with Amber. Though he seemed fine when she introduced him to Moretti, she sensed tension in the way he held himself and how his gaze kept darting to his ex as if he were keeping an eye on a threat.

As much as she would have loved to talk to Moretti all night, Alex did find relief when the party wound down and the guests prepared to leave. She exchanged final words with Moretti on his way out and noticed Mark return from starting their car. Snowflakes dotted the shoulders of his dark coat.

"It's really starting to come down out there," he told his dad. "It's a good thing everyone's heading out."

Alex exchanged a look with Riley, and he pulled out his phone. His taut expression didn't signal anything good.

"Looks like the storm shifted farther south than they predicted."

He showed her the radar. The big, dark blue blotch she'd been watching earlier had moved over their area, and the worst of it was still coming.

"Do you think we can make it to Boulder at least?"

He didn't answer, his lips pinched. Shoving his phone back into his pocket, he turned to Mark. "When you drive out, let me know how the roads are."

Mark nodded. "I will, but judging by how heavily it's already snowing, I wouldn't recommend heading back to Aspen Creek."

"We just need to make it to Boulder."

Mark and Kayla left a couple of minutes later. While Riley's parents said goodbye to the remaining guests who filed out, Alex took a seat on the couch, and Riley joined her. They were both quiet as they waited. Five minutes later, Riley's phone buzzed, and he answered it. Alex couldn't quite hear what Mark said on the other end, but Riley's short replies didn't sound hopeful.

When he hung up, his parents walked into the now-quiet living room.

"How are the roads?" Alex asked.

"Mark says they're getting slick. The plows are out, but he's not sure there will be many between here and Boulder. At least not for a while. By that time, the brunt of the storm will be hitting." He sighed. "If we take it slow, we should be fine."

"Nonsense." Mrs. Conrad joined them. "It would be foolish to risk it when you can stay here tonight. It could take you hours to get to Boulder, if you do at all."

Riley looked over at Alex. She read the hesitation in his eyes. She wasn't keen on staying either, but his mom was right. People died in blizzards, and neither of them was dressed for the weather. He'd probably sooner get them each a room at a nearby hotel than stay here, but why waste the money by rejecting his mom's invitation and creating even more conflict?

"Maybe it would be wise to stay?"

In the end, his concern for her safety would outweigh how much he wanted to leave, and he nodded.

His mom smiled. "Good, I'll prepare the guestroom for you."

Heat crept up Alex's neck. She should have been prepared

for such an assumption. This wasn't anything like staying with her Christian parents. She scrambled for what to say, but Riley beat her to it.

"I'm sure Alex will be comfortable in the guestroom. I'll sleep in my old room."

Mrs. Conrad's perfect brows lifted in mild surprise. "Oh, all right. I'll get you some of your dad's pajamas, and I'm sure Jenny still has something here for Alex."

She walked away, her heels clicking. Alex sent Riley a grateful look for handling the awkward situation. None of this was ideal, but she had to believe it was better than risking a snowy highway in the middle of a raging blizzard. She remembered past blizzards that had knocked out power and left people stranded for days. She winced. What if they were stranded here? Riley would go insane.

In the quiet of the living room, Mr. Conrad picked up a remote control and turned on the TV above the fireplace. He tuned in to the local weather station where a young meteorologist talked about the downward shift of the storm and how it was stronger than anticipated. They now predicated white-out conditions in most areas and cautioned people to remain indoors. Alex looked at Riley again. It seemed they'd made the right choice.

Mrs. Conrad returned several minutes later and addressed Alex. "I found a pair of Jenny's pajamas for you. I also found jeans and sweaters. If any of them fit you, you can wear them home tomorrow."

"Thank you, Mrs. Conrad. I appreciate it."

"Would you like me to show you the guestroom?"

Alex nodded and rose from the couch. She looked down at Riley. "I think I'll go to bed." It was late, and the day was starting to catch up to her.

They traded goodnights, and Alex followed Mrs. Conrad through the house. When they stepped into the guestroom, Alex

JAYE ELLIOT

took in the space with wide eyes. But then, she shouldn't be surprised that it was every bit as grand as the rest of the house. Really, it was like a fancy hotel room and even had its own bathroom.

"There are toothbrushes and toothpaste in the drawers, and anything else you might need. If you can't find something, just let us know."

Alex thanked her again and then closed and locked the door. The moment she was alone, she kicked off Mindy's heels and sunk her toes into the luxurious carpet. It felt so good to have them off. She hadn't noticed how much her feet ached until now. She found the set of fleece pajamas Mrs. Conrad had left on the bed and carried them into the bathroom where she took a hot shower to wash the hairspray out of her hair. The high-tech shower head was like a massage, and she enjoyed every minute of it.

Once she was cleaned up and cozy in the pajamas, she pulled down the plush satin bedspread and crawled into bed. Resting back against the pillows, she grabbed her phone and sent Mindy a video call.

A moment later, Mindy's face appeared on her screen. "Hey!" Her voice warbled a bit until the video and audio cleared. "I was wondering when we'd hear from you. I can see you're obviously not on your way home."

"No. When we found out the storm had shifted, Mrs. Conrad invited us to stay. Riley wanted to try to make it to Boulder, but we decided it was probably wise to just stay put."

"Yeah, I was worried about you guys. It's really coming down here." Mindy gave her a probing look. "How do you feel about staying?"

Alex tipped her head. "More comfortable than Riley does, I think. He'd probably attempt to drive back if it was just him. Or get a hotel."

Mindy made a face. "Poor boy. Must be hard for him."

262

"Yeah."

"So how was the party?" Mindy asked, getting animated again. Behind her, Alex caught Zach making faces, and she laughed. Mindy looked back and gave him a light smack on the shoulder. Still laughing, Alex said, "It wasn't too bad. I had the most amazing time talking to Moretti. He's such a nice and fascinating guy. He said he loved my work, and he and Mr. Conrad plan to try to get it into McKinley."

Mindy squealed just as Alex knew she would.

"That's awesome! This is what you've been dreaming of. How soon will you know?"

"Moretti is going to call me when he has a meeting set up with the art director. It should be soon."

"I'm so excited for you! Now I'll always be able to say that I knew you before you were famous."

"I'm not famous yet."

Mindy shrugged as if that particular fact were inconsequential. "So, did you meet any interesting members of the Conrad family?"

"Well, I met Riley's younger sister. She seems nice. Her boyfriend is a creep though. He kept checking me out."

Mindy screwed up her nose. "You should have walked up and slapped him."

"And cause a scene?" Alex shook her head at Mindy's nonsense. She paused. Why was she even thinking about this? "I also met Riley's ex."

Mindy's brows shot up to her bangs. "And?"

Alex blew out a hard breath. "And I'm trying really hard not to be jealous. I know Riley isn't into her anymore, but she's very... persistent. I don't like her."

"I wouldn't either."

"I just wish I didn't feel so . . . threatened. I mean, I know Riley won't betray me, but I can't help this nagging fear. I know it's just my insecurities, and I wish it would go away."

"It's natural to feel threatened, but Riley is a good guy. Remember, I've seen the way he is with you, and I can't imagine him betraying you. Don't worry about it."

Alex breathed slowly now. It did help to hear Mindy say that. Her phone chimed, and a text appeared at the top.

"He just texted me. '*You all right for the night?*'"

She sent a text back that she was. A moment later, he responded, *I'll see you in the morning.*

"See," Mindy said, "he's thinking about you, not her. And if it's still bothering you tomorrow, talk to him about it. It's better than holding it inside and letting it grow into unfounded suspicion."

"I will. Thanks."

They said goodnight, and Alex ended the video chat. She sent a quick text to her mom about the evening's developments and then sat for a moment thinking over the day before reaching to switch off the lamp and scooching down farther beneath the covers.

After Alex went to bed, Riley found himself alone in the living room. His dad had wandered off somewhere, probably to get ready for bed himself. He stared at the fireplace for a couple of minutes and then looked around the room. He had grown up in this house. Much of it was the same, yet more modern and updated. And it obviously didn't have kids staying at home anymore.

His stomach growled. He'd been roped into too many conversations with old acquaintances to take advantage of the table of hors d'oeuvres. The housekeeper had already cleaned up everything before leaving for the night. He pushed himself up from the couch and wandered into the kitchen.

Did his mom still get those good artisan crackers she had always loved? He opened one of the cabinets and smiled faintly. A box sat right where she always kept them. Surely she wouldn't mind if he had a few. He set the box on the long, marble-topped island and opened the fridge. In one of the drawers, he found a wedge of Asiago cheese.

He shrugged off his suit coat and draped it over a stool on the other side of the island and loosened his tie. He then searched the drawers for a knife to cut a few slices of cheese.

Leaning against the counter, he munched on the crackers and cheese, satisfying his hunger. A couple of minutes later, footsteps approached. Dad walked into the kitchen. He too had shed his suit coat, though his tie was still properly in place. He glanced at Riley but remained silent as he approached the counter and drew a wine glass from a rack under the cabinets. He then pulled a bottle from the wine rack, one of his old favorites. He poured himself a glass before looking at Riley again.

"Wine?"

Riley responded with a brief nod. If his dad was feeling kind enough to drink with him, he wouldn't turn it down. He sipped from the glass of the red wine Dad handed him. He'd once stolen a bottle of it from the wine cellar to share with teammates after a football game. That stunt had gotten him benched for the next game. And it probably would have for the game after that too if they hadn't been facing their arch rivals. They should've benched him for the season.

"I'm glad you brought Alex tonight," Dad broke the silence between them. "James was impressed with her. I'm confident that, between the two of us, we can get some of her work into McKinley."

Riley smiled, something that rarely came easily around his dad. "She deserves it. She's gone through a lot to get where she is."

Dad took a sip of wine, eyeing him as if he were measuring his worth. Riley held his gaze in a refusal to be intimidated.

"And what about you?" Dad asked finally. "What is it you're working toward?"

Riley bit back a sigh. Could they not share a moment of peace between them?

When he didn't answer immediately, his dad pressed on, "You can't expect to get by forever working at a bar. You're not in your twenties anymore. You should be well established by now, especially if you intend to support a wife and family." He inclined his head toward the door, clearly indicating Alex.

Riley gritted his teeth. He knew exactly what he wanted for his life, he just didn't know yet if he could attain it. And the last thing he wanted was to share his desires with his dad who had a habit of bulldozing right over his dreams.

"I don't know what the future holds." He would keep working toward opening a coffee shop, if that was the future God had planned for him. Beyond that, he didn't have an answer.

Dad shook his head, his forehead creasing. "So much potential and you simply waste it."

Riley set his wine glass down and straightened away from the counter. "How would you know my potential when you've never taken the time to truly know me?"

"You're a Conrad. That should mean something to you. We don't just drift along in life. We make things happen."

Riley shook his head, his temper boiling up. He was a Conrad all right. "That doesn't mean I can't have my own life or that my pursuits are any less worthy than Mark's or Jenny's. The moment I showed the smallest bit of interest in cooking you shoved me right into culinary school. You never paused for one second to learn who I am or what made me tick."

He paused just briefly, but he'd gone too far to stop now. "Do you even realize you and Mom never showed up for a single one of my football games? I was good, Dad. I might've gone into sports professionally if I'd only had your support. I had dreams. I still have dreams. But you don't seem to think they're good enough. I'm sick of trying to measure up. It's why I enlisted. It may have been an escape, and I'm truly sorry for whatever it cost you, but I'm proud to have fought for this country. I'm proud to have fought alongside heroes like Alex's brother. But the worst of it is, I don't think you share that pride."

"Of course we're proud of your service, but it doesn't negate the fact that it took away thirteen years of your life and now you're left with nothing but scraping together a living from a bar job."

Riley shook his head again. Dad just didn't get it. He was lucky to have a job when so many homeless veterans would've done anything to be in his place. But just because his last name happened to be Conrad, it wasn't good enough. Never good enough.

"I'm thankful to have that job and am trusting God for the rest."

Dad scoffed. "Trusting God."

"Yes, God," Riley snapped. "The one who saw fit to bless you with the wealth and success you enjoy even though you and Mom have never acknowledged Him. I may never enjoy such success, but at least I know exactly where I'm going when this life ends. Wealth and success here mean nothing in the end, so whether or not my life ever measures up to your standards won't matter."

He sucked a hard breath, guilt grating on his conscience. Here he'd had the perfect opportunity to share his faith in love, but instead he'd spat it out in anger. His dad would never be receptive to that.

"Fine." Dad's voice rose to match his. "Throw your life away. You've already done a perfectly good job of it. I had an offer for you, but if you'd rather slog along as you are, be my guest."

267

Riley narrowed his eyes. "What offer?"

Dad paused for a moment and adjusted his tie as if composing himself. When he spoke again, his tone was all business. "As you may remember, I own the Royale Restaurant downtown. The head chef is looking at retirement. Were you in any kind of mood to do the smart thing, he would be willing to take you on and teach you everything he knows. Once he retires, he would hand his position as head chef over to you. The restaurant would be yours to run."

He set his empty wine glass aside and stepped closer to Riley. "Think about it. This may be the last decent chance you'll ever get."

He then stalked past him and out of the kitchen. The silence he left behind was oppressive. Riley hadn't expected such an offer, but the question of what to do with it just stoked the turmoil raging inside of him. One part of him felt it might be wise to accept. A larger part of him seethed with the idea his dad thought this offer was the only way he would succeed at anything—that he would be a failure if not for his parents' intervention.

Unable to banish the emotions, he put away the cheese and his mom's crackers and headed upstairs to his room in a foul mood. What he wouldn't give to be back home in his apartment right now with only Tux for company. That old punching bag of his would probably have seen quite the workout. While under his parents' roof, he felt as if his life wasn't his own—like he was that immature, rebellious teenager again, struggling to find his way.

When he stepped into his room, he paused. Nothing had changed since he'd left for the military. His desk and old computer still sat in the corner and a couple of rock band posters remained on the walls. He probably still had *Sports Illustrated* magazines or worse stuffed under his mattress, as if that wasn't the first place his mom would've looked. And all at once, memories of Amber assaulted him.

He closed his eyes and fought to banish the past. If only he could go back in time and talk to the kid he used to be—the kid who wasn't concerned with the future, only the present. If only he could tell himself that his actions would have consequences, even now.

He yanked off his tie and changed into the flannel pajama pants and white undershirt his mom had left folded on the bed. Exhaustion weighed heavily, but he could not stay in this room. Grabbing the pillow from the bed, he walked back out. In the hall closet, he found a heavy blanket and returned quietly to the living room. He turned the fireplace on low and made himself comfortable on the couch. Though he craved sleep, he spent a long time praying before it ever came.

Chapter Twenty-nine

ALEX STRETCHED, SURROUNDED BY DOWN COMFORTER AND FLUFFY pillows. For sleeping in a strange place, she'd slept really well. Of course, the party and earlier preparations had tired her out. She probably would have slept like a baby anywhere.

She pushed down the comforter that half covered her face and looked toward one of the windows. White, crisp snow covered everything. From here, she guessed they had gotten several inches at least. She reached for her phone and her glasses. A text from Mom had come in late. She said she was glad they hadn't driven in the snow and told Alex how beautiful she looked in her dress.

With a smile, Alex dialed her mom's phone. A couple of rings later, Mom answered.

"Hey, I thought I'd give you a call after last night. I wanted to before bed, but I was exhausted."

"How did it go?" Mom asked.

Alex filled her in on all that had happened at the party, getting giddy all over again about meeting Moretti. She shared a little bit about Riley's family and let her know that she and Riley had spent the night in separate rooms. It was a way to keep accountable.

They kept the conversation brief, and after saying goodbye, Alex crawled out of bed. She inspected the clothing Mrs. Conrad had left for her and found a pair of jeans that fit pretty well and a long, comfy sweater. She loved the dress she had worn last night, but she would choose jeans any day.

After freshening up in the bathroom and braiding her hair, she wandered out of the guestroom. The house was very quiet, but the alluring scent of coffee led her into the kitchen. The room was huge, with tall stained cabinets, marble counter tops, and state of the art stainless steel appliances. It looked like a page out of a luxury home magazine. It probably was. Her attention shifted to Mrs. Conrad, who turned when she entered. Though dressed more casually today, she still projected refinement in a pair of dark corduroy pants and an ivory cable knit sweater.

Her open smiled comforted Alex. Though she could be intimidating, so far Alex liked Riley's mom. She'd been so afraid both of his parents would hate her.

"Coffee?" Mrs. Conrad asked.

"Yes, please." Alex approached the counter where she poured a mug. "I'm a bit addicted."

The woman's smile widened. "Riley always was too. I think he started drinking it when he was thirteen, against my better judgment."

Alex grinned to imagine thirteen-year-old Riley with his coffee. Is that when his dream of a coffee shop had taken root? She would have to ask him.

"Is he up yet?"

Mrs. Conrad tipped her head toward the doorway out of the kitchen. "He's passed out on the couch in the living room."

Alex frowned slightly. Hadn't he planned to sleep in his old room? In a house this big, surely he had somewhere besides the living room to sleep, but his mom's expression said she didn't understand it either.

"I'll bring a mug in to him and see if he's awake yet."

She poured another large mug of coffee and fixed it with cream and sugar the way Riley liked it—sweet, though not quite as sweet as she liked hers. She then carried both mugs into the living room.

The sight of him bundled up on the couch in a heavy quilt, his hair half falling out of his hair tie, brought a smile to her face. She could more easily imagine him as a young boy now. It seemed everyone looked younger in their vulnerable sleeping state. If only she could cuddle up with him, but she promptly whisked that thought out of her mind. Instead, she set his mug on the coffee table and contented herself with sitting on the unoccupied section of the couch near the fireplace. She hated to wake him after the long night, so she sipped her coffee quietly.

A large album on the end table caught her attention. She reached for it and flipped it open. Old Conrad family photos greeted her. She grinned to herself at a photo of Riley and his siblings on Christmas when they were little. Now she didn't have to just imagine him as a boy. He looked like an adorable little troublemaker at that age. After scanning the rest of the photos, she flipped to another page.

A few minutes later, the scent of coffee must have roused Riley. He shifted under the quilt and stretched. When his eyes blinked open, she said, "Good morning."

He looked at her. "Hey." His voice was groggy.

"I brought you coffee." She nodded to the mug on the coffee table where a little steam still curled around the rim.

He glanced at it, and then sat up. He rubbed the sleep from his eyes and reached back to pull out his hair tie, freeing the rest of his hair. Finally, he grabbed the mug and took a sip before breathing a sigh. His mom did make good coffee. That's probably where he had learned it from.

After a moment to let him fully wake up, she said, "I thought you were sleeping in your room."

Something of a wince crossed his face. "It brought back too many things I didn't want to remember." He seemed to avoid her eyes.

She didn't know what he meant at first but then realized she had a pretty good guess. She looked down at the photo album in her lap again while she processed that discomforting thought.

"I didn't know Amber would be here last night. If I had, I would've warned you."

She looked up and nodded slowly. "It's okay." The insecurity still needled her, but she wouldn't let it be a thing.

"Last I heard she was married. I didn't know they were divorced."

She shrugged, working to let it be unimportant. "It doesn't make any difference." She hesitated, but then added, "Does it?"

He shook his head. "No."

And Alex would leave it at that. To change the subject, she held up the photo album and grinned. "You were quite adorable when you were little."

He laughed quietly, chasing the discomfort from his expression. "I haven't seen those photos in years."

She scooted over to his side, and they scanned the album together as they enjoyed their coffee. They laughed at certain photos, and he gave her background stories. When Mrs. Conrad came in to tell them breakfast would be ready soon, he got up to get dressed and Alex closed the album.

They all gathered in the dining room several minutes later. Riley wore his suit again, though he'd abandoned the coat and tie and hadn't bothered pulling his hair back. Whether that contributed to it or not, definite tension existed between him and his dad. They both avoided looking at or even acknowledging each other this morning. Had something happened after Alex had gone to bed? They'd seemed on fairly good terms during the party.

Breakfast consisted of savory egg bake with sautéed mushrooms and onions. Alex wasn't sure if Mrs. Conrad had made it or if their housekeeper had prepared it ahead of time. Either way, it was delicious. She expected nothing less. She couldn't quite imagine the Conrads beginning their morning with a quick bowl of cold cereal.

Mrs. Conrad led the conversation, mainly talking to Alex about her art. Mr. Conrad joined in here and there, but Riley remained stubbornly silent throughout the meal. The moment each of their plates were empty, he pushed back his chair.

"We should get going." He sounded as if they couldn't leave fast enough. "The roads should be clear by now."

Alex nodded and excused herself to gather up her purse and dress. When she rejoined Riley, Mr. and Mrs. Conrad followed them to the foyer.

"I will send the clothes back," Alex said as she slipped on her coat.

Mrs. Conrad shook her head. "There's no rush. You can bring them next time you visit."

Alex glanced at Riley. If his mood was any indicator, he wouldn't be up to visiting again any time soon. However, she did anticipate seeing Mr. Conrad in the near future with his offer to help her get a meeting with the art director at McKinley.

As Riley pulled on his own coat, his dad stepped closer to him. "I hope you've given thought to our conversation last night—to my offer."

Alex looked between the two of them, taking particular note of the tired and worn expression that crossed Riley's face in response to whatever his dad referred to.

"I need time to think about it. I can't just give you an answer right away."

"This opportunity won't wait forever."

Riley sighed, and spoke a bit shortly. "I'll give you an answer on the second. Is that soon enough for you?"

"Very well."

Riley turned toward Alex, nodding to his mom, and reached for the door. Alex traded quick goodbyes with his parents before following him outside. Apparently someone had come along to plow the Conrad's driveway for them, for which Alex was grateful. They would have had to trudge through nearly knee-deep snowdrifts otherwise. Riley's truck started up with minimal hesitation, and he turned it around, driving out into the streets of Denver.

Alex peered out the window for a few minutes, enjoying the snowy scene, but when the silence stretched out, she looked over at Riley. "What did your dad offer you?"

He sighed again and didn't answer for a moment. "A job."

She lifted her brows.

"He wants me to take over a restaurant he owns. The head chef is retiring and apparently has agreed to teach me everything he knows."

She let this news sink in. On the surface, it was a great opportunity—a chance to jump right into a job that could pay off big. However, Riley had already told her that he could never see himself in a fancy restaurant. Not only that, but it would mean him leaving Aspen Creek.

"Are you thinking of accepting?"

"I don't know." He glanced over at her. "I'd have to move here to Denver."

"Don't let me stop you if you think this is something you should do. I'll support any decision you make. So please, don't base it on me. Do what you believe is right for you. We can make it work."

"It would be the smart choice."

Though he didn't go on, she heard a huge *but* in his statement. To accept this job—to work in a place his dad owned—went against every reason he had joined the military and left all of this behind in the first place. He would end up exactly in the place he'd tried to escape from, and she struggled to know what to say or how to help. Would it be wise and responsible to accept an offer that would give him stability and certainty for the future?

Or should he hold on to his dreams? *Lord, what do You want for him?* She prayed God would give him the answer. He only had three weeks to make his decision.

Chapter Thirty

THE BAR WAS QUIET ON TUESDAY AFTERNOON. LUKE HAD GONE out to run errands, leaving Riley to take care of things. With no customers currently, he found himself free to focus on his own thoughts—not that it was such a good thing. All he'd thought about for the past couple of days was his dad's job offer. He'd never faced a harder decision. Even enlisting had been easier than this.

Responsibility dictated securing his future, especially if, as his dad had said, he wanted to provide for a wife and family. But accepting the job meant giving up on everything he'd ever wanted. He spent just about every waking moment praying for direction, but God seemed silent in this decision. He just hoped that silence would break before he had to give his dad an answer.

The bell on the door jingled, and he turned, banishing his thoughts to greet the customer. The sight of blonde curls and grinning lips sent his heart tanking into his stomach. As if he didn't have enough to contend with.

"Amber, what are you doing here?"

A smirk played on her mouth, and she slid up onto one of the stools across from him with comfortable familiarity. "I couldn't picture you working in a bar, so I had to come see for myself."

Riley fought down the aggravation welling up inside him. Thank God the bar stood between them. It felt safer that way. The sooner she left the better.

"Can I get you something?"

She tipped her head. "What do you recommend?"

He wouldn't fall for her flirting. He dropped all pretense of professionalism. "What do you want?"

He hadn't meant to sound so harsh, but he wouldn't play her games.

She straightened, her expression losing its smirk. Instead, her eyes deepened, her lips turning pouty. "I was hoping we could talk."

"About?" He grabbed a glass to dry from the sink. It felt too intimate to give her his undivided attention.

"About us, Riley. I wanted to talk at the party, but you wouldn't let me."

She was unbelievable.

"I thought I made it clear there is someone else."

She forged on, undeterred. "Things change."

He shook his head. No wonder she and Dean had split.

When he didn't speak immediately, she leaned over the bar. Good thing her coat was zipped up to her throat. "Come on, Riley, just come back to Denver. Accept your dad's job offer. Give us another chance. Think of what a power couple we could make."

He narrowed his eyes. "How do you know about the job offer?"

She straightened again. "My dad mentioned it. It's a good offer. The Royale is one of the best restaurants in Denver. I know you could do amazing things with it."

He pinched the bridge of his nose. This woman was going to give him a migraine. "What is it about me? Why does everyone try to push me into doing what they want without ever asking what I want?"

She gave him a look like she was humoring him. "All right, what do you want?"

He looked her dead in the eyes. "For starters, I want Alex."

Her face soured, but he didn't give her a chance to protest.

"I want to stay here in Aspen Creek. I want to have a house just outside of town with a couple of horses. I want to get up in the morning and go riding with my wife. I want to raise a family here. I want to start a business that's mine and that I can take pride in, not some plan of my dad's."

The words poured out—dreams he'd never even fully formed until this moment, but they had been inside of him for a while now.

She nodded slowly. "Well, it would take some getting used to, but I could adjust to small town living. It's not like we're far from Boulder."

He almost laughed in disbelief at the sad scene that played in his mind of that scenario. "You know as well as I do you'd be miserable, and so would I. And ignoring every time I mention Alex won't change things."

He grew very serious now. It was time to end this ridiculous game she was trying to play. "We're done, Amber. We were done when you walked away. That was a different life. I'm a new man now, and I have no interest in revisiting the past or the old me. Now if you're here to buy a drink, I'll serve you, but if not, then you should go."

Her eyes rounded, moisture gathering at the rims. He folded his arms. Those fake tears wouldn't work on him. Not anymore. She blinked, the tears vanishing just as quickly, her eyes growing cold. He half expected her to throw a tantrum. Instead, she slipped stiffly off the stool and turned away. He thanked God when she disappeared through the door without another word. With a huge sigh, he put his elbows on the bar and rested his head in his hands, praying the past would finally stay where it belonged.

A minute later, the door opened again. His stomach twisted, and he straightened, brushing his hair out of his face. He did not have the patience for this. However, instead of Amber, Alex slowly approached the bar. Had she seen Amber? Would she think—

"I take it that didn't go well."

So she had seen her. Riley sighed. "No."

Alex nodded and rested her gloved hands on the bar. "She wants you back, doesn't she?"

"Yeah, but it's not happening." He watched for any uncertainty in her eyes.

"I know." She walked around the bar to stand facing him. "That's why, when I saw her through the window, I stayed outside. I knew you'd handle it, and I didn't want to complicate things."

Her trust meant the world to him. Amber had been insanely jealous if he even spoke to another girl, and she'd always made sure he knew it. Alex was in such a different league, he couldn't imagine how he'd ever thought he loved Amber.

He couldn't help himself. He reached up and cupped her cold cheeks in his hands and tipped her head just enough to press his lips to hers. Of all the dreams he'd rattled off to Amber, Alex was the one he wanted most. It didn't matter where or what it would take, he would do whatever he could to hold on to her.

She kissed him back, and he didn't want to stop. However, he forced himself to pull away and put more space between them before either of them could get caught up in the moment and head down a dangerous road. If nothing else, the last couple of days had shown him just how important it was to keep things right between them. He didn't want to face more consequences in the future. He may not be able to change his past, but it was squarely on his shoulders now to keep his present self on the path God intended.

Forcing himself to focus, he asked, "What are you doing in here on a Tuesday anyway?"

She smiled. "I wanted to let you know I got a call from your dad this morning. I'm meeting him and Mr. Moretti at McKinley on Saturday morning." She drew a deep breath, her face a mix of excitement and nerves. "In just a few days, I'll know whether or not my art dreams will come true."

"I'm sure they will. If there's one thing I know about my dad it's that he doesn't give up. But, in the end, it's all you. They wouldn't do this if your work wasn't amazing."

She seemed to blush a little, though it was hard to tell with her cheeks already pink from the cold. "Thank you. I've dreamed of it for so long, I can hardly imagine what it will be like." She hesitated. "I'm not sure how long it will take, but I'll probably be a little late to work on Saturday. I hate to keep doing this to Luke. I feel like I'm taking advantage of his generosity."

"Don't worry about it. He'll want you to go."

She nodded and then gave him a pointed look. "I know you're thinking about taking me, but I'm a big girl. I'm perfectly capable of going on my own. I don't want to drag both of us away from work again."

He crossed his arms. She knew him too well. "Are you sure?" He'd be there for her in a heartbeat if she asked.

"Yes."

The bell rang, and a couple of regulars walked in. Alex glanced at them before saying, "I need to get groceries, but I'll see you tomorrow."

She flashed him a smile and headed out the door. While she didn't flirt like Amber did, the way she looked at him was far more alluring.

Alex never could have imagined how much life would change a few months ago. The day she met Riley had started a whirlwind of events that would never have even crossed her mind. Now today she would be taking her art into the McKinley Art Gallery. She almost had to pinch herself to make sure it was real.

Though barely even light out yet, she stood in front of her mirror to make sure she was ready. She wanted to look professional this morning while still maintaining her own artistic style, so she chose the wool skirt she usually saved for church and a soft red sweater. Paired with warm tights and a cute pair of low heels, she was pleased with her look. She'd French braided her hair and with a few pieces of jewelry to finish the look off, she was as ready as she'd ever be.

In the kitchen, she gathered up her purse and keys and checked her phone. Riley had texted her to see how she was doing. He'd also asked her to text when she made it to the gallery and when she was on her way back. His sweet concern always brought a rather dreamy smile to her face. Before pulling on her coat, she texted him that she was about to leave. A moment later, he responded that he was praying for her. Just knowing that did help her nerves.

Outside, she started up the Jeep and drove out of Aspen Creek. Thankfully, the forecast didn't call for any snow today despite the cloudy sky. She turned on the radio, filling the Jeep with Christmas music, but she kept the volume low as she contemplated and prayed about today. She wasn't sure what had her more nervous—the meeting at McKinley or the plans she'd made for afterward. Plans she hadn't shared with Riley yet.

She passed the forty-five minute drive with a steady stream of prayers—some silent, and others spoken out loud. Pulling into the parking lot of McKinley Art Gallery brought back memories of college. She had come here often and even dragged Mindy along on more than one occasion. It had been so inspiring to see the work of artists she was studying and to daydream about someday seeing her art displayed here. Today that daydream could become reality.

She pulled into a parking spot as close to the entrance as she could so it would be easy to get her paintings. She then grabbed her phone to let Riley know she had made it before getting out of the Jeep. Smoothing her skirt and taking a deep breath, she walked to the wide front doors and went inside. The interior was open and airy with a glass tiled ceiling and angled supports. Riley's dad had designed this building nearly twenty years ago. Alex didn't think it looked outdated at all.

But she wasn't here for the architecture. Just inside, she found Mr. Conrad and Moretti waiting for her. Riley's dad was in one of his usual clean business suits. Moretti wore a dark navy blue suit today, not quite as creative as the one he'd worn at the party, yet a lime green tie and pocket handkerchief added a splash of bright artistic color. Alex was convinced he could wear a fuchsia suit and still pull it off, unlike Jenny's boyfriend.

She greeted both of them with a handshake. The tap of heels drew their attention to a middle-aged woman in a charcoal skirt suit, her dark auburn hair pulled back in a loose bun. She greeted Moretti first, obviously old friends, and then Mr. Conrad. Finally, she turned a kind smile to Alex.

"You must be Miss Jennings. I'm Celia Ray, Gallery Director here at McKinley."

"I'm very pleased to meet you." Alex shook her hand lightly. "This was my favorite place to visit while I was in college. It's been too long since I've been back."

The woman seemed pleased and gestured toward the galleries. "Would you like to take a walk through and see some of our newest pieces? James just brought in a few last week."

"I would love to."

The three of them followed the woman into one of the gallery rooms, and they discussed many of the pieces. However, this was not just a simple stroll through the gallery. In between discussing the art, Celia asked questions about Alex, her time in college, and the art she had done. Alex worked very hard to answer well and professionally and not let her nervousness show overmuch. Mr.

Conrad and Moretti sprinkled in praise here and there, which she would be eternally grateful for. They obviously had confidence in her abilities, and the last thing she wanted was to disappoint them.

Finally, when they had seen most of the art, Celia turned to Alex. "James has told me good things about your work. I would like to see some samples of it."

Alex nodded, breathing deeply to keep the fluttering of panic in her chest from becoming more than that. She reached into her purse and withdrew the folder there. "I have my portfolio, and I have some pieces in my car if you wish to see them."

She handed the portfolio over, which was actually one of the scarier things she had done in her life. All this woman had to do was take a quick look and decide her work wouldn't fit here or wasn't good enough. Just like that, it could be over. But Alex reminded herself it wouldn't mean an end to her art career. McKinley was only one of many avenues she could pursue. It was, however, the one she desired most.

It was almost impossible to read Celia as she flipped slowly through Alex's photos. Alex held her breath nearly the entire time. She glanced at Moretti, who gave her a nod and slight smile. Hopefully, that was a good sign. After all, he knew Celia a whole lot better than she did. She still couldn't believe she was standing here with the endorsement of her favorite artist. Whatever happened now, she thanked God for giving her this amazing opportunity.

At last, Celia looked up. "I would like to see the pieces you brought."

Alex let her breath out slowly, careful not to let it whoosh out in one big gust. If Celia wasn't intrigued with the portfolio, surely she would have just turned her down here and now.

"I will get them."

Mr. Conrad and Moretti both followed her out to her Jeep and helped carry in the five pieces she had brought with her into

Celia's office, where they laid them out to peruse. Celia inspected each one with Moretti, discussing the different features as Alex stood to the side with Mr. Conrad. Her heart nearly beat itself out of her chest while she waited. She had never had her art scrutinized to this extent before.

When Celia turned to her after inspecting the final piece, her expression was professional, and Alex fought not to jump to any conclusions.

"How many more pieces like this do you have?"

Alex quickly swallowed to moisten her throat. "Finished, I have about a dozen."

Celia nodded. "Why don't you bring me another five to display with these, and we'll go from there."

Now Alex's breath did gush from her lungs. She couldn't stop it. It was really happening. She was really going to have her art displayed.

"Thank you so much for giving me this chance." She struggled mightily between sheer disbelief and the effort to remain professional.

Celia seemed to understand. "I think our customers may find your work very much to their liking."

All of Alex's pent-up nerves came out in a breathless laugh. Mr. Conrad and Moretti both congratulated her and shook her hand.

"Welcome to the ranks of represented artists," Moretti said.

Alex could hardly do more than grin. Her art may fail to sell in the end, but for now, she was just delighted to have made it this far.

After the moment of celebration, Celia discussed terms with Alex and had her fill out the necessary paperwork. They talked briefly afterward before parting ways. Outside, Alex turned to Mr. Conrad and Moretti. "Thank you both so much for doing this for me. It never would have happened without you."

"I believe you would have made it eventually," Moretti said. But, given her history of discouragement, Alex wasn't sure she would have been persistent enough. As they walked slowly toward their vehicles, Mr. Conrad said to her, "A day like today deserves celebration. I know you talked about having coffee with me and Julia, but it is getting close to noon. Would you join us for lunch instead at the Royale?"

Alex recognized the name immediately. She should be getting back to Aspen Creek for work, but she did have something important she needed to do first. If she didn't do it today, she'd likely lose her only chance before it was too late.

"I'd love to."

"Excellent." He looked at Moretti. "Would you care to join us?"

Alex panicked for a split-second. If she was going to follow through with her plans, she needed to talk to Riley's parents in private.

But Moretti said, "Sorry, Wife's got an ultrasound I have to get to. Today I find out if I'll be the proud father to a little boy or little girl. Whatever it is, if they're as smart and good looking as their mother, I'll be happy."

Mr. Conrad and Alex both smiled.

"Make sure to tell her we missed seeing her at the party," Mr. Conrad said.

"Will do."

He turned and strode toward a flashy red Chevy Camaro, but then Alex remembered something.

"Mr. Moretti, could I ask you something, if you have a minute?"

He turned back to her. "Sure. Have at it."

Alex looked at Mr. Conrad. "Do you want me to meet you at the Royale?"

He nodded. "I'll pick up Julia and see you there."

He walked away, and Alex turned her full attention to Moretti. "I was hoping you might have some advice for me. When my brother died three years ago, I really struggled with my art. For a long time, I just wasn't happy with any of it, and I felt that maybe I had lost any talent I had. It has gotten better, but I'm afraid now that I won't be able to produce the kind of work Celia is looking for."

Admitting it out loud was a scary thing. She'd just gotten her chance, but if she couldn't produce more paintings, then it was all for nothing.

Moretti nodded as if he understood. "Have you tried pouring those hard emotions caused by your brother's death into your paintings?"

She hesitated, not quite sure what to say, or even really what he was asking.

He started again. "All of your paintings I just saw are bright, happy—sunrises, spring landscapes. Have you tried something darker—nightscapes, sunsets, stars, tears, that sort of thing?"

She shook her head.

"Instead of trying to push the emotions aside and ignore them, try letting them out. Project them into your paintings. If you're sad, paint something sad. If nothing else, it'll be good therapy, and who knows, you might produce some of your best work. Pain is part of life. Instead of fighting it, find the beauty in it." He spoke as if from experience.

She nodded slowly. He actually made a lot of sense. "I'll try that. Thank you."

He reached into his coat pocket. Handing her a business card, he said, "If you have any more questions or need anything, give me a call. You should come to dinner sometime. My wife would like you. And bring your boyfriend. I never got a good chance to talk to him, but he seems interesting."

Alex almost laughed. Hadn't Riley said the same thing about Moretti? "I'd like that." To think, she'd just gotten her art into a gallery for the first time and had even been invited to dinner by her favorite artist. Life was crazy.

Moretti got into his car, gave her a quick wave, and then zipped out of the parking lot. Still smiling, Alex climbed into her Jeep and grabbed her phone. She called Riley and put it on speaker so she could drive. She didn't want to be late to lunch.

When he picked up the phone, Alex was near to bursting with excitement.

"I'm in! My art is going to be displayed!"

"That's awesome!" Riley's voice was a little distorted over the phone, but she could tell he was excited for her. "I knew they wouldn't turn you down."

"Celia, the Gallery Director, even wants me to bring in more pieces. Now I just have to pray they will sell."

"They will."

She took a quick breath. "Listen, your dad invited me to have lunch with them. I'll try not to be too long. I should get back before things get busy later."

"Take your time. I've got it covered."

"Thanks. I'll see you later."

They said goodbye and hung up, and she drove through the city. The Royale wasn't too far from the gallery. She found an empty parking space in front of the restaurant and waited until a sleek black car pulled in. When she saw that it was the Conrads, she got out. It was a good thing she was dressed appropriately for fine dining, though the other diners might give her old Jeep odd looks.

She met them at the entrance, and Mr. Conrad opened the doors for them. Alex scanned the interior. It was pretty much the exact opposite of Penny's Diner—sparkling chandeliers, round tables draped with white tablecloths, waiters and waitresses in crisp uniforms. She never would have chosen to eat here on her own. She had no idea how much dining here would actually cost, but she had a pretty good idea a family dinner might come close to her full month's rent.

An attendant at the front desk greeted them, obviously familiar with Mr. Conrad, and guided them to a small but elegant table next to the window. Mr. Conrad pulled out a chair for his wife first and then for Alex. They were each supplied with a menu full of fancy fonts and even fancier words. Alex had no idea what half of the food was or how to pronounce it, and the pricing along the side confirmed her suspicions.

In the end, she ordered a chicken and pasta dish, at Mr. Conrad's recommendation. They were each served a glass of wine with the meal. The pasta was mouthwatering. Though Alex was perfectly content with burgers, home cooked beef roast, and other everyday staples, she wouldn't mind these fancy dinners once in a while. Not that she could ever afford such luxury. She'd have to be the next James Moretti for that, and she didn't see anything like that happening, at least not any time soon.

Well into the meal, she took a small sip of her wine and hesitated. The atmosphere had been pleasant so far. Mr. and Mrs. Conrad seemed to have adopted her as a second daughter. She really hoped she wasn't about to destroy that, but in the end, this was more important than maintaining their perfect opinion of her.

She took a deep breath. "There's a reason I suggested we get coffee after visiting the gallery. I wanted to talk to you both about something."

They looked at her, appearing open to whatever she had to say, but how long would that last? "I really hope you do not take offense, especially because I'm so grateful for everything you've done. But it's important for you to know how much Riley means to me. He has done more for me than I am able to tell you. Because of that, I feel I must take a stand for him as he has for me."

She paused. Neither of them said anything, but Mr. Conrad's face took on a cool, more business-like expression. She already felt his goodwill slipping away.

Alex forged on before her fear could strangle her words. "I know there have been hurts and disappointments on both sides. I don't argue that. Even Riley knows it . . . but I think you may be basing your opinions of him on who he was in college rather than who he is now. Thirteen years is a long time. It might look like he has nothing to show for it, but just the fact that he survived and is home when so many others don't come back . . . that is something to be thankful for."

She swallowed hard. She didn't want to bring her emotions about Josh into this, but that was difficult to avoid. "You should be proud of what an honorable man your son is. I've waited so long to meet a man like him. Not only that, but you should be significantly proud of his service to this country. He doesn't talk about it, and neither did my brother, but I know they both witnessed horrible things that Riley will never forget. And they willingly faced those things so people like us don't have to. That takes a lot of courage. Riley didn't just run away from his life here; he chose over and over to keep facing those awful things, even when he didn't have to."

She paused again, this time waiting to see if they would say anything. Riley's mom nodded slowly, her eyes welcomingly soft and a little misty.

"You're right. His choices have been difficult to accept in the past, but we have not given enough consideration to what he has gone through. We *are* proud of his sacrifices; we've just failed to show him that. I hope we'll still have the opportunity."

Alex smiled a little and glanced at Mr. Conrad, who gave a slight nod of agreement. It was progress at least. "I also want you to know he is truly giving a lot of thought to your job offer. I can tell it has been on his mind all week. He knows it's a good opportunity. His past decisions may not attest to it, but he's a very responsible man—one I trust wholeheartedly."

His dad nodded more noticeably now. "I'm glad to know he is taking it seriously."

"Very." Alex reached into her purse for her phone. This would seem random at first, but she had one more point left to make before she could leave this restaurant. She opened up her photos and set her phone on the table in front of Mr. and Mrs. Conrad. "Do you see these?"

She swiped through a few photos of latte art. Hopefully Riley wouldn't be mad at her for this.

Mrs. Conrad frowned lightly at the apparent change of subject, but said, "They are lovely."

Alex left the phone sitting with a photo of a latte art flower—one of the newest ones Riley had been practicing and her favorite. "Riley did all of those."

His mom looked up from the phone, her face registering surprise. "Riley did?"

Alex nodded. "I've watched him do it. He has only shown a few other people besides me. I don't know if he'd be all right with me telling you, but I feel you should know what he's giving up if he accepts the job here at this restaurant. Riley isn't just wasting away his life as it might appear to you. He has real dreams. Ever since moving to Aspen Creek he has wanted to open his own coffee shop. He has a real passion for it. I can see it when he talks about it and has me try new coffee blends he creates in his spare time. There's this beautiful old building in Aspen Creek that used to be a coffee shop but closed a couple of years ago. Riley wants so much to buy that building and reopen it. He's been saving up ever since he started working at the bar."

She sighed and looked Mr. Conrad in the eyes. "If he accepts your job offer, it will be because he believes it's the wise and responsible thing to do, even if it means giving up his true passion.

So please, if he does accept, know what it's costing him. There's so much more to him than you give him credit for."

She fell silent now, her heart throbbing loudly in her ears. She couldn't believe she had gone through with this, but for Riley, she was willing to step way outside of her comfort zone.

After a long moment, Mr. Conrad said, "You're a brave young woman for sitting down with us like this."

She let out a tiny laugh of air. She didn't feel brave.

Mr. Conrad continued. "We'll keep your words and insight into Riley's life in mind."

Chapter Thirty-one

WITH CHRISTMAS ONLY A WEEK AWAY, ALL OF ASPEN CREEK WAS in a festive mood. And after her meeting at the art gallery yesterday, Alex took particular joy in the season. She was even tentatively hopeful her conversation with Riley's parents would lead to good things. They had parted on good terms, which was a huge relief. As it was, she hadn't mentioned the conversation to Riley, but she would have had to if his parents suddenly wanted nothing more to do with her.

Pastor Ellis's sermon this morning was a Christmas message Alex thoroughly enjoyed. After the service, everyone mingled and talked about their Christmas plans. Alex had really come to love it here at church. She was even making friends with the young women her age, particularly those who were still single, even into their thirties. She might have Riley now, but she still knew the struggle. God didn't just drop guys like him out of the sky, unfortunately.

Once they'd made their rounds, Alex and Riley met up with Mindy and Zach in the parking lot and headed over to the diner for lunch. This had become a tradition for the four of them. They slid into their booth, Alex next to Riley on one side, and Mindy and Zach on the other.

After they ordered and were waiting on their food, Mindy asked, "So what are your Christmas plans?"

Alex looked at Riley. So much had happened lately they hadn't really discussed it. "Well, my mom did not-so-subtly hint that she would love for us to come down there again. What did you do last year, Riley?" If he had any Christmas traditions, she didn't want to mess them up.

"I helped serve food to homeless vets in Denver. It seemed better than sitting at home alone feeling sorry for myself when I should just be grateful to have a home. I could just as easily have been one of them." He took a sip of his coffee. "But we can visit your parents again."

He sounded fully on board, yet Alex had a niggling feeling his words held slight disappointment.

"Actually, I'd be happy to go with you to Denver to volunteer."

He turned a little in the booth to look at her. "Really? You want to do that for Christmas?"

It certainly wouldn't be the traditional Christmas she was used to, but if it made Riley happy, then it would make her happy. "Sure. There's always so much emphasis on family during the holidays, but never enough on giving. Like you said, we're blessed with homes and jobs and food. Just because someone doesn't have those things doesn't mean they shouldn't have a good Christmas. Besides, we can always visit my parents another time."

Riley smiled, the warmth of his eyes melting into her core. Yes, she was definitely happy with this decision.

"Well, if you two will be gone on Christmas, why don't you come over to our place Christmas Eve?" Mindy invited. "Maybe even open some presents." She grinned like a child. "That way you can still have a traditional Christmas celebration and volunteer."

<hr>

Christmas Eve arrived with a light snowfall that accompanied Alex and Riley into Boulder mid-morning. Between them sat a small pile of brightly wrapped gifts for each other. Alex kept glancing at hers, wondering what Riley had gotten her. She had spent the last few weeks scouring the stores in Boulder as well as the internet finding gifts for Riley. It had been harder than she had anticipated, but she wanted them to be perfect.

When they arrived at Mindy and Zach's house, they carried the gifts up to the front door, and Alex nudged the doorbell with her elbow. Shadow and Bella's barking echoed inside, and a moment later, Mindy opened the door with a huge grin.

"Come in!"

The dogs met them with wagging tails and slobbery tongues, but Alex didn't mind at all. She breathed in deeply. Mindy's house always smelled so good thanks to her love for candles. A delicious scent of food cooking drifted from the kitchen.

Zach stepped into the entryway. "Here, why don't you let me take the gifts and put them under the tree."

Alex and Riley piled the presents into his arms and then shrugged off their coats and shoes.

"I have Christmas cookies and coffee ready to go," Mindy said as she led them into the kitchen. "I put a couple of chickens in the oven earlier, and Zach helped me with potatoes and salads. It's not quite a full Christmas banquet, but it's just the four of us."

"It sounds great. Smells good too." Alex's mouth watered, especially at the cookies on a platter on the island. Mindy had them decorated perfectly in Christmas colored icing and sprinkles. "Do you need help with anything?"

Mindy shrugged. "I still have a few things to put together, but there's no rush. I figure the cookies will tide us over until dinner is ready."

Alex agreed. She and Riley each poured a cup of coffee and took a cookie. For a while, the four of them hung out in the kitchen together before Riley and Zach disappeared somewhere discussing guy stuff while Alex helped Mindy finish up in the kitchen.

"So, have you been working on any new paintings?" Mindy asked, mixing together a fruit salad.

"I did start a new one this week. It's different than I've done before, but I really like it so far." Alex pulled out her phone to show Mindy a photo of her progress. It was a snowy, nighttime landscape. The colors were a lot darker and cooler than she normally used, but she'd taken Moretti's advice to heart. Though the scene was rather stark, she had added a sprinkling of stars above the spiky black tree silhouettes, with just a hint of pastel colors in each one that added beauty to the dark landscape.

"Oo, I like that a lot. It's definitely different, but I think it would look gorgeous hanging above a fireplace or something. I can't wait to see it in person."

Alex smiled with satisfaction warming her chest. It had been a long time since she'd created anything she was proud to show off. She would have to let Moretti know his advice was helping. "Hopefully Celia and customers to the gallery will like it."

"I'm sure they will. I'd buy it myself, but it's worth a whole lot more than I could give you. I'm so glad things are starting to work out with your art."

"Thanks. There's still a lot of unknown, but it's been a long road just getting this far."

"Speaking of long roads, has Riley made his decision?"

Alex shook her head. "I don't know. It's weighing on him, that's for sure. But he hasn't discussed which way he is leaning, and I don't want to press him. I want the decision to be his and not sway him."

"It'll be tough one way or another, won't it?"

"Yeah, I think so. And now he only has a little over a week to make up his mind. If he takes the job, he'll stick with it even if he hates it. He wouldn't back out again after dropping out of college. I know many people have jobs they dislike. But this is different. Living in Denver, running a restaurant owned by his parents—he'd always be in their shadow and feel the constant pressure to live up to their standards. He wouldn't just be giving up his dreams, but in a sense, his freedom. I hate the thought of that. It doesn't seem right."

Mindy gave her a commiserating look. "Zach and I are praying for him. I'm sure God will help him make the right choice, whatever it is."

"Thanks. It's so hard wishing I could do something to help, but I can't. I really don't want him to make his decision based on me. It's his life. I'm part of it, but he's the one who will have to live with what he chooses."

Mindy gave her a quick, comforting side hug before asking Alex to hand her a bag of mini marshmallows. Alex took a couple and popped them into her mouth, still brooding until Mindy sent her a mischievous look.

"On a lighter topic, do you think you might be getting any special bling for Christmas?"

Alex shook her head. "We've only been dating since August."

Mindy shrugged. "I know, but sometimes things move quickly. I think Zach would have proposed after a couple of months if I hadn't been away at college."

"With everything that's coming at us lately, I doubt either one of us are in the right mindset to make that sort of decision."

"True," Mindy acknowledged.

"Not that I haven't been thinking about it."

Mindy's grin broke out immediately. "Well, I won't count the chickens before they're hatched, but I'd be mighty surprised if that's not where your relationship is headed."

Alex smiled again, more to herself than Mindy. Marriage had been so far from her radar a few months ago, but now she could hardly imagine life without Riley. More and more she wanted to spend the rest of her life with him.

Once they finished up in the kitchen, they joined the guys in the living room. A football game was about to start, and they all sat down to watch. Since it wasn't the Broncos, Zach allowed

Mindy to sit with him after an over-exaggerated display of reluctance, making them all laugh. In the end, he snuggled her against him and gave her a kiss on the cheek. Alex craved that kind of simple intimacy. It made things rather difficult considering how such feelings could lead to dangerous places while unmarried. That's probably why marriage entered her mind so much. Was Riley thinking about it too? She prayed for patience and that if this was what God intended for them, their relationship would progress in His time. A lifelong commitment wasn't something to rush, after all, and she had absolutely no intention of becoming part of the world's sobering divorce statistics.

Between football, conversations, and Mindy's delicious Christmas Eve dinner, the afternoon passed with all the Christmas tradition Alex loved about this time of year. Though she missed her parents, she couldn't imagine a better way to spend the day.

When evening approached and the living room was lit by a couple of lamps and the glow from the Christmas tree, Mindy turned off the TV. With steaming mugs sitting on the coffee table between them, they turned their attention to the gifts. Alex and Riley gave Mindy and Zach their gifts first. They had gone shopping together earlier in the week and bought their friends a few things for the house and for the dogs. Mindy was especially delighted by the adorable pink fairy sweater with sparkly wings Alex couldn't resist getting for Bella. They all laughed as Bella walked around, her stubby tail jiggling. Alex had a feeling Mindy would never take that sweater off the dog.

Mindy and Zach passed out their gifts to Alex and Riley next. They turned out to be several bags of coffee each, plus delicious-looking chocolate truffles.

Then it was time for Alex and Riley to open each other's presents. Alex offered hers first, a bit nervous, hoping he would like what she had bought him. The first gift he opened was a distressed Ford trucker cap that Alex had to admit she'd bought mostly because she loved it so much. His next gift was a navy-blue hoodie with a distressed flag emblem that was an exact match to one he wore so often. It had ripped just recently from such regular wear. She'd spent hours online searching for it before finally winning a bid on eBay. She could tell by the way his face lit up that it was the perfect gift, just as she'd been hoping. His last gift brought a cute smile to his face. A denim apron.

"You probably have one at home, but you could keep this one at my parents' so you have your own when we visit."

He gave her a warm smile that caused her stomach to somersault. "Thank you."

Now it was Alex's turn. Her first gift from him was a watercolor mug with flowy script that read *Good Morning, Beautiful.* She grinned. She would definitely be using this mug often in the mornings. The second gift was a layered copper necklace with small arrow charms that had a lovely blue-green patina. It was exactly the sort of Bohemian style she loved, and she put it on right away. Her final gift was rather heavy. She set it in her lap and pulled away the wrapping to reveal a journaling Bible that had become so popular lately. She'd been thinking about getting one for a while now.

"How did you know this is exactly what I wanted?"

He shrugged. "I can't take all the credit. I talked to Bradley a couple of weeks ago, and his wife has one she loves. When I heard about it, I knew you'd probably like it."

"I *love* it." What could be better than mixing her love of art with Bible reading? "Thank you so much."

She leaned over to give him a quick kiss and then flipped through the Bible, already imagining what sketches or doodles she might add to the pages.

Chapter Thirty-two

IT WAS STILL DARK OUTSIDE WHEN ALEX GOT UP ON CHRISTMAS morning. She dressed in a pair of jeans and a warm red sweater with a white snowflake design. After finishing in the bathroom, she thought about making coffee just so she could use her new mug from Riley, but he would no doubt bring her some. Instead, she made a quick plate of eggs and toast for breakfast. Knowing her parents were always up early, she called them while she ate to wish them a merry Christmas. She told them all about yesterday and the gifts Riley had given her. Though they were a bit sad she and Riley weren't there today, they were very supportive of her plan to go to Denver instead.

She kept the call brief, and by the time she finished her breakfast, Riley knocked on her door. She grabbed her coat and purse and followed him to his truck. Along the way they listened to Christmas music on the radio and shared Christmas memories from when they were young. Alex also gushed over how excited she was about her journaling Bible, and noticed how he was wearing the hoodie she had given him yesterday. She hoped he could enjoy today without thinking too much about his upcoming decision.

Once they arrived at the community center in Denver that Veterans Affairs was using to host the Christmas dinner, Alex followed Riley hurriedly inside. The breeze had picked up, making her shiver on their way across the parking lot. Thank God the homeless vets they were feeding today would also have a place to warm up and seek shelter from the frigid temperature.

Activity buzzed inside as volunteers of all ages set up tables with white plastic tablecloths and festive red and green napkins. A Christmas tree stood in the corner surrounded by a mountain of gift bags. No doubt they were care packages to give to the veterans after the meal. From the back of the large room came the delicious smell of turkey, ham, potatoes, and other traditional holiday foods.

As they stepped farther into the room, a tall black man with a wide smile broke away from the group to meet them.

"Riley! Good to see you, brother."

They greeted each other with a handshake and a quick man-hug.

"You're looking good," the man said.

"Yeah, I was still a bit hobbled last year, but I've made a lot of progress." Riley turned slightly. "This is my girlfriend, Alex."

The man gave her a big grin and shook her hand. "Pleased to meet you, Alex. I'm Dak."

She greeted him in return, drawn to his friendly disposition. She'd never met any of Riley's friends before.

To Riley, he said, "Looks like you've done real good for yourself over there in Aspen Creek." He sent Alex a wink.

Riley chuckled. "Definitely can't complain."

"Well, we're all grateful to have you two joining us today," Dak told them. "We're a bit low on volunteers this year."

"Just point us where you need us," Riley said.

"We could use some more help with the tables. We'll be opening the doors soon and want to make sure there's enough seating."

After taking off their coats and hanging them with the others, Alex and Riley went to work helping the other volunteers arrange and set the tables. Alex soon got talking with a couple of other women, who both had brothers in the military. It felt good to talk to them and share experiences about how difficult it was. They were incredibly sympathetic and supportive when she told them about Josh.

About an hour before noon, the room started to fill with homeless veterans from all around the city as volunteers picked them up in borrowed or rented vans. Many of them were older—a lot were Vietnam vets—but Alex found herself surprised by how many were around Riley's age. There were a good number of men and a few women with scarred faces and missing limbs. Her heart squeezed painfully to see them here. Didn't they have families who could help and take them in, at least for the holidays? It felt so wrong that so many who had fought for their country were reduced to this. If only there were a way she could help them all.

When it was time to eat, they helped carry plates full of food to each veteran as others in the kitchen dished them up. Once everyone was eating happily, the volunteers received their own plate of food. Alex took hers and followed Riley to a table with two empty seats amongst a large assortment of men. They all greeted each other and introduced themselves. They seemed very happy to have people to talk to and celebrate with.

To see how comfortably Riley spoke with them had Alex's heart swelling with love. He was so at ease in a setting like this—with regular, everyday people. He was the same way at the bar. It might not have been his dream job, but he was good at it. He would be equally good at running his own coffee shop—at getting to know the regulars and creating a comfortable place to hang out. If only she could know for sure if that was his future. She ached to see his dreams come true.

Though being the sister to a fallen soldier drew Alex into the conversation regularly, she often found herself just watching and listening to Riley. He was in his element here. It clashed horribly with the thought of him at the Royale. It would never be anything like working at the bar or at a coffee shop. It would stifle him and force him to be someone he was not. He deserved to be the man she was falling more and more in love with—a man who wore jeans and hoodies, flannel shirts and baseball caps, a man who rode horses with her and her dad and tinkered on vintage trucks. That man didn't fit in a world of white linen tablecloths, polished silverware, and gourmet meals that cost a fortune. If he took his dad's job offer, he would have to change, at least while he was working. Could he be both men? She knew he would try, but would he be happy doing it? She sighed quietly to herself. If only there was a perfect solution.

The afternoon passed with more food, talk, and laughter, which Alex thought was probably the best gift of all for the people here. As each one left, they were given one of the gift bags containing a coat, hat, scarf, gloves, and hygienic products, as well as packs of jerky and trail mix. Alex helped hand out some of the bags and was touched by how grateful they were. If only she could just gather everyone up and take them home with her. She was never going to feel complaintive again when she couldn't afford coffee or other luxuries.

When all of the veterans had left, Alex and Riley joined in on clean-up, clearing the tables and washing dishes. By the time they said goodbye to Dak and the other volunteers, the sun was setting. Alex shivered as they stepped out into the icy wind, and Riley put his arm around her. In the truck, he turned the heat on high, and Alex stuck her hands in her pockets until the cab warmed up. She looked at the few cars left at the community center, her heart both full and heavy—full with the smiles and thankfulness she had witnessed, but heavy with how many people didn't have homes or family to go to tonight. And this was just in Denver. All over the country were people just like the ones she had met today.

"I'm really glad we did this," she said as they pulled away. "I was sad this morning not to see my parents, but this was so much more important. I wouldn't have wanted to miss it. It wasn't traditional, but it was a perfect Christmas."

Riley smiled at her, and she could tell he thought so too.

On the way home, they shared some of their thoughts about the day, and how much they both wished there was more they could do to change things. By the time they made it back to Aspen Creek, they'd already made plans to do more volunteer work together, and Alex anticipated this becoming a new Christmas tradition.

When they parked in front of Alex's apartment, she hated to say goodbye. It would be so nice to just go inside together, have some coffee, sit under a warm blanket, and keep talking. It was entirely too tempting, and while it might start out completely innocent, she didn't want to take any chances. She quickly reached for her purse to divert her attention.

"Before I go in, I have one more Christmas present for you." She pulled an envelope out with a red ribbon around it. She really hadn't needed to get so fancy, but it was Christmas. He looked surprised when she handed it to him. "You can open it when you get home, or you can wait until morning. It's up to you."

"I don't think my curiosity will wait until morning," he said with a smile.

She grinned back at him before growing more serious. "I love you, Riley. All I want is for you to be happy."

He gave her that tender look that would never fail to make her melt inside. "That's all I want for you too."

He then leaned over, and they shared a kiss. With a quiet goodnight, Alex got out of the truck before her emotions could betray her good sense and hurried up to her apartment.

Chapter Thirty-three

RILEY FIXED HIMSELF A MUG OF COFFEE AND SAT DOWN AT THE table. Tux followed and jumped up onto the tabletop where he tried to stick his nose in Riley's mug. Riley moved the mug away.

"No, I'm not sharing my coffee, and you're not supposed to be on the table."

He picked the cat up and set him down on a chair instead. Tux gave him an ornery look before proceeding to bathe himself. Satisfied his coffee was safe, Riley focused on his Bible. He didn't always do the best job, but he made a point of sitting down to read in the morning, or at least sometime during the day, even if it was just ten minutes after work at night. He spent a few minutes praying first. Alex and their relationship were a big part of his prayers now. He was determined to honor both God and Alex, and he wasn't about to believe Satan wouldn't try every which way he could to ruin that.

He also prayed for his family and for their salvation. It was another area Satan would attack relentlessly. Riley hated that his own antagonistic feelings toward his parents played right into that strategy. In order to reach them he would have to forgive them and let go of any bitterness, but that proved difficult when the situation was ongoing. He just prayed God would change his heart and provide the right opportunities.

After praying for the people in his life, Riley's prayers turned to a plea for wisdom. He still hadn't made up his mind on the job offer. There was so much to consider, and each choice had its pros and cons. He'd prayed for a clear choice, but after two weeks, God was still silent about it. He fought frustration and prayed that, when the time came, he'd make the right choice.

Once Riley turned his attention to his Bible, he tried to focus on the pages and find wisdom in the words, but his mind kept drifting, always toward his decision. Over and over, he weighed the options, looking for the clear choice.

Finally, after over an hour, he sighed and closed his Bible. He'd probably read the same three paragraphs in Ephesians six times. He grabbed his phone to check the time. The sight of Alex's photo on his lock screen managed to draw a smile, and he reached for the letter she'd given him last night, skimming the words again. It wasn't very long but everything he'd needed. She'd told him that, no matter what decision he made, she would be behind him one-hundred percent. She encouraged him to do what he believed was right and to trust God with the rest. A little of the frustration died. With her support, he could take on any challenge, including the restaurant if that was what it had to be.

Energized, he got up and brought his empty mug to the sink. After making sure Tux had enough water and food, he headed downstairs and out the back of the bar. He had one week until he had to give his dad an answer. He would have to make up his mind one of these days, and a drive might help. Getting into his truck, he started up the engine, let it run for a minute, and drove away from the bar.

Across town, near the grocery store, Riley turned onto a street he'd probably almost worn a path to. Sitting a little off from the other shops along the street rose the old brick building with tall, red-trimmed windows. The decorative wrought iron hook overhanging the door used to have a sign for the old coffee shop. Everything was exactly the same as the other times he'd driven past except for one particular detail that was glaringly absent.

With a sinking feeling, he pulled up to the curb and shut off the truck. Stepping out, he studied the windows but didn't see any indication of the *For Sale* sign that had sat in them for so long. A bell jingled, and the front door of the old shop opened. A dark-haired woman stepped out, and he recognized the realtor he'd talked to in the past. It wasn't until she had locked the door and turned that she noticed him.

"Riley."

He could tell by her look what news she would give him. "It sold?"

She nodded. "It did. I'm sorry. I know you were interested."

He forced a shrug, hiding the true extent of the disappointment piling up inside of him. "It couldn't just sit here forever." He looked up at the building. He hadn't realized until now just how much of his dreams he had placed on it. How often he had imagined himself inside of it, brewing his own coffee blends and serving customers. "Who bought it?"

"The new owners don't want to give any information until the deal is finalized later this week. I'm sorry."

Riley shook his head. "That's all right. I was just curious." Probably one of the big coffee chains wanting to capitalize on having a place in a small tourist town. Hopefully it was one of the better ones at least.

"I can let you know if any other buildings come up for sale."

With a smile, Riley thanked her, but that wouldn't be necessary anymore. He returned to his truck where he pulled out his phone and texted Alex. He then pulled away from the building and down the street to drive around the quiet back roads outside of town.

⌇

Alex was happy to accept Riley's text invitation to lunch. She'd spent all morning working on her latest painting and had just put the final details on it when it was time to get ready to go.

She didn't want to get too excited just yet, but she was pretty happy with the painting, and she prayed whatever slump she had been in was officially over. She thanked God for Moretti's advice. When Riley knocked on her door, Alex was excited to share her painting success; however, something about his smile stopped her. It just wasn't quite as bright as usual.

"Ready to go?" he asked.

He sounded normal, but the nagging feeling in the pit of her stomach didn't subside. It was probably his decision weighing on him, and it hurt not knowing how to help.

"Yeah." She slipped on her coat and followed him out.

They were both quiet when they drove away from her apartment. She searched for something to cheer him up, but he ended up speaking first.

"Thanks for the letter." He looked over to give her a smile that was warm and genuine. "It means a lot."

"You're welcome. I just wanted to make sure you knew I was with you no matter what."

He maintained his smile for a few moments longer but didn't say anything else until they reached the diner. Once they were seated in their booth and had a pot of coffee, he finally opened up. Alex was just stirring sugar into her cup when he said, "I took a drive this morning, hoping for some clarity about my dad's offer."

He paused, and she looked up to meet his eyes.

"I drove past the coffee shop. It sold."

Her heart and stomach sank. "Oh, Riley, I'm so sorry." No wonder he was bothered.

He shrugged. "I always knew it was likely to happen one of these days."

Her throat squeezed as she recalled the times they had dreamed of him buying the place. He had wanted it so badly. *She* had wanted so badly for him. "I really wish there had been something I could've done to help you buy it."

"It was always a long shot. And if that's where God had wanted me, it wouldn't have sold, right?"

She nodded slowly. It was true, but that didn't make it any easier. Though he did his best to hide it, Alex keenly sensed his disappointment, and her eyes watered a bit. As she had told him last night, she just wanted him to be happy. It didn't feel like it was supposed to go like this.

"Do you know who bought it?"

"No. Probably some corporation. Maybe it won't even be a coffee shop." He stirred his coffee but didn't take a drink. "I guess this is the sign I've been praying for."

The resignation in his voice broke Alex's heart.

<hr/>

The rest of the week passed quickly, at least for Alex. She found it difficult to determine how Riley felt after their lunch at the diner. He acted like he was fine, but he was a soldier. He could be dying inside and never show it. They didn't really talk about the coffee shop anymore. He seemed to have let it go, yet Alex couldn't help asking God why it had turned out this way. Why He would put Riley somewhere she couldn't see him happy.

Saturday night was New Year's Eve, and according to Luke, the busiest day of the whole year at the bar. He needed all hands on deck, including Kat. Alex had never once imagined herself in a bar for New Year's Eve, but despite the rowdy, boisterous crowd and abundance of alcohol it wasn't too bad. The patrons were good people, if not more than a little tipsy as the night grew late. Mindy and Zach surprised Alex by showing up to celebrate with them.

Despite working well past midnight to help make sure everyone too intoxicated to drive got rides home and helping clean up, Alex was still up to go to church with Riley the next morning. A large mug of coffee helped ward off sleepiness during

313

the service. They visited with everyone for a while afterward before Riley drove her home. She had a feeling they would both be taking a nap later this afternoon. At least she would.

When they arrived at Alex's apartment, Riley shut the truck off, and the cab fell silent. He looked over at her, wearing the same dejected look as when he'd told her about the coffee shop.

"My dad asked to meet me here in town tomorrow. We're going to meet at the diner at eleven." He paused and took a breath. "I'm going to accept the job offer."

She gave a slow nod. Heaven knew how much they had both prayed about this. If he felt that was what God was leading him to do, then she would support him all the way. "I'm sure you'll make a fantastic chef." She attempted a grin. "Do you think there will be a girlfriend discount on the food?"

He released a quiet chuckle. At least she had managed that.

"Once I'm head chef, I guarantee it."

They shared a smile.

"Will you come with me tomorrow?" he asked.

"Of course."

Chapter Thirty-four

ALEX WOKE UP EARLY, A LITTLE BEFORE SIX O'CLOCK, AND COULDN'T get back to sleep. Today would change life as she had come to know it for the last few months. Riley would accept his dad's offer and probably move to Denver right away. It meant Alex would have to decide whether to look for a new job or not. Luke had already told her that he could adjust her schedule to work when he did. She appreciated that, but it was hard to think about working at the bar without Riley. He was the only reason she'd felt comfortable with the job in the first place. As much as she hated the thought of leaving the quiet atmosphere of Aspen Creek, relocating to Denver might be in her future as well.

However, more concerning to her than deciding whether or not to keep her current job was Riley's situation. Everything pointed toward it being the choice he was supposed to make. So why did she feel so uneasy about it? And did he feel it too? It was probably still the disappointment of losing the coffee shop. She had really believed he would do it one day. It still bothered her to think of him giving it up, but life was far from perfect, as she well knew. Sometimes you just had to make the best of a difficult situation.

With no hope of sleep now, she dragged herself out of bed and dressed warmly. In the kitchen, she brewed a pot of coffee. She sure would miss Riley picking her up for work or to go see Mindy and Zach and bringing her coffee to try. They'd been spoiled with how easy it was to see each other whenever they wanted.

Once she'd filled her mug, she sat down at the table with her journaling Bible and her favorite set of colored pencils. Opening to Psalms, she read a couple of chapters and then let the artistic side of her brain take over. She added pretty doodles and drawings in the margins, highlighting her favorite verses. It helped dispel some of her gloomy mood.

Riley showed up shortly before eleven. He had his hair pulled back and under his leather coat he wore the dark blue shirt and black tie he often wore to church. When he greeted her at the door, he seemed ready for this meeting, but it was hard to tell if that was really true underneath his strong exterior.

Down at the truck, he opened her door for her as always; however, she didn't get in right away. Instead, she turned to face him.

"Are you okay?"

He didn't answer immediately, but with a bit of a smile, he said, "I'm alive, one way or another I have a job, and I've got the best girlfriend in the world. I've got nothing to complain about."

Alex had to smile at the compliment. They were both blessed, and whatever today meant for the future, they would make the best of it. If this was God's plan, then it must be leading somewhere better than if Riley turned down the offer.

She climbed into the truck, and they drove to the diner. The Conrads' black car wasn't yet in the parking lot, so Alex and Riley went inside to wait for them and ordered a pot of coffee. Alex had just poured herself a cup when Mr. and Mrs. Conrad arrived. She and Riley both stood to greet them. Mr. Conrad seemed to be in a good mood judging by the way he greeted Riley, which was warmer than Alex had witnessed in their past meetings. He was probably feeling confident Riley would accept the offer.

The four of them sat down, Alex next to Riley and across from his mom. He and his dad sat facing each other. Once the waitress had asked if Mr. and Mrs. Conrad wanted anything but coffee, she left them alone. A moment of silence hung between them. Alex wasn't sure who would speak first, but then it was Riley.

"Why don't we get right to the point?" He kept his tone businesslike, not giving away how hard she knew this must be for him. In a sense, he was handing over his life to his dad, probably the last person in the world he really trusted right now. "I accept your offer."

Her heart sank a little. He shouldn't have to do this. Riley, however, held his dad's gaze steadily. If he had any second thoughts this morning, he didn't let them show.

Mr. Conrad, who had been about to take a sip of coffee, set his mug down. "I'm glad you took the decision seriously. However, before we move forward, I have a second offer for you."

Alex looked between the two of them as Riley's brows drew together, a stormy look brewing in his eyes. Alex's stomach cramped. She prayed this wasn't some sort of game Mr. Conrad was playing. This had been hard enough for Riley without suddenly being forced to make a second decision on the spot.

"What kind of offer?" Suspicion laced his voice. She couldn't blame him after the history between the two.

"You can take the job at the Royale . . ." Mr. Conrad turned to his wife who fished a thin stack of papers out of her purse. He set them on the table in front of Riley. "Or you can take this."

Riley frowned down at the documents. Alex tried to see what they were but couldn't figure out just what she was looking at.

Riley shook his head, looking up at his dad again. "What is this?"

"That is the deed to the empty coffee shop on Martin Avenue."

Alex's jaw might have smacked the table had it fallen open any faster. Riley's face just went blank. A moment later, his brow furrowed again.

"*You* bought the shop?"

She couldn't tell if his tone was accusatory or just stunned.

Mr. Conrad nodded. "I did."

"Why?"

Mr. Conrad let out a long breath, cast a glance at Alex, and then looked at his wife before facing Riley again. When he spoke, something about him seemed to have softened.

"This is not easy for me to admit, but I realize I've not been entirely fair to you. I've pushed you in ways I shouldn't have, and you were right when you said I never made an effort to learn who you are. We were very disappointed when you dropped out of college, but that was a long time ago. You're not a child anymore, and I understand that now. I also realize that just because you make different decisions than I would doesn't always mean that I am right and you are wrong."

Alex hadn't known Mr. Conrad for long, but she'd never imagined seeing him so uncomfortable. It must have taken an awful lot to admit he was wrong. And probably his wife supplying a lot of the right words beforehand.

"Thanks, Dad," Riley said slowly, appearing just as disquieted judging by how he shifted in his seat. He was looking at his dad like he wasn't sure it was really him. "But I still don't understand what you're offering."

"I'm offering something I hope will begin to make amends between us. The coffee shop is yours. All you have to do is sign the papers. I'll give you full ownership. It will be yours to do with as you please, and I'll even loan you the money to get started if you want. We offered our help and support to get your brother and sister where they are. It's time we did the same for you."

Complete silence settled. Riley stared down at the papers now with a look of utter disbelief. Alex had never seen anyone in real life rendered truly speechless. Tears threatened to pour into her eyes. She had never for even the smallest fraction of a moment dreamed of anything like this. She glanced at Riley's mom. The dignified woman had tears in her eyes and a small smile on her face as she looked at her son.

Mr. Conrad reached into his suit coat and withdrew a pen. He held it out to Riley. "Just sign them and it's yours."

Riley moved to take the pen as if in a trance, still looking at the papers. His hand hovered over them for a moment before he looked up at his dad again.

"This is for real?"

It was painful that he had to ask, and Alex's heart pounded with a plea that this would be a new beginning in his relationship with his parents.

"Yes." Mr. Conrad actually looked emotional. "There are no strings or conditions attached."

Alex watched Riley slowly go through the papers. She could hear his heavy breathing and couldn't imagine the emotions he was experiencing. Observing him sign his name, the tears burned her eyes. She just knew they were going to start flowing down her cheeks any moment now. He was getting his dream.

When he signed the last paper, his dad reached into his coat again. "Here are your keys."

He set them on the table with a clink. Riley looked at them as if he wasn't even sure they were real or that they wouldn't just vanish in front of him. Alex wasn't sure herself.

"I look forward to seeing what you do with the place," Mr. Conrad said.

He and his wife quietly slipped out of the booth. Mrs. Conrad stopped at Riley's side and put her hand on his shoulder.

"We love you, Riley." She kissed the top of his head before following her husband out of the diner.

Alex and Riley sat alone in the booth. Riley just stared at the keys and the papers that officially made him the owner of his own coffee shop. Alex had not seen such emotion on his face since they had visited Josh's grave. Tears glimmered in his eyes. How could someone look so broken yet so relieved at the same time? Especially someone so strong?

After a moment, he broke from the daze. He looked around as if only now realizing his parents were gone before pushing up out of his seat.

"I'll be right back," he said, his voice huskier than usual.

Alex remained in the booth and looked out the window as he left the diner. He hurried across the parking lot to where his parents were just about to get into their car. They stopped and turned to him. Though she couldn't know what they said to each other, Alex watched as Riley gave his mom a hug—a true, full hug. He then shook hands with his dad before the man pulled him closer and embraced his son. It was brief and awkward, but one of the most wonderful things Alex had ever witnessed. The tears flowed now, dripping off her chin. She half laughed, half cried with the joy and thankfulness that bubbled up through her. The tears kept falling, but she just couldn't help smiling.

"Thank You, God," she murmured.

A couple of minutes later, Riley's parents got into their car and drove away. Riley stayed standing in the parking lot, his hands on his hips, for another minute or so—probably to collect himself.

When he returned to the diner, Alex worked to blot the tears away from her cheeks with a napkin and get rid of the smudges to her glasses. As soon as he reached the booth, she got up, grinning. He smiled back at her, and she put her arms around his neck. It was all she could do. She was so happy for him. He wrapped his arms around her, holding her tightly. And there went her tears again.

"You did this, didn't you?" he murmured in her ear. "You told them about the coffee shop."

She slowly let go, her heart giving a hard thump. He loosened his hold, though he still kept his arms around her as she looked up into his face.

"Yes, I did. I hope you aren't upset. I just really wanted them to know who you are, the way I do."

She opened her mouth to start babbling her explanation, but his lips promptly captured hers and cut her off. She melted into the kiss, but the spell was broken momentarily by the sound of cheers and applause. Alex's cheeks flushed when she peeked around the diner and found the rather large lunchtime crowd watching them. She ducked her head bashfully, but Riley didn't seem to care one little bit.

She turned halfway to their table and picked up the keys sitting there. Looking back at him, she held them up.

"Should we go see your new coffee shop?"

Alex stepped out of the truck in front of the coffee shop, still in a bit of a daze. This had never even come close to entering her imagination when she had sat down with Riley's parents at the Royale. All she had wanted was for them to have a greater understanding of their son, the man she loved. God had taken her feeble efforts and done more than she had ever dreamed. She was still in danger of crying just thinking about it.

Riley approached the door to the shop, and Alex pulled out her phone. "This is a momentous occasion. We need to have a picture of it."

Keys in hand, Riley smiled, and she snapped a couple of pictures of him. Then, as she was about to slip her phone back into her pocket, he motioned her closer.

"Come on, we need one together."

She grinned and hurried to his side. He put his arm around her, and she held out her phone to take a selfie of the two of them in front of the door. This was a moment she knew both of them would remember for the rest of their lives.

Finally, he turned to the door and unlocked it. They stepped inside, and Alex could barely contain the joy and thankfulness that overflowed within her. She hadn't been inside the shop in almost two years. All of the furnishings she remembered were gone, but the empty space held such potential. The brick walls and high ceilings gave it an old industrial atmosphere. A spiraled iron staircase led up to an open balcony rimmed in iron railing that nearly doubled the seating area. She had always liked sitting up there. The counter and work area was off to the left side, and some coffee equipment still sat there. Riley walked around the counter to inspect it.

Alex stood in the middle of the space and turned in a slow circle as her artistic mind went to work. "Ignore me if this is nothing like what you have in mind, but leather couches would look amazing in here. Maybe some iron tables and those vintage bentwood chairs. And some Edison bulbs for light fixtures would be really cool. You could put up string lights under the balcony and around the railing. It would be really cozy. You could probably find some really great pieces at flea markets this summer to make the place really unique."

She stopped turning when she faced the counter. He was grinning at her.

"And put some of your art on the walls."

She walked up to the counter to stand across from him. "This morning you said I was the best girlfriend in the world. Well, you're the best boyfriend in the world."

They shared a smile and might have kissed again if the counter wasn't between them. Alex's phone buzzed in her pocket. She pulled it out and read the text on the screen.

"Mindy wants to know about the meeting. Should I call and tell her?"

"Go ahead."

Alex dialed Mindy's number and waited. It only took two rings for her to answer. "So, how did it go?"

Grinning to herself, Alex said, "Hold on, I'm going to put you on speaker." She wanted Riley to hear the reaction, which was sure to be explosive. After setting the phone down on the counter, she asked, "Are you ready for this?"

"Um, yeah." Mindy's confusion practically radiated from the device.

Barely restraining her glee, Alex said, "Riley's parents bought the coffee shop for him."

Instead of her usual squeal, Mindy actually screamed. Alex and Riley both laughed. The pure happiness in his expression made Alex's heart soar.

"Are you serious?"

Loving every moment of this, Alex nodded even though Mindy couldn't see her. "Completely."

"I'm coming over. Can I come over? I have to see it!"

Alex laughed again and looked at Riley, who was nodding. "Sure, if you want to."

"All right, I'll be right over."

Just before she hung up, Alex shouted, "No speeding!"

She wasn't even sure Mindy heard her. Laughing lightly, Alex ended the call and looked at Riley.

"Be prepared. She will have a bundle of ideas." She glanced at the dusty coffeemakers. "So how does everything look?"

"Not bad," he replied, turning to look at them too. "They'll need cleaning, but I think they'll work."

"So, when are you going to start getting things ready?"

"No reason not to start right away. Try to get it open before tourist season."

Alex couldn't stop smiling. "I can't wait to see what it will look like. And I'm more than happy to help get it going, if you want."

"I wouldn't want to do it without you. I wouldn't even have it if not for you."

Alex ducked her head and shrugged one shoulder. "I was scared to death to talk to your parents. It was definitely more God than me."

For the next twenty minutes, they shared ideas and discussed what work would need to be done. They talked about new things they could do as well as some things they could bring back. When Mindy arrived, it was as if the Energizer Bunny had walked in. She was absolutely bubbling with excitement.

They spent hours at the coffee shop, ordering pizza to celebrate. They sat lined up along the serving counter while they ate, trading their ideas. Mindy was quick to offer her services as a photographer and Zach's website expertise to create one for the shop and help promote it once it opened. By the time they all left and Riley drove Alex home, she was sure his head was spinning with everything they had discussed. However, she wasn't sure she had ever seen him look quite so happy.

Chapter Thirty-five

ALEX STOOD AT THE SINK BEHIND THE BAR AND WASHED BEER glasses while Riley and Luke served the customers. The last two weeks had whisked by in an exciting whirlwind of activity. She joined Riley at the coffee shop nearly every morning before work and on their days off. They'd cleaned up all the dust that had gathered, and Riley was looking into acquiring the permits he needed. His dad even came by once so they could discuss finances. It wouldn't be long before Riley ordered furnishings and equipment.

Laughter from a group of older gentlemen at one of the tables brought a smile to Alex's face. The bar was nearly full tonight with the NFL championship games on. Though Denver had missed out this year, people still showed up to watch the games with friends. Busy nights like this could be overwhelming, but the atmosphere was festive. Alex just might sort of miss moments like these when she no longer worked here. She and Riley had already talked about her working at the coffee shop with him. Even Luke was supportive of these plans. While it would mean having to hire new employees, he was very pleased for Riley, and even offered his help some mornings when he had time to spare.

As Alex turned to put clean glasses away, Riley came to stand at the tap next to her, filling them almost as fast as she cleaned them.

"Hey, my mom texted me earlier," she said. "One of their friends has a bunch of those bentwood chairs. I don't know what

325

shape they're in, but I think he has about a dozen of them. If you want them, Mom said they can pick them up for you. They've been talking about coming for a visit and are excited to see the shop."

Though his attention was on the taps, Riley smiled. "Sounds great. As long as the chairs are sturdy enough, we can fix them up."

"My dad said he could do some work on them, too, before they bring them."

The bar remained busy until closing time. Once everyone had left, Alex, Riley, and Luke went through the usual routine of locking up and cleaning before calling it a night. When the three of them left through the back door, Alex shivered in the frozen air. It was supposed to drop to nearly zero degrees tonight. Saying goodbye to Luke, she and Riley got into the truck. She pulled a pair of gloves from her pockets as Riley started the engine and pulled away from the bar.

"I should've come out and got the truck warmed up before we left," Riley said.

She sent him a smile. "That's all right. It's not like we have far to go."

Really, it was only a couple of blocks to her place. They would be there in less than five minutes. She could stand a bit of cold. Still, she looked forward to spring and all the outdoor activities it would bring. She intended to hold Riley to his promise to teach her how to fly fish.

When he pulled up to the curb in front of the duplex, he put the truck in park and looked over at her. "See you in the morning."

With a sappy grin, she echoed him and opened her door, sliding out of the truck. She hurried up the walkway to her porch, and then up the stairs to her door. After a quick wave to Riley, she slipped inside her warm apartment. She was used to these late nights now, but she couldn't wait to crawl into bed with the fresh flannel sheets she'd put on this morning. And maybe a wool blanket too.

⌒⌒⌒⟶

On the short, quiet drive back to the bar, Riley thought about the coffee shop. It had been a lot of work already and would take a whole lot more work before opening. Even so, it held a certain enjoyment. There was something deeply satisfying about soon working for himself. He might not be his dad, but it was still in the Conrad blood to want to run your own business. It might never amount to the business empire his father had created, yet a small-town coffee shop was all he'd ever wanted or needed.

Despite how busy the place kept him, it hadn't escaped his mind that he'd be stuck working in Denver right now if not for Alex. He would've made it work, but he wasn't going to pretend it would've been easy. None of this would be happening if not for her. She'd been with him through each up and down that had brought him here, and he intended to keep it that way. It was probably about time to make that official. He just had to pick the right moment.

He pulled back into his spot behind the bar and got out. Using the dim light from the truck cab to locate the bar key before it went out, he walked up to the door. As he fiddled to find the keyhole in the dark, footsteps crunched the snow and ice behind him. Who in their right mind would be walking around this time of night in the freezing temperatures? He turned.

Something crashed the side of his chin. He stumbled sideways but quickly regained his balance. In the dark, he spotted four black silhouettes standing in a semi-circle around him, backing him up to the bar. One of the assailants lunged toward him again. Military training took over in an instant. Riley dodged the wide strike and rammed his fist into the attacker's stomach. With a grunt, the guy doubled over. Riley sensed someone behind him and swung his arm back. His elbow crunched against bone. A loud yelp preceded an eruption of swearing.

Before he could switch his attention to the other three, a rock-hard object smashed into his side. The air burst from his lungs and streaks of pain shot through his ribs. He staggered. His bad leg gave out, and he fell to one knee. He scrambled to get back up, but the object he now identified was a baseball bat swung down again. It smacked against his lower back, forcing him to his hands and knees.

His heart raced with the pounding need to get up, much like the day he'd been shot. If he could just get into the bar and reach Luke's gun! He lunged toward the door, but a fist latched onto his coat, jerking him back.

"Not so tough now, Captain America."

Riley recognized that voice. He balled his fist to take a swing, but Tony rammed the bat into his gut, doubling him over again. He gasped to recover what little air he could. Every attempt to take a breath set fire to his chest.

"You didn't think you could hit me and get away with it, did you?" Tony scoffed. "Nah, nobody hits me and gets away with it. Once we're done here, I think I'll pay a visit to your girl. She's home alone, isn't she? Of course she is, 'cause you just dropped her off like you do every night."

Alex.

The pain vanished, and Riley shoved to his feet. He grabbed Tony by the jacket and slammed him into the side of the truck. However, two pairs of hands yanked Riley back. He fought to free himself. The bat cracked against the side of his head. The next moment he was on the ground. Everything was foggy. He blinked hard to clear his vision and struggled to get up. A fist plowed into his face. A second blow landed him on his back, and this time he couldn't hold onto his fading consciousness.

Alex rolled from one side to the other. A minute later, she rolled onto her back and blew out a sigh. She hadn't had this much trouble getting to sleep in months. She glanced toward her nightstand. It was almost one-thirty. She closed her eyes, taking a deep breath and willing herself to relax. It didn't work. A creeping, cold sensation still lingered in her limbs. Something was . . . off. Ever since she had gone to bed, things just felt . . . wrong. But why?

Surely it was just her imagination messing with her. Nighttime was notoriously bad for that. She reached for her phone just to check if there were any texts or messages. The screen showed nothing. She brought up Riley's contact, and her thumb hovered over the call button. She shook her head against her pillow. She was being silly. Why wake him up? He'd been working so hard. He needed all the rest he could get.

Then again, he would probably tell her she should call, even if it was silly. She pressed call and put the phone to her ear.

It rang.

And rang.

After several rings, it went to voicemail. He was probably sound asleep just like she should be. When it was time to leave a message, she said, "Hey, it's nothing. I was just feeling weird and can't sleep. But I'm fine. It's probably just random anxiety because I'm tired. Well, I'll talk to you in the morning."

She ended the call, and the room went dark as her screen turned off. Her heart thumped in the silence, heavier than it should while resting. There was no reason to worry that Riley hadn't answered. No reason at all.

So why was she so worried?

She drew a deep breath. "I'm being irrational, Lord. Please calm me . . . and please don't let anything be wrong."

For the next minute or two, she found herself praying Riley would call her back. However, instead of his ringtone, a police siren echoed faintly outside. Her heart gave a jarring thud in reaction. She shook her head again. Now she *was* being ridiculous. The police station wasn't far from her apartment. She'd heard the sirens at night dozens of times. It could be any number of things. Returning her phone to her nightstand, she pulled the covers up to her chin and forced herself to calm down. The minutes ticked by.

A knock at the door sent an icy jolt straight to her core. She bolted upright, holding her breath. The knock came again. She slid out of bed and tiptoed into the hall. Who on earth would knock at her door at this time of night? If it were Riley, he would have called first. A chill skittered down her back. Should she even answer it? She was all alone here. Who knew what kind of person could be on the other side?

A muffled voice filtered in from the outside.

"Alex, it's Luke."

Her body seized, frozen for a second. But then she flipped on the light and rushed to the door. She yanked it open. The taut, grim expression on Luke's face told Alex her world was about to be rocked again. Just like she'd known when her dad had called to tell her about Josh. Even before he'd said a word, she'd known it was bad. Her legs shook, and she couldn't get her voice to work.

"Alex," Luke said gently when she just stared at him.

In the following split-second, she didn't want him to speak. She didn't want to hear it. She didn't want to know. She didn't want her life to fall apart again.

"Riley's been beat up. He's being taken to the hospital."

Her knees almost buckled, and her lungs expelled a harsh breath. Her voice barely rasped past her throat. "Is he all right?"

Luke's face morphed into that sympathetic look people gave to try to comfort someone. She had seen it so many times after Josh had died. So many horrible times. "I don't know. Why don't you get dressed, and I'll take you over there?"

Paralysis clung to Alex's limbs like ice, but she snapped out of it. Spinning around, she ran to her room and changed out of her pajamas as fast as she could. *Please, God, let him be all right.* He had to be all right. She couldn't lose him too. Not after how he'd helped her deal with Josh's death. If she lost him . . .

She rushed back into the kitchen where Luke waited at the door. Tugging on her coat, she grabbed her purse and followed him outside. In his car, she fought to control her breathing, but her heart raced out of control. This couldn't be happening. She begged herself to wake up and discover it was only a nightmare. But the tight, gnawing ache in her stomach knew this was real.

She looked over at Luke. "What happened?"

He shook his head, the street lamps flashing on his face as he drove through town well above the speed limit. "I'm not sure. I was at home and realized I forgot my phone at the bar. I was going to wait until morning but decided to go back for it. When I got there, Riley was on the ground by his truck."

"Was he conscious?"

"No."

Alex wrapped her arms around her stomach that threatened to heave itself up her throat. She was no doctor, but even she knew it wasn't good if he was unconscious for any length of time. Not to mention how cold it was outside. What if Luke had never gone back?

She squeezed her eyes shut against the burning tears. Finally, she looked at Luke again. "How bad is he?"

He glanced at her but didn't speak immediately.

She gulped in a breath. "Tell me the truth. I need to know."

His jaw twitched. "It wasn't good. He was pretty messed up."

She hunched in her seat, still clutching her stomach. A couple of tears finally made their escape. "Who would do this? *Why* would anyone do this?"

"Whoever it was stole a bunch of liquor from the bar."

She shook her head dismally. A robbery? Someone had beaten Riley up to steal liquor?

The moment they pulled into the nearly-empty hospital parking lot, she jumped out of the car and ran in through the emergency entrance. Luke followed right behind her. At the receptionist desk, she fought to calm herself though she was one step away from full-blown panic.

"My boyfriend, Riley Conrad, was just brought in. He was beaten up."

The middle-aged woman must have seen the tear streaks on her face and gave her a gentle look. The kind of look that only heightened her desperation every time she saw it. "The doctor is looking after him now."

"Do you know if he's all right?" Riley could be awake, dead, or anything for all she knew. Surely the nurse could tell her *something*.

"I'm sorry, I don't. Why don't you have a seat? The doctor will be out to see you as soon as they're done treating him."

Alex stood, unable to move or process any of the emotions boiling inside of her until Luke's hand settled on her shoulder. "Come on, Alex."

She numbly let him lead her to the waiting area, and they both took a seat. Her knee bounced, and she rubbed her tingling hands against her jeans. Even with Luke sitting right there, she felt suddenly alone. He was her friend and all, but he wasn't Riley.

Battling another onslaught of tears, she pulled her phone from her pocket. She fumbled to dial Mindy with trembling fingers. It was as if her blood wasn't reaching her extremities. Three rings droned in her ear before her friend answered.

"Alex, is everything all right?"

She gulped and struggled to speak calmly. Her voice shook. "No. Riley is in the hospital. Someone beat him up."

Mindy's voice rose in volume and pitch. "Is he okay?"

Alex's cheeks grew hot and wet. "I don't know. He's in the ER. Luke said he was in pretty bad shape and unconscious." She sniffed and swiped at her face. The urge to sob tightened her chest.

"Alex," Mindy said, speaking in a soothing yet serious tone, "we'll be right over, okay? Just hold on. We'll be there soon."

"Okay," she choked out.

She ended the call and hung her head. *Oh, please God, let him be all right.* She fought unwelcome thoughts of losing him. To even contemplate it would send her into a meltdown she didn't know if she could escape. She needed to be strong.

Time dragged for eternity. Alex sat fixated on the door to the hall of examining rooms, waiting for a sign of Riley or a doctor. Cold waves of fear and dread rolled through her stomach and outward into her limbs. Her knee bounced furiously, and she trembled as if caught outside in the snow without a coat.

"Riley's the strongest guy I know." Luke's voice broke into her spinning thoughts. "He survived getting shot. I'm sure he'll be fine."

She cast him a look and attempted to smile. "I'm sure you're right."

But she wasn't.

Mindy and Zach arrived after what seemed like hours. The moment they walked in, Alex got up and Mindy pulled her into her arms, holding her tightly.

"I prayed the whole way here," Mindy said. "Have you heard anything?"

Alex shook her head against her friend's shoulder. "Not yet."

"Everything will be okay." Mindy embraced her even tighter. "We're right here with you, no matter what, and God is taking care of Riley."

Alex squeezed her eyes shut, but the tears still leaked out. If only she could snatch even an ounce of such confidence.

They all sat down, and Zach questioned Luke about what had happened. Mindy held Alex's hand, lending her support, but Alex's attention fixed on the door again. Why hadn't they heard anything yet? Riley had to have been in there for over a half an hour. Surely someone had news. What if no one told her how he was? She wasn't technically family.

At last, the door opened and a man in scrubs stepped out. Alex's heart thumped sluggishly and sent ice cascading through her body. The doctor walked toward them, and they all rose.

"Are you here for Riley Conrad?"

Alex nodded. "Is he all right?"

"We've treated him the best we can, but due to the trauma and extent of his injuries, we feel it's best to transfer him to Denver. He's being prepped for transport now."

Chapter Thirty-six

THE BLAND BEIGE WALLS OF THE WAITING ROOM AT UNIVERSITY of Colorado Hospital in Denver sported colorful fine art prints that did nothing to soothe Alex's raw emotions. She clasped her hands tightly in desperate prayer and a battle to remain hopeful. Mindy and Zach sat to her right while Mr. and Mrs. Conrad were to her left looking for the first time like regular people. No fine suit or meticulously applied makeup. Just jeans and sweatshirts and worried eyes.

Across from them sat Luke and Kat, Mark and Kayla, Jenny, and Grandpa Joe. A somber silence surrounded them as they waited for news of Riley's condition. Alex hated the wait. Her insides clamored to do anything but sit still, but she had already called her parents on the ride to Denver with Mindy and Zach. They were on their way now and would arrive in about an hour and a half. Another thing she had to wait on. Though she had Mindy and Zach, the little girl inside her cried for her mom and dad.

She leaned back in her chair, straightening her shoulders. After sitting hunched for so long, they were starting to ache. Mindy reached over to take her hand again. Alex squeezed it and attempted a wobbly smile. What would she do if she had to face this alone? If Mindy and Zach weren't around and she had no relationship with Riley's family? But they were here. She wasn't alone this time. Not only that, but Zach had called Pastor Ellis so he could share the news with the congregation and gain even more support through prayer.

An hour passed. Alex's knee bounced uncontrollably again. A nurse kept them updated about where Riley was, but none of the news was encouraging. He had not yet regained consciousness and had gone through CT scans and MRIs to determine the extent of his injuries. What if he died? What if the words he and Alex had shared in his truck when he'd brought her home were the last words she would ever hear from him on this earth? Her head buzzed, her stomach threatening to upend, and she swallowed hard to keep it in place.

An electric shock jolted through her when a man in a white coat walked into the waiting room.

"Mr. and Mrs. Conrad?"

Everyone shot to their feet. The man was dark haired and on the heavier side. Behind a pair of black glasses, his eyes spoke of kindness. Alex needed that. As much as she wanted information, the fear of bad news left her body barely strong enough to support her.

"Yes?" Mr. Conrad responded.

"I'm Dr. Gordon. I've been looking after your son."

"How is he?"

Alex held her breath. Dr. Gordon spoke in a positive tone, but she could tell he wouldn't sugarcoat things.

"We have him settled in the ICU. He has several broken ribs and a bruised kidney. Those will heal with time. Right now our biggest concern is the head trauma he sustained. There's some brain swelling we're monitoring closely. Should it increase, we may need to perform surgery. As of right now, Riley is in a coma."

Alex wrapped her arms around her stomach, a sob rising up and catching in her chest. A coma? Mindy put her arm around her and hugged her close. Dr. Gordon must have noticed this reaction because he offered her a sympathetic look.

"Now, obviously I can make no guarantees, but I'm optimistic Riley will regain consciousness before too long. Typically coma patients come out of it within two to four weeks if not much sooner. The good news is that he's breathing on his own and has not needed to be put on a ventilator."

A long moment of silence followed as they all processed the doctor's information. Alex's mind spun, creating all kinds of horrific scenarios. She'd been around military families enough to know head injuries weren't like broken bones. They didn't just heal and go back to normal. The consequences could be much more terrible.

"Will he have any permanent mental or physical damage?" Her voice trembled.

So many brain trauma victims were never the same again. Riley might survive, but would it change him? When he woke up, he might not even be the same man she had fallen in love with. What then? What if he was a completely different person? Would he still love her?

Dr. Gordon answered gently. "I'm afraid we won't know until he regains consciousness and we can perform some tests."

Like a slow motion movie, Alex saw her world crumbling all over again.

"Can we see him?" Mrs. Conrad's voice echoed the longing that pounded deep within Alex.

"I can take a couple of you."

Alex's heart jumped and then sank. She loved Riley like she had never loved anyone, but she wasn't family. Not officially. Riley's parents and siblings were. Surely they would see him first. She would have to wait. Her chest ached as if her ribcage were being split right down the middle.

But then Mrs. Conrad turned to her. "Come with us."

Alex could have broken down and cried right there she was so grateful. Holding in the tears, she followed Riley's parents and Dr. Gordon through the sterile hospital halls. It seemed very quiet for a hospital. Then again, it was only around three o'clock

337

in the morning. She shivered. It wasn't exactly cold, but a chill crawled along her skin. What would it be like to see Riley, knowing he was in a coma? Her heart had pounded with the desperate desire to see him ever since Luke had shown up at her door, but now... Was she even prepared?

When Dr. Gordon stopped at a door and opened it, Alex slowly stepped into the room after Mr. and Mrs. Conrad. Her gaze landed on Riley lying in the hospital bed, hooked up to an IV and various monitors, and her breath caught in her chest. The tears that had come and gone over the last couple of hours returned, dribbling down her cheeks and blurring her vision. Yet, it wasn't enough to block out the sight of Riley's bruised and swollen face, and the bandage around his head.

A tiny sob broke free with the air trapped in her lungs. She would have given anything for him to wake up right then and tell her that he was okay. To see him like this—to not know if she would get him back—tore open her heart with familiar wounds that had only just healed.

"Oh, God." She didn't even know what to add to the half-whispered prayer.

She stepped to Riley's bedside across from his parents and took his hand.

"Riley." Her voice cracked. His complete lack of response only drove the pain in deeper. "I'm here," she choked out around her tears. "I'm right here."

They let Alex remain at Riley's side as the others came and went. His mom stayed too. They sat, watching his breathing that was a bit labored due to his ribs, and listened to the steady rhythm of his heart monitor. Sometimes they spoke to him and sometimes to each other. And in the midst of it, Alex begged God for healing.

She didn't know how long it had been—minutes seemed like hours in a hospital—but the door opened quietly and Mindy stepped into the room.

"Your parents just got here." She glanced at Mrs. Conrad. "Luke also has news from the sheriff in Aspen Creek."

Alex gazed for a long moment at Riley's battered face. She didn't want to leave him, even for a moment, but she did desperately need to see her parents. She pushed herself up from the chair the doctor had provided. Now that the adrenaline was wearing off, her limbs responded sluggishly, like trying to walk through syrup. They followed Mindy back to the waiting room. Mom immediately took her in her arms when she walked in, and Alex laid her head on her shoulder. Dad put his arms around both of them. In their protective embrace, Alex allowed herself the real cry that had been building all night. Her mom whispered soothing encouragement in her ear.

They held her until she was able to calm herself, and then they sat down. Wiping her face with tissues from a box Mindy handed her, Alex looked at Luke. "You have information from the sheriff?"

He nodded and spoke coolly. "They found out who did this. It was Tony Vargas and his friends."

Alex's heart took a dive toward her stomach. It didn't come as a shock, yet to hear it was like a punch to the gut, and her tears flowed once more.

"Stupid, punk kids," Joe growled. "If I ever get my hands on them . . ."

Luke cast him a look of agreement. Every man in this room probably had half a mind to go after the guys themselves, and Alex would have cheered them on.

"I guess Tony brought his brother into the ER with a badly broken nose," Luke went on. "Said he slipped and fell, but the doctor thought it was suspicious. The sheriff questioned them separately. When their stories didn't quite add up, Tony's brother caved and confessed. They even found the stolen liquor in Tony's car. They're going out to pick up their two friends now."

Alex swiped her sleeves across her face, but it did little to stem the flow of tears. "Why would they do this? Why does Tony hate Riley so much?"

Luke let out a long sigh. "Apparently this isn't his first run-in with someone from the military. Sheriff said Tony has warrants in both Pennsylvania and Michigan for assault against military servicemen, though this is the first time he put anyone in the hospital. The sheriff didn't have much information, but it sounds like Tony's dad was military and abusive when Tony and his brother were kids. I guess he now holds a grudge when it comes to anyone in uniform."

Alex squeezed her eyes shut and ground her teeth together but could summon no sympathy for Tony. A terrible childhood gave him no right to beat anyone half to death.

"Now that he's been apprehended, he'll have a lot to answer for," Luke said.

But what comfort was that? Tony might pay for his crimes, but it didn't mean Riley would leave this hospital the same, if he left at all.

⌁

Nearly thirty-six hours passed. A lifetime, as far as Alex was concerned. She couldn't sleep or eat during that time, despite how her parents and Mindy encouraged her to try. Monday morning dawned with a bright sunrise that didn't quite make it into the room. Mindy and Zach had left the evening before since Zach had to work, but Mindy promised to return at some point today. Luke and Kat had left too. Kat assured Alex she would check in on Tux and make sure he had enough food and water and was well taken care of for as long as Riley remained here.

Alex remained glued to her spot at Riley's bedside, holding his hand. Her mom and dad had sat with her most of the night, as well as Riley's parents and Grandpa Joe. Around mid-morning, Riley's parents reluctantly departed. Mr. Conrad had to take care of business, and Mrs. Conrad wanted to change her clothes, but they both said they would return shortly. Alex's parents left the room as well in order to get breakfast with Joe.

Alone with Riley, Alex stared at him and squeezed his hand. Though Dr. Gordon was pleased with his progress and assured them the brain swelling was going down, Riley showed no outward sign of recovery.

"Please come back," she whispered. Tears welled in her eyes and rolled down her cheeks. "Please come back to me. I love you so much."

She closed her eyes, fighting the pain rising in her chest. She wanted so badly for this to be over. To go back to the life they had made in Aspen Creek. Back to the bar and the coffee shop. Back to the dreams she had for the future. Dreams that all included Riley. Would this be the end of it all? Would she have to create yet another life from broken pieces? How could she do that again? She had come too close to failing last time.

A buzzing jolted her from her thoughts. It resonated from the table next to Riley's bed where a nurse had set a bag of his personal belongings. After the second buzz, Alex pushed up from her chair and reached into the bag to withdraw his phone. Even before she read the name, she recognized the picture on the screen— his best friend Bradley, who he mentioned so often. Her heart clenched painfully. She should have tried to get in touch with him the night this all happened. She hadn't even thought of it.

Hands shaking, she accepted the call and put the phone to her ear. "Hello?"

A noticeable pause followed before a male voice asked, "Is this Alex?"

"Yes."

Another pause before Bradley's low, serious tone came through. "What happened?"

She drew a deep breath, only now noticing how weak and shaky her body was from lack of sleep and nourishment. She sat down so she wouldn't get lightheaded and faint. Making a valiant effort to hold herself together, she told Bradley about the attack and Riley's condition. Her voice wobbled and cracked a few times with the tears that didn't want to stop.

When she finished, Bradley remained quiet for a moment before he said, "Will you keep me updated?"

"Of course." She wiped her face with her sleeves and grabbed her own phone. "Give me your number so I can put it in my phone."

He did, and Alex added him to her contacts.

Just before they hung up, Bradley said, "Hey, Alex, we'll all be praying for him. Remember, he survived war. I don't think he is going to let a few thugs take him down."

She managed to smile. "Thanks, Bradley."

Chapter Thirty-seven

THE NEXT MORNING, MOM AND DAD TALKED ALEX INTO COMING with them to the hotel they had booked to shower and change. She forced her heavy, aching body to move and followed them out of the hospital. Walking outside was like stepping into a different world. It felt like she hadn't been out in weeks. The world still moved. People still lived their lives.

They didn't say much on the short drive to the hotel. When they reached their room, Alex trudged into the bathroom and turned on the shower. For a long time she just stood under the hot water, trying to pretend for just a moment that none of this had happened—that she was back in her apartment, getting ready for Riley to pick her up for work. Back to the wonderfully normal routine she had grown to love.

Numbness engulfed her as she finally stepped out of the shower and put on the clean clothes Mindy had brought. Working the tangles out of her wet hair with her fingers, she looked into the mirror and peered at the girl with red, shadowed eyes. Though she had slept a little last night, curled up on the chair in Riley's room, it hadn't been nearly enough. Everything hurt this morning.

The reflection staring back at her was nothing like the girl who had felt like Cinderella only a few weeks ago. This girl looked broken. Shattered. When she recalled the night of the party and witnessing Riley's awestruck reaction to her dress, all the emotion crashed in at once to cripple her. Sinking to the floor against the bathroom wall, she couldn't hold back the sobs building in her chest. They broke free, each one a little harder and more painful than the last.

Mom's voice filtered through the door, but she couldn't respond. A moment later, the door opened a crack before swinging open more fully. Mom sank down next to her and put her arm around her. Dad sat down on her other side, laying his hand comfortingly on her back. Alex sobbed inconsolably, the pain and fear of the last couple of days consuming her. She'd fought to hold it back for so long. She'd fought to be stronger than this, but she couldn't do it anymore.

"I'm scared."

Dad rubbed her back. "Riley is a fighter. I'm sure he'll come through this just fine."

But Alex shook her head. As terrified as she was for Riley, the fear that gripped her now was something else—another fear that had crept in, growing with every passing hour.

"If I lose him, I'm afraid I won't want to live." The truth broke out with a choked sob. "I'm afraid I'll sink again."

She wanted to believe she was stronger than that, but she knew herself too well. She had fallen once; she could so easily fall again. Already she struggled to understand why God would allow this to happen. Why bring Riley into her life only to take him away? Hadn't she lost enough?

The struggle between her faith and her fears pressed down like an enormous weight on her chest.

Mom hugged her close, her voice low. "We're here with you, Alex. No matter what happens, you don't have to face it alone this time. We'll help you through it."

Alex buried her fingers in her hair and held her head against her palms, crying harder.

"I know it's hard," Dad's thick voice murmured near her ear, "but whatever happens, God has a plan. You have to trust Him, Alex."

Her human nature didn't want to hear that. She didn't care that there was a plan. She just wanted Riley back. But she fought desperately to hold on to her tattered faith. She had battled too hard to regain it.

They sat together on the bathroom floor for a long time while she cried and let the emotions drain out. Eventually, the tears slowed, though she wasn't sure she could even stand up. Any bit of strength she'd clung to over the last couple of days seemed to have poured out with her tears. But she did need to get back to Riley. Her dad helped her up, and after she finished drying her hair, they returned to the hospital.

For the remainder of the morning, she sat at Riley's bedside. This was the longest she had gone without having a conversation with him since they had met. She missed his voice. And smile. It had become such a huge part of her everyday life. She'd never imagined just how noticeable the absence of it would be.

After a quick lunch in the cafeteria with her parents, Alex excused herself. The morning emotions had taken a toll on her mentally and spiritually. Wandering the hospital halls, she found her way to the hospital chapel. She slid into one of the short pews and gazed at the large wooden cross hanging on the wall. She didn't need any particular place or building to pray—she could reach out to her Heavenly Father at anytime, anywhere—but this little chapel was the only place that didn't feel like a hospital.

Bowing her head, she spent a while in silent prayer. She confessed all of her fears and doubts and struggle to keep trusting. She told God how afraid she was to sink again and how desperately she wanted to make it through this stronger, not weaker.

For a long time, silence engulfed the small, intimate space. Eventually footsteps entered behind her. She didn't look up until they drew near and stopped at her pew. Her eyes widened. Mr. Conrad. Without a word, he slid into the pew next to her. She just stared at him. He was the last person she would have expected to visit the chapel. Men like him relied on their own power and abilities, not spiritual ones. What should she say to him? Her muddled, sluggish thoughts wouldn't cooperate, but he spoke first.

"I haven't been in a church since Mark and Kayla were married." He paused for a moment, staring ahead at the cross as if thinking and speaking to himself. "My mother was religious in her later years after my father died. I like to think it counted for something and she is in a better place. We didn't always have it easy while I was growing up."

Alex took a deep breath. Why did she always feel inadequate in these situations? It should be so easy to share her faith. After a silent prayer, she said, "If your mother truly placed her faith in Christ before she died, then she is in heaven."

Mr. Conrad nodded slowly. "When Riley and I talked after the Christmas party, he said something about being sure of where he was going when he died. I haven't thought much about life beyond this one. But this is the second time I've seen Riley in the hospital, both times with life-threatening injuries. I'm also not getting any younger." Finally, he looked at her. "Is it really possible to be certain of life after death?"

Alex looked into his cool eyes. He was such an imposing sort of man but was clearly searching. She had never imagined for a moment she would have this conversation with him, but she didn't want to waste the opportunity.

"Yes, it is." *Lord, give me the right words.* "Anyone who believes they are a sinner and puts their full faith and trust in Jesus's death, burial, and resurrection can be certain of their eternal future. Salvation is through faith alone, in Christ alone. Nothing more, nothing less. Riley believes that, and so do I." She drew a breath to settle her nerves. "I've struggled in my faith a great deal and was angry with God for my brother's death. But I know He never gave up on me even if I did. He wants to extend the same grace to everyone who will accept it."

She held her breath. Would he say or ask anything more? After a few silent moments, he offered her a quiet "thank you" and rose to leave the chapel. Once more, she sat alone and in silence, but hope stirred within her that, as hard as it was to worry about Riley, it might lead to his dad's salvation.

The time of prayer and heartening conversation offered the boost Alex needed. While still exhausted and uncertain, her world didn't seem quite so fragile when she left the chapel.

On her way back to Riley's room, she entered the waiting area where a familiar figure stood with Mr. and Mrs. Conrad.

"Mr. Moretti."

He turned to her. "Alex."

"What are you doing here? Is everything all right with your wife?"

He nodded. "I heard what happened. I wanted to drop by and offer my support. My dad died after a car accident several years ago, so I know what it's like to be stuck in a hospital waiting for good news."

Alex summoned the best smile she could muster. "Thank you, I really appreciate that."

Her parents lingered nearby, and she motioned them closer to make introductions. They hit it off well with Moretti and spoke for a little while before he prepared to leave. Focused on Alex once more, he said, "As soon as he wakes up, you tell that boyfriend of yours I expect him to make a full recovery. You two still haven't taken me up on my dinner invitation."

Alex's smile bloomed a bit more easily. "I'll tell him."

Once he had gone, Alex returned to Riley's room. She spent time on her phone, answering messages on her social media accounts. Many people from their church asked about Riley. At one point, she opened his Facebook profile and read him all the notes their friends and acquaintances had left for him. She prayed he would be able to read them himself soon.

That evening around suppertime, Alex caught movement out of the corner of her eye. She sat up straight, her attention fixed on Riley. Had she just imagined it? She held her breath. Her pulse quickened. Finally, she had to let her breath out. Disappointment took its place. She wanted this so badly she was beginning to imagine things.

However, only a few seconds later, Riley moved his hand. It wasn't imagined.

"He moved!" Though only a tiny thing that maybe meant nothing, she hadn't seen him move for three days.

The room fell silent, and they all focused on Riley. Another moment later, he moved his head against his pillow, a slight grimace crossing his face. His mom leaned over the bed.

"Riley, can you hear me?"

Alex, her eyes stinging with tears of hope, stared at his face. *Please, respond.* He didn't; however, a new energy of anticipation filled the room.

"I'll go find the doctor," Mr. Conrad said.

While he was gone, they took turns talking to Riley, holding their breaths for even a small response. When Mr. Conrad returned, Dr. Gordon was with him. Alex stepped to the side with her parents to give him room. She wrung her hands, desperate for good news.

After a thorough examination, Dr. Gordon turned to them with a smile. "Riley is starting to show signs of regaining consciousness, though it still may take a few days before he is fully aware of anything."

A cool, numbing sensation, as if all her muscles were finally relaxing, washed through Alex, her legs going a bit wobbly. Her dad put his arm around her shoulders, and a couple of tears dripped down her cheeks.

"He's not in a coma anymore?"

Dr. Gordon shook his head, still smiling. "No."

Chapter Thirty-eight

HOW COULD SHE BE SO ANXIOUS FOR RILEY TO WAKE UP, YET SO scared at the same time? Alex had sat glued to his bedside for two more days now, anticipating the moment he would regain consciousness. He'd shown increasing signs of it. She prayed for the moment to come; however, her anxiety and fear grew. What might happen when he *did* wake up? Any number of things could still go wrong. What if he wasn't the same? That question pierced her heart like a knife blade wedged between her ribs. She would stick with him no matter what, but it still scared her more than anything she had ever faced before.

Shortly before noon on the fifth day since the attack, Alex sat with her phone, texting Mindy, when the blankets shifted. She looked up as Riley stirred. It wasn't the first time this morning. Usually, he stilled again and was quiet. This time his eyes fluttered open. Again, it wasn't the first time; yet, after a couple of blinks, they stayed open. She jumped up from her chair.

"Riley."

His parents joined her.

"Riley, can you hear me?"

He blinked a few more times as if disoriented, but then his gaze focused on her. "Alex."

He barely whispered, but a grin broke out on her face. She grabbed his hand and squeezed it gently. "I'm here." Her own voice wasn't much more than a squeak.

JAYE ELLIOT

Mr. Conrad turned to get the doctor once again. Riley glanced in his direction, and his brows below his bandage furrowed. He looked like he might slip back into unconsciousness, but his eyes opened when Dr. Gordon entered a minute later, and they gave him room.

"Riley, I'm Dr. Gordon. You're at University of Colorado Hospital."

It took a moment before Riley seemed to comprehend.

"Do you remember what happened?" Dr. Gordon asked.

Again Riley hesitated, but then clarity smoothed his expression. "I was jumped outside the bar." His eyes widened, his skin going pale. "Alex."

At the desperate way he spoke her name, she moved closer and took his hand again. "I'm right here."

He looked up at her almost as if he were in pain. "Did he hurt you?"

She frowned. "Did who hurt me?"

"Tony?"

"No, he didn't hurt me. I wasn't there."

Riley closed his eyes and released a slow sigh. Finally, he looked at her again. "He said he was going to your apartment."

Alex's breath died and grew cold in her chest. If he had showed up at her door, what would have happened? Goose bumps crawled along her arms. Thank God that Luke had arrived first. She shook her head almost as much to assure herself as Riley.

"He never showed up. At least not before Luke came to get me. He went back to the bar for his phone and found you. I think Tony was too busy taking his brother to the ER with a broken nose. That's where the sheriff questioned them and found out what happened."

"So they were caught?"

"Yes. Tony's brother confessed to everything."

350

The tension released from Riley's face, and Alex once again battled tears.

"It's so good to see you awake. I've been so worried." Just seeing the concern for her on his face had already done her heart a world of good, and she thanked God.

"How long was I out?"

"Five days."

At his look of surprise, she said, "You were in a coma."

He seemed to struggle with this information, and his eyelids grew heavy again. He didn't say much more before unconsciousness reclaimed him. Dr. Gordon assured them this was normal and that he would become more alert over the next few days.

For the rest of the day, Riley passed in and out of consciousness, sometimes briefly, sometimes for longer. Alex thanked God for every moment she gained, to be able to talk to him and hear his voice. Dr. Gordon still had to perform tests, but she rejoiced that, for now, Riley didn't seem changed.

When he awoke the next morning, he seemed nearly normal besides the fact he was lying in a hospital bed and still sporting bruises from the attack. Once in a while, Alex did pick up hints of pain from his rib injuries, but he had medication to manage it. He even smiled at her and said that he was fine. She laughed, something that felt so good after so long, and had to wipe a bit of moisture from her face. For the first time since the attack, she dared to hope everything would be all right.

Dr. Gordon came in a short time later, and everyone stepped out so he could give Riley a full examination. Though Alex hated to go, she followed her parents to the cafeteria to get coffee and a breakfast sandwich. She hadn't eaten nearly enough in the past week and would have to start taking better care of herself now.

Riley would insist on it. She didn't need him worrying about her when he should focus on his own recovery.

After eating, they all sat and waited for Dr. Gordon to come get them. Alex sipped her coffee and thought about how much she missed Riley's blends. Even the best, most expensive coffee in the world would never taste quite like it.

When Dr. Gordon joined them, Alex couldn't help but hold her breath. He was smiling though. Would he smile if he had bad news?

"How is he?" Mr. Conrad asked.

"His injuries are healing nicely," Dr. Gordon answered. "I don't see anything to worry about there. I performed several tests to assess any damage from the brain trauma. While it's impossible to say if there will be any long term effects from the attack, I didn't find anything overly concerning. I do, however, have to tell you that, at this point, Riley is unable to walk."

Alex just about crushed her coffee cup and put her free hand to her chest. Beneath it, her heart gave a sluggish beat.

"He's paralyzed?" Mr. Conrad said.

"Not in the traditional sense. It's not a spinal injury; it's a brain injury. Riley still has feeling and mobility in his legs, but the area of his brain that gives the commands needed to walk has been injured. It is fully possible he can walk again, but it will take a lot of dedication and rehab to relearn."

Alex couldn't seem to breathe until her dad put his hand on her shoulder and gave it a squeeze. Riley was alive. That was the important thing.

"I know this is tough news to hear," Dr. Gordon said sympathetically, "but given the circumstances, if this is the extent of effects of the brain trauma Riley suffered, then I think I'd have to call him blessed. I've seen much worse."

Alex forced a nod. He was right. But did Riley feel the same way?

"Can we see him now?"

Dr. Gordon smiled at her. "Yes. He has asked to see you alone first before everyone comes back in."

Her heart thumped. Was this a good thing or bad thing? How would he feel given the results of his examination? Would he take it hard or would he be happy, as she was, that he was alive?

With a glance at Riley's parents and then at her own, she hurried down the hall to his room. She took a deep breath at his door before letting herself inside.

Riley was sitting up in bed, a wonderful sight after how many days he had just lain there so still and unresponsive. She raised her brows, trying to gauge how he was feeling. He lifted his hand and held it out to her. She walked quickly to the bed to take it and sat down on the edge facing him.

"Are you okay?" she asked.

He nodded, a hint of a smile on his lips. "Yeah. Are you?"

She squeezed his hand. "Yes. I'm just glad you're here. I was so afraid I'd lose you even if you did wake up."

The emotions of the last week built like a boiling pot inside her and tears rushed in and overflowed, running down her cheeks. Riley pulled her closer and put his arms around her. She curled up against his chest, careful not to hurt his ribs. It felt so good to have him hold her again, and her tears kept flowing, both with the release of how hard this had been and with joy.

Once she had her tears back under control, they talked quietly for a few minutes before she went to get the others. With their parents there, they talked about a lot of things, including plans for the coffee shop. It would be more difficult now, and Alex had no idea when Riley would be able to work on it again. Yet, he didn't seem dissuaded by his current disability. All Alex knew for sure was that she would do whatever she possibly could to help him open the shop whether he could walk or not.

At one point, Riley video chatted with Bradley. Though not an actual face to face meeting, Alex was happy to "meet" Riley's friend more officially. After that, she helped him open and read all the get well cards he had received from their friends and church family back in Aspen Creek. While life might not be completely normal for a long time, Alex finally felt like she could breathe again.

Chapter Thirty-nine

ALEX BACKED INTO RILEY'S RECOVERY ROOM WITH TWO Styrofoam cups in her hands and nudged the door closed. Riley sat in bed, fully alert when she turned to him. She was surprised to find him alone. His parents must have gone out while she was at the hotel showering. Perfect. They'd finally have a moment alone. There had been precious few of those since he had woken up. The doctors had kept Riley for observation, but Alex sensed his anxiousness to get out of the hospital. That, however, brought a whole new set of challenges and questions they had to face. Now might be just the opportunity they needed to discuss it.

"Hey, I brought you coffee. I'm not sure Dr. Gordon would prescribe it for your recovery, but . . ." She shrugged.

He grinned as she handed him the cup. "Thanks." He took a sip, nodding appreciatively. His face still bore the bruises from the attack, but most of the swelling had gone down.

She kicked off her shoes and took a comfortable seat on the edge of the bed. She'd never imagined nor wanted to have to get so comfortable in a hospital room, but it was nearly over now.

"So Dr. Gordon said you can leave in a day or two."

Riley nodded, looking down at his coffee cup. She waited through the contemplative silence for him to look up at her again.

"I don't think going back to my apartment is an option. And I don't see myself being able to work at the bar if I can't walk."

She drew a deep breath. They'd been through so much already. "Neither do I."

"I'll have rehab here in Denver. That will be multiple times a week."

Now she nodded. She'd prepared herself for that. "So, for the time being, we need to find you a place to stay here in Denver." She hated the thought of not having him in Aspen Creek, but that was the last thing she would complain about when God had brought him through this alive.

"My parents have offered to let me stay with them, in the guesthouse."

"Okay," she said slowly. It did seem like the best choice. If he wasn't working, he'd have to stay somewhere rent free, plus have easy access to food and other necessities. His parents were the obvious ones to provide that. She studied his face closely. Their family relationship might be on the mend, but that didn't necessarily mean it would be entirely comfortable for him.

"How do you feel about it?"

He scratched his hand near his IV needle and didn't speak immediately. "I don't think I have much choice. I can't afford to stay anywhere else, and I can't ask my parents to pay for a place when they have an empty house that would work just fine."

She gave him a wry look. "I guess we all just have to do what we have to do. Isn't that what both our lives have been all about the last couple of years?"

He breathed out a short laugh. "Yeah."

The door opened a moment later, and his parents entered. While Mr. Conrad had been at work more the last couple of days, Alex found it very sweet how often he still came to check on Riley. It proved he cared, even if he hadn't been the best at showing it over the years.

Once they had settled into their usual spots, Mr. Conrad looked at Riley and said, "Have you given it some thought?"

"Alex and I were just talking about it." He looked at her, and she tried to silently convey her support in whatever decision he made. Finally, he looked over at his parents. "I appreciate and accept the invitation to stay in the guesthouse. I just have one request."

A guarded look flashed across Mr. Conrad's face, a subtle tightening around his lips, but he showed restraint in not letting it taint his voice. "What is that?"

Alex wondered too since he hadn't mentioned it her.

"I'd like Granddad to move in too, and be able to stay after I go. He belongs with family, not with strangers. If you can afford to put him up in an assisted living place, I'm sure you can afford a home care nurse to look after him."

Silence met the request, though Alex considered it a good sign Mr. Conrad didn't immediately shut it down. Awkward tension stifled the room. Riley's mom dipped her head as if embarrassed or ashamed. She then looked to her husband. Some unspoken communication passed between them.

With an audible breath, Mr. Conrad looked at Riley again and nodded slowly. "All right. We can make that happen."

Alex smiled to herself. To share the house with his grandpa would surely make Riley more comfortable with the arrangement. It would probably help him emotionally as well. Having to say goodbye to his job, his apartment, and everything that had been a normal part of his life in Aspen Creek would no doubt be depressing. He needed to keep his spirits up. That would be an important part of his rehab.

"I'll start making arrangements right away so everything is ready as soon as you are discharged," Mr. Conrad said.

⌐——→

A pitiful, kitten-like mew echoed from the crate in the passenger seat of Alex's Jeep.

"I know, buddy, we're almost there." She glanced briefly at Tux's black and white face pressed to the bars of the pet carrier.

He hadn't ceased to remind her every few miles how much he disliked this car ride.

"Just wait until you get to see Riley. It'll all be worth it."

In just a few minutes, she pulled up in front of the Conrad's guesthouse. Riley had been released from the hospital and moved in yesterday. A new wheelchair ramp took the place of the front steps.

She unbuckled her seatbelt and glanced in the rearview mirror at all the boxes and totes she had stuffed into the back of the Jeep. She had slept in her own bed for the first time in days last night and had been up bright and early to help Luke and Kat pack up the majority of Riley's belongings at the apartment, including one very mopey kitty.

Another meow from Tux, which clearly said he would die if he wasn't released soon, hurried Alex out of the Jeep and around to the passenger door. As she opened it and lifted the crate out, the front door to the house opened. Riley rolled out onto the porch in his wheelchair. It was so good to see him in regular clothes again instead of a hospital gown.

She smiled and held up the crate. "I have someone here who is very anxious to see you."

She walked up to the porch and set the crate on Riley's lap.

"Hey, boy," he said.

Tux stuck his paws through the bars and pulled on Riley's shirt before releasing another mournful sound.

"We better get him inside," Riley said.

"Yeah, before he never forgives me for being the mean lady who locked him in there." Alex opened the door and let Riley go through ahead of her.

Joe met them in the entryway.

"Alex," he said with a big smile.

"Hi, Joe." She gave him a hug, and then turned back to Riley, who opened the crate. Tux crawled out onto his lap and immediately started purring as Riley rubbed his chin. Alex smiled. It was good to see them reunited.

"Ah, another bachelor for the bachelor pad." Joe stepped closer, and Riley introduced him to Tux. The cat accepted a brief ear rub before jumping off of Riley's lap to explore his new domain.

"Well," Alex said, "I brought as much stuff as I could fit in the Jeep, except for your furniture."

Riley looked up at her with a smile. "Thanks. I appreciate it."

Joe reached for his coat. "Let me help you bring it in."

The three of them headed outside. Alex told Riley that she and Joe could handle it, but he insisted on helping, so she piled the lighter items in his lap. Even with his wheelchair, his broken ribs wouldn't make it easy to get around. Alex wasn't about to let him overdo it and watched closely for any signs of undue pain. With the three of them, it didn't take long before they had everything piled inside where Riley could easily sort through it.

"I think it's about time for lunch." Joe motioned them toward the kitchen. "Riley's not the only one who can cook. I made tomato soup. It was his grandma's favorite recipe. I'll get some grilled cheese sandwiches going."

Alex grinned at Riley, and they followed Joe into the kitchen. Though smaller than in the main house, the room didn't lack any of the elegant furnishings. It didn't exactly suit Riley's style, but at least it was temporary. One way or another, he would have his own place again.

"Alex, there are bowls and glasses up in those cabinets, and silverware in the drawer below if you want to get them down," Joe said as he stepped to the stove where a pot steamed. A warm tomato scent filled the air.

Alex opened the cabinet. She handed three bowls, plates, and glasses to Riley, who took them to the dining room table.

"Are your parents still in Aspen Creek?" he asked as they set the table together.

"Yes. They plan to leave the day after tomorrow. They want to make sure I'm settled back in first."

"Are you?"

She shrugged. "Pretty much. I mean, it's no different from before I met you, but it just doesn't feel the same without you there."

"Hopefully it won't be for long."

Of course, he had every intention of being able to walk again as soon as possible. At the same time, Alex realized it would probably take longer than he wanted to admit. Even then, they had no one-hundred-percent guarantee he would even walk again.

"Luke said he'll keep the apartment for you."

Riley shook his head. "You should tell him to rent it out. I'll just find someplace else once I move back."

"If you're sure, I can tell him when I start working again. Kat is going to pick up your shifts for now, and they've both agreed to pick me up and bring me home." She could have driven herself, but the thought of going home alone so late at night gave her chills even if Tony and his friends were locked up now. There were too many evil people in the world.

"That's kind of them."

Alex agreed. "We've also worked out a schedule so I can take you to your rehab."

Riley shot her a frown. "You don't have to come all the way here just to take me to rehab. Between my parents, Mark, and Jen, there's no reason they shouldn't be able to get me there and back."

"I know, but I want to be there to support you." Before leaving the hospital, Alex had asked Dr. Gordon if there was anything she could do to help Riley recover. He'd answered that encouragement and support would be the most important things for Riley, especially if he hit times of frustration and discouragement. While Riley's parents were making a great effort, Alex

360

couldn't quite trust them yet to be everything Riley needed, emotionally and spiritually. Their lives were so full and busy. She just wanted to make sure nothing would slow Riley's recovery. After all, how many times had he inconvenienced himself to support her?

Riley looked like he had a bit more to say on the subject, but Joe walked in with the pot of tomato soup.

"The sandwiches are just about done."

Alex smiled and followed him back to the kitchen to help before Riley could try to dissuade her from her plans. He had been there for her time and again. It was her turn to be there for him.

When the three of them had taken their places at the table, Joe passed the plate of grilled cheese wedges around. Alex put a couple on her plate alongside her bowl of soup. Before they began, Riley asked, "Granddad, is it all right if we pray before we eat?"

Joe didn't seem bothered by the request at all. "Sure, go ahead."

They bowed their heads, and Riley said a short prayer. Alex added her own silent request for Riley's recovery and that, even if this was not where he would have chosen to be, God would use it for good.

Alex slid into the back seat of Mindy and Zach's SUV outside of her apartment on Sunday morning and buckled her seatbelt. "Thanks for picking me up."

Mindy turned to give her a quick smile. "Glad to."

Today would be her first Sunday back at church without Riley. She would have to get used to it and a lot of other things now. She'd offered to pick him up for church, but he refused to let her drive to Denver and back twice in one day. He still wasn't fully on board with her taking him to rehab either.

"Too bad your parents couldn't stay for church with us," Mindy said.

Alex shrugged. "They would've liked to, but they really needed to get back to the farm. Uncle David has been taking care of things, but that's a lot of work when he's got his own stuff to take care of."

She had loved having them stay the last couple of days, and she missed their presence. Thankfully, she was busy enough with Riley that she didn't have time to dwell on her empty apartment and how strange it felt not to have Riley only a few blocks away.

When they arrived at the church, they had barely entered the building before people swarmed Alex to ask how Riley was doing and to give her messages for him. She was actually surprised by just how many people, even those they hardly knew, were so concerned about him and said they were praying for his recovery. It touched her deeply, and she couldn't wait to tell Riley about it.

Once she had sat down with Mindy and Zach just before the service, she said, "I sure wish Riley could be here. He's really going to miss these services. Bradley emailed him links to videos he could watch on Sundays, but I know it won't be the same. He really likes Pastor Ellis's teaching."

Zach leaned forward to look at her. "I'll have to talk to Pastor about it, but I was thinking maybe I could set up a webcam. Then Riley won't have to miss the messages. He won't actually be here with us, but it'd be the next best thing."

Alex grinned. "He'd love that." She thanked God for Zach's technical skills. After all, Riley would need spiritual encouragement more than anything during his recovery.

Chapter Forty

ALEX CLIMBED INTO HER JEEP AND CLOSED THE DOOR, CAREFUL NOT to get her skirt caught in it. She hadn't anticipated the opportunity to wear her dress from the Christmas party again so soon, but Valentine's Day provided just the right occasion.

She set the velvet heels she'd borrowed again from Mindy on the passenger seat to wear later. Mindy might be able to drive in heels, but Alex wasn't going to attempt it. Pulling away from the curb, she steered in the direction of Denver. She couldn't wait to see Riley. When she'd made Valentine's Day plans, she had told him to dress up but hadn't supplied any other information. She hoped he would like the evening she had planned for them. He needed to get out and do something out of the ordinary.

The now familiar drive to Denver dragged a bit, but her excitement returned when she pulled up to the Conrad's guest-house. It had become almost a second home to her in the last couple of weeks. She'd spent more time here than in Aspen Creek. She had even driven over early the last two Sunday mornings to watch Pastor Ellis's message with Riley since Zach had set up the webcam. She could tell it meant a lot to him. And the best part was that Joe had joined them in front of the TV both mornings. By all appearances, he enjoyed the messages, and it created an excellent opportunity for Riley to talk to him about spiritual matters.

Hurrying up to the door, she knocked and waited briefly for it to open. Riley met her on the other side with a smile.

"Hey," he said.

She echoed his greeting, and he backed his wheelchair up for her to step inside. He wore a dark pair of jeans, the blue shirt she always loved on him, and his black suit jacket. Wheelchair or not, he looked very fine. He eyed her up too, and when he got to her feet, his smile widened.

"Nice shoes."

She glanced down at her completely-out-of-place winter boots and laughed. "I wasn't as daring as Mindy to think I could drive in stilettos. Seemed like the best choice until we get where we're going."

Joe stepped into the entryway then and looked at Alex with a grin. "That's one good looking date you've got there, Riley."

Riley just smiled up at Alex with agreement warming in his eyes. She blushed a little under his gaze, and he turned back at Joe. "You going to be fine here tonight, Granddad?"

Joe nodded. "Your parents have like five-zillion channels. I'm sure I'll find something to entertain me. You kids go have fun."

They traded goodbyes. Alex opened the door and let Riley out first. She grabbed her other shoes from the Jeep, and they headed over to the car Riley's parents let them use since it was the easiest for Riley to get in and out of. She opened the passenger door for him and braced his wheelchair while he hoisted himself into the car. While he might not be able to actually walk, at least he was still able to somewhat use his legs to maneuver himself. Alex was always afraid he'd hurt his ribs, but so far he just kept soldiering through any pain they caused. Once he was seated, she put the wheelchair in the trunk and walked around the car to get in the driver's side.

As they drove away from the Conrad's and toward downtown Denver, Riley said, "It's usually the guy who makes the Valentine's plans like this."

Alex shrugged and glanced over at him. "Who ever said we had to be a traditional couple?"

She would be more than happy to let him make the plans typically, but rehab took a lot out of him every week, especially since he was prone to pushing himself more than he probably should.

Ten minutes later, they pulled into the parking lot of the Royale. To think, she had dined here with Riley's parents just a couple of months ago. That one simple, albeit rather terrifying, decision had changed everything.

The parking lot appeared completely full, but after a bit of maneuvering, she managed to find an empty spot.

"You know," he said, "the Royale is usually booked solid months before Valentine's Day."

She sent him a little grin. "Not if the girlfriend of the owner's son needs a reservation. Your dad was more than happy to make sure we had a table when I asked him."

Riley laughed quietly. "I'm beginning to think you could get my parents to do almost anything."

"Oh, I doubt that, but I'm glad it's worked so far."

She reached down to pull off her boots and slipped on Mindy's shoes. She then stepped out of the car, collected Riley's wheelchair, and helped him into it. Standing behind it, she wheeled him toward the entrance.

The place was packed, just as expected, but Alex confidently approached the greeter. "Reservation for Conrad."

The man smiled and gestured to the dining room. "Right this way."

He led them past dozens of dining couples to a table in the corner. It wasn't exactly private, but it sat a bit away from the others. She had to smile. No doubt Riley's dad had specifically reserved this table for them. He might be intimidating, but she was willing to bet he had a bigger heart than most people would give him credit for.

Once seated across from each other and left alone with their menus, Alex said, "Don't hold back on what you decide to eat. Your dad also offered to foot the bill. I doubt either of us will be able to afford to eat here again any time soon."

They browsed their options.

"So what are you thinking of getting?" she asked.

"I haven't been here since college, but I remember the filet mignon was excellent. What about you?"

"That sounds delicious. I've never had filet mignon before."

They ordered several minutes later and shared prosciutto-wrapped mozzarella and cherry tomatoes as an appetizer. Wiping her fingers on the cloth napkin in her lap, Alex looked at Riley in the romantic candlelight and held his gaze for a long moment.

"So how are you?" she asked finally. The last few days she had taken him to his rehab, he'd seemed quiet and kind of down. It was understandable, of course, considering all that had happened, but she hoped tonight would go a long way in cheering him up.

"I'm doing all right."

She gave him a bit of a prompting look. He could say that all he wanted, but she sensed more behind it.

He shrugged. "I guess it's not the easiest being the one who needs help instead of the one giving it."

She could understand that. It seemed to be a pretty universal man thing.

"I know, but it won't be forever." At least she prayed it wouldn't, for his sake.

"I suppose I had hoped to see more progress by now. I know it's only been three weeks and will take time. I've been through it before, but at least then I still had one good leg to walk on."

She reached out and laid her hand on his. He was always such a strong and capable man. Taking away his ability to walk surely felt like he'd been robbed of that. "Maybe, once your ribs heal, you'll see more rapid progress. You're kind of limited right now while you're still healing."

He breathed out a long breath as if his ribs pained him now. "I already miss working and Aspen Creek." He gave her a sad smile. "I miss spending time with you that doesn't involve hospitals and rehab centers."

Her heart swelled at his sweet and open honesty. "I know, me too. We need to figure out how to change that."

His smile faded then. "I really think you should stop taking me to rehab. You can't keep driving to and from Denver all the time."

He was right. She couldn't sustain the cost of fuel for long. Though she wanted for tonight to be romantic and carefree, she did have something to tell him. "I won't be for much longer. I gave Luke my notice last week. Thankfully, he has already found someone who can replace me. Friday is my last day. I'm moving in with Mindy and Zach for now, so it'll only be a twenty-minute drive from there to here. And on Saturday, I start working at that coffee shop we visited after seeing Dr. Gracin."

His brows lifted, and Alex smiled. "It's only a couple of days a week, but it'll work. Mindy and Zach are refusing rent money, so as long as I have enough for gas and to help chip in for food, it'll be enough. And I thought I could gain some coffee shop experience for the future."

Riley mulled this over, his expression too guarded for her to read his thoughts in the matter. "So you're leaving Aspen Creek?"

"For now."

He shook his head. "You shouldn't be doing all of this. You should be focused on your art, not uprooting the life you built just for me."

She squeezed his hand. Of course he would protest, but she'd given this a lot of thought and prayer. She had no doubt this was the right decision.

"I learned something from my dad when we were there for Thanksgiving. Turns out, he had dreams of being a pilot. I had no idea, and I asked him why he never pursued it. He told me that, in the end, a life with my mom was his greatest dream."

She took a deep breath, a comforting confidence forming into words. "Art has always been my passion and what I've dreamed of since I was little. I thought it was the one thing that defined me, but I've come to realize it's not. *Things* don't define us. Our faith and how we live it does. I'll always be deeply passionate about art, but I have dreams beyond being an artist—bigger dreams—dreams that involve you. I'm not about to give up my passion for art, but right now, what I really want is to be here for you—to do everything I can to help you walk again, and to help you open your coffee shop. That's what I want most."

He sat silent for a moment before shaking his head again. "Are you sure about this?"

"Completely. I know it'll be hard with rehab and the distance between here and Aspen Creek, but I think you need to start working on the shop again. You need to get it open. It won't be easy, but I want to help you do it." She caught sight of a couple of servers coming their way. "So what do you say?"

There was no mistaking the love in the smile that grew on his face. "Sounds like a plan."

Chapter Forty-one

ALEX SAT DOWN ON THE TAILGATE OF HER GRANDPA'S OLD RED Chevy her dad had given her for her birthday last month. It still hadn't sunk in that she'd turned thirty, but she was more than happy with her life right now. That happiness leaked out in a smile as Riley rolled his wheelchair to the truck and then slowly stood up and lifted himself onto the tailgate beside her. He let out a long sigh, but it was the sort of contented sigh after a long day of hard work. They'd been up and moving since the crack of dawn.

In the last light of gathering dusk, Alex looked up at the building Riley's parents had bought for him. A decorative sign hung above it now reading *All Things Coffee*. While most would never realize the significance, the two of them would forever hold the reference to Romans 8:28 close. Just below the sign a banner fluttered in the evening breeze: Grand Opening May 1st!

Alex leaned into him. "Can you believe you're opening tomorrow?"

He shook his head. "No."

Neither could she. For two and a half months, they'd worked like crazy to get this place up and running. It would have been impossible without all the help they'd received from family and friends. That and a whole lot of prayer and determination. By the grace of God, despite everything that had been thrown against them, they'd managed.

She gazed at Riley until he noticed, and they shared a smile. The last couple of months had been such a whirlwind. She'd hardly been home and had painted very little, but she was okay with that. She'd made her choice, and that choice was Riley. She didn't regret it for a moment.

"I'm so happy for you right now," she told him.

His gaze shifted between her eyes and her lips.

"None of it would have happened without you." He leaned in to kiss her.

Alex welcomed it. Though time slowly dulled the raw and fearful emotions of those days in the hospital, each kiss, or hug, or smile felt like a gift she had nearly lost for good.

As content as she would be to just sit here for a while, she broke off the kiss after a moment. "I suppose we should get going. Everyone is probably waiting for us."

He nodded, but sneaked in one more quick kiss before sliding off the tailgate to return to his wheelchair. Alex watched to make sure he didn't need help, but he managed it on his own. He wheeled around to the passenger door of the truck. She opened it for him, and he got in. Once she'd put the wheelchair in the back and had climbed in herself, she started up the truck and pulled away from the coffee shop. She loved having her own old truck to drive now.

A few blocks away, they pulled into one of the family restaurants in town. It was no Royale, but that was perfectly all right. Inside, the greeter guided them to two big tables pushed together to accommodate them all. As Alex had expected, everyone was there—her parents, who had driven up to help with final preparations, Riley's parents, Mindy and Zach, and grandpa Joe. They had all done their part in making Riley's dream a reality.

They took their seats at the table and joined in on the lively conversation. What a joy to see everyone sitting here together. When Alex had first met Riley, she couldn't have imagined the progress he would make with his family. Now they even got along well with her parents. It was a miracle, really.

Their food arrived a short time later, and they paused so Alex's dad could say a quiet prayer. Neither of Riley's parents seemed to mind. They all ate the celebratory meal in high spirits. About halfway through, Alex called for everyone's attention and raised her glass of soda.

"To family, friends, and a God who makes all things possible."

The others raised their glasses, and Joe said heartily, "Hear, hear."

Alex had to laugh. As a newly saved Christian, Joe was quite enthusiastic, his joy infectious. Even Riley's parents and Mark showed increased interest. Jenny not quite so much, but Alex still had hope. God had shown His awesome power and love so many times over the last several months. He would never give up on Jen. Neither would Riley and Joe, for that matter.

They remained at their table late into the evening until the restaurant had nearly emptied. On their way out, Riley's parents stopped near him and Alex.

"We'll be back tomorrow for the opening and to pick up your grandfather," Mr. Conrad told Riley. "Mark is planning to stop by sometime as well."

"See you tomorrow then," Riley replied.

His mom touched his shoulder as she passed. "We're proud of you."

Riley smiled. "Thanks, Mom. Goodnight."

Outside in the early spring air, Alex said goodnight to Mindy and Zach, and they all headed to their vehicles. At Alex's truck, Joe got in first and then Riley. Once Alex climbed in behind the wheel, Joe chuckled. "I haven't had the middle seat since I was a kid."

Both Alex and Riley laughed, and they drove away from the restaurant. Across town, they pulled up to the apartment complex where she and Riley had each rented an apartment a couple of weeks ago. Now that they would be working at the coffee shop, it had been time to leave Denver and Boulder. Though her new apartment wasn't nearly as charming as the one she'd rented from Mrs. Santos, Alex was just happy to be home.

Inside, she walked with Joe and wheeled Riley down to his apartment door. When he'd unlocked it, Joe said goodnight and walked inside, but Riley lingered in the hall.

Alex smiled at him. "I know it probably won't be easy thinking about tomorrow, but try to get some sleep."

"I will."

Bending down, she gave him a soft kiss and a loving smile. "Goodnight."

He echoed her, and then she turned to rejoin her parents and head up to her second floor apartment.

Alex turned slowly in a circle, taking in the sight of the coffee shop one more time before it would officially open for business. It had that perfect cozy and welcoming atmosphere she loved about coffee shops, while artistically highlighting the industrial aspects of the building. She couldn't imagine that it wouldn't be one of the most popular places in town once it got going.

She stopped facing the counter where Riley gave final instructions to the employees he had hired—previously unemployed veterans his friend Dak had put him in touch with. They all looked excited to start their jobs. Alex smoothed her hands down her apron. She was excited too, and thankful for the experience of working at the coffee shop in Denver, even if it had been brief. She'd even begun practicing her own latte art with Riley's instruction.

He turned his wheelchair away from the counter and caught eyes with her, breaking into a smile. He wheeled closer.

"Are we ready?"

She looked around. "I think so."

He glanced at his watch. "Two minutes. I think you can open it."

With a grin, she walked to the front door. She cast one more quick look at Riley and then turned the sign to *Open* and unlocked the door. Outside, a group of familiar faces from their church had formed. Pulling the door open, she greeted them all with a big smile. "Good morning, everyone. Come on in."

They stepped in one at a time, greeting her and then Riley, shaking hands with him and congratulating him on the opening of the shop. Pastor Ellis and his wife were among the group, as well as Mrs. Santos. Luke and Kat came in next, followed by a steady stream of people they knew from town. The shop filled with the sounds of conversation and the delicious scent of coffee just as it should be.

Though Alex spent most of her time behind the counter filling orders, her attention often sought Riley. Her heart filled with an overwhelming joy to watch him interact with his customers. It was everything she had ever wanted for him. This was where he belonged, and she thanked God for making it possible.

Alex stifled a yawn as they closed up shop for the evening. It had been a perfect opening day. Nearly the whole town had stopped in at one point or another. When the other employees left for home, Alex stayed to help Riley finish clean up and make preparations for tomorrow. Though they didn't actually work there, Alex's parents and Mindy and Zach had stayed throughout the day, making sure people were happy and helping where they could. The way Mindy was with people, she *should* work there. She had talked about it as a part-time job alongside her budding photography business.

Done straightening and wiping tables in the balcony, Alex walked down the stairs. Her parents and Mindy and Zach had disappeared. Probably waiting outside for her and Riley to finish up. Putting away the cleaning supplies and hanging up her apron, she walked around the counter to join Riley.

"I think that's it. Are we ready to lock up?"

He moved a little closer and set the brakes on his wheelchair. "There's just one more thing."

Using the counter for balance, he pushed himself to his feet.

She frowned. "What?"

He took one step forward with a bit of effort and slowly lowered himself to his knee. He slipped a little. She reached out to help him, but he held up his hand with a smile. "I'm fine."

She stared at him. What was he trying to do? But her heart beat faster as he looked up at her from this position.

"Today has been one of the greatest days of my life," he said. "I couldn't have asked for more. I can't imagine a better way to end it than this."

He reached into his pocket and withdrew a small black box. She gasped, her heart nearly leaping out of her chest now.

"After all we've been through together, Alex Jennings, will you marry me?"

He opened the box. A brilliant silver ring studded with tiny sparkling diamonds in the shape of a North Star sat nestled in the white satin.

A cross between a laugh and a sob broke from her swelling chest. Tears flooded her eyes, but a grin split her face. She almost squealed. Was this how Mindy felt on a daily basis? "Yes! Absolutely, yes."

His grin matched hers, and she held out her hand for him to slip the ring onto her finger. The tears dripped down her face, but she had never been so overjoyed in her life. Though she'd known for a while now she would marry him, tonight had been a surprise of the best possible kind. Dropping down to her knees, she threw her arms around him and continued to cry her tears of joy. He was her best friend in the whole world, and she couldn't wait to live with him for the rest of their lives.

After a moment, he pulled away just enough to kiss her until she was out of breath and just a bit dizzy. He then grinned at her, lifting her glasses just enough to wipe the tears away from her cheeks.

"Whatever date we set, I plan to be standing at the end of that aisle waiting for you, and then I'm going to walk down it again with you as my wife."

"I look forward to that day, but I want you to know that, even if you never walked again, I would marry you right here on the spot. You mean so much to me, Riley Conrad. I was a terrible mess before I met you, but even though I had given up, God hadn't. When I walked into the bar that day and met you, everything changed, and I know it was not by chance."

Epilogue

THE CHIRP OF AUGUST CRICKETS DRIFTED IN THROUGH THE OPEN window with the light breeze and scent of warm sunshine. God couldn't have provided a more beautiful day for Alex to be sitting in one of the church's back rooms in a wedding dress. She brushed her fingers lightly across the white lace and satin draping her body. The dress was the perfect blend of country and elegance. She had no doubt Riley would love it.

Her mom, Mrs. Conrad, Mindy, Jen, and Mrs. Ellis all bustled around her, chatting happily as they helped with the finishing touches. Alex glanced at the clock. Only another twenty minutes. Her stomach fluttered, but her excitement to marry Riley far outweighed any nerves. Exactly one year to the day she had walked into the bar and met him for the first time, they would become husband and wife. She had never imagined what joy would bloom from that first meeting. Instead of taking her life, she had met the man of her dreams.

Mindy whisked around in front of her, a bundle of radiant energy. Of course, her glowing face had more to do with the adorable little baby bump just showing through her navy blue matron-of-honor gown than any of her makeup. Her pregnancy had come as a delightful surprise to everyone, including her and Zach. Alex could hardly wait to become "Auntie Alex." First, however, she was going to become Mrs. Conrad.

"Are you ready?" Mindy asked with a sparkling grin.

"Very."

She stood up now that Mindy had finished double checking her hair. Her eyes suddenly watery, Mindy put her arms around Alex.

"I am so happy for you. You deserve the most amazing day possible."

Alex smiled and hugged her friend tightly. Despite her energy, Mindy had never been one to get overly emotional. That is, until pregnancy. "Thanks, Min. I don't know what I would have done without you this past year."

Mindy pulled back but gripped Alex's shoulders as she looked her in the eyes. "You might be marrying your dream man today, but you can always count on me to be there if you need me."

"Thanks. You're the sister I never had."

She then turned and caught her mom's teary but happy gaze. Alex stepped forward to hug her too.

"You look beautiful," Mom murmured as they embraced tightly.

"Thanks, Mom."

With time quickly counting down to the ceremony, they left the room to get to their places. Alex walked with her mom to the waiting area outside the sanctuary. There Dad awaited them. His strong, stoic expression wavered upon seeing her. His quiet smile meant more to her than any compliment. In it he conveyed all of his love and pride.

When she reached him, they too hugged. This one lasted longer than the others. It must be difficult for him to let her go like this, yet he had expressed nothing but support for Riley and their marriage.

"You're so beautiful, sweetheart," he whispered just before they parted.

Now Alex's eyes watered. "Thank you, Dad."

The next couple of minutes passed in a bit of a blur as they all got into position. Just before it was time to walk out, Dad turned to her.

"God brought you a good man," he said. "I'm not sure I'd be very happy about standing here right now if He hadn't."

She laughed, though her throat squeezed. "Yes, He did."

A moment later, the music started, signaling the beginning of the ceremony. Alex drew a deep breath and wrapped her hand around her dad's arm. She gave it a gentle squeeze and cast him a wide smile before they followed the wedding procession into the sanctuary.

Once they passed the doors, her attention shifted from her dad to the end of the aisle. Standing straight and tall with no wheelchair in sight, Riley waited for her, just as he'd said he would. Tears flowed into her eyes even as she grinned at him. *Lord, I love him so much!*

His smile filled her chest with a flutter of anticipation and giddiness. She held his gaze until she and her dad reached him. Here, she gave Dad another quick hug before he offered her hand to Riley. Riley's strong but gentle fingers wrapped around hers, reminding her of the first time they had ever held hands.

He guided her toward Pastor Ellis where they stood facing each other. Alex couldn't stop grinning through the entire ceremony and spoke her vows with pure joy. Her pulse seemed to rise with each passing moment until, at last, Pastor Ellis pronounced them husband and wife. More than ready for this moment, Alex melted into Riley's arms as he pulled her in for a kiss. Their first kiss as a married couple.

When they faced their gathered family and friends, he took her hand again and led her confidently down the aisle. Alex could find no hint of the fact that he had needed a wheelchair to get around only a couple of months ago. Outside, he helped her climb in and situate her dress inside his truck that was decked out in balloons, streamers, and a *Just Married* sign.

Before she could buckle her seatbelt, his hand captured her face, and he bent in to give her a deep, lingering kiss only appropriate for a married couple. Alex relished every glorious second of it. When they parted, she grinned breathlessly at him. From this day forward, she would never have to leave his side and would never be forced to say goodbye at the end of the day. Ready to spend every moment together, she took hold of his suit vest to pull him close again for one more quick kiss before he rounded the truck to get in and drive them to their wedding reception.

About the Author

JAYE ELLIOT IS AN AWARD-WINNING AUTHOR, COUNTRY GIRL, AND hopeless romantic at heart. She loves a good hero and will always sigh happily during the lights scene in Tangled. She writes from her home in the Northwoods of Wisconsin, which she shares with three cats she considers her kids. When not writing romance novels, she pens fantasy and adventure stories as Jaye L. Knight.

www.jayeelliot.com

Like adventure fiction?
Check out Jaye's other books written as Jaye L. Knight.
Visit: **www.jayelknight.com**

ILYON CHRONICLES
Half-Blood (Prequel Novella)
Tyra (Free Short Story)
Resistance
The King's Scrolls
Samara's Peril
Exiles
Bitter Winter
Lacy (Novella)

Made in the USA
Monee, IL
09 June 2024

59309168R00229